"NO . . ." She Moaned Just Before His Lips Came Down Firmly on Hers. . . .

Alexander was laughing, a low rumbling sound that caressed her . . . drawing her to her feet and into his embrace. Arms that bruised her back, crushed her to a chest hard as a rock, muscular thighs pressing insistently against her.

There was no time or space, only a spinning, tumbling void. A rushing sound in her ears, small coils of tension in isolated corners of her consciousness that were unbearable and sweetly agonizing. All feeling was concentrated in her lips. She tasted Alexander, the wine, the scent of tropical flowers. She felt his tongue, warm and pulsing, the sudden shock of his teeth along her lower lip. She was filled with yearning. She was soaring to a rendezvous on the far reaches of the cosmos, and he was part of it. She knew real desire for the first time. . . .

Dear Reader:

We trust you will enjoy this Richard Gallen romance. We plan to bring you more of the best in both contemporary and historical romantic fiction with four exciting new titles each month.

We'd like your help.

We value your suggestions and opinions. They will help us to publish the kind of romances you want to read. Please send us your comments, or just let us know which Richard Gallen romances you have especially enjoyed. Write to the address below. We're looking forward to hearing from you!

Happy reading!

Judy Sullivan
Richard Gallen Books
8-10 West 36th St.
New York, N.Y. 10018

Dream-tide

KATHERINE KENT

PUBLISHED BY RICHARD GALLEN BOOKS
Distributed by POCKET BOOKS

This novel is a work of fiction. Names, characters, places and incidents are either the product of the author's imagination or are used fictitiously, and any resemblance to actual persons, living or dead, events or locales is entirely coincidental.

A RICHARD GALLEN BOOKS *Original* publication

Distributed by
POCKET BOOKS, a Simon & Schuster division of
GULF & WESTERN CORPORATION
1230 Avenue of the Americas, New York, N.Y. 10020

ISBN: 0-671-41783-5

First Pocket Books printing May, 1981

10 9 8 7 6 5 4 3 2 1

Printed in the U.S.A.

Why did I laugh? I know this Being's lease,
My fancy to its utmost blisses spreads;
Yet would I on this very midnight cease,
And the world's gaudy ensigns see in shreds,
Verse, Fame, and Beauty are intense indeed,
But Death intenser—Death is Life's high meed.

Keats

Dream-
tide

Chapter 1

She sat bolt upright, heart pounding, palms sweating. Terror ran along her veins in icy rivulets. The echo of her scream hung in the smothering darkness.

Nick jumped, then reached for her. "Good God, Liz, what is it?" One arm went around her as he fumbled with the switch to the bedside lamp.

Liz blinked as the white light snapped her fully awake. "I . . . don't know. I felt . . . overwhelming fear. But I don't remember having a nightmare. What time is it?"

"Midnight. Straight up. The witching hour." He pulled her down beside him and grazed his face along her breasts.

Liz was shivering. "Please . . . just hold me."

He rolled on to his back, leaving his arm stiffly under her shoulders. "Seems you're always restless when I stay all night. You know, babe, I'm beginning to wonder if we'll be one of those married couples who have separate rooms."

Saturday, she thought. Nick and I are getting married on Saturday. I'll be able to really relax with him then. Why am I so hopelessly old-fashioned about this. He loves me. I love him. . . . She had learned long ago there were some thoughts it was better not to share with him. She said only, "I don't know what's wrong with me. . . ."

He ran his hand tentatively over her stomach, slid his fingers between her thighs. Needing his nearness and the comfort of his flesh to press away the nameless fear that had disturbed her sleep so often on the stroke of midnight, she did not push him away.

Those other midnights she had been alone and, not knowing where Nick was, wondered if the sudden awakenings were the result of the uncertainty of living with Nick's abrupt changes of mood. Of not knowing when he would disappear on one of his jaunts—or, worse, when she would learn of another of his infidelities.

Tonight he was here, beside her. And still the faceless horror had stalked her sleep and brought her, tingling with fear, to a strange state of anticipation. What?

Nick had laughed at what he called her attacks of 'women's intuition' and said they made her even more feminine. She had declared angrily that most premonitions were really psychological warnings, based on common sense. Pointing out that on several occasions her premonitions had been chillingly accurate, had merely provoked another argument in which her logic was met with teasing battle-of-the-sexes banter. He was infuriatingly macho, but then, wasn't that what had attracted her in the first place?

He pulled her on top of him, fondled her breasts again and moved impatiently under her. "Come on, babe, it was only a nightmare. A little loving will help you go back to sleep."

She wasn't ready; had never learned how to be ready as quickly as he was. Her heart still thudded painfully against her ribs in pulsing aftershocks to the panic that had come while she slept.

Prodding her dry and unresponsive flesh, Nick groaned with frustration. He pushed her back down under him and demanded a response from her with his lips and tongue.

Out of the corner of her eye Liz saw that the hands on the clock had moved safely past midnight. When Nick climaxed he fell asleep again immediately and, after a time, Liz slept, too.

When she opened her eyes again the room was filled with dusty gold light. She licked her lips, feeling the dryness of the morning air. Her body was hot, although she was covered only by a sheet. She was alone in the bed. The voice that had awakened her came from the radio in the adjoining room.

". . . the desert winds come roaring out of the canyons, searing the air to tinder dryness. When the harsh winds blow the smallest spark ignites chapparel that has been without rain for many months. There are brush fires every year in Southern California. We have a fire season as other regions have a snow or ice season."

Liz slipped out of bed and went to the open door. Nick was dressing, his back turned to her. He reached over to turn up the volume and the announcer continued, "Sometimes—and this season appears to be one in which this happens—the brush fires are driven by ferocious winds into populated areas. The cost in burned homes and human misery is difficult for this reporter to describe. From where I'm standing I can see smoke and flames all along the top of the hills. Below me people are frantically wetting down roofs, while fire trucks go screaming toward the blaze . . ."

Nick turned and saw her and snapped off the radio. His brown hair had a bronze underglow and was tousled from sleep. His dark eyes regarded her with that look that her friend, Maggie, always claimed reminded her of a hound who knows his prey is treed. Nick buttoned his shirt and yanked on his jeans, giving her a casual grin but not slowing the pace of his dressing. "Everything's burning, babe, and I'm on my way."

"I'll go with you. Just give me a minute to dress."

He frowned. "The Highway Patrol will be closing the area soon. If I don't get in before they do, there'll be no pictures."

"I'll be ready by the time you get the equipment into the car," Liz said, already reaching into the closet for a cotton shirt.

He was backing the car out of the carport when she raced up to the passenger door. The tires squealed as he floored the accelerator. They went roaring down the deserted early morning street toward a smoke-shrouded sunrise.

From the set of his mouth and the way his hands gripped the wheel, as well as his reckless speed, she knew what he was feeling. She did not say, as she had so many times in the past, that they were partners, and if they shared everything else they should also share the risks. Nick's idea of their partnership was that she should stay in the studio, shooting the photos of babies and animals which were *the bread-and-butter* of their business, while he went out into the field. Even when he was merely going to shoot some routine shots—model homes, a new shopping mall—there was always the chance of a news story breaking.

She understood how he felt and loved him so much she rationalized: Not that he did not want to share the limelight, but rather that he gallantly wanted to protect her from danger. After all, he had been a Pulitzer Prize-winning news photographer while she was still in college.

Liz pulled a comb through her hair, static electricity crackling through shades of gold and sun-streaked platinum that burnished honey-colored waves falling just past her shoulders. She wore no make-up, but her love of the outdoors had tinted her cheekbones and bridge of her nose to a warm peach, and the blue depths of her eyes were lit by a violet glow. Nick complained sometimes that she looked too young and a little make-up wouldn't hurt.

"Quit primping and start loading film," Nick growled.

Liz complied. He was never at his best first thing in the morning.

A black pall of smoke hung over the Santa Monica mountains, rising and billowing. Nick swerved suddenly to the curb and slammed on the brakes. "You drive from here on. And bat the big blue eyes at any cop who tries to stop us. You bring your press card?" He swore when she shook her head. "Get into the driver's seat, anyway. I want to be ready to go into action."

Liz took the wheel and they joined the procession of emergency vehicles streaming toward the conflagration. County Sheriffs and Highway Patrol officers were busy evacuating the threatened houses.

People were running back and forth from their houses to their cars, carrying valuables. Some stood on rooftops, playing the dwindling supply of water through hoses to keep the shingles wet. "Nick, we've got to park the car. How are those people going to get through?"

She pulled over to allow a station wagon packed with children to detour around a fire truck.

Nick's chiseled features were set in angry lines. He grabbed his camera and leaped from the car, not bothering to close the door behind him. He was quickly swallowed by the crowd.

Liz stumbled out, too, becoming a part of the desperate scene. She ate smoke, helped evacuating homeowners carry their possessions, snatched a hose from a weary old man and wet down his roof. She did not take any pictures.

A sobbing young girl told her a breeding ranch had been engulfed and there was no way to reach three hundred animals, large and small. Liz lost track of Nick, who moved through the destruction oblivious to the human emotions around him.

Hours slipped away. Was it noon when she grabbed a quick cup of coffee from the Red Cross? It was hard to say, as the smoke now darkened the sky and wind-whipped flames licked at the first house. A corner of the roof caught and exploded into an orange ball of flames. Sparks flew to the next structure, which ignited on impact. Half a dozen homes were soon blazing out of control.

Liz helped where she could. Nick would get the pictures. He always did. Eventually, eyes stinging and limbs twitching with exhaustion, she wandered into an untouched neighborhood, crept into the back seat of a parked car and slept.

The following dawn she stood wearily on an unknown street, unable to believe her eyes. One section of the mountains might have been covered in snow; it lay beneath a thick layer of white ash. Beyond the devastation, the fire was cresting yet another ridge, determined to blacken everything in its path all the way to the sea.

She stumbled blindly in the direction of the bluffs along the coast highway, stopping at the end of the street. Below, on the beach, were at least a hundred horses, tied to every imaginable type of stake. There was also a pet goat and even a pet duck.

Nick came looking for her when he was almost out of film. His clothes were smoke-blackened and he needed a shave, but his eyes glowed with satisfaction. "Where the hell have you been? No, never mind, let's get out of here. I want to get these developed and into print."

Liz opened her mouth to say the fires were far from being under control, but only a hoarse groan came from her lips. She climbed into Nick's car, taking the driver's side. They had to detour around the reinforcements of firefighters, County Sheriff's cars and emergency vehicles screaming into the area. Suddenly they were on an ominously deserted dirt road.

"Turn back," Nick ordered.

Liz braked, slid to a stop. They heard it then, the terrified screaming of horses. Liz stumbled from the car, heedless of Nick's yell. The horses were locked in a corral, there was no one else in sight. Behind them, the fire crackled down the hillside.

Trying to shield her eyes from the smoke and glare, Liz looked with dismay at the frantic animals, rearing and charging at the imprisoning gate. If she were to open it, there would be little time to escape the stampeding hoofs. She glanced back toward the car and saw, disbelievingly, that Nick was up on the hood, camera in hand. He's waiting for the flames to reach them, she thought in shock and horror. Then she was racing toward the gate, choking on the smoke, blinded by whirling ash.

The moment she slid the lock, a huge chestnut stallion crashed through the opening, pinning her between gate and fence. The other horses followed in a thunderous roar of hooves and a great cloud of smoke and dust. Clinging to the fence, which threatened to collapse against her as the maddened animals surged through the opening, Liz prayed for the strength to stay on her feet and not be sucked under the thrashing hooves.

Suddenly there was a blast of water nearby, deflecting the rush of horses. A moment later a fireman was at her side. The whites of his eyes stood out starkly against his blackened face. He didn't speak, merely grabbed her and dragged her back from the flames, now racing across the corral.

She had lost track of time and had no idea how long she had clung to the fence as the horses stampeded by. Had the fireman and his life-saving hose appeared, fortuitously, or had he been summoned by Nick? Since Nick left her immediately to rush back to develop his film, she did not have time to ask.

Two of Nick's photographs made the wire services the next day. The first was a silhouetted fireman against the flaming backdrop of the Santa Monica mountains. The man was a shadow only, yet every line of his body expressed exhaustion and the helplessness of losing the battle.

The second picture was of fear-crazed horses, with

bulging eyes and flaring nostrils, caught in an almost choreographed variety of poses; rearing, running, stumbling, falling. Hard on their heels was the specter of the fire.

Liz studied the picture in the newspaper, wondering again if Nick had raced back for help. Even if he had, he had first taken time to get that picture.

The key turned in her door and Nick came in, grinning. He dropped his lanky frame on to the couch. "Come here," he invited, holding out his arms. When she made no move toward him he said, "You OK?"

Liz said carefully, "They told me at the hospital I suffered mild smoke inhalation. I suppose that's what you mean? That was yesterday. Today I guess I'm suffering mild doubts about a man who feels a picture is more important than either human or animal life."

"Hey, babe," Nick said reproachfully, "I didn't get that shot until after I brought the fireman. And who the hell do you think was holding the hose while he got you out of there? I'd have come after you myself, but he had a respirator and there was no sense in both you and I keeling over from smoke inhalation. And I did call the hospital to ask about you, soon as I got back to the studio. They said you'd been treated and released."

As always, there was a plausible explanation, Liz thought. She didn't remember the fireman wearing a respirator, but then nothing about the incident was clear in her mind now. It must have been Nick, however, who played the hose about her while the fireman risked his life to plunge into the mass of smoke and dust and panicked horses.

"Come on, Liz. You know you're more important to me than any picture."

Silencing a small protesting voice, she went to him;

to arms hard around her back and lips that kissed briefly, quickly moving down the column of her throat. He began to unbutton her blouse the minute she sat down, his hand going under her breast, pulling it up for his lips and tongue. He nipped playfully, hurting her, and she winced.

Instantly his touch was tender, stroking gently, caressing downward over her slender body. As always, her flesh melted at his touch. The lonely hours of smoke and fear and misery were forgotten. His hands slid down her back, lingering to press lightly in the hollow above her buttocks, slipping around to probe her inner thighs. He was nibbling at her breasts, bringing the nipples to hard little peaks of tension.

"Oh, Nick, I love you so." She did not hear the despair in her voice as his fingers caressed and entered her.

He sucked at her nipples and desire raced through her, bringing her skin to a pink glow. He laughed softly, pushing her over on to her back, then stood up and, watching her eyes, took off his clothes.

His body was deeply tanned and his muscular chest and arms seemed to retain the heat and power of the broad California sunlight. He stood still, poised with his legs apart, studying her face. She knew that he wanted to see how much she wanted him, and she knew that in spite of everything, her need showed plainly. He could make her want him more than anything in the world.

He lay down next to her with elaborate gentleness, running his hand from the insides of her knees, pausing tantalizingly to play with the tight curls of her hair, to her breasts. She nestled in closer to him, trying to dissolve in the warmth of his huge arms, drinking in the scent of his skin. Suddenly Nick rolled on top of her, and pulled her roughly by the chin so that they were eye to eye.

"Liz, you have to know how much I need you. You can't leave me, don't ever leave me." His words were a command, but there was the disappointment of a little boy in his tone. "You can't, you can't. . . ." he repeated, opening his mouth over hers so that her answer was stifled. But he knew, as Liz knew, what that answer had to be.

She opened her legs under him feeling his hardness stroking her delicately and insistently. At the next moment came that incredible feeling of being filled, stopped, unable to feel anything but the size and strength of him inside her. It sucked all the breath out of her and she just clung to him wanting to hold him like that forever. He began to thrust slowly, then slower, until all at once he gripped her shoulders so hard she cried out and she could feel him exploding inside her. She listened to him gasping for several moments before she realized how quiet her own breathing was, how hidden and faraway.

He dropped his head down to her breast and lay silent, watching the shadow of the curtains on the dim ceiling. She felt outside her body somehow, as if Nick hadn't really touched her. When he slipped from her after a short time, and began to sleep blissfully like an infant, she felt too tense to lie there with him. She had to get up and move.

She went into the bathroom and turned on the shower. She had never achieved orgasm with Nick during intercourse, although there had been times she was so close she could have died from it. He could bring her to a climax after his own ejaculation, and usually did. But she still felt she was missing something important.

After Saturday, she thought, stepping into the jets of warm water, I'll lose all my inhibitions after Saturday. Her wedding day. It would be the magical metamorphosis, she was sure of it. She had yielded to him because she loved him, but her belief that sex outside of the total commitment of marriage was empty was too deeply ingrained to fade before his derision at her old-fashioned morality.

"Marriage is a commitment to continuity—to the future, not only of ourselves, but humanity," she had told him.

"You're talking about children."

"Of course." She smiled. "Our immortality."

"Marriage *si*—kids, no way," he had said.

The phone rang shrilly, and she grabbed a towel and ran, remembering Nick's admonishment that she should take the phone off the hook. She got to it on the second ring. A strange male voice said, "You must be Liz Holly. Nick said it was OK to call him at this number. I'm Elliot Moore, an old friend of his."

"He's here, but he's asleep. We covered the fires. The studio is closed for business." She was about to add, for our wedding and honeymoon, but stopped herself. "Nick told me about you. Are you still a wire service reporter? Could I give him a message?"

"I'm freelancing. I'll call back. You can tell him that I'm going to need him for the pictures we talked about. This Saturday."

There was a crackle of interference on the line, and the buzzing echoed in Liz's brain. "This Saturday," she repeated, glancing toward Nick sprawled on the couch, passion spent, oblivious to the world. "He promised to shoot pictures for you *this* Saturday?"

"I wasn't sure exactly when I'd need him, but I told

him it probably would be this weekend. I want pictures of a movie stunt and they're doing it this Saturday. He knows all about it. Tell him Adam Eastman has agreed to do it and can get us on the set. I'll call back in an hour."

Resisting the impulse to claw Nick awake, she stood watching him and trying to deal rationally with her emotions. The question, Liz old girl, she told herself, is whether or not you can continue your relationship with him with or without marriage. Because if you can't, you'd better end it now. It would have been easier to decide whether or not to amputate part of her body.

When Nick opened his eyes, yawned and stretched, she was fully dressed, sitting across the room watching him. He recognized the look. He gave her his little-boy-guileless grin and sat up. "You're beautiful, Liz. Naked or dressed, you're the best. Hey, I'm a poet."

"This dress was part of my trousseau," Liz said. "That's an old-fashioned word for the clothes a bride-to-be buys for the early days of her marriage." She tried to sound sarcastic, but her eyes gave away her true emotions.

"Why didn't you save it for your honeymoon, then? I'm going to shower." His tone was light and he whistled under his breath as he padded, barefoot, across the floor to the bathroom.

She called after him, "Your old reporter-buddy Elliot Moore called."

He stopped and turned around. "I did ask you to take the phone off the hook."

"Tell me about the pictures you're going to shoot for him, Nick."

"Elliot's doing a series of articles on Tinsel Town. The real Hollywood, you know. And you know how tough it is for a photographer to get past their unions to take any pictures."

"He mentioned a movie stunt, and someone named Adam Eastman."

"Adam and Elliot and I went to school together. Adam is the best stuntman in town. It seems some producer is re-making an old silent movie, recreating some famous stunt. They're keeping it secret until they see if it works. The only reason I'm in on it is because we're all friends and it's an independent production."

"So we're postponing the wedding again?" Liz asked carefully.

"I was going to tell you—but then the fires started. . . ." he gestured vaguely. "Oh, come on Liz, it's no big deal. We'll get married Sunday instead."

"The chapel will be in use then."

"So we'll go to a Justice of the Peace, for Christ's sake. It's just a formality, isn't it? Liberated women no longer insist on a ceremony, right? Unless they're planning to get pregnant. You wouldn't do that to old Nick, would you?"

Liz counted silently to ten, battling anger and hurt and loss of pride. "If you don't want to get married, Nick, will you please tell me?" she said at last, her voice controlled. "If you aren't ready for that kind of commitment by now, then you never will be. Let's just go our separate ways."

He was immediately contrite. "Liz, I love you. I do want to marry you. More than anything. I couldn't get along without you. I guess I feel we're good as married now, the ceremony itself isn't important to me."

"It's important to me, and this isn't the first time you've called it off," Liz snapped, anger beginning to dominate her other emotions.

His arms went around her and his breath was warm in her ear. "OK—forget the chapel. Let's fly to Vegas after I've shot the pictures. We can get married there."

"You know how I feel about the Wayside Chapel." Her parents had been married there and, she had been baptized there. All of her friends had been invited to the little glass chapel on the cliff overlooking the Pacific's serene beauty. "I don't want to get married in Vegas surrounded by glitter and one-armed bandits."

"Then make another reservation at the chapel, soon as you can." His lips pressed the words to her cheek, closed her eyes with their sensual promise, and her misgivings faded again.

Liz went to the telephone, dialed a number and waited. "Hi . . . Maggie? You sound like you're choking. What? I thought you were on a diet. No, nothing important, we're just postponing the wedding for a few days. Listen, would you mind calling around to tell a few people?"

Nick came up behind her and kissed the nape of her neck, patted her behind and departed in the direction of the bathroom. A moment later he stuck his head around the door. "Hey, Liz, I forgot. There's going to be a party to launch the movie, if the stunt goes off OK. You can go along and meet movie stars. Barry Gerrard is starring. And you'll never guess who Adam is shacking up with . . . a living legend, no less—"

Liz covered the receiver. "Would you excuse me, Nick, while I try to explain to Maggie why our wedding is being postponed for the third time?" Her voice quivered slightly but the sheathing of armor she had fashioned over her heart held fast.

"OK. Give my love to your fat friend."

Maggie's voice hissed down the wire. "I heard that.

God, that man doesn't deserve you, Liz. Don't let him do this to you. Run—now, while you can hold on to a shred of your sanity."

Liz was silent. Her own feeling of insecurity did not need to be fueled by Maggie's dislike of Nick. Liz tried to change the subject. "How was the convention today?" Maggie was a travel agent and had spent the day meeting her peers.

"Interesting. Perhaps prophetically so."

"What do you mean?"

"Remember you asked me to come up with a honeymoon hideaway for you and Nick? Well, for a few minutes I thought I'd found it. An island. A tiny dot in the South Pacific—privately owned by a man who leases it out if he likes the sound of the prospect. A veritable paradise, from what the Hawaiian agent who handles it told me. You even have to travel the last leg of the journey by outrigger canoe, because nothing larger goes there."

"Maggie! It sounds marvelous. What's it called? Is it available?"

"Hold on! It's called Falconer's Island and it *is* available—but you can't have it. Not unless you want to go on your honeymoon alone. The owner is eccentric. He only leases it to one person at a time. Apparently there's just a primitive grass shack, big enough for one. The owner doesn't want anyone to stay too long and one person alone isn't likely to—they just go there to work."

"Oh," Liz said, disappointed.

"Maybe you should go—think things over before becoming Mrs. Nick Kane," Maggie suggested slyly, revealing her real reason for mentioning the island.

Liz eased her way gracefully out of the conversation. While she waited for Nick to finish showering, she thought about the island retreat. Perhaps, if she and Nick could find somewhere like that, they could escape from all the pressures and really find each other. But when Nick emerged from the bathroom she did not tell him about Falconer's Island. She pushed it into a corner of her mind and temporarily forgot it existed.

Chapter 2

"Tomorrow," Maggie said. "Friday. Why not? The chapel is available and I can call everyone tonight. If you're determined to marry him, then do it, for God's sake, and end the suspense. I for one can't take it anymore." She tugged at her skirt, loosened her belt, and sat down, sighing with relief.

"All right," Liz said. "I'll call him. He's at the studio picking up the equipment he'll need for the pictures Saturday."

"Call him now," Maggie advised. She was pretty in a flamboyant way, despite the excess poundage. A complete extrovert, she liked everyone. Except Nick. They had hated each other on sight.

Maggie thinks she's calling his bluff, Liz thought, amused. She picked up the phone and dialed the studio number. Nick listened silently when she told him the wedding could take place a day earlier. There was a split second's pause, and then he answered. "Hey, babe, that's great. I felt bad about postponing it again, but I owe Elliot a favor. And Adam once showed up with a chopper in 'Nam when I really needed a lift. Look, I won't come over tonight, so you can have an early night. I'll call you first thing in the morning."

Liz replaced the receiver and smiled across the room at Maggie. "OK?"

Maggie's cupid's bow mouth managed a wry smile. She glanced about. "The apartment was neater when I lived here."

Liz flushed and began to straighten the crushed cushions on the couch. It had been embarrassing to ask Maggie to move out, but it had been even more embarrassing when Nick disappeared on his jaunts and Maggie found her alone.

"Luckily, I didn't return any of your gifts this time," Maggie added. "Some of them were getting long in the tooth for a return trip. You want a night out—your last fling of freedom?"

Liz shook her head. "I'd better wash my hair. Get my beauty sleep."

That night, hair washed, an overnight bag packed and her wedding dress pressed and ready, Liz soaked in a bubble bath and then retired early. She had fallen into a deep sleep when the phone shattered the vaguely disturbing dream she was having.

Nick's voice, low and slightly slurred, registered slowly on her mind. "Babe, I'm sorry—I'm going away for a couple of days. An assignment. I'll be back in time for the party Saturday night."

She shook her head, disbelieving. "Nick, what about our wedding tomorrow?"

"Put it off until next week. There's too much happening right now. Look I'll explain when I see you."

Groping in the darkness for her alarm clock, she saw it was 2 a.m. "Where are you? Nick . . . if the wedding doesn't take place tomorrow it's off permanently. I mean it. Nick . . .?" But there was no answer, the phone was dead.

She spent the following day explaining that her wedding had been called off. Maggie was sympathetic, did not say I-told-you-so. Liz's emotions alternated between humiliation, rage at Nick's cavalier attitude, and fury at herself for not ending the affair before she arrived at this state of degradation. She wondered bitterly if she had persisted in trying to arrange the wedding after that first postponement merely to prove to Maggie and her other friends that Nick really did want to marry her. Her own doubts about marriage to Nick had become eclipsed by her desire to prove everyone was wrong and, she admitted ruefully to herself, to save face. Now she saw the price she had paid to gain those temporary victories had been great, indeed.

As the day wore on, Liz began to realize she would also have to end their business relationship. When she told Maggie of this decision, Maggie said gently, "Why don't you just keep quiet about your future plans until after you've seen Nick, face to face? I've seen you in a white heat of rage about him before, but after you get together again . . . I mean, does he hypnotize you, or something?"

"Not this time," Liz declared firmly.

Liz had forgotten Elliot Moore and his pictures of the movie stunt when, early on Saturday morning, there was an angry pounding on her front door.

A short wiry man with sandy hair and an unkempt appearance stood on her doorstep. He had a cocky swagger, a jutting chin and the hungry look of a freelance writer. Liz knew who he was before he announced, "I'm Elliot Moore. Is Nick here?"

"He had to go out of town on an assignment." She had said it so many times the previous day she almost believed it herself.

"Goddamnit, he *promised* me," Elliot breathed through clenched tobacco-stained teeth. "What the hell am I going to do now? The stunt is being performed today."

"I could take the pictures for you," Liz offered. "Nick and I are partners."

He looked her over carefully.

"Get someone else if you want to." Her patience was wearing very thin.

There was a pause. "Nick said I wouldn't have to pay him until I get paid for the article."

"All right. What's the job?"

"I'll explain on the way. First we go to the marina."

As he helped her load the equipment into his car he said, "I wanted my own pictures—not the stills, nor any taken by a studio photog. I've sworn to keep quiet about the fact a stuntman is doubling the star and I want you to keep his face out of it."

Liz listened silently, not really giving a damn. Her pain over Nick kept clawing at her mind, preventing concentration on anything else.

Elliot was asking, "You ever hear of an old movie called *The Black Pirate?* Made back in 1925 or '26? It was a classic in its day. Douglas Fairbanks was the star and there was a famous scene where he evaded his pursuers by sliding down the sails of a ship—ripping his way with a dagger."

Liz shook her head.

"I'll fill you in on details as we go."

The moment they pulled into the marina parking lot she saw it; masts and spars and weathered wooden hull rising above the gleaming white power boats and toy sailing boats. An old sailing ship, looking like a dowager queen surrounded by dwarf commoners. If the rigging had not been stirring in a gentle breeze, the ship would have looked as though it were painted on the sky by a loving artist.

Liz stared mesmerized.

"That's what I want you to photograph first," Elliot said. "It's an exact replica of a fighting galleon, built by a millionaire movie producer back in the twenties, before the crash. He was a sailing buff and he wanted to make a movie on a real ship—no mock-up on the set and models in a tank. They say every detail is authentic. It was never used in a film, however. It's been down in San Diego as part of a maritime museum. A crew of sea scouts sailed it up here."

"Will it be used in the film you mentioned?" Liz asked.

"They're hoping to sail her to Hawaii to use at least for some scenes where she'll lie at anchor. And for interior shots. First they'll work on her here, to be sure she's completely seaworthy."

Liz looked around. "I don't see a movie crew."

"The actual stunt isn't going to be done here. I wanted you to get some shots of the ship first—then we'll drive out to a ranch where the stunt will be done."

Elliot followed her as she walked around, measuring distances and assessing patterns of light and shadow. He said, "In the re-make, there'll be a close-up of the star climbing out on a spar. Then they'll cut to a long shot of the stuntman ripping his way down the sail. But for my article I want you to superimpose a shot of the stuntman over a shot of the entire ship—not just a mock-up of the rigging."

She nodded, wanting only to be finished with the assignment so she could return to her solitude and her emotional upheaval over Nick. She had always known she would have to accept him on his terms, or give him up. Knowing this had not helped ease the pain, or make the choice. Even now, with the decision made to end their relationship completely, she worried about the magnetism of his sheer physical presence when they met again. I must not see him alone, she decided, recalling Maggie's warning. There must be the insulation of other people around when I tell him it's over.

She worked quickly and efficiently. A brief vision of the early days with Nick flashed into her mind.

In the beginning, she had re-loaded his camera, hauled his tripods, wrestled with vicious strobe lights and generally acted as stage-manager for Nick's shots. She was the one who chased the errant reflector screen when it blew away during a session in the desert. Or dealt with anxious celebrities, pushy Hollywood mothers, and curious bystanders.

If she dared to venture an opinion as to a possible better angle or different method of lighting, Nick would quickly put her in her place with a raised eyebrow or an acid comment. That had always been the trouble, she reflected, squinting up at the ship's masts etched against a brilliant sky. He had never acknowledged her as a person, a colleague, a separate entity. He looked on her merely as an extension of himself.

For her part, she had ached with envy at his skill with the camera, and wished passionately she could acquire his single-minded dedication to his profession. She had also been bowled over by his jaunty, devil-may-care facade of reckless bravado. He'd made his name as a news photographer in Vietnam and kept it alive by dashing to every potential insurrection, coup and terrorist raid. Wherever blood had been shed in the name of political idiocy, Nick Kane had been there.

It was beginning to occur to Liz that she had perhaps formed a movie screen idea of the world-weary war correspondent/photographer, complete with turned-up collar trench coat, reckless eyes and cynical grin—and that Nick had come along to match the image perfectly.

When she had finished photographing the sailing ship, they climbed into Elliot's car and headed toward the San Fernando Valley.

"I guess Nick told you that he and I and Adam Eastman were college friends?" Elliot asked as they blended with the stream of weekend traffic on the freeway.

"He mentioned you," Liz answered cautiously, remembering Nick's comment that Elliot Moore was a "cocky little bastard forever biting off more than he could chew." Nick claimed he'd constantly had to rescue him from perilous situations. "But I don't remember Nick ever telling me about your stuntman friend before."

Elliot's head jerked upward and he glanced sideways, reminding her of a badger sniffing the air for prey. "I bet he never told Adam about you, either."

When he did not elaborate on this statement, Liz said, "It's been some time since your college days. I've only known Nick a couple of years."

"Oh, we've kept in touch, the three of us," Elliot replied cryptically.

Liz felt at a disadvantage. Nick had never introduced her to any close friends and she had presumed he had none. He had kept her on the outskirts of his life and she had not questioned his motives. Nick was a man who seemed to have sprung, full-grown, camera in hand, from some distant battleground; having no past of family, college days or fraternity friends. She had been excluded from his life before they met, sharing neither memories nor former friends.

"Adam Eastman is the best of the current crop of stuntmen," Elliot continued. "If someone says a stunt can't be done, he'll do it. He was a college athlete, been a stunt flier, too. But the real passion of his life is sailing. Which is why he agreed to do this particular stunt. They wanted him because he makes a good double for the star, Barry Gerrard, even looks a little like him—wears the same heavy moustache."

Liz was silent, remembering that Nick told her Adam Eastman was "shacking up with a living legend," adding this to the news that he resembled the impossibly handsome Barry Gerrard, and dismissing the stuntman as another Hollywood type she would not care to get to know.

"Same height, but more muscular," Elliot went on. "He'll wear a mask for this stunt and any of his other shots where his face might be visible on film. Barry is touchy about using a double, and Adam doesn't look that much like him in his features."

"I'll keep his face out of my shots," Liz promised.

"There's going to be a last-minute war council to discuss the stunt. We should be there in time to sit in on it. Hopefully Adam will be there and you can study him before you take the shots."

The meeting was already in session when they arrived at the ranch. A glance about the sun-lit room disclosed no one answering the description of Adam

Eastman. One harassed looking man, evidently the director, was explaining to the others—apparently new to the project—what he hoped to accomplish.

"Today's stunt is a re-enactment of the famous scene from *The Black Pirate* that starred Douglas Fairbanks back in the twenties. Fairbanks was marooned by a gang of pirates and in order to revenge himself he promised to capture a ship single-handedly if they allow him to join them. In the action, he is about to be overcome by the crew when he sees a line that passes through a pulley at the top of the mast. He grabs the line and ties the other end to a brass cannon, pushes the cannon over the side and is pulled up to the crow's nest. His opponents come climbing up the shrouds after him. He climbs out on the top yardarm, plunges his dagger into the sail and slides down the sail, ripping the canvas and holding on to the hilt of the dagger. He repeats this process with the lower sails, past his incredulous pursuers. He escapes—and they capture the ship."

He looked around the room expectantly and a young woman with a notebook stood up and spoke. "There's been a lot of speculation over the years as to how the stunt was done—whether Fairbanks did it himself as he insisted, or whether a stuntman performed it. His director claimed the dagger was attached to a pulley arrangement behind the sail and there was a concealed platform on which Fairbanks rode. However, the director lost credulity by adding that Fairbanks smiled all the way down and in the print of the film you can't even see the actor's face, much less a smile. Donald Crisp was the original director before he fell out with Fairbanks and was replaced. Crisp says they tried the stunt many different ways—Fairbank's arm in a cast, a wire down his pant leg . . . he told so many confusing stories that in the end even he couldn't remember for sure how they actually did it. Then there was a stuntman named Chuck Lewis who says they got some canvas and hung it up and just tried sliding down it on a dagger. He says he did it and Doug did it—everyone did it."

The director interrupted, "And fifty years after the stunt, a film buff presented two reels of out-takes from *The Black Pirate* to the library of Congress—and lo and behold, there is Doug Fairbanks himself, sliding down sails over and over . . . ripping the canvas to shreds. The sails weren't on a ship, they were on a back lot . . . but there was no gimmick of hidden platforms or wires. That was when we decided to remake the film."

An earnest-looking man joined the conversation. "We've come up with a specially heavy-weight canvas, over a quarter of an inch thick, which the experts say will offer more than enough resistance to allow a man's weight to rest on the hilt of a dagger for a not–too–rapid descent."

"And the movie is to be an exact remake of *The Black Pirate?"* someone asked.

"More or less. We're making it longer and throwing in a few subplots. And since our star isn't here at present, I might mention that our stuntman—Adam Eastman—will be doing virtually all of the action scenes—the swordplay, climbing the ship's rigging and so on. He'll wear a mask—in fact, we're writing in the mask, and might even change the title to *The Masked Pirate,* just to be sure the audience doesn't realize Barry isn't in the action scenes. I want everyone to remember that Barry Gerrard is putting up the lion's share of the money for this film, and his ego bruises easily. If it gets out that he's only doing the close-ups. . . ." He paused significantly, then gestured that he was ready to answer another question.

Another voice asked, "Has Eastman made any practice runs of today's stunt?"

"No. Apart from the fact that we're trying to keep the whole project secret, he felt it would either work the first time and we'd get it in the can—or. . . ." The director shrugged.

"I didn't see a net out there."

"He refuses to work with one. Claims there's always a difference in the way a stuntman moves when he knows he's safe, no matter what."

"Where is Adam, anyway?"

All of their voices were running together. Liz let her gaze drift to the window. The canvas sails had been hung from a scaffold and were formidably high, to duplicate the rigging of a ship. Beneath lay the hard, sun-baked earth of what was evidently a corral.

A voice more resonant than the others cut through the technical jargon being tossed about the room. "If you're all finished discussing it, I'm ready to rip canvas for you."

Liz turned from the window, her eyes still blinded by the sunlight. The man standing in the doorway wore a bandana tied over his hair, a black mask covered his eyes. With the heavy moustache, the effect was almost comic-opera exaggeration and Liz was disappointed. She concentrated on visualizing the broad back and muscular arms wielding the dagger, the long legs sliding down the canvas.

Adam Eastman held her hand a second longer than necessary when she was introduced to him as Elliot's photographer. He said with mock alarm, "Well, Nick Kane, you've certainly changed since we met last."

"Nick couldn't make it, Adam," Elliot said. "Liz Holly is his assistant."

"His partner," Liz corrected automatically.

"I'd rather have Miss Holly take my picture anyway," Adam said. "Is Liz short for Elizabeth? A lovely name. Old-fashioned, and lovely. Makes me think of gracious ladies—flower petal sachets and starched petticoats and homemade apple jelly."

Liz looked up at him in surprise, but before she could answer, a female voice cut in, "He's teasing you, darling. Don't pay any attention to him." The tone of the voice was distinctly patronizing.

She came into the room on three-inch heels with short impatient steps, dressed in a stark white dress that, combined with silvery-blonde hair and almost translucent skin, was dazzling in its impact. She slipped a heavily ringed hand through Adam's arm in a manner clearly designed to indicate possession. Her eyes were hazel, with flashing pin-points of green, and they regarded Liz coldly, despite the smile curving the sensuously full lips. Similar eyes had been fixed on small animals as a bird of prey watched them.

Liz recognized her at once. Gwynna Duvalle. Famous for her husbands, her wealth, and her constant publicity, rather than the few mediocre films she had appeared in.

"Could we get started?" Gwynna asked, her smile never slipping. "Tonight is the party night, and I must go home to supervise the arrangements."

The meeting broke up and everyone moved outside. Liz began to set up her equipment, barely listening to Elliot Moore's instructions.

Somewhere in the confusion of shouted commands and the murmur of conversation, Liz heard Gwynna say, "She looks rather young and inexperienced to do justice to the stunt and to Adam, don't you think? Does she know he *must* look like Barry? Of course, there will be the stills too, if she blows it. But didn't you say you need the pictures for an article deadline, Elliot?"

Liz concentrated on her camera. It was not the first time her looks had been declared an impediment to her ability.

Adam Eastman climbed the mock-up of the rigging with practiced ease. He waited on the topmost spar while the crew made ready below.

Looking up, Liz felt a twinge of anxiety. What if they were wrong about the canvas ripping slowly enough to allow a man to descend without smashing himself to pulp on the hard ground at least a hundred feet below?

Dodging film cameras, swinging booms and dollies, Liz moved into position with her own camera. Bringing the stuntman into focus she tried to quiet her fears for his safety, telling herself that Nick would be concentrating on the shot to the exclusion of everything else.

The director called for the action to start and the babble of voices was instantly hushed. Adam swung out on the spar, glanced over his shoulder as if at his pursuers, then pulled his dagger from his belt. Plunging the blade into the canvas, he dropped from the spar.

There was a gasp as he fell rapidly, the canvas tearing with a hideous wrenching squeal. At the bottom of the first sail he dug his feet into the canvas, slowing his descent slightly. Then the daggar went into the next sail and he hurtled downward, leaning further into the canvas, digging in with his feet, tensing his muscles against the pull of gravity. He arrived with terrifying speed at the next spar.

He was tearing down the next sail and the ground was rushing ever nearer. Liz snapped off shots in rapid succession, unaware she was holding her breath until she found herself gulping air into her lungs as the stuntman's feet hit the ground.

Everyone crowded around him, congratulating him. Gwynna was squealing and kissing him at the same time. Liz heard Eastman nonchalantly offer to do the stunt again, before Elliot came to her. "He came down much faster than anyone anticipated. You get the shots?"

She nodded. "I'll have them for you tomorrow." Her fingers were shaking as she replaced the camera into its case and snapped it shut.

Elliot helped Liz carry her equipment back to the car. On the drive home he said, "Would you go to the launching party with me? I hate to go to Hollywood parties alone, but I have to attend this one, for my article."

Liz hesitated, searching for a polite refusal. Then she remembered that Nick had also mentioned going to the party. It would be just like him to forget about the stunt but remember the party and show up to make amends with Elliot. Perhaps this was the answer to her apprehension about seeing Nick again, she thought—the insulation she wanted around them when she told him they were finished.

Elliot was watching her with an eager expression that gave his heavy-jawed face a certain childish appeal. "Do you have any idea how many parties a guy who looks like me goes to alone?" he asked with a too-casual grin. "If I show up with you tonight my stock will be up for months around this town."

Liz smiled gently. "I'd be happy to go with you, Elliot."

Adam Eastman had always been a paradox to those around him. There was the physical contradiction of a boxer's brawn combined with the grace of a dancer; he moved like a lithe animal, every muscle controlled. There was the hint of barbarism in his features that was belied by compassionate eyes. Above all, there was his reckless daring and sheer vital courage that gave only the barest hint his soul was nurtured by the gentler pursuits of music and poetry.

His friends, like Elliot and Nick, described him as a "man's man" and did not seem to notice, or care, that their wives and women friends allowed admiring eyes to drift in Adam's direction. Perhaps the reason for this was the complete trust he inspired in those around him. Adam Eastman had never been known to think or act other than honorably.

Their first year in college, he and Nick and been roommates. Each had been fascinated by the other's alien background. Nick was the product of affluent parents who indulged him with expensive photographic equipment, a car, and a generous allowance so long as he stayed in school; thus avoiding the Vietnam draft. Nick chose the easiest courses and made no secret of his boredom with higher education; whereas Adam, in school on an athletic scholarship, worked every weekend, studied half the night and then arose before dawn to go through the Athletic Department's mandatory body punishment of jogging, weight-lifting and swimming.

From Nick, Adam learned the social graces which he had never been exposed to having grown up in a circus family, and later as the ward of the affable old-timer, Gene Eastman, one of Hollywood's first stuntmen.

Adam loved Gene with a quiet and steadfast loyalty. Never for an instant did Adam feel that the now crippled man was an anchor that kept him from fulfilling his dream of sailing around the world. Gene urged him constantly to finish building his boat and sail on the long-planned cruise. But Adam would grin and say the boat wasn't ready.

They would discuss Adam's stunts before he attempted them and in addition to his own carefully planned and scientific approach, Adam often made use of the older man's experience. Gene's heart was a hammer in a forge until the stunt was over, because he knew that Adam always gave more than was demanded of him.

Adam and Nick first met Elliot Moore when a diminutive ball of rage came hurtling down the steps of one of the college buildings where a member of the Black Panthers was addressing a class.

He'd been physically thrown out because of his insistent questioning. "The press has a right to know," he repeated through bruised lips.

Nick and Adam were en route to the library, but Adam paused to help the bleeding and disheveled Elliot to his feet. Glaring defiantly, he promptly started up the steps again.

"Hey, whoa," Nick called after him. "Those cats believe in segregation more than Wallace does."

Adam sprang to catch him, pulling him back. "He's right, you know. That's a Black Panther meeting and they don't care for white visitors. Why do you want to go in there any way?"

Unable to free himself from Adam's grasp, Elliot mustered his dignity and said hoarsely, "I'm a journalist. I just wanted the story."

"I admire your guts, fella," Nick told him, introducing himself. "But you'd better let one of their newsmen write it."

Elliot smiled, showing a chipped tooth. "I'm Elliot Moore," he said. "Will you please ask your gorilla friend to turn me loose?"

After that, Elliot, who was on the newspaper staff, frequently approached Adam for news of his team's activities, and occasionally got his chief editor to use Nick's photos. Elliot was already hopelessly addicted to tobacco, booze, and the written word. A journalism major, he wrote short, incisive sentences that cut straight to the heart of the matter. He wanted, however, to write the great American novel.

Unfortunately, his imagination usually foundered on the rocks of writer's block around chapter two. But as a journalist, Elliot was a feisty featherweight constantly finding himself in trouble with giant adversaries because of his unrelenting search for truth. He would persist in questioning reluctant sources to the point of being slugged. Nick and Adam constantly bailed him out of such situations.

Nick was invited to join an exclusive fraternity and asked Adam and Elliot to accompany him to a get-acquainted dinner. Adam declined awkwardly and Elliot later got Nick on one side and told him, "Haven't you any tact? You idiot, have you ever seen Adam wear a jacket or a tie? No. That's because he doesn't own one. His scholarship pays his tuition, but he still has to take care of room and board, plus his books, plus he supports his old man. You must have known."

"Well—sure, I knew he was working his way through as a stuntman. Haven't I tried to get him to introduce us to some Hollywood starlets? He told me he learned his stuff from his old man. Didn't he retire last year?"

"Retire to a wheelchair, man. A horse dragged him in a Western. No insurance—no company would take him on with his profession."

Nick frowned. "Suppose I just buy a dress shirt and tie and rent a suit . . . leave 'em on Adam's bed?"

"You've got to be kidding. You want to humiliate him? Forget it."

"Oh, the hell with the fraternity then," Nick said, and never gave it a second thought.

Elliot was surprised that a man of Nick's apparent single dimension could be capable of such loyalty to a friend. Elliot did not believe that nothing mattered to Nick but the images he caught on film.

Even in those days, Nick and Adam had had the same taste in women. Elliot waited on the sidelines, mentally keeping notes, as his two good-looking friends vied with one another for the company of the prettiest girls on campus, trying to determine which of the romances would end their friendship. None did.

Then, half way through his senior year, Elliot went to cover anti-war protests and was arrested with the demonstrators.

Adam and Nick were shocked by his appearance when he was released on bail. His eye was blackened and his lip had been stitched. He gave them a puckered grin as he swaggered toward them. "Lost my glasses some place. You guys want to make some fast notes for me, before I forget?"

They had, in common with their peers, agonized over Vietnam. America's part in the conflict was winding down and no one wanted to come home in the last body bag. Campus activists openly solicited donations for the Viet Cong, while the army recruited for the other side. French boys had been born after the outbreak of hostilities in Indo-China, had grown up and died there. American boys who were in kindergarten when the French withdrew were now being maimed and killed on the same bloody battleground. Madness, they agreed. A waste of a lot of lives. No question.

But Adam said, "They only way anyone is going to see if what we're doing there is right or wrong will be to look at the country *after* we've pulled out. If we pull out of a no-win war and things get worse, then we've at least delayed the deterioration."

"Some of the pictures that came out of World War II were fantastic," Nick commented. "Raising the flag on Iwo Jima . . . imagine being there at a moment like that with a camera in your hand."

"Some of the demonstraters in jail with me were veterans," Elliot said. "They didn't want other kids to go through what they went through. Yet on the outside I talked to vets who feel we should go all-out and win—to make some sense out of it for all the kids who died or came home maimed. Guess you'd have to be there to really know . . ."

"I'd have tried for the Navy, if it hadn't been for Gene and his dream of a college education for me," Adam said. "But after I graduate . . ."

Two months later Elliot dropped out of school and flew to Vietnam. Immediately after graduation Nick packed his camera and followed. Adam worked for a few months, doing the stunts no one else wanted, then hired a male nurse for Gene and enlisted. Having some flying experience, he was taught to fly a chopper and assigned to a medical unit evacuating the wounded.

He and Nick and Elliot didn't meet again until the fall of Saigon. Elliot was a wire service reporter by then, a sun-shriveled, cigar-chewing, hardbitten inquisitor with a nose for news, a flamboyant journalistic style, and the still unfulfilled ambition to write the Great American Novel.

Nick had already won the Pulitzer Prize for news photography. He emerged from the conflict with an icy poise that distracted attention from a keenly developed sense of self-preservation. Although he had a knack for choosing the subjects most likely to evoke a sense of outrage, he never actually placed himself in combat danger to obtain them.

Adam had been twice wounded and twice decorated for gallantry under fire, but was less vocal about his experiences than either of his two friends. When it all fizzled out, they were too changed to resume a close friendship, but kept the memory of their Three Musketeer days intact.

Elliot became a freelance, his articles sold well when he wrote them, but he spent more time pursuing the elusive novel that he never finished. Some of his old fire had dissipated in the bloodbath he witnessed, but he was basically still the little runt who tackled bullies twice his size and usually came out the worse for the encounter.

Nick turned down a couple of invitations for reunions and, hurt, Adam did not try again. He did not know that Nick had met Liz, the one woman he did not want to introduce to Adam.

Chapter 3

"Why is everyone scurrying about and giving the impression they only have a minute to live?" Liz asked Elliot that evening.

"They worry that someone will think they aren't working. The worst thing that can happen to anyone in this town is to be out of work. See the guy by the door, making his apologies to our host?"

Liz recognized the good-looking actor who had starred in a smash-hit television program in the late sixties. His face had not been seen anywhere for several years. "He's leaving early—pretending he has to go home to finish a screen treatment that producers are clamoring for—that's the old actor-turned-writer excuse for not working. Or there are several others, each as phony as the last."

Beside them in the tightly-packed room a woman was

saying, "I've been out of the country and haven't seen the trades. What are you doing now?"

Her companion said, "I never go to Hollywood premiers," as though this were an answer to her question. "Premiers are for out-of-work actors. What? Oh, I'm a producer."

Elliot winked and whispered to Liz, "Excuse number 47. To be a producer, all you have to do is *say* you're a producer."

"Hey look . . ." the woman beside them said excitedly, "Paul Newman and Joanne Woodward just arrived—and I heard Jon Voight is here. Oh, wow . . . there's Francoise Brent."

"Who is she?"

"The town's buzzing about her . . . no, I haven't seen her film yet, but they say . . ." The couple drifted away and Elliot said to Liz, "That's the best part of fame for them, when they're new and fresh. When the town is reporting that so-and-so is full of promise, destined to be a super-star. They're all so desperate for it to happen to them. Even when it does it's usually fleeting. Most of the soaring stars crash before they hit the heights. This is a very cruel town. A people mill—grinds them up and spits them out."

Liz was not really interested, she watched the new arrivals to see if Nick was among them. Elliot did not notice her silence since he was talking about the articles he was writing.

". . . one of a series of articles about movie making and Tinsel Town. One segment will be about the stuntman because he's part of the magic. The actor gets all the credit, but guys like Adam take their lumps. Oh, there's always an actor who claims he does his own stunts, but I never met one, and I doubt if many of them would have the guts, even if the insurance underwriters would allow it. I guess it might have been different in the old days when Doug Fairbanks made *The Black Pirate.*"

The party was taking place in a sprawling tri-level house, high in the hills. From the wall of glass that formed part of the living room the lights of Los Angeles spread out like a jewel-encrusted cloak. Guests packed the room, standing in tight clusters, making animated conversation. Others had spilled out to the redwood deck on the other side of the enormous sliding window. Beneath the fixed smiles and tinkling laughter, the atmosphere hummed with tension and anxiety.

Liz had been introduced to her host, a slightly-built, flamboyantly dressed man in his forties with silver hair, silver chains around his turtle-necked sweater and a silver cigarette holder clamped between dental advertisement teeth. Since only first names had been exchanged, Liz knew him only as "Colby." Elliot added later that Colby was one of the picture's backers.

"Does Colby have a wife?" Liz asked now.

Elliot smiled. "He doesn't care for women—not romantically. I guess I should have told you, he's Gwynna's brother, Colby Duvalle. This is her house—Colby lives here too, but she owns it. He's her business manager; watches over her like a hawk."

"If she lives here, why haven't we seen her yet?"

"She likes to make an entrance, even to her own parties. Besides, neither Barry Gerrard nor Adam Eastman have arrived yet, and they are her current interests. Barry's been out of town and Adam doesn't care for parties, he'll wait until the last minute. He's probably working on the boat he's been building for years. It's always been his dream to have enough money to sail around the world. I guess that's why he takes on stunts other stuntmen turn down."

"But surely he's made enough for that already?"

"He might have, if it weren't for his father."

"He supports him?"

Elliot nodded. "Old Gene was a stuntman, too—originally came from a circus, I believe high-wire or something. Worked in the early days of movies and did some hair-raising stunts . . . falls, car wrecks. Then he had to double an actor being dragged by a horse in a Western. The stunt went badly: the doctors said if Gene hadn't been such a tough old hombre he would have been killed. He's been in a wheelchair ever since. I sometimes think that's why Adam never married."

"Or fulfilled his ambition to sail around the world?" Liz asked. "He probably couldn't leave his father."

"The old man is as much of a character as Adam is," Elliot mused, side-stepping deftly to avoid a lurching young actor making a beeline for a well-known director who had just arrived.

"Old Gene doubled in a lot of the old swashbuckling melodramas. He could fence and wield a sword or cutlass with the best of them. He taught Adam all he knows about fencing. Of course, they don't make swashbucklers any more, more's the pity. That's why *The Black Pirate* is such a gamble."

"I've heard the cost of producing costume dramas is prohibitive," Liz murmured.

All conversation died suddenly as Gwynna Duvalle made her entrance.

Gwynna was a vision in floating white chiffon, jewels sparkling in the silver blonde hair. Every movement and gesture, from the way she tilted her head so that the light reflected on frosted eye shadow and gleaming white teeth, to the graceful sweep of red-tipped fingers, were designed to catch and hold attention. Although Gwynna was a frequent guest on TV talk shows and news of her comings and goings was always faithfully reported in the news media, she had not actually made a film for many years. She had, however, gone through seven or eight wealthy husbands.

Elliot said, *sotto voce,* "Mirror, mirror on the wall, who is the fairest . . ." as the guests surged forward to greet Gwynna.

"Among the more interesting rumors about Gwynna is the one that she slips away in the middle of her parties for a nap, a bubble bath and a session with her hairdresser. She also has a second identical dress to the one she's wearing, so that no matter how long the party lasts, she'll look fresh. It's also rumored she'll only make love if she can sit on top of her lover—so she doesn't disturb her hair-do and make-up," Elliot said wryly. "I wonder if Adam would punch me out if I asked him if that's true?"

Liz was silent, thinking that Gwynna Duvalle made every other woman in the room look under-dressed and unglamorous. She tried to make a quick calculation of Gwynna's age, but other than realizing with a start that Gwynna had already been a star while Liz was still in high school, it was impossible.

The evening wore on, the house becoming more crowded and the conversation louder. Gwynna held court, surrounded by her admirers. Her only acknowledgment of Liz's presence came when she greeted Elliot Moore and added, "And you brought your little photographer with you, darling. How nice."

Elliot told Liz, "She's going to announce later on that she's coming out of retirement to star in *The Black*

Pirate. That's the real reason for the party tonight. You'll notice the news media is well represented."

"I thought you said it had already been cast months ago."

"Everything but the female lead. Barry Gerrard is playing the old Doug Fairbanks part and Gwynna's been wanting to make a movie with Barry for years. They were a hot item in the old days and rumor has it Gwynna's been carrying a torch for him—all her other husbands and lovers notwithstanding. I suspect her interest in Adam Eastman may only be because of the very slight resemblance in looks. I'd be worried about my friend getting hurt if it weren't for the fact that Adam is something of a rake himself. But I wonder how Barry will feel about having Adam on the set. Apart from Gwynna, Barry and Adam did not hit it off the last time Adam doubled for him."

A short time later, when Liz had decided Nick was not coming, she was grateful when Elliot suggested they leave. In a bedroom, sorting through a jumble of wraps and coats to find her own, she was suddenly aware of a prickling sensation along her spine.

The room was illuminated only by a bedside lamp, turned low, and when she raised her eyes he was standing in the doorway, a slightly-built silhouette against the light from the hall. "I don't blame you for leaving," he said. "It's a zoo, isn't it?" The voice was unpleasantly peevish. She recognized the diminutive shadow as Colby Duvalle, Gwynna's brother. He was saying "I understand you took photographs of the stunt today."

"You'll probably see some of them in the papers tomorrow. Elliot kept the best for his article."

"And the great Barry Gerrard will take credit for

what the stuntman accomplished. I suppose, like the rest of the female guests—including my sister—you're disappointed Mr. Wonderful Gerrard isn't here yet? He will be coming later, if you'd care to wait." Colby Duvalle spoke with a hint of a nasal whine, not quite disguised by a polished European accent. "Knowing Barry, I'm sure he'll take a bow for someone else's performance without a qualm," Colby added, with a petulance creeping into the comment that told more about himself than Barry Gerrard.

"It's a lovely party and I'd like to stay, but I'm rather tired," Liz said. "And I was hoping my partner, Nick Kane, would be here."

"Ah, yes. I met the gentleman. Tall, lean, reddish-brown hair, a cocky grin."

"That's Nick," Liz said, finally finding her wrap. Colby moved closer to help her with it, and she was aware of an overpowering scent of cologne and the jingle of chains around his neck. She wanted to run from him, without knowing why. As his hand casually touched her arm, she felt a shiver crawl up her spine. She moved quickly to the doorway.

Searching the crowded room for Elliot, she heard the conversation swell suddenly into a chorus of greetings. At the same instant she saw the two new arrivals. Nick. Her heart skipped. At his side was the unmistakable presence of Barry Gerrard, moving into the room with an actor's control over his body, greeting the other guests with that famous smile, slapping the men lightly, hugging the women. The distinctive moustache was exactly like the one worn by Adam Eastman, but Liz noted immediately that Barry Gerrard was smaller in stature and considerably older than the stuntman.

Nick saw Liz and made his way toward her. He swept

her into his arms. "Liz, babe, I'm glad you came. I've big news." His dark eyes were alive with excitement.

He's forgotten that today was to be our wedding day, Liz thought, trying to pull away from the embrace.

Nick was asking, "Did you see who arrived with me? The great Gerrard himself. Babe, we're going into the movie business. It's all set. I've talked to Barry and the other backers and they're letting me invest in *The Black Pirate*. I couldn't tell you on the phone the other night; I was afraid I wouldn't pull it off. I wanted to give you a really terrific wedding present, Liz. They'll be shooting part of the film on location in the Hawaiian islands and we can have our honeymoon there. What do you say to that? Liz, babe, look, I'm sorry, there wasn't time to explain. I'd been waiting for an opportunity to talk to Barry Gerrard and the other backers. I'd been after him for weeks, then the other night I suddenly got a phone call that he was going to Palm Springs for a couple of days golfing and he'd see me there. I drove down right away. I didn't even remember about Adam's stunt until this morning when Barry said he'd have to keep out of sight for a couple of hours as he was supposed to be doing the stunt. I guess Elliot can use the stills for his article." Nick was bursting with enthusiasm and did not appear to notice either the expression on Liz's face or the way she pulled away from him.

"I took the pictures," she said.

He gave her an animated smile. "I can always count on you. What would I do without you?"

"I don't know. But you're going to have to . . . do without me, that is. We're through." As usual, his explanation was plausible, knowing Nick, she also knew he would forget everything but the pursuit of the immediate goal. He had not deliberately hurt and humiliated her.

Conversation and laughter swirled and hummed around them. Nick blinked, leaned closer. "I didn't get that—what did you say? Oh, hell, let's get out of here. I can discuss the deal with the other backers tomorrow." He grabbed her hand but she stood her ground.

"I said we're through, Nick," she announced in ringing tones.

There was a momentary lull in conversation and several guests glanced at them with amusement. Nick flushed. "OK, babe, so I'm in the dog house. Let's go home and talk about it in private."

"I came with Elliot. He's taking me home."

"Fine. I need to talk to the Duvalles anyway." He turned angrily and pushed through the crowd toward Gwynna Duvalle.

Liz looked around for Elliot but he was nowhere in sight. Feeling uncomfortable under the scrutiny of nearby guests, she wandered out on to the redwood deck and sat down to wait, glad for the concealing darkness.

It would have been desperately easy to accept Nick's explanation. He had told her many times that the natural progression for a photographer was from stills to movies. Although she didn't agree, seeing photography as a separate art form, she could understand Nick's excitement at the opportunity of working with stars of the magnitude of Barry Gerrard and Gwynna Duvalle.

Just then she saw that Adam Eastman was coming directly toward her. Her first instinct was to melt backward into the crowd, but there was something honest and earnest about his expression that made her feel that she would be injuring him disproportionately by neglecting to recognize him.

"I'm so glad to see you here. I have the feeling that you're probably the only person here that I can talk to," he told her.

She was instantly on her guard, too battle-ready from her struggles with Nick.

"Oh, really," she said, "what exactly has your old friend told you about me?"

"Nothing," Adam said simply. "And it is certainly obvious why he didn't want to mention a thing about you. He's a very lucky man; though as fond as I am of him, I can't quite understand what brings you two together. You seem entirely different."

"Variety is the spice of life," Liz answered, but she was suddenly self-conscious, realizing how vulnerable her tough-lady repartee was beginning to sound.

"He's really hurt you, hasn't he?" Adam studied her softly.

All at once Liz was afraid that Adam was going to make her cry—there, in front of every one. She glanced up sharply into his eyes and he almost winced at the pain he saw on her face.

"Excuse me, please . . ." she mumbled and turned, leaving him stranded amidst the glowing tans and boring talk that had gradually drifted out onto the deck. She found her way into a small library where expensive antique books decorated the shelves, obviously never being disturbed by a reader. She didn't know how long she had sat there seeing nothing but the maddening pity in Adam Eastman's eyes when a door opened.

Colby Duvalle's voice interrupted her thoughts. "I'll be glad to interpret for you."

She looked up. "I beg your pardon?"

"The language they use. A crash course in the vernacular. All you have to do is throw in an appropriate comment. 'Boffo' or 'socko' are good. Then there's 'fairish' or 'trim.' Or if you really want to penetrate a conversation, then you should discuss a specific film. Be sure to look down on any films that are entertaining . . . use terms like 'superficial visual eye' and 'visual metaphor.' Better yet, throw in an observation about subtle thematic nuances."

Liz felt uneasy listening to his sarcastic outburst, particularly since she had observed Colby fawning upon all of the celebrities present. She murmured non-commitally and was relieved when Gwynna Duvalle's voice called from the door, "Colby, darling, what are you doing in there? Do come out, sweetie, Barry wants to talk to you." She took a step inside, peering near-sightedly to see who her brother was talking to, then went back out.

Colby said, "A certain director once remarked that they're all like cattle. Actors and actresses, that is. I heartily agree."

He walked across to the door and paused for a moment. Liz saw that he was unaware that he was slowly emptying his wineglass on to the floor as his rather delicate hand trembled and then relaxed at his side. The light from the house illuminated his face and Liz was startled to see his expression was one of hatred rather than disgust. His delicately handsome features were so contorted that she wondered uneasily who he was watching.

Chapter 4

Maggie found Liz going through a pile of old photographs, which she hastily tossed back into a file drawer.

"Why don't you stop torturing yourself?" Maggie asked. "Get away for a while—by yourself. Think things out."

"What do you suggest? Your shangri-la in the South Pacific? What was it called . . . Falconer's Island?"

"I made a tentative reservation. When you called to tell me it was off again. The wedding, that is."

"Maybe I should go there and work. I was just looking at those old photographs and thinking the story of Liz and Nick would make a novel. You know, one of those photonovels that are all the rage."

"Good idea. I'd like to see you get something out of the Nick Kane experience besides heartache."

Liz made small talk with Maggie, told her briefly that

Nick had invested in *The Black Pirate*. When she began to rationalize that this was the reason for the sudden trip out of town and the cancelled wedding, Maggie cut her short.

"Okay, Liz, if that's what you want to believe. But spare me the gory details. I've never been able to understand your obsession with him. I've a hunch you fell in love with his photographs—long ago when you knew that's what you wanted to do—then you just tailored Nick Kane's image to fit what you wanted your dream man to be. There's a theory around that women fall for the men they'd like to be. But you'll never be like him, you care too much about people, so you're doomed to lose him."

Liz handed her a cup of coffee and sat down across from Maggie's ample body lounging on the couch. "I had no idea you were a philosopher. All the time we roomed together you gave no hint of it. But it's all beside the point now, anyway. I told you, Nick and I are finished."

"I know what you told me," Maggie said darkly. "I also know that Nick isn't going to give up so easily."

Liz sipped her coffee and deftly changed the subject. After Maggie left, Liz pulled out the folder of pictures again. The photonovel had not been a spur of the moment invention so Maggie would not see her pain, the idea had come to her the last time Nick disappeared abruptly.

He'd called her from Hong Kong, the overseas wires crackling and hissing his explanation that he'd gotten fed-up with L.A. and needed to breathe.

Liz decided to sort her files and found there was a series of pictures that told the story of the two of them, from their first meeting. Some she had taken, others Nick had taken. His composition was always better than hers, but she caught the more expressive gestures, the revealing glance of his dark eyes or twist of his mouth. The photographs of the two of them together had been taken by several different people and ranged from candid to excellent.

Photographic novels were the latest rage in Hollywood, usually with film stars telling the story. Adult comic books, Nick had sneered when he was approached to do one. But many were much more than that.

Although the current crop of photonovels were all based on movies and contained frames from the film with cartoon dialogue, there was no reason a skilled photographer could not do the same thing with an original story, she felt. Why not tell the story of two photographers? Partners who loved each other and made each other miserable. She could include some of Nick's Vietnam pictures, the ones that had made his name, won him a Pulitzer Prize, and forever changed him.

Perhaps it would make some sense out of her willing descent to a level of despair that no human being had the right to inflict upon another. Perhaps it would be good therapy.

Perhaps it would be a gift to Nick, showing him how intricately interwoven their lives had become. A gesture of her love.

That had been her original intention. Now she thought perhaps the photonovel was still a good idea, it would be a cleansing process, washing Nick out of her life forever.

She had not seen him since the night of the party. He had phoned to say he would take the rest of Elliot's pictures for the articles. Nick was curt, businesslike, and made no mention of their personal status.

Liz was caught off-guard. She had expected him to batter her senses with his usual surfeit of charm, beg her forgiveness, and plead that she see him. When he did not, she was forced to take the initiative.

"We'd better discuss our business partnership," she said in a small tight voice. "I think we should terminate that, too."

"I have to run. I'll call you tonight," he said.

Late that night Liz watched a television talk show which featured Gwynna and Barry Gerrard talking about the re-making of *The Black Pirate.* Liz had waited all evening, nerves taut, rehearsing what she would say, waiting for Nick to call. Finally she flipped on the television to try to relax.

Barry was saying, "Naturally, since Doug Fairbanks did all his own stunts, I'll also be doing mine." He gave a careless smile, made more roguish by the heavy moustache.

Liz felt a twinge of indignation, remembering Adam ripping down the canvas sails.

". . . and darling, my wardrobe is fabulous," Gwynna put in. "This film is going to bring back the swashbucklers. Women will flock to see it, believe me. We're all so tired of anti-heroes and unhappy endings and all the harsh realities of modern life. We want romance, darling, with a capital R."

The talk show moderator leaned forward on one elbow and said, "There are rumors of a jinxed set. That you've had several setbacks. Accidents. Is that true, Miss Duvalle?"

Gwynna's smile did not falter, but her eyes flickered warily in Barry's direction. His face was carefully blank.

"Nonsense, darling," Gwynna said. "There was a tiny fire at the marina and it did a little bit of damage to an old sailing ship we're going to use. Nothing to do with the film crew at all."

The moderator interrupted smoothly, "But wasn't there also some trouble at the studio? Scripts that disappeared and a mock-up that collapsed? Cameras breaking down?"

Barry Gerrad said, "Movie people are superstitious. A couple of minor problems and they exaggerate into a jinx. There's no truth in any of the rumors you've heard. We've found that we need a great many script changes, that's all. Audiences today are more sophisticated than they were in the twenties."

Hearing Nick's key in the front door, Liz switched off the set.

"Turn on the TV," Nick said, before he closed the door. "Gwynna and Barry are talking about *The Black Pirate.*"

Liz started in disbelief as he crossed the room. "I've waited for you to call all evening. I'm not going to wait another second. Don't you understand—I don't give a damn about your stupid movie. I want to talk about splitting up all the equipment we bought together, about buying out your interest in the studio goodwill, although God knows you've done damn little to build it up. I want to talk about getting Nick Kane out of my apartment, out of my business, and out of my life. Permanently."

He shot her a quizzical grin, fumbled with the television, cursed softly when the picture came on and the sequence with Gwynna and Barry was ending.

"Nick—damn you!" Liz yelled. Her hand closed around an onyx vase standing on the coffee table and she hurled it in the direction of the television set. She missed the set and the vase crashed into the wall. Nick ducked, leaping behind the couch in feigned alarm.

"That's more like it," he said. "You had me worried with that icy calm ultimatum. When you're fighting mad at me I know you still care." He was inching along the back of the couch toward her.

Liz drew a deep breath, resisting the urge to pick up the twin to the vase and throw it at him. Inwardly she railed at herself for losing control. "I was merely trying to get your attention. What do you want to do about the studio and the equipment?"

"Will you just listen to me for a moment, first? Liz, I know I should have leveled with you. I was afraid you'd try to talk me out of it . . . and honest, babe, I was just doing it for us." He was beside her now and, despite her anger, his nearness sent old sensory messages impossible to ignore.

"Leveled about what?" she asked coldly.

"I put every dime we have into the movie—including a loan I took out, using the studio and all the equipment as collateral. I even used the money we saved for our honeymoon. But in a couple of weeks we can honeymoon in Hawaii. Liz, babe—just listen while I explain everything—OK?"

"Nick, are you out of your mind? Everything I put into this—my time, my love, my money—you had absolutely no right to do this without asking me. You do everything without asking me!"

He interrupted, bursting with enthusiasm, "When Elliot first contacted me about the article he casually mentioned that no one wanted to risk an expensive production of a costume drama, since they've been out of style for so long. But Gwynna had her heart set on doing one and she persuaded Barry Gerrard to star in it—and he's instant box office. She and Barry were putting up most of the money and were looking for investors for the balance. Liz, a re-make of a famous old movie, with those two starring in it, will make a fortune. The fan magazines have kept alive that story of them being starcrossed lovers since they were kids. Well, right now they are both divorced again, so the PR people can whip up a feverish romance off-screen, too. *The Black Pirate* is going to be a blockbuster. Adam Eastman is the best stuntman in town, as well as being an accomplished swordsman, so he'll double Barry in all the action scenes. And Liz, I've saved the best part till last—the film will be great because guess who is going to advise the camera crew . . . none other than the great Nick Kane himself."

Liz stared at him, marveling that his little-boy eagerness still had the power to make her want to protect him from disappointment. "Nick, it's too late. I've already resigned myself to life without you. I suppose we'll have to continue our business partnership until after the film is made, but I want you to stay away from me."

"You don't mean that. I love you, Liz. And you haven't stopped loving me. Just give me a chance to make amends. Liz, I want to give you the whole world. I saw an opportunity of making a lot of money and I grabbed it. But it won't mean a thing if you aren't at my side."

His dark eyes caressed her face as his fingers tentatively closed over hers. His eyes and his touch were pleading for forgiveness, while the fear of rejection manifested itself in the husky hesitation of his voice, the way his teeth came down over his lower lip in a gesture of suppressed pain, and the slight trembling of his hand. In spite of her resolution, she was deeply touched. Nick was as close to groveling as she had ever seen him, but she felt no satisfaction in his capitulation. She was wrenched apart with emotion, her heart and body wanting to melt toward him, while reason screamed at her that she would be hurt again.

"Nick—I don't know . . ." She looked away from the intensity of his gaze and did not see the flicker of triumph that passed briefly over his face.

Dropping down on her side of the couch, his voice broke slightly as he said, "I've missed you so, the last couple of days. I thought I'd go crazy, wanting to come to you, but afraid you'd turn me away. I didn't really want to watch Barry and Gwynna on TV when I came in—I was just trying to play it cool. Liz, inwardly I was crying with fright that I'd lost you. God, I need you . . . He played with the buttons of her blouse.

"If everything we have is invested in *The Black Pirate*—what if anything goes wrong? We'll lose it all." She tried to think about business, about the studio, about anything but the old longing for him. His fingers were finding their way inside her blouse, stroking her breast.

"Nothing can go wrong. Listen, tomorrow I'm going down to the set. Come with me. Watch them shoot the ballroom scene." His brown eyes sparkled with childish hope and excitement, happiness radiated from his flushed skin. His lips were warm against her throat, moving downward to take her nipple. She was breathing raggedly, feeling herself slip away to that mystic state that numbed her mind while it quickened her senses.

"You won't believe the magic of Barry and Gwynna," he whispered. "They were doing a torrid love scene today. Believe me, this movie is going to be a smash. See, Barry takes Gwynna in his arms, like this . . . kisses her—so . . ."

In spite of her misgivings, Liz relaxed as his lips

moved against hers, his tongue seeking entry to her mouth. Her body betrayed her will by responding as he pushed her backward and pressed his body close, his erection straining to find entry between her thighs. He smiled down at her, dark eyes alive with mischief. "Note that I keep my best profile turned to the camera at all times. When I kiss you—like this—I hide you from the camera completely." He gave a dazzling smile to the imaginery camera and Liz felt her last qualm slip away. He had always been able to restore her good humor, and stifle her misgivings, with such antics. She smiled, amused, and relaxed completely.

He was sliding her jeans down, caressing her soft pubic hair, kissing her eyelids, her mouth. Then he stood up and tore off his own clothes. Liz watched him, aware again of the power he had over her.

She had agonized a hundred times over why he could arouse in her such a fever pitch of passion. Wanting him desperately, feeling the magic of desire, why then did their lovemaking always leave her suspended in limbo? Loving him, she assumed the fault was hers; that some flaw in her response left her irretrievably behind. She felt sometimes as though they were racing each other to see who could be first to crash over the edge of fulfillment. Nick, of course, was always the winner.

Nick was kneeling between her legs, teasing her unmercifully, stroking her and then pulling away. At every flick of his tongue she shivered, wanting him, rising to meet him. Liz was sure of her own sensuality, she felt it in every nerve ending and in the mind-numbing desire that sent waves of dizziness over her. She longed for the fulfillment that always eluded her. If only they were married . . . no, don't think of that now. Abruptly Nick swung himself the other way and she felt a stab of disappointment when she realized there was not going to be intercourse.

She enjoyed oral sex only as foreplay, but increasingly for Nick it had become the means to climax. Vaguely she wondered about his fear that she would become pregnant. Was that the reason? Surely he trusted her not to force fatherhood on him? As much as she would like a child . . .

As usual Nick climaxed before she did. Her nerves were afire and her body was taut with tension when he suddenly shook with the spasm of his ejaculation and lay limply against her legs. Almost as though nothing had happened, he immediately began to talk about the filming of *The Black Pirate* again.

Liz felt a silent scream race from her brain through her aching senses.

The ballroom scene was being shot on a lavish set, with a milling throng of extras in elaborate costumes, a confusion of cameramen and equipment, script girls, a harassed director, and, it seemed to Liz, almost as many spectators as performers.

She saw Colby Duvalle in conversation with two make-up men, presumably about Gwynna, who had not yet emerged from her dressing room and was holding up shooting.

Nick was speaking animatedly to Barry Gerrard, who was resplendent in an embroidered satin coat over skin-tight breeches. The moustache isn't right, Liz thought, and his hair is too short.

Almost instantly, a second Barry Gerrard, identically attired, appeared on the set. Adam Eastman. Liz was startled at how much they resembled each other from a distance. Both wore masks, but the disguise seemed unnecessary. One of the associate producers was handing out satin masks to all of the extras, whom he addressed as "atmosphere people."

A heated argument was in progress near where she stood. A team of writers disagreeing over script changes. No doubt the finished production would bear little resemblance to the original silent movie.

The director called for silence to explain what would take place. "Gwynna has been married by proxy to a man who wants only her fortune. Her ship was captured by pirates and she's fallen in love with the dashing Sea Wolf—Barry, of course. The masked ball is to present Gwynna to her husband's family and friends, however, her pirate lover sneaks in wearing a mask. He is pursued by a rival pirate, who gives them away. A duel ensues."

"All right—everyone take their places. I want screams from the women and panic from everyone as they rush off the floor to make room for the duelists. Adam, are you ready?"

Adam was ready, but Gwynna had not yet appeared. Everyone waited.

Liz was thinking she should have gone to her studio, or perhaps called on some of the agencies to drum up business, when she looked up to see Adam Eastman approaching.

He bowed extravagantly. "The bewitching Miss Holly. What do you say to a breath of clean air when this charade is over? There's a freshening breeze and my boat would fly on swift wings across the bounding main with you as a passenger."

"I came with Nick—" Liz began.

"Who is going to spend the day telling everyone how the movie should be shot. There'll be take after take of this scene and you'll be bored to tears. The other double and I will do the duel once and get out of here.

Come on, let's put ourselves in the hands of fate. See what comes of this acute sense of awareness I get when you appear on the scene."

Liz looked beyond him to where Nick stood, gesturing toward the camera, as he spoke to Barry. "Nick and I are getting married on Saturday. You really are too much, Adam. Everything I heard about you is true."

"What did you hear?" Behind his mask his eyes expressed mock alarm.

Nick had warned her, en route to the set, that in the old days he and Adam had made a game of making a play for the woman the other was interested in. Nick claimed they had both declared their ambition to be famous ladies' men and that Adam had come close to fulfilling the role. She said, "That you're a professional rake."

"Not true. Are you really going to marry Nick?"

"You make it sound like I'm contemplating marrying the Prince of Wales."

"Unless Nick has changed radically in the last few years, I'd say that the Prince of Wales would be a better bet. Let's have dinner tonight and discuss it."

Liz said impatiently, "Aren't you needed somewhere?" She was about to move away when Gwynna swept out on to the mock ballroom floor. She wore yards of rustling satin and her powdered wig was ablaze with diamonds. She stopped, seeing Adam in conversation with Liz, and her voice was shrill when she spoke, "Really, Barry, must you have all these hangers-on cluttering the set?"

Adam turned toward her, giving a mock salute "Gwynna, you just made your director's day. Mistaking me for the star, that is. But I believe you owe Miss Holly an apology. It sounded as though you were referring to her when you said hangers-on."

"I *was* referring to her," Gwynna said. "And to everyone else who has no business here."

Adam turned to Liz. "Now how about that sail? To hell with all this."

They were surrounded by a babble of voices. The director, Nick, Barry Gerrard, all pleading with Adam to go straight into the duel. Gwynna remained tight-lipped, glaring defiantly. Nick grabbed Liz's arm and whispered in her ear, "What's the idea of getting cozy with Adam? Let me handle this."

Liz jerked her arm free of his grasp. "I think I'd better leave before I say a great many things I may regret later."

Nick did not try to stop her and Adam did not see her leave as his view was blocked by the director. Only Colby Duvalle met her eye, lifting his shoulders in resignation. He wore a silk shirt with an abstract black and white design and what looked like raw silk black slacks. As usual his throat was encircled with silver chains matching his stylishly sculpted silver hair.

There was a peculiar malevolence to his stare as he watched her go. Liz thought, in passing, that like his sister, he was a diminutive peacock of exotic plumage; except that Gwynna's rages flared on the surface, his seethed somewhere deep inside.

Half an hour after she arrived back at her apartment, Liz's phone rang. At first she didn't recognize the strained voice. "I wanted to apologize for Gwynna. She didn't mean anything really, she's touchy about younger women on the set and under a strain because she hasn't made a picture for a long time."

Adam Eastman, Liz thought, annoyed at his presuming to call.

"She mistook me for Barry. She doesn't care enough about a humble stuntman to give that kind of exhibition of jealousy. Your friend Nick was doing an admirable job of placating her when I left."

"What's that supposed to mean?" Liz asked sharply.

"Nothing. He's got a vested interest in *The Black Pirate* hasn't he? He was just protecting his investment. But since they're busy, how about you and I having lunch?"

"No. Please don't ask again."

"I really could use your company. I just had a narrow escape from a rather messy death on the set."

"You're kidding, aren't you?"

"Maybe the rumors about a jinx aren't just rumors. One of those fancy chandeliers came down—missed me by inches. I'd just finished the duel and was holding my position until Barry came to take my place for the close-ups."

"I'm sorry, but the answer is still no. Look, we've met briefly on two occasions connected with the film. No doubt we'll cross paths again—but please, let's not complicate either of our lives by imagining we will have anything but a business relationship."

She replaced the receiver firmly and then called Nick's apartment. There was no answer. She called their studio and got the answering service.

Making herself a sandwich, she thought of all the appointments she could have made for this week. It should have been their honeymoon, she thought with a pang of regret. Nick wants all of the advantages of marriage but none of the responsibilities. He wants to be free to come and go as he pleases; no ties. Why can't I feel the same? Did every man feel that way? Perhaps there was no other type of man left in these sexually liberated times.

Since making up with him again she had not been able to face Maggie, who had called to tell her

Falconer's Island was still available if she wanted to get away for a while.

Liz had tried to rationalize that Nick's preoccupation with the film had dimmed his ardor, once the white heat of their making up had faded, but the qualms were returning. The incident on the film set smouldered in her mind and with it the certain awareness that it had been a mistake to make up with Nick.

She called the answering service again late that afternoon to see if Nick had checked in. He had not. An hour later the service called back.

"An urgent call for you at the studio," the operator told her. "I told him you could be reached at home, but he said he didn't have time. An Elliot Moore asked if you could go to Gwynna Duvalle's house right away. The one you went to for the party. He said you'd know where it was and that he'd meet you there."

"Now?" Liz asked, perplexed. "Did he say what for?"

"No. Just said try to make it within half an hour. It was important."

Liz scribbled a note for Nick and drove up the secluded canyon toward Gwynna's house. There was no sign of Elliot's car on the driveway and, when she approached the front door she saw it was wide open. She stepped into the hall uncertainly. "Anyone home?"

Music drifted down the staircase, but no one answered. She crossed the hall, pushed open the living room door, and looked into a deserted room.

Feeling uneasily like an intruder, she went quickly back to the front door and almost collided with Colby Duvalle. "Why—Miss Holly, were you looking for someone?" He looked pale and fragile in the daylight, and with his pink silk shirt and white slacks, more feminine than ever. It was easy to see why it had long been rumored that Colby's preference was for his own sex.

Again Liz noticed the malice in his expression. There was something about the hatred that exuded from this man that seemed to Liz to be not pure hatred but . . . well, impure hatred. She could not help smiling at this thought, and Duvalle studied her smile, without smiling back, seeming to sense that she was not trying to be friendly. His look would almost make you sorry for him, she thought, except that there's something ruthless and cruel about it. He looks not only as if someone has made him suffer unbearably, but as if he would kill that person first chance he got. Not wanting to encourage any conversation, she came to the point.

"I had a message to meet Elliot Moore here. I'm afraid there must have been some mistake," Liz said, embarrassed.

"Ah—I see. He's probably upstairs wih Gwynna. I thought I heard her greet a visitor a little while ago. And there was some talk about photographs for his article."

"But I didn't bring a camera."

"Well, I could be wrong. Why don't you just run upstairs and see what he wants. You know how Gwynna is, she'll require several conferences on what she's going to wear and the lighting and so on before you actually take the pictures."

When Liz hesitated, he said again, "It's all right, she always receives visitors upstairs in her room. Second door to the right."

Reluctantly Liz went up the stairs toward the sound of the music. She didn't recognize the piece but it sounded like something from a forties' film. Colby

Duvalle watched her ascent for a moment, then went back outside.

Reaching the top of the stairs, she heard Gwynna's throaty chuckle over the strains of the music. The second door was slightly ajar. Liz raised her hand to knock, then pulled it back.

The crack in the door was wide enough for her to see Gwynna's naked white body, reflected in mirrors on walls and ceiling. She was sitting astride the man who lay on her white satin bed, riding him, her full breasts swinging back and forth as she rose and descended. Every platinum blonde hair was neatly in place and her diamond earrings flashed on shell pink ears. Liz thought, in that split second, that Elliot had been right about Gwynna not destroying her coiffure while making love.

Then Liz was running back down the stairs, biting her lip to keep all of the shattering pain contained inside her.

The man Gwynna had been energetically servicing was Nick.

Chapter 5

Liz felt a moment's panic as the outrigger canoe pulled away, bouncing through the surf beyond the reef, leaving her alone on the shimmering beach. She watched the sails disappear over the horizon before stooping to pick up her bags.

Only the sound of the sea and the occasional call of a bird broke the silence. He'll never find me here, she thought, no one will. Damn him, I'm finished with him. I'm not running away from Nick. I just need to be totally alone to work on the project. How he'd laugh at it. Will I ever show it to anyone, or is it just a cleansing I have to go through?

She tried to welcome her impending solitude as she walked up the beach toward the stone steps cut into the cliff. As she reached the top step the sunlight blinded her. Blinking, she hesitated before proceeding. Despite the warmth of the trade winds caressing the island and the heat radiated by midday sunlight, she shivered suddenly.

She scanned her surroundings carefully. The grass shack lay ahead, protected by a cluster of coconut palms, blooming trees and shrubs of every description. She recognized white ginger, plumeria, bougainvillea. Giant conch shells marked the path to the door. It was all exactly like the photograph she had seen in Honolulu.

Feeling uneasy, she glanced back over her shoulder, telling herself she was merely in a highly emotional state of mind. Below was a sheltered white sand beach, encircled by wind-bent palms. The center of the island was volcanic rock. Beyond the grass shack lay a dark pool into which a waterfall cascaded.

"You can rent it for a month. The only stipulation is that you must be the only guest," the travel agent had told her. "The owner is eccentric. Never goes there himself, but doesn't want people tearing up his island . . . having barbecues on the beach and littering the lagoon. He figures one person alone will go there to work, or rest. An artist, or a writer, for instance."

"I'm a photographer," Liz had said, "But I am doing a book. I do want to be completely alone to work."

And to get away from Nick, she thought. He tore me to shreds with his moods, his jaunts, and his infidelities; but he taught me a lesson with his final humiliation. No man will ever make me suffer like that again.

"A book of photographs?" the travel agent asked politely, as he produced a rental agreement for her to sign.

"Yes. Sort of."

Maggie had been glad to help with the arrangements, packing, and a loan to cover what Liz could not pay for out of what was left of her savings. "Do the photonovel, sell it and pay me back from the proceeds," Maggie said. "I'd like to see you get something out of the experience of Nick Kane."

Liz flew to Honolulu, from there to Tahiti. The last leg of the journey by outrigger canoe. Already it was an adventure.

The trunk she had sent on ahead was lying in the middle of the dirt floor of the one-room hut. The trunk contained prints, a manual typewriter, paper, pencils. An assortment of bikinis to wear in the gentle climate—a good place to "use them up" since the style had disappeared from California beaches this year. Several lengths of printed cotton material to use sarong-style, if she felt the need to cover up. The travel agent had assured her, with a smirk, that she could take no clothes at all, if she wished, since her isolation would be complete until the outrigger returned for her. There was no telephone, but there was a radio, for emergency use, and she was instructed in its use. Liz had once sunbathed in the nude, and burned her nipples painfully. She decided to sleep and swim in the nude, but to wear the bikinis the rest of the time.

There was a month's supply of food. Cans, dried food, and a creaky icebox that would function until the block of ice melted. Liz looked around at her spartan room. A narrow bed, two chairs, cupboard, rickety desk, the ice box. The shack consisted of coconut-palm fronds woven into a canopy overhead, connected to half walls supported by wooden posts. The upper half of the walls were open. No need for either glass or screens in the benign climate. Why shut out the warm caress of the trade winds and the fragrance of the flowers, or the view of sparkling water falling over dark lava rocks into a sapphire pool?

Liz found the can opener and opened a can of orange

juice. Later, when she had changed clothes and unpacked, she could go and pick some of the fresh fruit the travel agent assured her grew in profusion. She unlocked the trunk and pulled out the file of prints, rough photographic proofs that she would mark for cropping and assembly. Some would be combined, superimposed.

She held up the first picture of the two of them together. Nick's lanky frame was propped against the Piper Cub he had recklessly flown in an air show shortly after returning from Vietnam. His arm was draped carelessly over the shoulder of a heartbreakingly young and vulnerable Liz Holly, still in college and yearning to be everything Nick Kane was.

"Hey, baby, you're holding the camera like it was burning your fingers. See, you have to caress it—stroke it gently, make love to it." There was his crooked grin, teasing dark eyes, chiseled features with movie-star handsomeness. He wore a stained battle jacket, tattered jeans and a baseball cap. His brown hair had a fiery underglow of red and was carefully styled, despite its apparent unkempt appearance. There was oil on his hands, but his nails were manicured. Everything about him, Liz thought, was contradictory.

"So you want an interview with the great Nick Kane." One bronzed eyebrow went up. "You realize I've turned down every wide-eyed chick with a tape recorder in her hand from here to Singapore? What makes you any different? For a college paper yet! Baby, I admire your guts."

She had been angry then, at his conceit and his bad manners. "Pardon me," she flared back. "I thought maybe your career needed a boost. I haven't seen anything worthwhile under your byline since you gave us all the blood and gore of Vietnam."

He looked her over appraisingly and although he kept on smiling, his eyes had narrowed. "Honey, with your looks you've got yourself on the wrong end of the camera. How about you posing for a few shots for me?"

"My name is Elizabeth Holly. I'm neither your baby nor your honey. You've been out of the country too long, Mr. Kane. I'm on the side of the camera I want to be on."

"OK, Liz, simmer down. I thought I was paying you a compliment. You've got perfect cheekbones, the biggest blue eyes I've ever seen and your hair is the eighth wonder of the world. Only I didn't know how to tell you that without sounding like a man on the make. How about buying me a cup of coffee and we'll talk about your interview? I mean, if you're one of those liberated women I've been hearing about, I guess the coffee will be on you? Oh, yes, how about opening the door for me too? But first . . . hey, Charlie, grab my camera and get a shot of me, the Piper Cub and the gorgeous blonde with the legs . . . for posterity, Liz baby—just in case something comes of this—interview."

The look on her face was partly defiant, partly shy. His expression was cocky, his attitude toward her already proprietary. She had been thinking she hated the label "blonde"; her hair was not exactly blonde anyway. It was a light tawny brown, but a life-time of sun and surf had bleached the top layer varying shades of platinum and gold.

What had happened to that Liz? The one full of fire and bravado and spirited enough to tackle anything or anyone? She had allowed Nick to gradually erode her confidence in herself and her ability. In her desire to become his ideal she had lost her own sense of worth.

Now she felt a little like a butterfly emerging from the cocoon.

Putting down the picture of the two of them and the Piper Cub, she stared out at the southern sea. The water was green near the beach, changing abruptly to deep indigo beyond the reef, where white combers broke in choreographed majesty.

She looked down at the picture on the desk again, wondering if she really wished they had never met. A shadow fell across the photograph and she looked around, surprised. She was alone. Totally. The mid-day sun was high in a clear blue sky. There was no other person and no cloud above to cast a shadow. Her heart began to thump painfully. The shadow lingered for a moment, then vanished.

Get hold of yourself, Liz. It's the total isolation. You've never been alone before. She had been in college, three thousand miles from her parents. She had continued to live in the dorm, then shared an apartment with Maggie after they graduated. Until Nick Kane came along. Maggie had never liked Nick. "He's not good for you, Liz," she said after meeting him for the first time.

"Oh, I'm sure I won't see him again after I've got all the interview material together."

"He's one of those macho men who sees a woman as a notch on his gun . . . a kind you always seem to attract. I suppose it's because of your fragile good looks. You look like an easy mark, Liz. There are still men who equate beauty with brainlessness, you know."

Maggie would relish telling Nick that Liz had gone away and there was no way anyone could reach her. She would also tactfully explain to everyone that Liz had at last come to her senses about Nick.

Liz tried to settle down to organizing the proofs in chronological order. She scribbled dialogue and narrative to link them, outlined the first chapter and chose the pictures. She had seen photographic novels that were well done; it was like seeing a film in a book. She hoped to achieve the same result. There had been adventure as well as romance in the story of Nick and Liz. Mostly his adventure . . . her mind wandered as the sun began to slip into the sea in all its red-gold splendor. The coconut palms reached slender black fingers toward the sky in silent homage. A shower of ginger blossom petals blew over her hair, borne on whispering trade winds.

She went down the conch shell pathway and strolled toward the beach. The sand was pink in the setting sun. She sat down on a warm rock and picked up a handful of sand, letting it sift between her fingers. Like time running out.

"Of course I love ya, babe. Though it's damned hard to be sure when you won't let me *make* love to you." His mouth twisted mockingly, one eyebrow raised. "I asked you to marry me, didn't I? What else do I have to do to prove I love you?"

She squirmed, tormented by the memory of that first time he made love to her. The exquisite tenderness, the slow and sensual lingering, each step of the way, until her mind was a kaleidoscope of flashing lights, brilliant colors, and breathless response. Her body tingled where he touched, caressed, kissed. She was spinning through a black velvet universe, stars exploding all around her, as she melted with need. Now on the lonely beach she felt desire again, remembering. She peeled off her bikini and plunged into the warm water, swimming to the reef and balancing on the sharp coral so she could feel the cooler breakers splash against her burning flesh. After a moment the jagged spires of the reef pricked the soles of her feet and she slid back to the sandy bottomed lagoon. Tomorrow I'll wear tennis shoes, she thought as she swam back to the beach, and explore the reef.

When she returned to the hut she was so tired she fell into a deep sleep that was filled with confusing dreams. Nick, laughing at her, teasing, turning to run away from her with his long loping stride. She tried to follow but her feet felt like lead, Then there was a shadowy figure, standing motionless, watching her. She did not recognize him. That he was a man she knew was a certainty, despite the blurred silhouette. The vague shape in the darkness exuded masculine power in a way that was both a threat and a challenge.

She awoke with a start, heart pounding, hands clammy. The unfamiliar surroundings intensified her fear. She did not remember her dream as every nerve in her body screamed that she must beware of danger—now—this instant. She knew before she found her watch that it would be exactly midnight.

Not daring to move, she lay still, listening to the rustle of palm fonds and the lullaby of the surf. After a time her anxiety began to ebb. The moment had again passed. She fell into a shallow sleep, drifting constantly to the surface of wakefulness.

She awoke to find the sunrise silvering the sea. She was trembling and uneasy, as though dreading some event about to happen. She took a swim before breakfast to wake up fully. She pushed her feet into her tennis shoes, snatched up a towel and went down to the beach.

Twice across the lagoon was enough to awaken her appetite and, deciding to leave exploring the reef for later, she swam back to shore. As she bent to pick up her towel her heart began to hammer again. A tingling sensation traveled slowly down her spine. She froze, afraid to turn around. Slowly she picked up her towel and wrapped it around her dripping body. Then she turned and saw him.

He stood with one leg braced against a rock, hands loosely hooked into the broad leather belt he wore and from which hung a sheathed knife. Liz barely noticed the loose linen shirt with wide sleeves and tight-fitting trousers which appeared to be made of leather. Her attention was riveted on the man's face.

His light grey eyes sliced into her with the impact of steel and the fierce expression on his swarthy features was heightened by the jagged scar that marked one cheek.

"Who are you?" she found her voice at last. Her fingers tightened on the towel she clutched.

He glowered, unblinkingly. His hair was black. So black there was no hint of blue or brown, and his eyebrows matched his hair, heavy and dark.

"You dare ask me who I am?" She barely had time to note the resonant voice, as controlled as an actor accustomed to projecting to an audience, when he added, "This is my island, wench. You have better have a good tale to explain yourself."

Chapter 6

Liz's eyes widened and her lips parted. She glanced down at her soaking wet tennis shoes. She was engulfed in gales of laughter, as much from fright as amusement. She sank down on the sand, choking. "Unless you are Mr. Falconer, the owner of this island, you really . . . shouldn't . . . be here." She gasped the words out between giggles, clutching the towel tightly. "At least you have a sense of humor about the way you scare someone out of their wits."

His foot came down from the rock. He wore short flaring boots. He moved soundlessly toward her across the soft sand with a curious rolling grace about his stride that held her spellbound. She felt she was watching an old oil painting come to life. That was it—the clothes, the black hair growing thickly, unfashionably long, about his shoulders—he looked like a man from another century.

He was beside her before she realized he had closed the distance between them. His eyes went from her face to her body, barely covered by the towel.

"Cover yourself, wench. Your scrawny form is already darkening with the sun. What have you done to yourself? I see from your white breasts that your skin is not naturally dark, like the maids of the Indies. And your eyes are blue-violet. Are you a castaway? What name do they call you and how came you here?"

Although his choice of words and phrases was odd, there was nothing stilted about his speech. An actor, perhaps? If so, a good one. He looked and sounded perfectly natural.

"My name is Liz Holly. And I suppose I am a castaway. By choice." If he is a madman, then I'd better not show fear. We are alone, I have no weapon and he has the brawn of a boxer. "And you, sir, may I ask again who you are? Are you Falconer?"

"I am Captain Alexander Bartholomew. I know of no Falconer. This island is my personal retreat. Not even my crew are allowed to land here. I brook no interference with my solitude. You'll be gone with the tide."

He was scrutinizing her with bold eyes, a puzzled frown crossing his high intelligent forehead. "What manner of wench are you? Are you a harlot that you go into the water naked? For a harlot you are uncommonly scrawny. Why, if it weren't for those round breasts, I would have thought you were a boy. You have no bottom at all, m'girl."

"And you have a hell of a lot of nerve, Captain Bartholomew. How did you get here anyway?" The joke was going too far.

"My ship lies at anchor beyond the reef." He shriveled her with his stare. "I should perchance ravish you anyway, despite your skinniness. It would teach you a lesson. No decent wench goes naked. And no woman dares laugh at Alexander Bartholomew. Nor do I like wenches who swear. You will not curse again in my presence." He paused, considering. "Liz. I don't like it. A corruption of Elizabeth affected by serving girls and tarts. I will call you Elizabeth. On your feet, Elizabeth, and get thee into yonder house."

"Look, Captain," Liz said, standing up carefully. "There seem to be several possibilities. Either you sailed here not knowing this is a private island, or there's been a double-booking of Falconer's island."

He extended his hand to help her, cupping her elbow in a firm grip and propelling her toward the shack. The electricity his touch transmitted was definite cause for alarm. Keep your wits about you, Liz, and think of something. The radio? Unless he's already smashed it? Play for time.

"Are you hard of hearing, woman? Have I not told you this is my island?" he said impatiently. "I was enjoying a peaceful rest until you dragged me out of my sleep."

"I didn't make a sound," Liz protested. "But please—go back to your nap. I promise I'll keep quiet."

Inside the grass shack her unexpected visitor looked around in undisguised amazement. He opened the ice-box; peered inside. He jumped when he depressed a typewriter key and a letter clicked up on to the paper. Liz was edging carefully toward the radio.

"What manner of machine is this?" he demanded, pointing to the typewriter.

"It's a manual typewriter. No electricity on the island. May I go behind the screen to dress?"

His attention was distracted. The bold glance returned to study the towel-wrapped Liz. With the single movement of a panther he was at her side. Arms like steel springs went around her and she was bent backward. For one second his face was just above hers and she was conscious of a faint aura, as though a soft blue light were playing about his head. Sight and sound faded as his mouth found hers.

She did not have time to cry out, even to be afraid. The kiss was a pulsating, throbbing exploration of lips and tongue and teeth like nothing she had ever experienced before. A vital force that left her limp when he released her an eternity later.

The triumphant look on his face brought reality rushing back. As he reached to tear away the towel, Liz fought him with fists and knees and feet. When he cursed with rage and flung her to the hard ground, imprisoning her with the muscular hardness of his body, she sank her teeth into his shoulder.

"Hellion. She-cat. Bare your fangs at me, would you." His lips took hers again, savagely, while his hands found the soft flesh beneath the towel.

Liz was thinking rapidly of the anti-rape class she had taken. Forcing herself to lie limply, she waited until his mouth released her. Odd, the rapist was not supposed to kiss like that. . . . Then she looked up at him and said, "Look, captain, let's start all over, shall we? The floor was uncomfortable and I'll be much more accommodating if we could go a little slower. How about a glass of wine first?"

His expression changed and he rolled away from her immediately. He was on his feet in a single leap, staring down at her contemptuously. "A harlot," he said. "I thought so." He turned his attention to her food supply, picking up a can of beans warily and turning it over in his hand. Next he sniffed suspiciously at a box of cereal.

Liz took the opportunity to reach for a sarong and wrapped it around her body. She was still shivering and trying desperately to remember how to use the radio.

"This structure—who built it and when?" he demanded. "It was not here on my last voyage. Who dared build a house on Bartholomew's Isle?"

"Apparently the island has been in the Falconer family for generations. According to the travel agent it originally belonged to a Frenchman named Louis de Letraz—" She was interrupted by the stream of colorful curses the moment she said the name. His face was livid, the scar on his cheek standing out in white relief against his swarthy skin. His eyes pierced the morning shadows of the hut with almost visible sparks. In spite of her trepidation, Liz stared at him, spellbound, wishing she could pick up her camera and capture the image of the most magnificently barbaric face she had ever seen.

He paced the floor for a moment, then turned and said, "Tell me all you know about de Letraz—and the Falconers."

Liz wished silently she had gathered more information than she had. "I believe Louis de Letraz was a sort of French Captain Cook—" Alexander looked blank at this, so she continued, "Louis captured several ships for France. He was rewarded by being given this island, among other things. He had no sons, but there was one daughter. Regine, I think her name was. She married an Englishman named Falconer. The Falconer line became lost a few times over the centuries, but apparently the present Falconer's grandfather managed to convince the French government of his claim to the island. Since it's only a small atoll, I guess it wasn't too difficult for Falconer. I mean, since it is totally uninhabited."

The thunderclouds raced across Alexander's eyes again. "Not quite uninhabited. So the whoreson Letraz claimed the isle for France, did he? When I catch him I shall keel-haul him, then strip what's left of his skin by inches—"

"I don't imagine he has much left on his skeleton," Liz remarked. "Since he's been dead for three centuries."

Alexander stopped short, his mouth open. Comprehension dawned slowly in his eyes. He looked carefully at Liz again, then swept the interior of the shack with a speculative glance, coming back again to the typewriter on the desk. "Dead . . ." he breathed the word ". . . three hundred years."

He sat down abruptly on the nearest chair. In the following long silence Liz felt a dizzying sense of unreality. Am I dreaming all of this? she asked herself once. But the man seated in her chair, rigidly upright, hands clasping the arms in a grip so fierce his knuckles stood out whitely, was all too real. So real that she did not at first digest his next words.

"Then I, too, am dead."

"What?"

"The last thing I remember is a compelling need to come here for the treasure I left . . . in 1688 . . ." His voice trailed away. He ran his hands over his arms, then his thighs, touched his scar. "And yet, if I am a ghost, by the saints, I'm a solid one." He leaped to his feet, grinning fiendishly. "And you, girl—when I kissed your mouth, 'twas a man you felt, not a spirit." He moved closer, grasped her arm in his strong fingers, marking her flesh. She looked down and saw the black hairs on the back of his hands, the blunt fingernails. "You feel my touch. My hands are warm on your flesh, not cold. Is it not so?"

Liz nodded. "You said you came here on your ship—is there a crew aboard?"

"Ah—yes, of course. But I do not allow them to know on which island my treasure is hidden. This is but one of a chain of islands and they put me ashore on a different one, with a small boat. They will return for me in five days."

"Then I should think that in five days we'll both be given a few explanations. There is one other thing we could try—I mean, to find out if you're a ghost or not."

"You doubt my word?"

"No. Just my own sanity. It's possible I'm dreaming you."

"What means could we use to prove I am a spirit?"

"You could let me take a photograph of you."

"Photograph?" There was no surprising him into giving away the fact that he was playacting. His expression was uncomprehending.

"I have a Polaroid," she said, disentangling his hand and going to her trunk. "I use it sometimes for a fast shot to get the composition right."

He looked alarmed when she pointed the camera in his direction, but he held his ground. A moment later she held a blank print in her hand. A second try produced an excellent shot of the interior of the hut, including the desk and chair behind where the captain stood. There was no man in the room.

Liz's palms started to sweat. She could see this man—feel him, smell his vague scent of sun and leather—but the camera showed absolutely nothing. Her head swam. She had been so exhausted and confused by everything she had gone through with Nick, by the dizzying complications of trying to tie up the studio and becoming involved with all the people on the movie. When she looked at Alexander Bartholomew she saw the swaggering costumed actors of *The Black Pirate,* she saw the splendid ship and Adam Eastman's proud figure hurtling down the rigging. But this was not a movie.

Alexander studied the picture in amazement, looking about him to compare the image on paper to his surroundings. "Then artists no longer exist in your time? But where am I—you pointed your box at me."

Liz looked pained. "Yes, artists exist—if you mean those who use paint or other media. We photographers consider ourselves to be artists, too. And as for where you are . . . that, Captain Bartholomew, is a very good question. I believe you may be in my imagination. I've been under somewhat of a strain lately."

His hand went under her chin, tipping her face upward, and his mouth moved in, brushing her lips then retreating. He chuckled, deep in his throat. "You imagined that, too, then. And if I ravish you, how shall you imagine it?"

"Would you mind if I had breakfast first?" Liz asked nervously. "I'm starving. I suppose if you're a spirit, you have no need of food?"

"On the contrary. I'm famished. Go then, and prepare my meal."

"If you're going to eat," Liz said firmly, "you're going to help. You can start by lighting the stove. I imagine since it's oil, you know how."

"You expect me to do women's work?" he roared.

Liz smiled sweetly. "This is the twentieth century. Women are no longer chattels. We aren't quite as liberated yet as we'd like to be, but we're getting there."

He glowered at her for a second, then turned on his heel and went to the door. "I'll cook my fish on the beach. I like not the appearance of your victuals, woman. I did not know you intended to eat shriveled pieces of parchment." He jerked his head in the direction of the cereal box she had picked up.

"Besides," he growled, "I need time to collect my wits. I'll not be able to think with an addle-brained female nearby."

Liz hurled the cereal box at his retreating figure and it hit the doorpost, sending a shower of corn flakes drifting through the room. She ran to the door, looking down the conch shell path to the cliff. There was no sign of her visitor.

"Wait! Come back!" she suddenly screamed. It had hit her all at once; she was not alone on the island, she was very probably in danger.

But then the sensation of his kiss returned. Although there was no one to see her, she flushed deeply, remembering how eagerly she had responded. His touch had been overwhelming, but not really threatening. She felt fear, she knew, but it was a strangely familiar fear; the trembling thrill of wanting. Oh God, what have I done to myself, she thought, wondering if her relationship with Nick hadn't done more psychic damage than she had believed. I did see him, I really did see him, she answered herself after a moment. He was here.

She blinked in the morning sun, turned her head and listened for the sound of footsteps. There was nothing but the slow rhythmic beat of the surf on the reef and the fragrant whisper of the trade wind through the palms.

Chapter 7

After she had walked the length of the cliff, studied the beach below, scanned the surrounding sea, and seen no sign of Alexander or his boat, she returned to the hut and ate the remainder of the corn flakes.

I was dreaming. But it was so real. Liz, old girl, you're cracking up. Funny, my dream man looked nothing like Nick.

Nick. Oh, God, will it ever stop hurting?

She sat at the desk, studying her notes and the proofs of the early days with Nick. There was a list of his most famous pictures, including those which won him the Pulitzer prize. *Napalm. Defoliation. Refugee. Boat of Fools. Soldier's Solitude. Last Patrol. Medic! Medic! Long road home . . .*

His pictures were grim, despairing, horrifying. They had moved a nation's conscience and had perhaps been instrumental in ending a war. No one but Liz had ever asked him how he could calmly stand and focus his lens on the face of a burned child, or the eyes of a dying young G.I.

"Hey babe, that's a disapproving look and them's discouraging words that should seldom be heard. I'm not a doctor, I'm a photographer. I do what I do."

"And the end justifies the means," Liz said.

"Putting the war into American living rooms via TV and on the front pages of newspapers with pictures like that is what ended it, Liz, so knock off the holier than thou act. It's no different me taking those shots than it is for the guy who snaps a suicide in midair, or a plane going down in flames. The cameraman is just recording what he sees."

Liz tried to tell herself he was right, that gruesome though his subjects were, they were effective, and that perhaps she was just jealous of the success and acclaim that was Nick's alone.

Was it a coincidence that it happened on a night that Nick did not keep their date? She got a busy signal when she phoned and, after waiting two hours, went around to his apartment. They had exchanged keys several weeks earlier, after an argument about Nick moving in with her. The exchange of keys had been a compromise. She let herself in to the dark apartment, saw the half-open bedroom door and the light. She hesitated, took a step toward the bedroom and saw their reflections in the mirrored wall.

The woman was thrashing wildly beneath Nick's lean and naked back. Both were gasping and nearing release. Liz fled. She paced the floor all night long, sickened, desolate. Telling herself she was naive, a fool, to grow up, it wasn't the end of the world, that monogamy was passé. . . . Nothing helped the hurt and sense of betrayal.

The following day, dry-eyed and calm, she went to face him. He was already en route to the Middle East, where fighting had again broken out.

At lunch with Maggie, needing someone to talk to, she poured out the story. She expected Maggie to scold and say she was making a mountain out of a molehill. But Maggie did not.

"It's the beginning of the end, Liz. I'm sorry, but you've got to face it. I'm not saying I told you so . . . but new sexual mores notwithstanding, fidelity is the only foundation for a lasting relationship. Believe me, no one knows better than I do." Maggie demolished her crepes and surreptitiously slid Liz's breaded veal onto her own plate. "You're not going to eat it anyway, are you? That's the difference between you and me—you'll lose your appetite over Nick's infidelity and in the same circumstances I'll go on an eating binge. Course I sometimes eat as a substitute for sex, too." Maggie tried to take her mind off Nick by going into an elaborate and hilarious comparison of various sex acts and items of food.

Liz smiled wanly and grew the first sheathing of armor over her emotions. When Nick returned in his usual cloud of glory, she blurted out that she had gone to his apartment that last night.

"The Israelis fight with a complete disregard for danger. It was incredible in Jerusalem. . . . What did you say? What last night? Oh . . . ah, I see what you're driving at." He cleared his throat and grinned engagingly.

"Now, babe it didn't mean a thing. Just a diversionary action. I was angry about something and when I'm angry I don't like to get into bed with a woman I care about. Much better to pick up some chick and vent my hostilities on her, right? Hell, Liz, that has nothing to do with us. It didn't mean any more than my grabbing a meal in a restaurant instead of coming home to your cooking."

"I don't cook," Liz pointed out.

"Just a figure of speech. Come on, you're not really upset about it are you?"

"No, I'm not upset. I'm shattered. My world is crumbling. I'm dying of a broken heart. Nick, I'm going to go with you on the next assignment. No matter where it is. Nick—?"

She shuddered in the sunlight, remembering South America, and decided to swim across the lagoon before lunch.

Captain Alexander Bartholomew was sitting on an upturned boat at the water's edge, contemplating the caress of the sea on the land.

"He must have slain me as I slept," he said without looking up, as she approached him. " 'Tis the only way that scurvy dog could have better'd me. Methinks when my ship returns, I shall be able to return to settle the score. God's teeth, I'll have a surprise in store for the whoreson." He looked up at her, his mouth set in a cruel smile and his eyes gleaming with ferocious anticipation. Liz stopped dead in her tracks.

"But—assuming you return to your own time—" she said, her curiosity overcoming her caution, "won't you then have to merely re-live what actually happened? Will you be able to change anything?"

Alexander frowned. "Then I shall re-live the time we fought for hours for mastery of the ship. Aye and I'll cut off his ear again. 'Tis a pity that in our last duel I spared his life because the Lady Amelia begged me."

He stood up, towering over her. She caught a faint

scent of old leather, rum, and a pleasantly masculine odor of skin washed with strong soap. She wondered about the Lady Amelia.

"You don't remember how he killed you, then?" Liz asked.

A perplexed grimace knitted his brow and he stared out to sea as though seeking the answer there. "The events just before my life ended are obscure and dark in my mind. I remember only a great urgency to come here to my island. I know not why it was so imperative. This I do know—only Louis knew how to find this island. Aye, he slew me, the hound."

Liz watched him, admiring his simmering rage that was curiously without rancor. She hoped he would explain who the Lady Amelia was, but he did not.

His eyes softened as he looked again at Liz. "You'd be an uncommonly pretty wench, were you not so thin. Tell me about yourself and how you came to be a harlot."

Liz bridled, resisting the urge to rush at him and slap his face. She must keep calm. Plan ahead. She was no match for him physically. "Look, Captain . . ." she began.

"Alexander," he corrected. "I like your spirit, wench. Since we're alone here there's no call for formality. Besides—" he gave her a suggestive smirk, "You will soon be mine."

"That's what you think. Alexander, I have a radio. I can bring the law here within a couple of hours. I suggest you stop playing whatever game you're playing and leave."

"I know not what a radio is. But it would be a merry jest to fight your law. I evaded the might of several Navies in my lifetime and sacked as many cities. Not to mention the ships I plundered. I make my own laws,

Elizabeth, and obey no others. I was the most feared seagoing outlaw of my day."

"I still think you're a prankster or a figment of my imagination. Caused by the total isolation and . . . my state of mind. For one thing, this is the Pacific Ocean. Didn't you seventeenth century buccaneers operate in the Spanish Main . . . the Caribbean?"

"Then you had heard of me?" he asked, pleased. "Indeed we did. But there was a time when I wearied of the blood-letting. I brought my ship around the Horn and discovered many hospitable islands. I was searching for a way through the Gulf of Darien to the Pacific Ocean. Alas, there is none. But I found this jewel of an isle—and buried a fortune here in gold and doubloons. But you are wrong that we plundered only the Spanish Main. Have you not heard of Sir Francis Drake? A countryman of mine—a boyhood idol—plundered the Pacific, aye, and was knighted for his trouble."

"I just never thought of Sir Francis Drake as a pirate," Liz said.

"Aye, t'was not thought of as piracy when king and country benefited," Alexander said with a cynical twist to his mouth. "Privateer was the favored term then. A euphemism to salve Royal conscience. Yet let some poor suffering sea dog plunder for himself, starving and ill-used though he be, and the wrath of the king's navy was upon him. No matter what circumstances brought him to it."

"And what about Alexander Bartholomew," Liz asked. "What made him become a pirate? With his obvious breeding and intelligence, why was it necessary?" Part of her mind rejected him as a hallucination, while some distant memory stirred restlessly, offering tantalizing glimpses of knowledge she did not know she had.

One black eyebrow arched up at her question. "You believe it was a life I was forced in to, then, and did not choose? Perhaps because you were forced into a life of harlotry. Tell me, girl, for I am interested in you, were you seduced and abandoned by some wretch—or perchance you were aboard a vessel taken as prize? Ah, yes, that's the answer. You should have chosen the burliest knave aboard and offered yourself to him alone. He would have protected you from the ravishing of the entire crew." He paused, a possibility crossing his mind. "Are you then a spirit also? Did they kill you?"

"No, I'm very much alive. I wasn't ravished by a pirate crew, either. Piracy—at least as you know it—no longer exists. Though there are some who think we've merely changed the name and the weapons."

"How did you become a harlot, then?"

"Damn it, I'm not a harlot."

"Are you a virgin?"

"No."

"Aha!" He took a step toward her and she tensed, waiting. Keep talking, she thought, measuring his size and wondering if she would be able to use his own power and momentum to throw him. "Is everything black or white to you, Alexander? I've given myself to only one man."

He paused. "You are betrothed to him?"

"Yes." Perhaps the existence of a fiancé would be a deterrent to further sexual advances.

"Then where is he? Why are you alone here, at the mercy of marauders? What manner of man allows his woman to place herself in such danger? And what manner of man has carnal knowledge of his bride-to-be? He should have protected your honor. Waited for the marriage bed before taking your virginity."

Alexander spoke rapidly and his thoughts were obviously moving even more swiftly. There was a controlled energy about the way he stood, gestured, turned his head. He exuded a vital force that would have made him a leader in any age. For a spirit, Liz thought, you are more alive than any man I've ever known.

"Things are different today. We've perfected methods of birth control—" she began.

"Birth control?" he interrupted with a puzzled frown.

"Preventing conception."

"You do not desire children from your union?" His amazement was evident.

"Only when we want to have them."

"I see. But there are other dangers. Disease, for instance."

"We've discovered a means for preventing disease also. We're able to have perfectly safe sexual liaisons other than marriage." Odd, even as she said it, she was sorry to destroy his illusions. Or were they her own? Fidelity is the only foundation for a lasting relationship . . . Maggie's words.

He studied her silently for a moment and the disappointment written in his gaze caused her a pang of regret. "Then I pity you," he said. "A true marriage is a rare treasure and the only worthwhile liaison—as you call it. Finding a soul-mate was hard enough in my time, but in yours it sounds impossible."

"Did you find one, Alexander? And if you did, what about all the ravishing you did? Or was it just the wife who was supposed to be faithful?"

He took another step toward her, his hand raised, and for a moment she thought he intended to strike her. Instead he said angrily, "I had no wife. But if I had, I would have been true to her. My way of life was not one I could ask a decent woman to share. And I never took a wench against her will. You're testimony to that, Elizabeth. Have I forced myself on you?"

"You came close, but I fought you, tricked you into stopping." What was she saying—don't goad him!

"A puny woman could not stop Alexander Bartholomew from having his way with her, if he desired her sufficiently." His lip curled contemptuously and he turned his back on her and strode toward a wooden structure he had started to build further down the beach. "Consider yourself lucky, wench, that I sated myself with the dusky beauties of the Marquesas before coming here. Besides, you appeal little to me, with your scrawny body and sun-burned limbs. Don't you know that a woman is more tantalizing if she covers herself? Your bare skin makes me think of boys—and I've no taste for boys."

Liz felt her fury swell and grow. "Why you . . . conceited . . . overbearing . . . bag of wind—" she screamed after him, as he ran from her.

His laughter filled the empty beach.

She stayed where she was, watching him. He had felled several young trees and was building a small three-sided hut. He stripped off his shirt and the bronzed muscles of his back rippled as he wielded an axe, cutting the wood to size. He stopped, pushing the black mane of his hair back from his brow, and gestured to her. "Come—you will help with the *boucan.*"

"I will not. And if you plan to live in that, I suggest you make it larger."

His laughter rang out again and he slapped his thigh delightedly. "The wench has wit, too. I take it you'd like to see Alexander smoking himself back to whence he came, in the manner I shall smoke the raw meat in the boucan."

"Ah, a smokehouse," Liz said. "You have fresh meat?"

"I killed a boar before you rose to greet the day. If you make yourself useful, I will share my meat with you. We'll have fresh roast pork today and I'll smoke the rest."

Boucan, she was thinking. *Boucanier.* Buccaneer.

"I have my own food."

"Dried up bits of parchment," he said derisively as he swung the axe again. "You need meat to put flesh on those bones of yours."

"It's a gag—right? Someone bet you you couldn't live off the land for five days, with only the tools a seventeenth century pirate might have. But they forgot to check with Falconer to see if his island were available. Or are you Falconer—and this is your way of amusing yourself. Rent to some lone female and then materialize as a spirit. Well, whatever it is, it won't work. You're no ghost, Alexander. You're a man." And what a man, I almost wish you weren't acting. Liz pushed the thought out of her head.

The axe's blade glinted in the morning sunlight, sliced effortlessly through the wood. Alexander was not breathing heavily and only a faint glow to his bare back hinted at exertion. Spirits don't sweat, Liz did not realize she had muttered the words aloud until he smiled, showing strong white teeth. She stared at his teeth as though mesmerized.

"But this spirit has all of his faculties. I feel the sunlight, smell the salt tang of the air, see the tawny hair of a wench shining about her shoulders . . . feel the hunger in my belly and the swelling of desire." He threw back his head and roared with laughter. "There!

I've admitted I find you desirable. Be patient, Elizabeth, you may yet be ravished."

She turned and raced back toward the stone steps in the cliff, almost tripping over the carcass of the boar lying in the shade of a cluster of palms. *You'll be safe from any wild boar* so long as you stay on the beach or the clearing where the shack is. Don't go into the interior—no further than the waterfall. She remembered the travel agent's words. Now if she could remember how to use the radio.

The equipment was of the old-fashioned emergency portable type, with limited range. There was a gasoline-driven alternator and a 50-watt transmitter, a receiver and a control unit fortunately connected to a telephone-type instrument. Liz had been assured she would have no problem in relaying a message to the island from which she had taken the outrigger canoe on the last stage of her journey.

Afterwards, Liz wondered in amazement why she had not simply requested the outrigger to return for her. It was almost as though she had stepped outside of herself and listened, disbelieving, as she asked them to wire Tahiti for all the information they could dig up on one Captain Alexander Bartholomew, a buccaneer captain who had perhaps visited the island before it was given to Louis de Letraz. Captain Bartholomew had died in 1688 . . .

Chapter 8

His father was Sir James Alexander Bartholomew, loyal to his king in the Civil War, who fought gallantly and died bravely at the hands of Cromwell's executioners. Sir James' estates were confiscated and his widow and two young sons were transported into slavery in the Indies. It was the will of the Lord, the Puritan Cromwell declared.

Their ship was packed with criminals, prostitutes, Scottish prisoners-of-war, other political opponents of Cromwell, and any Irishman who happened by. Along with black Africans sold to slave traders, all would go to the tobacco and sugar plantations of the West Indies. Some of the transportees were also landless laborers lured by the promise of free land in an earthly paradise.

Lady Bartholomew, young James and Alexander, found themselves surrounded by paupers, thieves and ex-soldiers, exposed to a section of the populace they had not dreamed existed in their wildest nightmares. Lady Bartholomew contracted a deadly flux and died before the voyage was half over. Her two young sons watched their mother's body casually tossed overboard. A week later James was dead, felled by a blow to the head when a crewman demanded the gold medallion James wore and the lad refused to part with it.

Alexander, the youngest transportee aboard the ship, crawled into the rat-infested hold and wept his tears of grief and rage in private. He was found, starving and shaking with fever, by a man named Tad Bowen who was starting a new life on a seven-year contract as an indentured servant, hoping to become an employer himself at the end of that time.

Tad was a giant of a man. Bulging biceps, red beard that curled about an incongruously cherubic face, long arms that were attached to the largest hands Alexander had ever seen.

"Blacksmith I were, young sir," Tad told him, "like me Dad and five brothers. Ah, but there's the rub. The smithy could support two families at best. And me the youngest. Come on then, Tad will take care of you, laddie."

Tad bathed his head with cool water while the fever raged, brought him soothing drinks, and shared his own food so Alexander would not have to eat the slops provided to the prisoners. When they reached Jamaica, Tad contrived to have Alexander at his side when the planters came to the slave auction.

A somewhat effeminate looking young man, holding a lacy handkerchief to his delicate nostrils to mask the stench of the transportees, came looking for Tad.

"Must be Sir Geoffrey's son. Keep your mouth shut

and let me do the talking," Tad said under his breath. He raised his hand in response to the auctioneer's call for the indentured servant for Sir Geoffrey Grindwald's sugar plantation.

"I be Tad Bowen, sir," he said, touching his forelock.

The young man sniffed disdainfully into his handkerchief and turned watery gray eyes in Alexander's direction. "There was no mention of a child. Is this one with you?"

"Aye, sir, that he is," Tad said, giving Alexander a sharp jab with his elbow when the boy opened his mouth to speak. "And I'll vouch for the work he'll do, sir. Strong, he be, though he's been poorly on the voyage and don't look it."

"He has a bold stare for a pauper. And where, pray tell, did he acquire those clothes? Ragged and reeking though they are, I detect a note of quality there. Are you sure he's with you and not one of the political prisoners?"

"Oh, no sir. He's my boy, he is. And you, young sir, may we ask your name?" Tad gave his most ingratiating grin. He looked, Alexander thought, like an oversized infant. All pink soft mouth and rosy plump cheeks. A huge baby wearing a false red beard.

"I am Sir Geoffrey's oldest son, Miles Grindwald. Steward of the plantation, at least until I can leave this Godforsaken hellhole. Come, then, my good man, the carriage is waiting. You will be coachman, stablemaster, blacksmith and my personal bodyguard. You are fortunate that you will not work in the fields with the blacks, however we shall require you to supervise the burning of the fields prior to harvest."

Miles Grindwald observed Tad's puzzled expression and added patronizingly, "The stalk is not harmed when we burn off the excess foliage. Sugar cane grows so densely it is impossible for a man to get through clumps of it without this." He spoke slowly and distinctly, as though explaining to a child.

Tad and Alexander were cautioned not to walk too closely behind their employer, but to be alert for thieves or escaped slaves and to protect their master with their lives.

When they reached the plantation and Alexander started to follow Tad into the servants' quarters his progress was barred with a sharp finger jabbing his chest. "Not you, boy. You will go to the slaves' quarters. Tomorrow you will be given a hoe and put to work in the vegetable patch. When you've grown a bit, you'll go into the cane fields."

But Alexander had been taught to read and write, his destiny was that of a leader, a gentleman, a man of means. Never a slave, nor even a servant. He rebelled; he ran away. He was caught, returned for a beating, and threatened with a branding if he tried again. He was put to work in the cane fields, whipped and driven like an animal. When Tad tried to intervene on his behalf, the blacksmith found himself dismissed to the slave quarters.

Miles Grindwald surveyed them both with cold eyes and twitching nostrils. "I loathe my life here. I loathe living with rabble like you. I live only to return home and never again set eyes on this cesspool. I will bring in my father's crops while I am steward here and I will do it better than anyone else because I drive my hands harder than anyone else. Slaves are the cheapest commodity we have. Remember that when you contemplate defying me again."

When Tad tried to protest he was not a slave, but a

freely indentured servant, Miles' thin lips curved in anticipation. Tad was strung up by his wrists, feet suspended above the ground, and left in the blazing sun all day without water. At nightfall he was flogged by a relay of three men, one taking over as another's energy flagged. Miles watched, lace handkerchief pressed to his lips, pale cruel eyes fixed on the blacksmith's oozing wounds.

Alexander cared for Tad through his delirium. When his back was sufficiently healed and he was put to work in the fields, it was time for the burning prior to harvest. Tad moved stiffly, his eyes still glazed with pain and shock, his mouth hanging open vacantly. He went where he was pushed, obeyed commands like a puppet, stared unseeingly at the fierce flames licking through the tinder-dry foliage. When the foreman raised his whip to force him to move quickly, Tad turned with a bellow rage. He seized the whip, snapped it like a twig and flung it into the burning cane. Then, eyes glowing as brightly as the flames, he picked up the foreman and hurled the man after his whip.

They heard his screams as they fled. Tad ran a zig-zag course, great long arms knocking aside all who tried to halt his dash to freedom. A few paces behind, Alexander was sickened at the briefly inhaled stench of roasting flesh and the certain knowledge that they could never be caught if they wanted to live.

Soon they were running toward another red glow in the sky and they stopped, puzzled; afraid they had run in a circle.

"Do you hear dogs?" Alexander panted. "Where are we? I thought we were running toward the sea."

Tad looked at him with vacant eyes and grinned foolishly.

He doesn't know what he's done, or even who he is, Alexander thought in fascinated horror. He grabbed Tad's hand and propelled him forward.

The pirates who were sacking the town had chosen to set several fires on the same day the cane fields were burned. As night fell most of the town was burning or smouldering and the pirates had retired to the beach with their loot and most of the town's women.

Concealing themselves in the sand dunes, Alexander and Tad watched the roistering of the Brethren of the Coast. Silhouetted against the pulsing glow of the fires, ruffians and sea dogs of every shape, size and color, in varying degrees of drunkenness, ate, swilled rum, and made brutal love in every way possible. There were no captains or leaders, each man claimed an equal share of the booty. At sea, one man was designated captain of their ship, but he enjoyed no special privileges and issued no orders ashore.

Alexander watched, listened, and learned. "In the morning," he whispered to Tad, "when they are all asleep, we'll slip into one of the longboats. But first we'll strip a couple of them of their clothes. I saw one who is almost your size."

Tad patted his head affectionately, lay down, and began to snore.

"Sorry, Miss Holly, no information on Captain Alexander Bartholomew. Most of the information on pirates is hearsay, written by seventeenth and eighteenth century novelists and poets. Except for buccaneers who became respectable—like Henry Morgan—no official records were kept. The only possible pirate story we turned up was a rumor that the Falconer family once dug up portions of the island looking for treasure and one excavation turned up several ingots of rough silver that could have been discarded as worthless by pirates who did not recognize the unpolished metal."

Liz was disappointed in one way, relieved in another.

Alexander had worked on his *boucan* all day and had not come to the grass shack. After a time the sound of the axe stopped and she heard him singing in a deep, true baritone. A bloodcurdling ditty that began:

> *"A little I'm hurt but not yet slain,*
> *I'll but lie down and bleed a while,*
> *And then I'll rise and fight again."*

Then in an abrupt change of mood, he sang of the girls he'd known in various ports. A ribald song that made Liz smile and bite her lip.

Black smoke rose from the beach and, some time later, the delicious aroma of roasting pork.

She had made a half-hearted attempt to work, eaten a papaya for lunch, washed her hair under the waterfall. The island was heartbreakingly beautiful, bathed in crystal clear air that carried the scent of blossoms brilliant in the dew-polished foliage of the trees. The endless vista of the blue-green sea with its ruffles of white lace along the reef as the rolling combers caressed the unseen coral, stirred indefinable longings deep in her soul as she listened to its sound.

But even as she savored the tranquility of her surroundings and tried to think of other things, the presence of Alexander dominated everything else.

Is it a dream? Is there life after death? The questions formed and faded away without finding answers. She was letting herself become fascinated by a man who made his own laws and was so dynamic in life that his spirit lived on through the centuries. She was aware of his presence on the island to the exclusion of everything else. Impossible, she told herself repeatedly. A spirit who kills, sings, eats . . . makes love? Only a real live man is capable of doing these things. Spirits are vague images that pass through walls, have no substance, are lifeless. Alexander Bartholomew can't be dead. He has more vitality, more sheer physical presence, more—

His voice broke into her thoughts. "The meat is ready, Elizabeth. You will do me the honor of dining with me?"

She spun around, dropping the photo she held. He was lounging against the doorpost, one hand hooked into the broad leather belt he wore, the other pressed to the post above his head as he leaned carelessly in an attitude of studied indifference.

The smell of the pork was tantalizing. The prospect of sharing a meal with the pirate even more so. He had shaved, donned a clean white linen shirt and showed no sign of fatigue for his hard day's labor. Liz hesitated only a split second. "Well . . . yes, thank you. I've been so busy I haven't had time to cook anything for myself."

He gestured casually toward the photo that had fallen from her hand. "You used your magic box to capture the likeness of a man. He is your betrothed?" Steel-gray eyes probed her as he asked the question and waited expectantly for her answer.

Glancing downward, Liz saw it was indeed a picture of Nick.

"I see from the look in your eyes that it is he. You will tell me about him during dinner. Meanwhile, you have a few minutes to set the table and make yourself presentable while I remove the meat from the spit." He was gone before she could speak.

I *am* presentable, she thought, irritated. Her hair was freshly washed and she had wrapped her sarong as modestly as possible. She considered dressing in the only outfit she had, the jeans and shirt she had worn for the trip by canoe, then quickly rejected the idea. Alexander would never understand a woman in pants and, just for tonight, Liz wanted to learn more about him without wasting time quarreling. She did have a long gossamer-sheer silk scarf and this she draped about her bare shoulders, pulled it in a cross over her bosom and tied it at the waist. A white ginger blossom added further softness to her new neckline. Experimentally, she held another length of cotton material in front of her. If I wrap it about my waist—under the sarong I'm wearing—I will have a floor-length dress. Why am I bothering with this? For a ghost?

"Ah," he said, "Now you look more like a woman." With a flourish, he placed an enormous platter of steaming pork on the table. Under his arms were two very ancient bottles of wine. "But you've spent all of your time primping and none in preparation for our meal. Where are the dishes? Tankards, glasses? Have you baked no bread? 'Tis no wonder you're worried that your betrothed finds you lacking in wifely virtues. For indeed you are."

Flustered, she flung plates and cutlery onto the table while trying to argue at the same time. "Nick doesn't see me as a servant, as you apparently do. Women are good for more than baking bread and cleaning up men's messes."

He looked around in surprise. "But you have not touched this house all day. The remains of your lunch is still in yonder bowl and your bed unmade behind the screen you so hastily pulled in front of it while I went for the meat. I, on the other hand, have worked industriously all day—in addition to killing our dinner."

"I have more important things to do. I work. My work takes precedence over household chores." Two forks clattered to the table.

"Work, work," he mimicked. "You tell me you do not work as a harlot. I see no signs you work as a laundress or a seamstress. What mythical work is this that prevents you from keeping an orderly house?"

"My work is a hell of a lot more to be proud of than that of a thieving pirate," Liz said, tilting her chin. Heightened color came to her cheeks, making her eyes light up with violet fire.

"You are swearing again. 'Tis unbecoming in a winsome wench," he said coldly. "And you are again completely wrong in your opinion. We Brethren of the Coast are heroes to our downtrodden brothers ashore, for we have escaped their miserable lot, broken all the master's rules, aye, and enriched ourselves in the bargain. Our lives may be short, but our deeds will be remembered by oppressed men long after we are gone."

He stood, arms akimbo, legs braced as though against the roll of an invisible ship, his oblique black brows drawn downward over ice-colored eyes. Liz felt the power of his stare drain her legs of all feeling, so that she had to lean on the table for a second.

"You did not answer my question about the work you do." He picked up a fork and studied it curiously. "What manner of tool is this?" he asked, without waiting for her reply to his previous question.

"A fork—to spear the meat and put it in your big mouth," Liz said, fuming. "And I work as a photographer. My pictures have appeared in newspapers and magazines. In addition, I run a studio specializing in portraits of children and animals." Liz's security blanket, Nick had called the studio. What the hell do we need a studio for, babe? It will just tie us down. Let's be footloose and fancy free—no anchors. Obstinately, Liz went ahead and rented a small shop and set up business anyway. Nick kept his distance for a time, but during one long dry spell when there were no assignments forthcoming and he ran out of ideas, he drifted in to help her. "I still say it's an anchor, but let's make it a partnership anyway," he declared generously. Of course it's an anchor, Nick—I don't know how to hang on to you and this is another way of trying—a place to come home to—shared work, even if we're fighting again in our personal lives.

Alexander said, "And the man in the photograph—that is the word? What is his work? Does he then bake the bread and—how did you phrase it—clean up your messes?" Alexander seated himself in the most comfortable chair, ignored the napkin beside his plate, used his knife to spear a chunk of meat, and proceeded to eat it with his fingers. "You forgot to bring finger bowls," he pointed out.

"Nick is a photographer too," Liz said shortly, sitting down opposite Alexander and unfolding her napkin with elaborate precision. "This is a napkin—you use it to clean your fingers and don't need a finger bowl. Nick and I shared all the chores. There's no 'women's' work and 'men's' work any longer. We're equals." There was no point in explaining that she and Nick had parted. She hoped the existence of a fiancé might prevent further overtures.

Alexander removed the cork from a wine bottle with

his teeth, and filled the glasses from a great height without spilling a drop. His eyes were alive with devilment, his scar sinister in the rapidly falling tropical dusk, and his sensual lips bared white hunter's teeth.

"He's puny, then. If Elizabeth is his physical equal. So you ran away from him to seek a real man." He drained his glass, filled it again and gestured airily, "And by all that's holy, you came to the right place." His teeth tore into a succulent piece of meat and he chewed slowly, savoring the taste, as his eyes devoured Liz.

She moved uneasily in her chair, trying to tear her gaze away from his insolent stare but unable to do so. Her fingers shook as she tried to wield knife and fork without looking down at her plate. There was a bowl of fresh fruit she had picked on her way back from the beach that morning and, along with the meat and wine, it completed a simple but festive meal. "I didn't mean I was physically as strong as Nick. That isn't the point nowadays. It's no longer necessary for mighty caveman to hunt the food and little woman to rake out the cave and gather the firewood." Wanting to strike back, she held up her fork. "This, Alexander, as I explained earlier, is a fork. You use it to pick up your meat. It is considered uncivilized to eat with your fingers."

He looked at the fork lying beside his plate, nudging it disdainfully with his forefinger. "My fingers have never placed food in someone else's mouth. Can you say the same for your fork?"

Liz tried to hide the smile that plucked at her mouth by reaching behind her for the candles and matches in the desk drawer.

Alexander's eyes widened when she struck the match on the tiny piece of folded cardboard. As she held the flame to the candle Liz noted his reaction to the book matches with some satisfaction. "A little more modern day magic. I wish there were electricity on the island so I could really show you something."

He shrugged his broad shoulders, unconcerned. "You think me a dolt if you think I did not anticipate many discoveries would come with the passing of time. I am, however, saddened by what you tell me of men and women. Here we are, dining together on a beautiful tropical island, the very air around us heavy with the wine of love, and the lovely Elizabeth does not deign to smile on me, even in jest. Ah, Elizabeth, a single glance from beneath fluttering eyelashes? A soft and winsome word? A voice lowered with the hidden promise of delights to come?" He leaned forward, one elbow on the table, watching her expectantly. He had a habit of pulling up one corner of his mouth in a mocking half-smile that revealed the existence of a deep cleft in his cheek. The scar was a zig-zag slash that resembled a lightning bolt.

Liz cleared her throat and sipped the velvet-smooth wine. "Excellent wine," she murmured. "How did you get the scar on your cheek and who is Lady Amelia?" She couldn't believe she had asked the question.

His smile widened and his square fingers went up to the scar, tracing its progress with rueful remembrance. "Louis de Letraz made one thrust with his rapier when I expected him to parry. A lucky stroke. I cut off his ear in retaliation."

Liz shuddered and took another gulp of wine. It was extraordinarily silken and delicious and the night was beginning to swim dizzily in and out of focus. Alexander's hair was black as the sky. His linen shirt was partially open, revealing dark hair on a strong sculpted chest. His large blunt fingers caressed his wine glass, following the contour of the stem with great tenderness as his eyes strayed suggestively to the white ginger blossom nestled over her breast. Liz could feel heat radiating beneath her cotton sarong. She felt tiny nerves awakening that she had not known she possessed. Her legs were numb.

"And the Lady Amelia?" Liz asked, appalled to find her voice had dropped to a husky purr that had nothing to do with the question.

Alexander knitted his fine black brows in a perplexed frown. "I spoke to you of her?"

"You said in your last duel with Louis de Letraz you spared his life because the Lady Amelia begged you. I just wondered who she was to have such power over you."

He studied the blank space above her head, searching his memory. "I have the feeling of a man awakening after a long slumber. My mind is not yet clear and memory returns slowly. Odd, but I can see my sword about to plunge into his scurvy flesh and hear a woman's scream . . . yes, it must have been Amelia." Alexander paused, reflective, then sighed extravagantly. "The Lady Amelia was the fairest prize of all. The young wife of a sugar planter, Sir Miles Grindwald. He was the reluctant steward of his father's Jamaican plantation and they were married by proxy. The ship bringing his bride to him was waylaid by pirates, and in a surfeit of gallantry, the young Alexander returned the lady to her milksop husband."

"You say his name with almost as much hatred in your voice as when you refer to Letraz."

"I should say it with more hatred. Letraz was a man I could understand. Greedy, lustful, reckless, courageous in his way—a thorough scoundrel and sea rover, not unlike myself. We were both too stubborn to join forces, or together we might have ruled the seas. But Grindwald was sickly, effeminate, cruel, dishonorable—an underhanded weakling who took pleasure in the suffering of others. Including his wife. Ah, but Amelia was fair. Golden curls, soft hazel eyes, plump pink shoulders, a tiny waist and magnificent hips. She had a way of looking up at a man with her lips slightly parted and her eyes half-closed . . ." his voice trailed away and he looked dreamily into space.

"I take it she was one of the ravishees," Liz said curtly, "that you didn't have to force." Recklessly, she drained another glass of wine. The room was now filled with a red haze. Sunset, perhaps, despite the inky sky that was as black as Alexander's hair? No—the haze was not the sunset, she could see a silver moon floating above Alexander's head. *And the moon is a ghostly galleon* . . . she tried to remember the poem . . . *sailing on a silver sea?* Liz, are you getting loaded? Don't!

Alexander was laughing, a low rumbling sound that caressed her ears. "So, Elizabeth—you are jealous. A good sign." How did he manage to be on her side of the table, drawing her to her feet and into his embrace? His arms bruised her back, crushed her to a chest hard as a rock, his muscular thighs pressed insistently against hers. "No . . ." she moaned just before his lips came down firmly on hers.

There was no time or space, only a spinning, tumbling void. A rushing sound in her ears, small coils of tension in isolated corners of her consciousness that were unbearable and sweetly agonizing. All feeling was concentrated in her lips. She tasted Alexander, the wine, the scent of tropical flowers. She felt his tongue, warm and pulsing, the sudden shock of his teeth along her lower lip. She was filled with yearning. She was soaring to a rendezvous on the far reaches of the cosmos and he was part of it. She knew real desire for the first time.

Chapter 9

She awakened to the sound of a shout from the beach. "Liz! Where are you Liz?" She thought she was still dreaming. She sat up, trembling as the memory of the dream surged through her consciousness, awakening all of the longing again. She could feel the scarlet stain of a blush on her cheeks as she stumbled out of bed. She was alone in the room. And alone on the island . . . unless . . .

Another hail from the beach. "Liz! Hey, babe, wake up."

Nick. It couldn't be. It was.

Liz wrapped her sarong as she ran to the top of the cliff. Nick was coming up the stone steps as the outrigger skimmed back out to sea. She shaded her eyes against the glare of the sun and, still bewildered and disoriented, waited for him to come to her. Her first reaction was overwhelming disappointment that he had interrupted her idyll with Alexander.

Nick gave her his little-boy-lost grin. The sunlight glinted on his hair as his rangy frame negotiated the stone steps, two at a time. He wore a wrinkled khaki safari jacket and there was a camera slung over his shoulder. His dark eyes traveled the length of her body appreciatively. "Dorothy Lamour, I presume?" he said, three steps from the top of the cliff. "When's the typhoon . . . or was it a hurricane? You know they still show that film in Europe and Asia. The original, I mean. Not the remake."

"Who told you where to find me, Nick?"

"Now, babe, what kind of a greeting is that for a man who's been on a plane a thousand hours—to say nothing of a choppy canoe ride." He was beside her, looking down at her with his most appealing expression firmly in place. Slowly he slid the camera strap from his shoulder, lowered the case carefully to the ground and reached for her. She was stiff and unyielding in his arms. His lips nibbled hers.

"Surely it wasn't Maggie? No one else knew—"

"Intrepid soldiers of fortune have their methods of finding lost damsels in distress. Maggie wouldn't give me the time of day. Come on, Liz, admire my resourcefulness. I searched your bedroom, found the address of the travel agent in Honolulu, and convinced him of my urgent need to see you." He chewed her ear, slid his hands inside the sarong. "Urgent need," he breathed.

Liz disentangled his hands. She forced herself to remain calm, detached. There would be no scrimmaging this time, no physical contest that could end in love-making. She was wise to his tricks. She said coldly, "I want to be alone. You shouldn't have followed me. I want you to leave me alone. Surely you of all people understand that need. You never hesitated to take off when you wanted to be alone."

"But I always let you know where I was. I was worried about you, Liz. It isn't like you to just sneak off. Are you OK?"

"I'm fine. You shouldn't have sent the outrigger back. You aren't staying. For one thing, the owner of this island only rents it to one guest at a time. Surely the travel agent told you that? We'll have to radio for the outrigger to come back for you." Oddly, she was more annoyed than angry. Had he lost the power to make her angry, she wondered.

"Not until tomorrow, babe. They told me I'd have to stay at least twenty-four hours until another canoe crew was available." He glanced in the direction of the grass shack. "Got anything cold to drink?"

Liz sighed and led the way, wondering where Alexander was and if he were watching. It was wise to be civil to Nick, she supposed, at least until the outrigger returned for him.

Nick saw the photographs and her notes instantly. Before she could stop him, he was at the desk, reading what she had written. She snatched the notes from his hand angrily, tearing the paper.

"So that's what you're up to . . . and you wanted it to be a surprise for me? Hey, babe, I'm sorry—I didn't mean to spoil the surprise. But why not let me help you with it? There's my side of the story too; you don't know all there is to know, pretty Liz. Come on, let me see it. I think you've really got something. Hell, our real-life story will make most of those photonovels look like Brenda Starr. You're going to make South America the climax, right?"

Her eyes flashed and the words were out before she

could stop them. "No, I was thinking of using a big-name movie star in a torrid love scene with you. A fitting climax, so to speak."

His expression was controlled, his eyes blank. "So you found out. I figured that must have been the reason for the sudden disappearing act. Hell, Liz, it didn't mean a thing. She was upset about you making a play for Adam Eastman and it was her way of getting even."

Liz slammed the folder of notes down on the desk. "I don't give a damn about what it meant to Gwynna Duvalle. What about what it meant to you—or to me?"

"All I could think of was keeping the movie rolling. We had a lot of money at stake. She wasn't even that great a lay."

Closing her eyes, Liz counted slowly to ten.

His arms went out, tentatively. He touched her shoulder lightly, played with a strand of her hair. "I'm sorry, Liz. I swear to you I'm going to be a plaster saint from now on. Come on home and let's get married right away."

She was silent, not really caring any more.

"A truce, Liz? For twenty-four hours? I told them to send the outrigger back for us tomorrow. Come on, give me a drink then let's explore your Shangri-la. I always wanted to be lost on a desert island with a beautiful babe."

"Woman, Nick. I'm a woman," she protested wearily, but there was no point in fighting with him for twenty-four hours. She could be civilized for that long. She did not forget how ingratiating he could be when he was on his best behavior.

"Sure you are. All the woman I ever wanted. Listen, I've an idea: let's pretend we're castaways for twenty-four hours. We just met on the beach. Don't know anything about one another. Remember how it was when we first met?"

"You're wasting your time. I'm not in the mood for games." She handed him a glass of juice. "It's over, Nick. Finished."

He drained the glass. "If I tell you I've accepted that, then can we just not talk about it again until I leave?"

She nodded, curiously unmoved by the soulful stare he gave her, or the twitching muscle in his temple.

Because it was easier than talking, she showed him around the island. After a while they made small talk. They had known each other too long and too intimately to behave like strangers. As the day wore on the ice between them began to melt a little around the edges.

They swam in the lagoon, lay on the warm sand of the beach, strolled through the groves of fruit trees and flowering shrubs, rinsed the salt-water from their bodies in the sparkling fresh water of the waterfall, splashed each other in the pool. Nick took pictures, of the island, of Liz. They talked, joked, laughed. It was like old times again. Except she would not let him make love to her. Napping lazily on the beach in the late afternoon she suddenly sat bolt upright. "The *boucan!*"

Nick pushed his bush hat off his eyes. "Did you say 'we can'? It's about time, I've had a hard-on all day." He stretched his arms lazily toward her but she was scrambling to her feet.

"Hey, where are you going?"

She was running along the beach, around the point into the next cove. She stopped abruptly, eyes sweeping the deserted dunes, scanning the sun-bleached rocks and sculptured driftwood. Yesterday Alexander had built his *boucan,* hung up part of the wild boar to dry in the smoke. There was no sign today that anyone had set foot on that stretch of beach for a long time.

"It *was* all a dream," she whispered, disappointed.

The sand crunched behind her as Nick skidded to a stop. "OK, let me guess. You're looking for Friday's footprints in the sand, right? Doesn't look like he was here, Liz."

"Nick . . . do you believe in ghosts?"

He laughed, bit his lip and gave her a quizzical glance. "Sorry, you're serious, aren't you? Looks like I got here, if you'll excuse the pun, in the nick of time. Whose ghost did you see? No, babe, don't get mad. It's the loneliness—I've seen strong men hallucinate after they've been completely alone for a while."

"And I'm only a weak woman, is that it?"

"To answer your other question, no, I most emphatically do not believe in ghosts. I do, however, believe in vivid imaginations. And you have one, Liz. It's part of your charm." He looked over her shoulder, at the white caps beginning to ruffle the surface of the sea. Black clouds were darkening the horizon. "There's a squall blowing in," he added. "You may have to put up with me for longer than one night."

A gust of wind whipped her hair across her face. A vivid imagination indeed. She had smelled the aroma of roasting meat, seen the plumes of smoke rise from the boucan. Felt Alexander's hard body pressed to hers, his breath warm in her throat. Yet everything after he took her in his arms last night had a misty quality. Had he made love to her, or had she merely wanted him to, desperately? There had been no real consummation, she was certain. Yet how could there be, with a spirit?

Nick was right, her ghost had been a hallucination. After all, pirates had been very much on her mind before she came here. Hadn't the filming of *The Black Pirate* precipitated all of the events that followed?

"A penny for them, Liz. More if they're worth it.

That's a very perplexed grimace you're wearing. Come on, it's going to rain. Let's go back to our little grass shack." He slipped his arm about her waist as they walked, the wind hard against their backs. "Tell me about your ghost. That's what you were thinking about, isn't it? What did your boogie-man look like?"

She hated the patronizing tone, the superior, teasing, must-humor-her manner. There had been many times he had asked a question about her feelings and when she had began to answer his eyes would glaze and despite the smiles and nods, she would know he was not really listening. "Oh, I was just thinking, supposing this island were a treasure island—I found out that it was used by pirates, long ago. Supposing they buried their treasure here. I understand the family that owns the island once turned up some silver ingots. Think of what we could do with some loot. Pay off the loan—buy new equipment. Another Hasselblad. You monopolize the one we have. In fact, a double issue of everything. Then we could go our separate ways."

"You don't really mean that." His hand crept around her shoulder, making a short exploratory journey over the swelling of her breasts. She pushed him away.

"Well . . . we could dig up a few dunes, if you like. So long as you're not afraid of awakening the ghost of old Blackbeard. Liz, babe . . .?" His voice was husky and his hand tightened on her waist. "You aren't going to freeze me out, are you?" They were half way up the cliff and he stopped, turning her to face him, pulling her close.

She didn't have time to answer. A vicious gust of wind howled in from the sea and at the same instant the stone step crumbled under his foot. He looked down, startled, and clutched at her as he fell. She felt his hand slide through her fingers, but did not lose her own balance. Almost as though an unseen hand steadied her. Nick fell only a few feet, his natural coordination coming to his aid as he bent his knees, leaned in to the fall and grabbed the first solid rock in his path. He lay still for a moment, catching his breath. The low rumble of distant thunder played a bass melody to the shriek of the wind.

"Are you all right?" Liz asked. He nodded, climbing to his feet. "Pretty dangerous—especially if a body is here alone. Your landlord had better be told about these steps." He picked his way carefully around the crumbled area. The rain began to pelt them as they hurried to the top and ran to the shack. Everything was blowing about and the coconut-palm fronds on the roof were flapping wildly.

Liz captured her notes as they skittered across the desk, pushing them into a drawer and slammed it shut. Nick was picking up prints scattered about the floor. A snowstorm of flower petals whirled around them and tree branches hammered against the roof. The wind howled through the open sides of the hut, bringing both sand and rain.

"Where are the storm windows?" Nick yelled, above the din.

"Aren't any . . . we aren't supposed to have storms here this time of year."

"Let's try to rig the blankets across the windward wall—grab that end and hold on."

They fought the flapping blanket in the gathering darkness and even when it was fastened to two corner-posts the wind still lifted it and sent cold rain down on them as they huddled in the meager shelter of the half wall.

"There's an oil lantern; can you light it?" Liz said. "I'll open a couple of cans of something for dinner.

Some wine will warm us up." She crawled across the floor on her knees, reaching up to the cupboard. "We just aren't supposed to get storms this time of year," she said again, teeth chattering.

Dinner was a miserable snack of cold beans, eaten in total darkness when the oil lantern blew over and went out and Nick couldn't find any more matches. The flashlight he always carried had a dead battery. They huddled together under his safari jacket, which was damp and smelled musty. Even Nick's perpetual ardor diminished rapidly as the dismal evening wore on.

"I hate to say it, Liz," he said after a while. She stiffened, knowing she would hate to hear it, whatever it was. "But, babe, this was one of your dumber ideas. If you thought you were punishing me for a little harmless roll in the hay with Gwynna, it was dumber still."

"I didn't come here to punish you, Nick. I came to be alone and make a few long overdue observations and decisions. I don't know how we became so involved with each other when we really have so little in common. Some sort of sensual obsession, I suppose. Whatever it was, it's over for me. I'd like to make a complete break and end our business partnership, too, movie commitment or no."

In the darkness she could not see his face and it had been necessary for her to shout the words over the din of the storm.

"You've been working too hard, babe. We should take a real vacation—together. Sure, we've had our differences, but we belong together, babe. You're the only one I always come back to."

He said something else, but the wind howled and lashed at the hut in a fury and the words were lost to her.

"We've got more than sex in common," he yelled, "how about our profession?"

The wind died suddenly, leaving an eerie silence broken only by raindrops dripping from leaves. "Nick, you're a blind man," Liz sighed. "Your only eye is your camera. You see the whole world through that damn lens. Nothing is real to you, it's all just a picture. It's the open-sesame that gets you into any place you want to go. You're just a man attached to a camera. You don't care about anything—I mean, really care."

Just then the moon sailed out from behind a cloud, illuminating his face. His mouth was drawn into a pout that had no little boy appeal. When he answered there was a self-righteous whine to his voice. "Jealousy, babe. That's always been your problem. On the line—under fire—I keep my head and get the shots. You forget you're there to take pictures and run around in circles making a nuisance of yourself. Hell, I've carried you since the day we met. You think any assignments would have gone to Liz Holly if she weren't Nick Kane's woman?"

"We'll just have to find out, won't we? Because I'm not going to be Nick Kane's woman in the future. I'll make it on my own. Besides, the studio is in the black—no thanks to you."

"Squalling brats and drooling Basset hounds," he mocked. "And you think it's art. Hell, we aren't artists, we're mechanics. Get the light and the angle right, use the proper lens . . . it isn't art, it's craft. And if you're going to move in a man's world, you'd better be damn sure you can keep your head. I'll be a gentleman and not throw South America in your face."

"And I won't mention you taking your time to set up a shot of a corral of burning animals, when you could have been leading them to safety," she flared back.

"Right—and damn near getting you and a fireman killed—"

Odd that she had never noticed before that his voice became so high-pitched when he was angry. He lapsed at last into sullen silence and when the rain stopped, Liz crept beneath the wet blankets on the bed while Nick pulled the two chairs together and was soon asleep on them.

She lay awake, listening to the sound of his deep and even breathing. Their quarrels never interfered with Nick's sleep.

The crackle of the radio awakened her. The day was sunny and serene.

Nick had already carefully checked his camera equipment to be sure it wasn't damaged. He turned from the radio and grinned at her. "They're sending the outrigger for us this afternoon. Funniest damn thing I ever heard—no storms reported anywhere else. They said it isn't unusual though at this latitude. Ships at sea have passed by a squall and seen lightning bolts and churning waves while they were on calm water under clear skies."

As though nothing had happened, Liz thought. No mention of the quarrel. She crawled stiffly out of bed. "I won't be leaving with you. I'm staying for the rest of the month." She slipped into a bikini, keeping her back turned to him. "I'm going for a swim. I'll pick some fruit for breakfast on the way back."

"Hang on, I'll go with you."

Nick in his swim trunks was all elongated sinew; trim, tapered, taut. He wanted her to see he was aroused. She avoided looking at him and went outside. There was little damage to the shack. A few palm-fronds were down, several tree limbs were broken and the boughs stripped of blossom. The design of the grass shack, with its half-walls, permitted the fury of the wind to pass through.

"I hate to point this out," Nick said as he fell into step beside her, "but the early morning is a bad time to swim. Better keep a lookout for triangular fins. It's feeding time for the sharks and we saw a mess of them from the canoe on the way in. We'd better stay in the lagoon and keep our eyes open."

Liz had not ventured beyond the reef, although she had been tempted to ride the breakers on the other side of the coral wall. The travel agent had warned her both of the danger of sharks and the inadvisability of swimming alone, in the event she developed a cramp. Inside the reef, the water was clear and warm and, except when there was an extremely high tide, shallow enough to stand up most of the way out to the reef.

Nick was a stronger swimmer and he headed for the reef with long, sure strokes, then turned and swam back toward her. "Feels good," he yelled. "Too warm, though. I'm more in need of a cold shower after all the enforced celibacy."

She ignored him while continuing to swim toward the reef. When she felt the sharp jab of the coral she carefully climbed to the top of the reef, intrigued to find it just below the surface of the water so that it appeared she was actually standing on the sea. On the ocean side the waves formed translucent tunnels, hovered, then broke with a diamond-bright cascade of foam.

"Behold, she walks on water. White goddess, show me some more of your magic," Nick called. He was floating on his back.

Liz was an expert body-surfer. She had surfed every beach from Malibu to Torrey Pines. Lacking the strength and stamina for hard swimming, she had learned to ride the waves instead, using the power of the sea to propel her faster, more smoothly than her slender body had muscle enough to do. She looked longingly at the breaking waves, glanced back at Nick, then dove off the reef and under the breaking wave.

She swam through the surf, waiting for the next wave to form, then, arms behind her, head up, she took the wave in a graceful swan-dive. Down, down the white bright spray, hurtling toward the reef faster than the speed of a freight-train. Not quite flying, nor yet swimming, but equal parts of both. A brief, exhilarating communion of sky and sea and her own weightless body. She was enclosed in a misty emerald that was shattering into a million sparkling, exploding prisms. Tucking out of the wave just before it crashed on the reef, she swam back out to sea.

After she had ridden three waves, Nick joined her. They were treading water, waiting for the next wave to form, when she saw the fear leap into his eyes. He was staring over her shoulder and, turning, she saw the gray fin cruising slowly back and forth between them and the reef.

"Let's get the hell out of here," Nick said in a small frightened voice. He put down his head and began to splash wildly through the water. The gray fin turned and sliced directly toward him. Liz flung herself on the next wave, catching it too late. She was flung head-over-heels, sucked up into the vortex, smashed under the churning white surface. She came up, gasping for air, was rolled underwater again, held there by the force of the breaker.

Breaking the surface again, she found herself several yards from the reef. There was no sign of the shark. Had he dived, ready to attack her from below? She looked around frantically. Nick was already in the lagoon, swimming rapidly toward the beach. There was an ominous splash nearby and she saw the shark then, only a few feet away. A small sinister eye regarded her pitilessly, the hideous inverted smile revealed razor-sharp teeth.

She moved her arms and legs, trying to back away without causing a flurry in the water that would bring an immediate attack. The shark followed relentlessly, closing the distance between them.

She did not see the boat approach. One minute she was alone with the gray predator and the next the longboat slid into view. Alexander was in the bow, knife gleaming between his teeth. He dove into the water, barely rippling the surface between Liz and the shark. There was wild turbulence, then man and fish came into view, thrashing in blood-stained water. Alexander's brawny arm was around the fish's body, just below the wicked teeth.

"Get into the boat, Elizabeth," Alexander shouted just before he disappeared under the water again. Liz reached for the boat, hauled herself up over the side and flopped weakly down inside, shaking all over.

It was all over in a few seconds. The boat was being washed against the sharply-pointed coral spires and Alexander swam alongside and pushed it into the lagoon, then he climbed in with her and picked up the paddle. "You had a bad fright, Elizabeth, but you'll be all right," he said gently.

She nodded, trying to stop the shaking of her limbs, content to let Alexander take charge. Near the beach he swung over the side of the boat, lifted her carefully into his arms and waded ashore with her. He placed her on the warm sand, massaging her hands and feet to bring life back to them. She was struck again by the warmth of his touch. No icy spirit this.

"I'm going back for the carcass," Alexander said, "our friend will make a tasty supper and I like not killing any beast unless for food. Lie here and the sun will warm you." He gave her a reassuring smile that softened the wildness of his features, then he was gone. She heard the sound of his boat scraping the sand, the splash of his feet in the water. Closing her eyes for a moment she lay still, letting the sun's warmth seep into her bones. Nick! She remembered his lean body flying through the water toward the beach, leaving her behind. She sat up and looked around. There was no sign of Alexander or his boat in the lagoon. Further along the beach Nick lay on his stomach, panting.

Liz stood up, shielded her eyes to scan the ocean again. It was empty. She walked slowly toward Nick and he looked up as she approached.

"That was a near thing, babe," he said hoarsely.

"You didn't see him?" she asked.

"The shark? You bet I did."

She opened her mouth to say, "No, the man in the boat. A magnificent, ferocious pirate with a zig-zag scar on one cheek, a mane of black hair and a knife in his teeth." But of course she did not say it, Nick would have thought she was mad.

Chapter 10

Until the very last minute, with the outrigger waiting on the beach, Nick believed Liz would go with him. Finally embarrassed by the grins of the dusky-skinned oarsmen, he said nonchalantly, "OK, babe. Guess I'll see you back in L.A. at the end of the month," gave her a mocking salute, and left.

Liz prowled the beach and the cliff-top with a scarcely concealed air of excitement and expectation. She washed her hair in the fresh-water pool, cleaned up the shack, raked up the fallen branches and palm-fronds. As evening fell, she prepared a meal of imitation Beef Stroganoff from a dried mix. Shortly after sunset everything was ready, including Liz with a fresh flower in her hair.

Alexander did not appear. Nor did he come the following day, or the day after that.

The weather resumed its pattern of cloudless skies

and gentle trade winds. She swam in the lagoon, never venturing beyond the reef into the realm of the predators again, and, eventually, went back to the photonovel out of sheer boredom.

All of the proofs and her notes were out of order, the result of being blown about in the squall. The pictures of the California fires were on top of the pile. She stared at a cluster of anguish-filled faces. So many houses had been burning by nightfall that it was impossible for the watching owners to tell if they were watching their own house burn or someone else's. She placed the picture face down and followed it quickly with the shot of the fear-crazed horses.

The next picture was of Nick, triumphantly riding a tank through the rubble-filled streets of a South American town following an unsuccessful coup. Liz had taken the picture, and the next day she had been caught trying to take pictures of pathetically young students being dragged to jail.

Nick had been furious. He had to bribe government officials, the police, the army. They were, he said, lucky to get out of there with their lives. He would never, repeat, never take her with him again.

"But we only got pictures of one side of the story," she protested. "What about the reason for the attempted coup? What kind of desperation drove unarmed students to go against tanks?"

"And what about reporters who get shot? Hell, I should have known better than to drag you along with me."

Dispassionately, Liz held the picture in her hand. Oh, Nick, she thought, whoever said love is blind didn't know the half of it. A strange new feeling was invading her mind. Relief? A comforting easing of the pain and anxiety that had been her constant companions. She no longer hated what Nick had done to destroy her love, nor did she hate Nick. In a moment of revelation she realized that the opposite to love was simply indifference.

Alexander's voice growled at her elbow, "He is gone. And not a moment too soon. My patience wore thin."

Liz jumped, dropping the picture. She looked up into Alexander's flinty stare. "Must you appear so suddenly?" she asked. "You frightened me."

He was stripped to the waist, his breeches were soaking wet and in his hand was a large, flat fish. He tossed it onto the table. "Breakfast," he announced. "I caught it. You will clean it."

"I will not."

He smiled knowingly. "You don't know how. What a useless wench you are."

"I do know how."

He raised a perfect black eyebrow, pulled his knife from the sheath on his belt, handed it to her and waited expectantly.

Liz looked at the fish uncertainly. It looked back at her with a faint sneer of triumph. She lifted the tail gingerly. "I didn't thank you for saving me from the shark. You said you were going back for the carcass—but you didn't come back. Why didn't you materialize when Nick was here?"

"I tried, but couldn't. I stood in front of you both but neither of you saw me. There's more to being a spirit than I realized."

"On the cliff, when Nick stumbled . . . was that your doing?"

Alexander's smile was enigmatic.

"And the storm that came from nowhere?"

He lifted his shoulders questioningly.

"You're enjoying this, aren't you?"

"Watching you fumble with that fish? Not at all. I fear our breakfast will be in shreds if I don't come to your aid. Give me the knife, girl, you're mangling my meal and getting fish scales all over you."

"I meant," Liz said haughtily, "you're enjoying seeing me at a loss in front of a ghost."

Alexander looked wounded.

"The shoe would be on the other foot if we weren't on this island, you know," Liz said, ignoring him. "I mean, I am grateful to you for helping me get away from the shark, but the whole scene simply would not have arisen, back in civilization. There it would be *me* in control, because you wouldn't have a clue how to deal with . . . things." She waved her hand vaguely, hoping to indicate the complexities of contemporary life. He was gazing at her, admiringly, but blankly. She plunged on, "It's just that here you're in your natural habitat, so to speak, while I'm out of my element—"

"Elizabeth, you've lapsed into gibberish. This isn't like you. I had begun to believe women were perhaps capable of logical thought after all."

"What I'm trying to say is that this isn't the way I normally live. But it is how you live."

"My home is a ship. Not an island."

"But it's primitive here. No modern conveniences. You're more accustomed to a primitive way of life than I am." She reached for a skillet to cook the fish, which he had gutted with a single deft stroke. She wished he would not watch her every movement with such intensity. "I suppose you became a sailor because you love the sea?" she suggested, deciding to try another tack.

"Love the sea?" he scoffed. "Do you know what a sailor's life is like? A ship is a floating prison. A dank and cheerless place of pestilence and hardship. The sea constantly seeks to gain entry through her planks, beats down her hatchways so that the lower decks are always awash. A sodden blanket, a hacking cough, ceaseless toil—that's a sailor's lot. And a flogging or a belaying pin across his back if he hesitates to obey an order."

Alexander paced slowly and majestically back and forth, illustrating each point with a jab of his knife in the air. "And that's before he wrestles with wet canvas, clinging to the yards in a shrieking gale. Or breaks his back, and his heart, at the oars. He eats in the dark, so he doesn't have to see the black-headed weavils in his bread or the maggots in his meat. If the scurvy or dysentery or fever doesn't kill him, and he survives his punishments, then the French disease will get him. And this before he ever goes into battle with cutlass or cannon to face.

"Then why? Why did you go to sea?"

"Because life ashore was harder," he answered, grinning.

"And why did you become a pirate?"

"Ah," Alexander said, "that's a long story. Belay, wench, you're about to overcook the fish." He leaped to her side and wrenched the spatula from her hand.

They ate breakfast in companionable silence. The fish was delicately flavored and delicious. Alexander had also provided fresh passionfruit. The sun was warm on their shoulders, hunger was appeased and there was no need for words. Liz was aware of all of her senses as well as a carefree lighthearted joy in simple pleasures that she had not felt since childhood.

Occasionally Alexander's eyes would meet hers in a glance both appraising and quizzical. Liz thought, I am as much an enigma to him as he is to me. I must remember that and not let him get me flustered.

Alexander finished eating and sighed contentedly. He leaned back in his chair, expression inscrutable for a few seconds. Then he said suddenly, "I would not have pushed him, but for the shock of seeing that hated face."

Liz looked up in surprise. "What are you talking about?"

"Your Nicholas looks exactly like Louis de Letraz—except your betrothed has a pair of ears and Louis lost one of his."

"How very strange. I wish you hadn't told me."

"Why? I saw Louis only yesterday—he lives on in my own time, or perhaps it is my memory of my time. Anyway, your Nicholas is not my Louis. He has neither the cunning nor the stealth and, I suspect, he also lacks the wit. But tell me why you would have preferred not to hear of his likeness to your Nicholas."

"Because it reinforces a theory of mine. That you are a figment of my imagination. You see, if Nick is Louis and Louis is your rival . . . then probably I am dreaming up a rival for Nick. A rival who will make me forget him."

Alexander jumped to his feet, thunderclouds in his eyes. He pounded the table, making the crockery rattle. "Hark ye well, wench. When it comes to women, I do my own choosing. Many a maid has fluttered her eyelashes at me coyly, but none has trapped Alexander. And by the saints, why would I be attracted to a scrawny, sunburned strumpet with no wifely virtues at all?"

Liz faced him squarely, chin tilted. "All right. I get your point. There's no need to shout, you barbarian. Since you can apparently appear or disappear at will, why don't you just disappear until I leave the island? I'm not going to argue with a raving madman who has no appreciation of a real woman."

Alexander paced silently, angrily, a caged panther in the confined space of the hut. "I know not why I tarry here. Nor why you of all women disturb my rest. Perhaps it is to avenge my own murder I come. If I cannot change the past, then perhaps I can change the future. If Louis smote me dead in my time . . ." He paused, considering.

Liz swallowed. "No—not Nick. You wouldn't . . ."

His eyes sliced into her thoughts and the cold steel of the glance brought her half out of her chair, her heart beginning to thump painfully.

"You care for him, even though he showed himself to you in his true colors. Your Nicholas is a coward. He may look like Louis, but Louis at least is not a coward. Your man left you as shark bait and saved his own skin."

"That's not quite fair," Liz said. "Nick thought I was swimming for shore with him. I would have been, except I took the wave too late and it wiped me out. It all happened so suddenly."

Alexander had stopped pacing. He stood looking down at her with a level gaze that went right to the center of her thoughts. "In defending him, you tell me you love him."

"I did. I don't. Oh, why don't you go and haunt someone else? My life is complicated enough."

He was silent, watching her. Liz had the feeling he was putting two and two together but coming up with considerably more than four. She was also acutely aware of his bare muscular chest and the way his biceps flexed as he swung his arms in the flamboyant gestures that punctuated his speech. No wraithlike spirit this.

When Liz conjured them up, she did it with style. Odd how she had never felt fear for her safety in his presence. Fear for her honor, perhaps. . . . Those feelings he aroused in her were real indeed.

"I am not sure," he said at length, frowning, "why I awakened in this place at this time. I have learned, however, that I can return to my own time at will. I merely take my boat and return to the island where my ship comes to pick me up. The *Avenger* appears and I board her and it is as though I still live in my own time. Yet I dream of you, and this island. Perhaps, Elizabeth, it is I who have imagined you—yet for what purpose I cannot conceive. Our link seems to be your man Nicholas, who is my murderer. Perhaps our answer lies there. Still I see nothing in Louis's character that portends his killing me by stealth; I died in my sleep, I am sure."

"To die in your sleep indicates a death from old age," Liz pointed out. "But you are a man in your prime. Since you apparently remember most of your life but don't remember an old age, your death must have come suddenly and unexpectedly."

Alexander fingered his scar thoughtfully, searching his memory. After a few seconds he shrugged and gave her a lascivious grin. "Forsooth, more men died in brothels than in battle. I will remember the how and when of it in good time."

"Tell me what comes to your mind when you think of your life," Liz urged.

Eyes as sharp as steel lit up with a wicked light as he replied, "Bone and brains in the scuppers, gold doubloons clattering on deck, smoking cannon . . . and a hemp noose about a sunburned scraggly neck. I belonged to the third oldest profession, Elizabeth, did you know that? The other two being prostitution and medicine." He chuckled, deep in his throat, watching her reaction.

When neither shock nor outrage appeared to disturb the rapt expression on her face as she leaned forward in her chair, listening intently, he moved toward her, took her hands in his and drew her to her feet.

"But I remember too the warm breeze billowing the canvas and the wake gleaming with phosphorous, marking a bright path into the dark horizon. I remember brilliant stars in an endless sky and moments of perfect stillness before a silver dawn lit up the sea."

His strong hands cupped her face, his fingers pressing lightly at her temples, his gaze probing for answers to the questions that plagued him—questions he was unable to ask her, for fear that if he pried too deeply into the why of their meeting she would melt away.

Her arms went tentatively around his back. They stood for a moment in a silent embrace, each acutely aware of the awakening passion that was already touched with the sadness of inevitable parting.

Liz did not want to think of the future; but she could not help being intrigued by the past. "Alexander . . . if you can come into my time," she said slowly, "I wonder if there is some way I can return to yours?"

"To what purpose? Verily, wench, you would not like my time."

"Perhaps we can find out how you died—who killed you and why. Perhaps then you could sleep on in peace. There are some who believe a spirit returns because of the unsolved riddle of his death."

She felt his body tense in her arms and he released her abruptly. She instantly regretted destroying the mood of the moment.

"And what do you propose I do with you? Take you aboard my ship? Have you at my side when we attack a prize, sack and plunder a city? Our articles forbid the presence of women aboard our ships."

Liz gazed in to the little demon of jealousy that lurked in the back of her mind and asked, "What about the Lady Amelia? Wasn't she aboard your ship?"

His eyes mellowed at some treasured memory. "For a few days—and nights—only. Until I was able to put her ashore. Her presence aboard the *Avenger* had to be kept secret from my crew. By the saints, Elizabeth, I'd like to show you the Lady Amelia, so you could see what a real woman is like—"

"I am a real woman," Liz shouted. "Oh, you're impossible. Go away and leave me to my work."

"Perhaps you would like to prove your femininity?" he suggested with a sly grin, moving closer.

She felt the electric tension generated by his nearness and spoke quickly to break the magnetism drawing her to him. "Alexander, how about telling me your story? Perhaps I could see something in it that you can't by the perspective of the years that separate us. I'm truly interested in how and why you became a pirate. There has been so much nonsense written about pirates and buccaneers that we really don't know what it was like."

"And in return, Elizabeth will tell me all of her story? For Alexander is plagued by the riddle of Elizabeth's passion for Louis—I mean, Nicholas."

"Why do you refer to us in the third person? It's—forgive me—spooky."

He laughed. "No reason. Come, we'll go to the beach so I can work on my boat as I tell you my story. In my day we believed Satan found work for idle hands."

"Funny," Liz said. "We believe the same thing today."

They went from the cool shade of the hut to the

blazing sunshine, picking their way carefully past the crumbled cliff-step.

"I was a callow youth when I joined my first pirate ship," Alexander told her. "I ran away from a sugar plantation under the stewardship of one Miles Grindwald. The law was after me and I had a companion to whom I owed my life . Tad Bowen. A great giant of a blacksmith whose mind broke under the brutal treatment of that monster in the guise of a milksop . . . Grindwald.

"We swam out to where the pirate ship called the *Tiger's Claw* lay at anchor, climbed aboard and hid in the hold while her crew were carousing ashore.

"They found us the following morning . . ."

Chapter 11

Tad Bowen and the young Alexander were discovered and hauled before a pirate council. The ship they had boarded was already out of sight of land, riding low in the water, her hatches bulging with loot. The *Tiger's Claw* was a brigantine, fast and versatile with her square sails; carrying ten cannons and a crew of a hundred men.

In the ship's steerage, quaffing rum and smoking foul-smelling pipes, the pirates argued among themselves as to what to do about the stowaways. The man Bowen was a windfall, they agreed, prodding Tad's blacksmith's muscles approvingly. Pity he was an idiot, but no doubt he could be trained to wield a cutlass and furl sail. The boy, however . . . still wet behind the ears and lacking a man's muscle. They shook their heads doubtfully.

"Give him to me," one black-bearded man of monstrous proportions suggested, grasping Alexander's arm in a flesh-numbing grip. Tiny black eyes glinted and rum-sodden breath fanned Alexander's cheek. "I'll see to the lad."

"And what about Article VI?" A scholarly-looking man who seemed out of place in the villainous-looking group asked. "Didn't we all sign the articles and wasn't number six that no boy or woman be allowed amongst us?"

Alexander shook his arm free of the bearded man's grasp and looked around at his captors. Some regarded him lasciviously while others muttered, "Toss the lad overboard and be done with it."

Only the scholarly-looking pirate seemed to possess the last vestiges of humanity and it was to him Alexander appealed, "I can reef and furl sail. Read and write, too. How many of you can say the same? Are there not times you wish to send a ransom note—or let your wishes be known to some island governor? I can shoot, too, my father taught me. Give me a pistol and I'll show you."

There was a burst of laughter and some grudgingly given comments about the boy's courage.

"Who is your captain?" Alexander demanded. "What manner of ship is this that has no leader?"

The scholarly-looking man tapped his pipe on the rough wood of the table in front of him. "This is a pirate vessel, lad, and every man aboard takes an equal share. Our captain plots our course and leads us into battle, and for that he gets two shares. But we elect who the captain will be. Aboard a ship that flies the *jolie rouge* we tolerate no tyrannical masters. Most of us fled from brutal skippers on other ships, or were ill-used on the land by lords."

"But you, sir," Alexander said quickly, "speak like a gentleman. Not an ignorant tar or a whoremongering wharf rat such as these others."

The scholar, as Alexander had privately dubbed him, laughed. The others bellowed with rage and indignation. The black-bearded one seized Alexander by the throat. "Methinks I'll teach the puppy to respect his elders," he roared.

At that moment Tad Bowen, who had been forgotten as they pondered Alexander's fate, sprang forward. He had been sitting on the sidelines, eyes vacant and mouth hanging open. At the sight of Alexander being roughly handled, however, Tad's cherubic features were convulsed with a fury that stopped every man's breath in his throat. The baby-faced giant became a punching, flailing, unstoppable machine of vengeance. The black-bearded man was the first to be laid flat on his back. Two more joined him in short order. One man pulled out his pistol, only to have it yanked from his grasp and smashed into his face. Cursing and trying to surround Tad in the cramped quarters, the pirates dropped before his blows. Daggers were drawn but never connected with flesh. Alexander waded into the fray at Tad's side, but he needed no assistance.

The melée ended abruptly as a pistol ball smashed into the bulkhead, filling the air with smoke and deafening every ear. In the moment's bewildered silence that followed, as every man checked himself for blood to see if he'd been hit, a silky voice announced, "Stand where you are, all of you. Let me see the half-wit and the boy who turns this crew into scuffling schoolboys."

Everyone froze, and Alexander turned around slowly, expecting to see a man at least as big as Tad or blackbeard. The man who stood with smoking pistol in hand, however, was slim and almost girlishly handsome. His sable brown hair waved as beguilingly as any wench's and he was much younger than the other pirates. The thin black moustache and goatee were obviously an attempt to disguise both his youth and good looks. But there was, Alexander was quick to note, a cold malevolence to the man's deeply set eyes that brought to mind the stare of a venomous reptile. The eyes and their pitiless stare quickly drew attention away from the lean, handsome features.

Someone pushed Alexander forward and he sprawled on the deck, inches away from the boots of the dandy who had quieted the crew. Tad stepped forward and helped Alexander to his feet, brushing the boy off gently and shaking his head in a worried manner. Alexander said, "My name is Alexander Bartholomew, sir, and this is Tad Bowen. Do I have the honor of addressing the captain of this ship? If so, we'd be pleased to join your crew for we're wanted for murder in Jamaica."

The scholar said, "Cap'n, the big one fights like a demon, we could use him. But look ye how he watches over the boy, he won't be any use to us if we kill the lad."

There was another outburst of grumbling and arguing among the crew that was interrupted by a shout from the deck above. "Sail ho! Three leagues to westward."

"Our prey, gentlemen," the captain said. His English was flawless, but obviously not his native tongue. Alexander noted the French accent as the captain poked him playfully in the chest with his pistol and said, "If your half-witted giant fights well today, we shall see. Perhaps I'll cast my vote to spare both of you."

Alexander turned to Tad, praying the man would

understand their peril. "We must fight with them, Tad. We've nothing to lose now—we can't ever go back."

The other ship flew French colors and attempted to run, but the pirate vessel ranged down on her starboard quarter. The captain climbed out on the bowsprit to order the Frenchman's captain to come aboard the privateer to discuss terms. The cold-eyed leader of the pirates seemed unconcerned at the prospect of plundering a ship flying the colors of his former country. The French captain of the merchantman answered with a volley of small arms fire.

Both crews retired to closed quarters and the *Tiger's Claw* brought her big guns to bear. The air was filled with the deafening roar of cannon and eye-stinging black smoke. The captain brought the pirate vessel about and rammed her bowsprit into the Frenchman's mainmast rigging. Alexander and Tad were issued cutlasses and pushed unceremoniously out on deck. The pirate crew was lashing their bowsprit to the other vessel and some of them were crawling along it while the rest swung over the sides. Once aboard, several pirates climbed the shrouds of the French ship in an attempt to cut down her yards. All the time the guns of both ships fired at point blank range.

Blinded by smoke, Alexander saw Tad swept along with the rush of men pouring over the side. When Alexander attempted to follow, he slipped on a pool of blood on the deck and went down behind a hatchway, fighting the nausea that threatened to choke him. He wanted to cover his ears to shut out the sounds of gunfire and clashing steel, the death cries of the mortally wounded, and the fearful sound of heavy bodies falling from the shrouds to crash onto the deck or splash into the sea.

Gritting his teeth, he picked up the cutlass and

climbed to his feet. Making his way carefully to the rail he realized the gunfire was now reduced to an occasional pistol shot. The pirates were swarming aboard the French ship, hacking away at boarding nets. On the deck of the merchantman they gained the closed quarters and dragged men out to dispatch them with pistol and cutlass. Other members of the French crew came up from below and hand-to-hand combat raged on the bloodied deck, the sailors knowing well that the pirates would give no quarter.

The cold-eyed captain of the pirate ship, scorning the usual cutlass, pranced gracefully about the deck with a rapier, a gentleman's weapon. The captain was engaged with three men, slicing and slashing quickly and efficiently. A small, satisfied smile played about his lips. Alexander watched, fascinated. Seeing the captain in full sunlight, Alexander realized he was only a few years older than himself. Despite his youth, he stood out as a swift and graceful eagle stands out against a pack of ungainly crows. He fought with unhurried precision, as though savoring every moment. Every line of his lithe body, and flourish of his rapier, bespoke breeding and self-confident control. His thin lips curled contemptuously as the three sailors frantically swung their cutlasses, trying to bring him down. He might have been playing with a pack of demented puppies.

Alexander looked away hastily as the captain's rapier plunged into the chest of one of his opponents. Looking down at the cutlass in his own hand, Alexander wondered if he could bring himself to plunge the gleaming blade into human flesh. All at once he had no choice. He looked up to see a Frenchman poised on the rail of the other ship, about to vacate his own ravaged vessel for the relative peace of the deck of the pirate ship. Only Alexander barred his way. The man crashed down on him, knocking the wind out of him. Alexander rolled over and scrambled for his fallen cutlass as the man raised a dagger and lunged for him. It was all over so quickly Alexander wasn't sure exactly what had happened. He felt his hands close around the hilt of the cutlass and he raised it as the Frenchman lunged. The man seemed to collapse on top of the cutlass, drenching Alexander in blood.

Dazed, he flung aside the body and staggered to the rail, wanting to vomit. Then he saw the pirate captain was in dire straits. The thin-bladed rapier had snapped in half under the impact of the heavier cutlass and the captain was vainly trying to defend himself with the broken blade. His two assailants were closing in. He was backed against the capstan.

Alexander wanted to cry out to warn him, but there wasn't time. He leaped over the rail and rushed to the captain's aid, slashing wildly at the back of the nearest man. A second later Tad Bowen appeared at his side and calmly picked up the other Frenchman and hurled him over the side.

The captain looked at the two of them and smiled, his pleasure not quite reaching his eyes. "You, boy, if you can cook you shall live until you are man enough to warrant a share of our booty. And you, Tad Bowen, are now a member of our crew. You have the honor to sail with Louis de Letraz."

Some time passed before Alexander and Tad learned that Louis was the son of a French nobleman who had offended his king and died in exile. Louis himself had barely escaped with his life and it was said he had been tortured during his imprisonment, although there were no visible scars. Only his cold and empty eyes, and his complete lack of mercy, showed what he might have suffered.

They stayed aboard the *Tiger's Claw* and learned all there was to know about stalking a ship and plundering a town. The Brethren of the Coast had their own unique way of life. No man had a past and few expected much of a future, therefore they lived life to the hilt. Favorite pastimes were drinking, sharpshooting and gambling. The pirates' favorite tipple was a mixture of gunpowder and rum, said to quickly separate the men from the boys.

The French, English and Dutch islands of the Caribbean were full of desperados like themselves. Riches slipped through their fingers as they spent their loot dicing, drinking and whoring. Alexander noted that the slim young captain did not indulge himself as freely when ashore. Upon questioning the scholar, Alexander learned that Louis cherished the dream of returning to France and regaining his family's former glory. To that end he saved his loot by burying it on a deserted atoll, knowledge of the whereabouts of which, the scholar pointed out, had cost several men their lives.

Alexander admired Louis' courage, his knowledge of navigation, his skill with a rapier, and his reckless disregard for danger. Alexander vowed he would excell in these areas himself and observed Louis carefully. But he deplored Louis' cruelty. Prisoners were shown no mercy and, while Alexander saw the wisdom in the adage that dead men told no tales, he saw no reason to torture men for the pleasure of it before killing them.

Tad Bowen never spoke to Alexander again after the night he flung the sugar plantation overseer into the flames, but Alexander was sure Tad understood when he spoke to him, for Tad often nodded knowingly.

"We'll break away from Louis and his cutthroats

when we can," Alexander told Tad. "We'll get our own ship. We must find a place to bury our share of the plunder and never let anyone know where we put it."

Few women of the day traveled as passengers unless their ship was escorted by heavily-armed Naval vessels and therefore avoided by pirates, but the *Tiger's Claw* made frequent calls at ports known for their favorite brothels and accommodating females. Alexander listened with growing curiosity to the tales the men told when they returned to the ship, for in the early days he and Tad were not allowed to go ashore.

Apparently the pleasures of a strumpet's flesh were worth the risk of disease. Alexander had duly observed that in looting a ship some of the pirates often made straight for the medicine chest, seeking mercury to treat their affliction. Yet he heard one man boast he had paid five hundred pieces of eight to a strumpet merely to see her naked. Alexander was growing to manhood mainly in the company of other men and vague longings had become urgent need by the time Louis appeared one night with three comely young wenches in tow.

The rest of the crew was ashore, except for the watch. Alexander was surprised when his captain, a giggling wench on either arm and the third behind him, stopped and invited Alexander to join him in his cabin. "You fought well today, Devil's spawn," Louis said, his voice slurred. He never called Alexander by name, but each time he addressed him with a new and insulting nickname. "Therefore Louis will reward you. Come."

In his cabin he lighted a lantern and motioned for the women to fill the glasses. The flickering light revealed plump breasts spilling over lacy bodices, long silken hair falling on soft shoulders, and red lips that parted to reveal glistening tongues. Louis sprawled comfortably on his wide bunk and two of the women flung themselves upon him, plucking at his belt.

"Our young friend hesitates," Louis said mockingly as he looked at Alexander over a rounded shoulder. "He fears I've brought diseased whores for the night's pleasure."

Three pairs of female eyes turned accusingly to Alexander, who stood uncertainly in the middle of the cabin, unsure of how to proceed, or even if he wanted to. Louis had a knack of reading a man's thoughts, Alexander perceived.

"We are the daughters of the largest plantation owner on the island," the oldest of the three girls said. "We are not whores—but, ah, Louis . . . who can resist him? And it is not our fault we were carried off by a pirate captain and forced to pleasure him in every depraved way imaginable." She gave a delicious shudder of apprehension and joined the sensual laughter of the other two. Alexander was not sure whether they were laughing at him or at convention. They certainly were well-dressed, immaculately groomed and did not appear to be prostitutes from their speech and manner.

"It's true, what she says," Louis murmured lazily. "Although, *mon ami,* she did not mention that this is not the first time they have allowed Louis to carry them off in the night."

He's drunk, Alexander thought. He calls me his friend. The clothing of the wenches was very much in disarray by now and one of them was mysteriously enclosed by Alexander's arms. The rum was scalding his throat and his blood pounded in his ears in a way it never had before. His hands were on the soft flesh of her breasts and her lips trembled and parted under his.

Dimly he heard Louis laugh somewhere in the shadowy background.

Alexander pushed the girl away, but held on to her wrist. "Come, let us find a private place," he whispered. He could see that Louis had buried his head in the thighs of one of the girls on the bed and was too busy to notice their departure.

He found a spot on the deck and undressed the girl in the moonlight, gasping at the perfection of her body as his manhood strained to be free of restraining breeches. He tore impatiently at his clothing and she cradled him in her hands, caressing him to the point of exquisite agony. Her thighs parted willingly and he thrust himself inside her as stars exploded in his brain and the warm tropical night spun away in a frenzy of passion.

She was a great deal more experienced that he, and, when his senses returned the following morning, Alexander realized he had been fortunate, indeed, that his first experience with the fair sex had proceeded so well. Having had a woman give herself not only willingly, but enthusiastically, Alexander wondered at the folly of his shipmates who paid for favors in filthy brothels. He did not consider that he was growing to be an exceptionally handsome man. He did not realize that his virility and devil-may-care attitude, as well as the indelible stamp of breeding, were magnets that would always draw women to him.

Nor did he realize that, whereas Louis made love with cold precision, in exactly the same manner he killed a man, women sensed that Alexander was a man who truly liked women and was as pleased by their pleasure as his own. It was a combination of traits that made Alexander irresistible to every woman who crossed his path, and there were many over the years.

Alexander was not sure of his age, but he believed he had passed his twentieth birthday when fate decreed that his path would again cross that of Miles Grindwald.

The *Tiger's Claw* had sighted a strange sail, which proved to be a lone English merchantman, apparently ripe for the taking. As the two ships came within range of each other, the buccaneer's cannon roared, sending the mizzen topmast of their prey crashing down.

Almost at once the English vessel's guns replied with a broadside. When the smoke cleared, the pirate helmsman was slumped over the wheel, his throat tore open with grapeshot. It was quickly evident that the merchantman was heavily armed and her crew determined to resist fiercely.

The battle raged for several hours and both sides took heavy casualties. By the time the *Tiger's Claw* was able to move in close enough to board, the pirate ship was almost as badly damaged as its prospective prize.

Grappling irons were thrown over the side of the merchantman and the pirates swung over to her deck, cutlasses slashing the boarding nets and pistols smoking. They were met with a hail of small arms fire and an incensed crew determined to go down fighting.

Battling desperately for control of the bloodied deck, Alexander had a moment's doubt about the outcome of the struggle. Louis had been getting more reckless of late and there had been murmurings among his crew that perhaps it was time to replace him as captain.

Alexander knew that Louis had shown his authority by ordering the attack on the heavily-armed English ship to proceed even though they had failed to disable her. The men would be angry no matter how rich a cargo was shared between them.

Looking into the bloody eyes of the English first

mate, and deflecting a murderous swing of his cutlass, Alexander was panting with fatigue and exertion as he lunged to administer the fatal blow. The man staggered, clutching his spurting wound, then fell forward. Springing backward to avoid being hit by the burly body as it fell, Alexander stumbled over a fallen comrade and crashed to the deck. Another English sailor saw his plight and, with a triumphant yell, leaped toward him, cutlass aloft.

Alexander rolled over a second before the blade buried itself in the deck beside him. Tad Bowen's cutlass dispatched his attacker. Giving a slack-mouthed grin of childish innocence that was more fearsome than the snarling cries of the other buccaneers, Tad then casually cut down three more sailors. There had been many past occasions when Alexander thanked providence that the blacksmith had come into his life.

By the time the pirates were in control, more than half their number lay dead or were mortally wounded. Both ships were badly damaged and it was obvious they would have to limp back into port leaving most of the cargo behind.

Alexander surveyed Louis across the body-strewn and bloodied deck, feeling conflicting emotions about the captain of the *Tiger's Claw.* As always, Alexander admired Louis for his cool courage under fire, but for the first time Alexander wondered if that reckless bravado masked an unconscious wish to die.

Louis never spoke to anyone of his previous life, but Alexander was sure that the young French nobleman felt his exile more keenly than men who had escaped life among the lower classes ashore. Alexander remembered his own carefree early boyhood with sad regret, but whereas he determined to make the best of things as they were, Louis was of a more brooding and vengeful nature. He frequently gave in to moods of black despair that were followed by suicidal orgies of violence. He seemed to invite death as other men recoiled from it.

Frequently he showed his contempt for his adversaries by the use of his lightweight rapier against the heavier cutlasses. He was always the first to board a prize; the last to leave a sacked and burning town. Alexander had seen Louis calmly turn his back on an opponent in the middle of a fight to bestow a compliment on a trembling, watching female. He had been known to stride arrogantly into a tavern and order the biggest, most surly outlaw present to rise so that he might sit in his chair.

Admiring Louis for the dashing rogue he was, Alexander had delayed their inevitable clash for leadership. Yet Alexander knew that he must lead and there could not be two captains aboard the *Tiger's Claw*.

Louis stood on the quarterdeck, resplendent in a crimson waistcoat, two pistols pushed into a matching sling that encircled his lean waist. The fine white linen shirt was spattered with blood, and his hat with the jaunty red feather had been lost in the battle. He stared morosely at the surviving pirates who clustered about him complaining of their losses. It was clear the *Tiger's Claw* was too badly damaged to either take on the other ship's cargo, or take the prize in tow. The angry growl of voices demanded to know the reason Louis had ordered an attack on a ship very nearly their match.

Prowling through the English ship to seek hidden valuables while Louis dealt with the mutterings of the crew, Alexander began to form a plan to deal with the situation to the benefit of both Louis and himself.

Ransacking the master's cabin, Alexander heard a faint whimper. Drawing his dagger, he lifted a blanket draped over the edge of the bunk. He looked into frightened eyes set in a pretty apple-cheeked face surrounded by golden hair. He noted a small, voluptuously proportioned figure clad in a well-cut velvet gown. Alexander closed the cabin door, shutting out the sound of the pirates arguing with Louis about leaving a rich cargo behind while Louis pointed out that if they did not, their ship would never reach port.

"Spare me, please, kind sir," the woman said. "My intended husband will pay a handsome sum to have me delivered safely to Jamaica." She crept out of her hiding place, smoothing her gown over her rounded hips.

Her betrothed must either be a dolt or did not actually want to marry her, Alexander thought, to send her sailing alone through the pirate-infested waters of the Caribbean. She was obviously a woman of quality and means, judging by her clothing and the impressive coat of arms emblazoned on the sea chest in her cabin. He felt a wave of compassion for her plight, as well as a stirring in the groin at the sight of her plump breasts straining at the soft material of her gown.

On the rare occasions the ships they took had a female aboard, Louis himself always took the woman and she was never seen again. Alexander surmised, correctly, that female captives were sold into white slavery when Louis was done with them.

"Who is your intended husband?" Alexander asked. Perhaps, he thought, Louis could be persuaded to ransom this one.

"Sir Miles Grindwald. He owns a plantation in the Indies to which I journey. He was unable to come to England to marry me because he has not yet found a buyer for his plantation. His father died, you see, and Miles inherited. My own inheritance depended upon my marriage before my twenty-first birthday. So we were married by proxy before I left England—"

"Grindwald," Alexander repeated the hated name thoughtfully. No doubt that fop hoped his proxy-wife would perish on the long voyage so he would be rid of her but in possession of her fortune. Grindwald . . . who had forced Tad Bowen and himself into a life from which they could never escape.

"Please, sir," the woman said. "don't give me to the crew. If I could . . . if *you* would want . . ."

Alexander ignored her as he thought rapidly. Louis had almost cost all of them their lives today. Louis would use the woman and then sell her. Louis had offered his own perverted form of friendship to Alexander, more because they were the only two gentlemen aboard the ship than from any personal liking. That friendship was predicated on Alexander forever maintaining subservience to Louis. But Alexander had for some time been preparing for the day he would challenge Louis for leadership.

He had secretly practiced fencing. He knew as much about navigation as Louis. He loathed the bloodthirsty abandon with which Louis mutilated captives. Yet Alexander had hesitated to challenge Louis because he felt he owed him his life. Now, however, he saw a way out of the dilemma.

"Stay here until I return for you," Alexander told the woman.

"I am the Lady Amelia," she whispered breathlessly just before he left the cabin.

On deck, two camps had been formed. One group wanted to take the crippled English ship in tow to save her cargo, while Louis and his henchmen wanted to abandon her to run for port and the necessary repairs to their own ship. Louis pointed out they would move too slowly and possibly fall prey to another buccaneer if they were to take a prize in tow in their own damaged state. Since such decisions were always decided by vote, a deadlock was causing tempers to run high.

Alexander sprang to the top of a hatch cover and shouted for their attention. Scowling, the men quieted slightly and turned to listen to him.

"We can solve our problem by splitting into two crews. Those who agree with Louis can remain on the *Tiger's Claw*. The rest of you can join me on the English ship, which I shall make mine. A few changes in her rigging—more guns—she will serve nicely as a buccaneer. I shall call her *Avenger* and strike out on my own as her master. I will fight any man who challenges me for the right to captaincy. I warn those of you who decide to come with me that I am writing new articles. I'll plunder with the best of you, but I won't be your captain only in battle or to handle the navigation of the ship. I will be your leader all the time."

There was a moment's silence at the announcement and then all eyes turned expectantly to Louis. He regarded Alexander with eyes narrowed to black slits, his foot tapping impatiently and his hand already on the hilt of the rapier at his side. "So, you strutting whelp. I offered you friendship but you stab me in the back."

"On the contrary, Louis," Alexander said, "I am offering to rid you of those men who dispute your leadership. You plan to abandon the English ship anyway. Let me have her."

"She'll never make port."

"Then you would be twice wise to let me have her."

"I wondered how long it would take for you to show your fangs," Louis said, withdrawing his rapier slowly. "You think Louis wanted you to be his friend? Louis does not need friends, he seeks only enemies. Take my rapier and give me a cutlass. I will fight this insolent puppy." The last was addressed to the scholar.

Before he could comply, Alexander sprang from the hatch cover. "Keep your rapier, Louis. If you must fight me, I'll use your weapon."

Louis hooted with laughter when Alexander dispatched Tad back to the *Tiger's Claw* to bring a rapier from his cabin. "You would fence with *me,*" Louis cried incredulously. "*Sacre bleu,* we have a mad man on our hands. His small successes have addled his brain."

Louis' scorn quickly turned to grudging respect when Alexander began to put him through his paces. Alexander was not as accomplished with the rapier as Louis, but what he lacked in grace he made up for in determination. He seemed utterly unaware of his opponent's flashing blade and, while he had none of the knowledge imparted to Louis by a succession of fencing masters in his youth, Alexander gained advantage by his unorthodox style and sheer reckless aggressiveness.

The thin steel blades clashed and rippled, as the watchers yelled encouragement and exchanged wagers on the outcome. Louis saw an opening and lunged, ripping open Alexander's shirt and leaving a deepening trail of blood as he sprang backward defensively. Pressing his advantage, Louis followed and the point of his rapier zig-zagged down Alexander's cheek. A shout of approval went up from Louis' supporters.

Enraged, Alexander fought back, swinging wildly. Later he realized it had been sheer luck that Louis slipped at the same instant Alexander managed to hook Louis' rapier hilt with the point of his own sword and flip it irretrievably out of reach. Alexander found himself standing over Louis, rapier pointing at his heart, while the cold eyes regarded him without fear, expecting death.

Slowly the red haze cleared from Alexander's eyes. "The *Tiger's Claw* is yours, Louis. You spared a boy years ago and I am sparing you."

"Better kill me now, whelp," Louis' voice hissed from between unmoving lips. "Because I will surely kill you for this day's work."

Alexander smiled condescendingly, then winced as the torn flesh of his cheek contracted. He wiped the blood away with his hand. "You've left your mark on me, Louis, why not be content?" he asked as he looked around for Tad.

In the excitement of the moment Alexander had forgotten the Lady Amelia, awaiting him in her cabin. He had also forgotten Sir Miles Grindwald, awaiting the arrival of his bride.

The Lady Amelia Grindwald looked up as Alexander entered the cabin. She was sitting on the bunk. Her hair had come loose and fell in golden curls about her shoulders. Slanted green eyes watched as he advanced into the circle of light cast by the lantern.

Slowly he unhooked the sheathed knife from his belt, unbuckled the belt, and dropped both to the floor. Next he kicked off his boots, moving without haste, watching her as intently as she watched him.

She licked her lower lip. "May I inquire . . . what is your name?" She squirmed slightly as he stepped closer and reached out to run his forefinger slowly down her cheek, caressing her throat and sliding lightly to the laces of her bodice.

"Bartholomew," he said, pulling the laces so that the velvet bodice sprang open. "Alexander Bartholomew." He lifted one plump breast from its velvet prison, caressing with a firm but gentle touch. "Are you a virgin?"

Her breathing quickened, causing her breast to rise and fall against the warm pressure of his hand. "I am married."

"By proxy, you told me. I take it, therefore, you are a virgin?"

The slanted eyes had the grace to look away as she answered, "I had a lover. A strolling minstrel who deceived me. I was seduced and abandoned. My father arranged with Sir Geoffrey Grindwald that I would marry his son Miles . . . in return for my dowry and the fortune I will inherit from my grandparents when I am twenty-one."

Alexander released her breast and stroked her hair. "You were ill-used by both your father and your proxy husband. They must have known the danger of sending you on an unescorted ship—heavily armed though she was—through these waters."

A bright fierce light flashed in the green eyes and she clutched his hand, pulling it back to the soft flesh of her breast. "I've no doubt they both wanted to see me dead. My father because I was disgraced and my proxy husband to acquire my fortune. It was rumored in London that Miles has squandered most of his family wealth. He is the eldest son and his younger brother was forced to join the Royal Navy because there was nothing left but the plantation in Jamaica, and that in dire financial straits."

"What would you have me do with you?" Alexander mused, almost to himself. "I can put you ashore where you can find an escorted ship and return to England . . . or I can deliver you to your husband." He fondled her breast again, since she seemed to expect it and Alexander felt it wasteful to refuse a willingly offered pleasure.

"But . . ." she said, leaning closer and looking up at

him from beneath half-closed eyes, "I thought I would be *your* woman now."

He smiled. "Alas, our articles forbid the keeping of women aboard our ship, or I would not be so ungallant as to refuse—"

Before he could finish she was on her feet, anger blazing from her eyes. A ring be-decked hand slapped his cheek and she stamped her foot in rage. "You . . . great oaf! How dare you . . . oh, I hate you, you!"

Tiny fists pummeled his chest and his eyes widened at the sight of bobbing breasts, now accentuated by hard little peaks at the center of rosy areolas. Trying to hide his amused smile, he ducked as she swung for his jaw, but seized her promptly when she tried to raise her knee.

"My lady, really . . ." he said, tossing her to the bunk, where she lay panting and furious. Her skirts were tossed up over well-turned thighs and Alexander noted that she was not wearing pantelettes. The minx not only expected to be ravished, she invited it with every gesture, from her heaving bosom to the way she parted her legs so that he could catch a glimpse of dark gold hair.

She looked around wildly for a weapon; flung herself toward the former captain's pistol lying on the sea chest. When Alexander shoved it out of her reach, she slid a satin slipper from her small high-arched foot and flung it at his head.

Alexander sighed and caught her arms, forcing her back to the bunk and imprisoning her with the hard length of his body. The green eyes looked up at him with an expression of triumph as his manhood stirred against her thigh, as usual independent of any willed command. She had, after all, admitted a prior lover . . .

He slid down her dress, revealing what little of her he had not already seen. He had surmised correctly. She wore nothing under the embroidered velvet gown. Her body was voluptuously curved; skin milky white and glowing with the heat of passion.

Small, greedy hands reached for him and when he bent to kiss her full lips they parted instantly to admit his tongue. She was whimpering in the back of her throat and her hips moved in slow circles beneath him, seeking to draw him into her moist warmth. Her fingers were busy—knowledgeably so—with the buttons of his breeches. The moment the object of her pursuit was free, she guided his thrust, rising to meet him with an enthusiastic fervor it had rarely been his pleasure to encounter.

Alexander wondered fleetingly if the admission of only one lover was a slight error when the diminutive body writhed and twisted, gripping him with fevered urgency and refusing to let go until he reached a white-hot climax even as she shuddered repeatedly as the after tremors brought cries of pleasure to her lips. Alexander hastily covered her mouth with his hand. "Lady Amelia, I beg of you—" he said, his voice still husky with fulfilled desire, "do not betray your presence to my crew. I am newly elected captain of this ship and I know not what will happen to either of us if the men learn I have concealed you. We will put into the nearest safe port for repairs to the ship and I will smuggle you ashore."

She was smiling moistly, her eyes serene and contented. Idly she allowed her hand to float down his chest, making small teasing circles.

Alexander sighed again, despite the gleam in his eye. It was going to be a long night.

Chapter 12

Liz looked at the pile of petticoats, the long lace-edged drawers, whalebone corset and voluminous dress. She picked up a white cotton stocking, fingered the bonnet and shawl, touched the gloves. She looked up at Alexander in amazement. "You've got to be kidding. I wouldn't be able to walk if I wore all that."

Alexander hooked his thumbs into his belt and shrugged indifferently. "If I take you with me—which is by no means certain—that's what you must wear. If you go dressed in the skimpy attire you wear now, they will throw you into the stocks, or maybe lock you in a brothel."

Liz tried on the bonnet experimentally. "What made you change your mind about taking me back with you."

"Curiosity. Nothing more. I wonder what the people of my time will think of you. You express your views like a man. I have never seen you resort to any of the wiles of the women I know, no tears or pouting, or flattering a man to get your way. Not that I'm saying I approve of your ways. Any strumpet could teach you how to get what you want from a man—"

"By showing subservience," Liz interrupted. "Flirting and weeping and pretending helplessness and ignorance so that men feel strong and protective and laugh at how foolish the little woman is."

Alexander turned his back. "You have the tongue of a shrew and the body of an undernourished boy. I know not why I bother with such a wench." He began to sweep the pile of clothes into his arms angrily.

Liz put up her hand to stop him. "Truce?"

He looked down at her and she was unable to read his eyes but there was something there, elusive and indefinable, that made her heart skip. "Will you wait for me down on the beach?" she asked quickly. "I'll try on the clothes and come to you."

He gave a devilish grin, raising one eyebrow questioningly. "I could help you dress. I am well acquainted with the intricacies of female clothing."

"I bet you are. But I'll manage." Liz felt like a fool for blushing.

"The color in your cheeks is becoming, Elizabeth. There's hope for you yet. But how will you lace your corset without my help?"

"I'll figure it out," Liz promised, shoving him through the door. As always, when she touched him it was a shock to feel the warm vibrance of his muscles.

She did not attempt to lace the corset and wore only one petticoat. Astonishingly, the dress was a perfect fit. It was a lightweight silk, a soft shade of blue with fine handmade lace edging a plunging neckline and the wrists of wide belled sleeves.

As she approached Alexander looked up from his task of preparing meat for smoking in the *boucan*. He stared at her for a moment, not speaking. His lips parted, then he blinked and said, "Your hair . . . isn't right . . . I will dress it for you." He seemed to be in a state of shock.

They went back to the hut and he took her hairbrush and swept her hair on top of her head, fastening it in place with pins he whittled from driftwood. When he was finished he stepped back to examine her again. Liz recognized both the awed admiration and a hint of raw masculine lust in the appraisal. She felt a moment's apprehension, thinking of the other men she would encounter if she accompanied Alexander back into his brawling time.

"How will you explain me to your crew?" she asked.

Alexander shrugged. "I have transported other females from time to time. Aboard the *Avenger* I am undisputed master. No man dares question me. I have a highly-trained crew who are well disciplined and satisfied with my leadership. They have lasted longer than other sea rovers because we never enraged the Royal Navy sufficiently to bring them after us and we showed mercy where our brethren did not. Indeed, were it not for Louis' self-proclaimed vendetta against me and Miles Grindwald's rage that I possessed his fair bride before he did, our lives would be almost a bed of roses." He threw back his head and roared with laughter. When his mirth subsided he looked at her again and said, "You look passing fair, Elizabeth. More like the woman you were meant to be."

Liz tried to keep the inexplicable wave of jealousy she felt from showing in her eyes. She ignored his compliment. "So you did ravish the Lady Amelia, after you took command of the *Avenger*. I assume you made it back to port for the necessary repairs."

Alexander's smile was blissfully reminiscent. He cleared his throat somewhat suggestively and sighed deeply. "Who knows what might have happened, had I not been committed to a life she could not share? As it was, I made one of my few noble gestures. I returned her safely to that faint-hearted milksop proxy husband."

Thunderclouds raced across his eyes as he remembered. He paced the room, anger written in every line of his body. "My ship was being repaired in a secret cove in one of the islands. Disguised as a priest, I accompanied Lady Amelia to Jamaica—leaving Tad and the rest of the crew behind."

Liz sat down, spreading her skirts about her becomingly. It seemed evident that Alexander was not yet ready to take her back with him. No doubt the clothes were experimental. He would move in his own good time and she knew better than to try to hurry him. Being so infuriatingly domineering, he would balk altogether if he felt she were attempting to command him.

"I'd no sooner returned Lady Amelia to the house of that cowardly knave and installed myself at an inn for a night's rest before proceeding back to my ship—than I was summoned by a note in the lady's handwriting. 'I beg of you, kind sir,' she wrote, 'come and fetch me, for I must return to England. My husband is already mistreating me because of my capture.' Now, Elizabeth—how could any gentleman fail to respond to such an appeal? How was I to know that sniveling cur had forced her to write the note?"

"Alexander, you fool, you didn't go? She wanted to

get even with you, didn't you see? She must have been furious with you for rejecting her."

He paused, considering. "Nay, Elizabeth—he forced her to write it. She did not wish to see me hang."

"But you didn't hang—or did you?"

Chapter 13

Alexander felt as if he had stepped backward into his boyhood as he cautiously approached the Grindwald plantation on a moonlit night, answering the Lady Amelia's summons.

Alexander tied the horse he had borrowed from the innkeeper to a tree on the hardpacked dirt road at the edge of the cane fields and made his way on foot toward the house.

Although the cane appeared to be flourishing, it was soon obvious that the plantation house and outbuildings were neglected and falling into severe disrepair. This appeared to be the result of lack of replacement material and the strain imposed by the tropical climate rather than lack of effort, for the grounds were free of weeds and the shrubbery neatly clipped. As he passed the row of slave cabins, with the flogging post casting its vile shadow on the moonlit clearing, he thought grimly that human flesh was still the cheapest commodity Miles Grindwald possessed. His slaves had been driven to superhuman effort to keep the plantation's appearance at this orderly and neat level, with very little to replenish crumbling masonry and rotted wood.

The house was illuminated only by a lantern flickering over the front doors, which were set at the corner of the house and flanked on either side by a roofed verandah extending all the way around the house. Ignoring the beckoning light, Alexander went to the rear of the house and swung silently over the balcony rail. Undoubtedly the chambers of Miles and Amelia would be on the upper floor, to take advantage of any cooling breeze.

In her haste and distress, the Lady Amelia had forgotten to indicate where she was imprisoned. She had written that Miles had locked her in her chambers and was threatening to deliver her to the nearest brothel because a pirate had carnal knowledge of her.

Alexander paused now, glancing toward the long row of slave cabins just visible through a protective barrier of trees, realizing what had troubled him as he passed by them on his way to the house. Oddly, there was neither light nor sound borne on the faint breeze coming from that direction. Alexander knew this to be unusual.

He had retired early and it was still long before midnight. Slaves worked until dark and often nourished their exhausted bodies with music and song when they returned to their quarters. But tonight there was no music, no plaintive cry of an infant awakening to hunger, nor even the mournful howl of a dog catching sight of the moon as it slid over the chimney stacks of the plantation house.

His instinct warned him he was walking into a trap,

but it was more than the desperate plea of the Lady Amelia that drove him to ignore the cautionary signals: Alexander was again on Grindwald property—perhaps within inches of confronting the man who had whipped and abused Tad Bowen and himself until they had been little more than driven animals.

Alexander wondered, as he pulled open the nearest window shutter, if he had returned Amelia to her husband with the express purpose of taunting his former master. Miles would know that he had lain with her. It was an offense that even a fop like Grindwald could hardly ignore. Perhaps, therefore, Alexander had planned all along that he would again face his boyhood tormentor.

The house was ominously dark and quiet. He went swiftly up the wide staircase to the upper floor. Noiselessly opening the first door, he looked into an empty room, the furniture shrouded with ghostly dust covers. The next three doors also proved to be empty guest rooms. A candle burned beside a canopied bed in the last room at the end of the landing.

Behind swathed mosquitoe netting, Amelia lay on a mound of satin pillows. She wore a black lace gown, filmy and sheer. As he stepped into the room, Alexander was struck by the fact that the misty netting surrounding her and the black lace gave the illusion of a plump little spider lurking in the center of a deadly web.

He did not have time to analyze the expression on the pouting lips and in the slanted eyes. A shrill voice shouted, "Seize him!"

A dozen slaves appeared from every corner of the room, springing into well-rehearsed action. One dived for his knees, bringing him down, while others fell heavily on his chest. Alexander managed to render two of them unconscious before his wrists and feet were caught by the rest.

He found himself spread-eagled on his back, staring up into the malevolent gaze of Miles Grindwald. With great deliberation and obvious relish, Miles nodded toward the brawniest slave and Alexander had a quick glimpse of the descending club before the world rushed away from him.

He was flung into prison and manacled by his wrists and ankles to a wall in a filthy communal cell with a dozen other lice-infested wretches and the rats which shared their quarters. All were awaiting the public hanging that was to be the highlight of a forthcoming holiday. Alexander was the only pirate in their midst and as such would be given special treatment. He was also to be drawn and quartered, his head impaled on a stake to warn off other members of the Brethren of the Coast.

These sentences were pronounced at the end of a brief, but, by the standards of the day, fair trial. However, the accused was not permitted to enter the witness box to testify on his own behalf and there were no witnesses for the defense.

"Alexander Bartholomew," the prosecutor thundered, "is a cruel, feared, hated arch-pirate, who has done the worst mischief, caused confusion and disorder both at sea and on land."

The three king's witnesses who were called to the box told outrageously fabricated stories or torture and murder and Alexander's counsel, under court-ordained procedure, was not allowed to cross-examine. Alexander himself refused to cross-examine the patently lying witnesses, knowing it would avail him little.

He stood in the box with head held high, his expression scornful and his eyes meeting those of his accusers unflinchingly.

"You have been tried by the laws of the land," the court clerk's voice droned in the warm still air. "Nothing remains but that sentence be passed according to the law. You shall be taken from the place from whence you came, and from thence to the place of execution . . ."

On the tenth day of his incarceration, Sir Miles Grindwald and the Lady Amelia came to the prison. The guard opened the iron-studded door and the three of them stood at the top of a flight of stone stairs leading to the straw-strewn floor below. All of the prisoners were chained. The ones awaiting hanging were manacled to the walls. Both groups received frequent and severe physical punishment, as well as being deprived of their small ration of bread and water at the whim of the guards.

Lady Amelia stood with downcast eyes, while Sir Miles kept his handkerchief pressed to his lips and nostrils. His small deep-set eyes quickly found Alexander. "He hardly looks cowed, guard," Miles said petulantly. "Have you not given him a taste of the lash? Must I report to your superiors that you are lax in your duty?"

"He's felt the knout and the cat, milord," the guard answered. "It's dark down there so you can't see his shoulders or his back. But I assure your lordship he's worn out two of my best men."

"They why does his head not hang on his chest like the other wretches?" Miles demanded.

"It was, milord. I reckon he's come to."

"No food or water, remember."

The guard looked doubtful. "They don't last long

down there without water, your lordship. And the hanging won't be for a few days . . ." he paused delicately, with a glance at the Lady Amelia.

"Water only, then." Miles sniffed into his handkerchief. "You see, my dear, the misbegotten rogue will pay dearly for his treatment of my wife. And before he dies he will tell us where my murderous indentured servant is hiding. Not to mention the rest of his scurvy crew of pirates. Oh, yes, Amelia, my sweet, your pirate will betray his own mother before we're done with him."

Amelia twisted her gloves and kept her eyes downcast. "Please, Miles, could we leave now?" Her voice was no more than a whisper. "I feel faint."

"You will wait here, my dear. I wish to approach the prisoner, guard. Please clear the way."

Miles drew his cloak tightly around his body and picked his way carefully down the steps, making sure he did not brush against the dripping walls. The guard went ahead, clubbing prisoners out of their path.

Alexander held his head high and regarded Miles Grindwald with a mocking smile. "So you have not yet escaped your hell-hole, despite your inheritance. But allow me to congratulate you on your marriage. Your bride is charming—"

Miles Grindwald's leather glove caught Alexander full in the mouth, cutting off the rest of his words. Alexander threw back his head and laughed until the guard's club rendered him senseless.

At the top of the stairs Amelia turned away as her husband examined the welts on Alexander's back and nodded, satisfied.

On the day of the public hanging Alexander was placed on a platform, wrists and ankles chained, and put on display in the center of the town square. As the prize capture, he would be last to feel the caress of the hangman's rope.

Carriages came from the outlying plantations and all morning the townspeople gathered in the square. Vendors hawked their wares and acrobats and musicians performed for the throngs of holiday-makers. Children were held up on their father's shoulders for a better view of the men awaiting death, while pickpockets and prostitutes moved expertly through the crowds.

Alexander watched the milling throng scornfully, holding his head high despite the agony of the oozing welts on back and shoulders. Miles Grindwald and the guards who had inflicted almost continual punishment on Alexander still did not know where the *Avenger* or the rest of his crew was hiding, but several cannons and heavily armed men were guarding the harbor in case the *Avenger* came to her master's rescue.

During the trial Alexander had been identified as the master of the *Avenger* and accused of the plunder of scores of ships, as well as the sacking of several ports, and the "ravishing" of men, women and children.

On the periphery of the crowd Alexander caught a glimpse of bright red hair, not quite covered by a bandana, then a cherubic smile. Tad!

He was surrounded by a group of urchins who were teasing him. Alexander did not turn to look at him, for fear of calling the attention of Miles Grindwald to his former servant. Grindwald and his bride occupied places of honor, front-row seats, shaded by a palm-frond umbrella. Amelia looked away when Alexander grinned at her and inclined his head in salute. Miles simpered behind his handkerchief, tiny eyes bright with anticipation.

Tad was moving closer to the platform, staring up at

the chained prisoners, his mouth hanging vacantly open. Out of the corner of his eye Alexander saw Tad's great hand playfully swat at one of his tormentors, then slip inside the loose leather gherkin he wore. A moment later Tad held a blacksmith's hammer.

Alexander caught his breath. Tad was going to attempt to break his chains, but it was a futile gesture, he would be seized instantly by the guards. Alexander took a chance and turned to look Tad full in the face. He shook his head firmly, mouthing the word "No!"

Tad looked bewildered, but did not move.

Miles Grindwald was on his feet, peering into the crowd to see who it was Alexander was looking at.

Inwardly Alexander groaned. He had already decided his only chance would come when his chains were removed just before he was led to the scaffold and the noose placed around his neck. At that moment Tad's help could have been the difference between life and death. But now Miles had seen the former blacksmith's bright red hair and he was calling to a guard.

At that moment a hush fell over the crowd. A black-hooded man, stripped to the waist, his muscles bulging, strode into the center of the square. The executioner had arrived.

Run, Tad, Alexander thought. But Tad stood rooted to the spot, eyes wide and trusting as he looked up at his captain.

Alexander's voice broke the silence. "Run! Go now. I'll meet you at the ship."

But it was too late. The guards were running, knocking women and children to the ground in their haste. Miles Grindwald's high-pitched voice shrieked that the big redhaired man was wanted for murder on his plantation as well as piracy. Tad blinked and turned around to seek a way of escape.

He fought valiantly but they brought him down by throwing a cargo net over him from aloft.

"Shall he hang with the others?" the captain of the guards asked.

"No. He must be brought to trial. We are not barbarians," Miles Grindwald said, sniffing disdainfully. But his glittering eyes said he wanted imprisonment for Tad so that his eventual hanging would be a merciful release.

Alexander saw them drag his friend off to prison and then watched the rest of the prisoners hanged, to the cheers and applause of the crowd. Then it was Alexander's turn. He flexed his shoulders slightly as his chains were struck. Guards encircled him, heavily armed. His limbs were stiff and he walked slowly, offering no resistance, but his eye was measuring the distance from the top of the scaffold to the nearest roof.

Other prisoners had attempted to cheat the hangman. Some had fought and some had begged for their lives, but none waited until the noose was placed about their necks to make their move.

Alexander was so calm and apparently detached that the two guards holding his arms at his sides were no longer clutching tightly. The hangman placed the noose in position and was about to tighten the knot when Alexander made his move, thanking the saints that the crowd enjoyed the sport of watching twitching limbs as a condemned man died and, therefore, his arms and legs were free.

He shook free the guards holding his arms and his hands went up to the rope about his neck. The next instant he was flying through the air at the end of the rope, holding it taut, well away from the lethal knot about his throat.

The first swing missed the roof he was aiming for and

he felt himself falling back. Shots rang out and pistol balls whistled past his ears. Screams and panic from the crowd. He swung in a slow arc over their heads, guards grabbing for him as he went by. Then he arched his body, kicking frantically with his legs to give him the momentum he needed. There would be no second try.

When the rope had swung to its full extent Alexander let go, jerking the noose off his head as he did so. For a second he was in midair, arms stretched toward the haven of the roof. His fingers touched, held. The next moment he was running across the roof while his pursuers ran in circles below, colliding with each other and the crowd, cursing and yelling their frustration.

Alexander did not give a second thought to the dozen bodies twitching at the end of their ropes, but the memory of the faithful Tad being hauled away spoiled the triumph of the moment.

The Lady Amelia was seated at her dressing table, brushing her hair and frowning at her reflection. Her husband was scouring the town with the rest of the searchers, looking for the escaped pirate. Amelia was wilting in the heat and bored with the plantation. The colony was indeed the hell-hole Miles said it was, and she wished he had been able to find a buyer so they could return to England.

Her proxy wedding had not been consummated. Miles had declared angrily that he would not take a pirate's leavings, but Amelia guessed there would have been another excuse if he had not had that one. The memory of the voyage with Alexander was with her constantly, as was her guilt at sending the message that trapped him. But Miles had threatened to send her home in disgrace, divorced for adultery, if she did not comply. Her family would have disowned her.

Amelia's insatiable appetite for the opposite sex had been awakened early by a virile young stablemaster in her father's service. Fortunately no one had learned of their trysts in the sweet-smelling hayloft. When she tired of him, she moved through a succession of tutors and even a brief fling with the local vicar in the rectory after Sunday school. But the wandering minstrel had been her undoing.

He alone of her lovers had aroused more than passion in her. She truly loved him. But he was penniless and her fortune was administered by a father who almost succumbed to an apopletic fit when she begged for permission to marry her beloved. She never knew what transpired, but the troupe of players performing in the village moved on hastily and she never saw her minstrel again.

A gossiping woman friend expressed malicious horror when Amelia told her a marriage had been arranged with Miles Grindwald.

"Oh, my poor dear!" her friend exclaimed. "Haven't you heard about *him?* My brother once shared a tutor with Miles and told me . . ." she lowered her voice, "Miles doesn't like ladies, or women either for that matter. He likes his own sex. They say his father sent him to be steward of the sugar plantation in Jamaica to avoid a scandal."

Amelia had thought that perhaps the marriage would be a good thing for both of them, since they were both social outcasts. She had met other men who preferred their own sex and Amelia had always found them charming in a gentle, sweet way, capable of deep and mutually satisfying friendships with women, perhaps because the element of sex was removed from the association.

But Miles had not proved to be one of these gentle souls. He was a diminutive dandy filled with self-pity and a raging violence at a world that seemed to have cast him aside. A vindictive bully, trapped, perhaps mercifully, in a small and delicate body.

Miles had shown evidence of being torn in two directions when he first saw Amelia. His admiration for her beauty was obvious from his quickly indrawn breath and the fluttering pulse in his temple as he stared at her, transfixed and speechless. A footman conducted her to Miles' study and announced her identity. Amelia stood demurely, head bowed and hands folded in front of her, relishing his astonishment. He was no doubt expecting a plain little mouse. A woman who brought a substantial dowry, agreed to sail through pirate-infested waters, and marry a man sight unseen, could hardly be expected to be beautiful into the bargain.

But when the significance of her survival in the hands of pirates at last penetrated his dazed senses, he railed at her, "A decent woman would have flung herself overboard rather than submit. Tell me, madam, how many of those filthy scum used you?" His angry glance raked her body with both contempt and lust. Amelia recognized the latter emotion from long practice. She was surprised by that look in his pale eyes, for it contradicted what she had heard about Miles' predilection for his own sex.

She lowered her eyelids modestly, but looked at him from beneath the fluttering fringe with a limpid glance she knew to be beguilingly inviting. "How could I bear to die without ever setting eyes on my husband? I beg of you, forget what has happened to my body. T'was a vile thing that was done to me, but my mind and my heart are still pure and belong only to you." She raised her eyes slowly, imploringly, to meet his cold stare, knowing that the golden perfection of her hair and irresistible slant of her green eyes had been the undoing of better men. Her husband's expression was sternly unforgiving. He demanded to know the name of the pirate captain who had possessed his bride and then had the audacity to return her in such a state to her husband.

"Bartholomew," she whispered. "Alexander Bartholomew."

Miles' head jerked upward and his eyes narrowed. He breathed through flared nostrils as a wave of fury passed through him. "And was there a great giant of a man by name of Tad Bowen with this Bartholomew? Bowen was red-bearded with the face of blandest innocence?"

"Yes—how did you know?" Amelia said, startled.

Miles paced up and down his study for a few minutes with precise and elegant steps, hands clasped behind his satin jacket. Watching him covertly, Amelia had to concede her husband was perfectly dressed and groomed, if a trifle foppish in his appearance.

At length he turned abruptly and said, "You will compose a note to your erstwhile partner in debauchery. You will deliver Bartholomew into my hands."

"But I know not . . ." Amelia began.

Her husband caught her hair in his fist, jerking her face close to his. "You will remember where he is staying this night and you will write a note he cannot ignore. If he does not come for you, then I will brand you with the mark of the adulteress and return you to England."

Amelia had meekly complied. There was not a man on earth she would risk her own fair neck for and there was a decidedly interesting aspect to her new husband's character she suddenly wanted to explore. Each was drawn to a kindred spirit, admiring in the other their own worst characteristics.

Amelia had not given much thought to Alexander's fate until the day of the hanging. Now he was loose somewhere on the island and Miles was searching for him, perhaps at this very moment running him to ground with the dogs. Amelia shrugged her white shoulders regretfully. It was a pity about Alexander. He was a doughty rogue of considerable charm and much manly grace. She closed her eyes briefly, remembering the passion she had stirred in him and the dizzying heights of sensual pleasure he had given her.

When the velvet draperies at her window moved she thought at first a welcome breeze had sprung up. Then she look disbelievingly at Alexander, wondering if her imagination was playing tricks with her. But he stepped into the room, bowing deeply, and said mockingly, "Forgive the intrusion, my lady. I correctly assumed you would be alone and I am in need of your help."

"Alexander! How did you get here . . . oh, please believe I didn't willingly send you that note."

He sat down on her bed. "I simply asked myself what would be the last place the Governor's men—and your husband—would look for me? And I am well-acquainted with your plantation, from my servitude here. Now, as to why I need your help . . ."

She moved to his side, her eyes wide invitations.

"Tad Bowen is in prison. I can't leave without him. You are going to get dressed and come to the prison with me. You will tell the guards your husband has sent you and your plantation steward to take Tad Bowen home. That the merciful Sir Miles has decided not to prosecute a half-witted wretch whose mind cannot distinguish right from wrong. Tad is to be brought home."

"No!" Amelia gasped. "I can't . . . what would happen to me?"

Alexander stood up slowly, unfastening his belt. "You will tell him what you told me. That I forced you to do it." He smiled and reached for her. She went willingly into his arms, her plump breasts rising and falling rapidly with excitement. He dealt rapidly with her robe and nightgown, lifted her to the bed and was soon eliciting sighs and moans of pleasure from her lips and a wild whirling dance from her hips.

Liz said, "And of course Lady Amelia melted into your arms, swooning, and begged you not to take her honor again."

Alexander answered, "She helped me to free Tad Bowen. It would have been difficult without her. She provided me with clothing which helped disguise me when we went to the prison, and her carriage took Tad and me to the harbor. She felt sorry that she had trapped me, you see, and wanted to make amends."

"And you didn't make love to her, to sweeten the deal?" Liz asked suspiciously.

Alexander regarded her with an innocent stare "When would we have had time? Surely only a fool would attempt a dalliance in the home of his enemy, while his faithful friend languished in chains!"

"So you and Tad made it back to your ship."

"With the unwitting assistance of Louis de Letraz, who had assumed that after the public hanging and with the great show of force the townsfolk would that night be the worse for merry-making and relax their vigilance. He decided to sack the town as they slept off their drunken binges—not knowing, of course, that armed men were searching for me. He brought his men ashore in piraguas, leaving his ship anchored well offshore. Ah, what a battle it was, Elizabeth. Tad and I fought with them, of course, and we all made good our escape to the *Tiger's Claw.* Although old Louis was somewhat disgruntled that they took little booty and barely got away with their lives."

"And that was the last you saw of the Lady Amelia?" Liz asked.

Alexander's expression was enigmatic. "No. It seemed that both Louis and I were fated to cross paths with Amelia—and swords with her husband's flunkies—on other occasions. Indeed, I fear I must confess that the fair Amelia was the cause of great animosity between Louis and me, even more than my defying his command. You see, when he learned I had kept her hidden from him when we first captured her ship, he was enraged. She was part of the plunder, and should have been turned over to the captain. Louis vowed he would bring me before a pirate council and would also possess the fair Amelia, one way or another. Apart from his anger at me, he felt he should also take vengeance on Miles, for costing him half of his men in the aborted sacking of the town. Louis and I parted amid shouted insults and dire threats."

"Go on, what happened next?" Liz asked.

"If I take you back with me . . ." Alexander said slowly, "You will see for yourself. For the next events are the ones I know I will re-live, when I row back to the island and go aboard my ship."

"Take me, please, Alexander. Take me back with you."

He regarded her curiously. "Why do you wish to go? What if I am killed before I can bring you back? What will become of you? What if you are trapped there with me? Elizabeth, we are both meddling with forces we don't understand."

"I want to see you in your own time. You've seen me in mine. Alexander, my life is never going to be the same, having met you. I was hopelessly trapped in a destructive love affair that has ended. I have the feeling that you've been carrying a torch for the Lady Amelia and I'd like to free you from her in the way you freed me from Nick."

"I know not what 'carry a torch' means—but if you imply I loved the wench, you are wrong. I never knew real love until "

"Until when?"

"Never. Love is for women, men have no time for such nonsense "

But Liz was not to be put off. She said, "You were going to tell me you did love a woman. Alexander, it isn't anything to be ashamed of, it certainly doesn't make you less manly. In my eyes it would make you more of a man."

"What care I what you think of me?" he growled, turning from her to hide his discomfort. "I know not why I tell you anything, wench. But if you must know, there are moments when that last part of my life flashes before my mind's eye. Within the blurred images I seem to see a face—yet I do not see it. Perhaps I sense the presence in my life of someone who became important to me. I am aware of emotions that I had not thought were part of my nature, of great tenderness and longing. Yet when I reach into my memory to seek out what ultimately led to my destruction . . . I grasp only shadows. All I know for sure is that I was on my way to my Pacific isle when I met my end. And that Louis de Letraz had sworn to kill me. I can't remember why. A disputed prize? A woman?"

Liz stared at him, fascinated. As he spoke, the ferocious expression faded from his face and the barbaric lines softened. Even the lightning bolt scar seemed more poignant than sinister. A tortured longing that seemed to come from his very soul was reflected in the clear depths of his eyes. His black eyebrows were raised like the wings of a bird in flight. In that eloquent gaze Liz could see that Alexander had indeed known a deep and abiding love. Had it been so painful that he had blotted all memory of it from his mind? She had thought his spirit roamed restlessly in search of his murderer; now she wondered, with a pang of acute jealousy, if what he sought was his lost love.

"Elizabeth looks pensive," he said. "Does she regret her impulsive request to return to my time?"

"No . . . of course not," Liz said.

But he sensed her inner battle with her doubts. "Elizabeth, I've taunted you with the charms of the Lady Amelia—and you are loathe to compete with her, is that it?"

Liz swallowed hard and resisted the urge to chide him for his conceit.

He said, "I should have been honest about her. She was a lady by birth and breeding, but not by nature. Her morals were those of a feline animal and her favors any man's for the asking. Not a woman Alexander Bartholomew would lose his head over."

"I haven't changed my mind about going back with you," Liz said. "How else am I going to get you to stop haunting me?"

Alexander laughed. "You are right. You should come with me and see for yourself what manner of man I am. A sea rover with a price on his head that only loose women would dare be seen in public with . . . while their high-born sisters welcomed me by stealth. So be it, Elizabeth. Together we shall re-weave the fabric of my life."

Chapter 14

The voluminous skirts were a hindrance. Alexander swept Liz up into his arms to carry her aboard the longboat. She did not protest, for fear he would change his mind about their venture into his time.

"It's no wonder women were so helpless in your day," she muttered against his chest. "They were so hampered by their clothing they could hardly move, let alone do anything for themselves."

"And Elizabeth isn't even wearing a corset," Alexander added, giving her waist a playful pinch. "Why in my day we thought women were fortunate that the practice of making them wear chastity belts had been discontinued."

Liz scowled at him. When he placed her in the boat she immediately picked up an oar.

"Nay, Elizabeth, rowing is man's work. If you blister

those delicate hands we shall never be able to pass you off as a lady. As it is I know not how we shall explain your sunburned complexion."

Liz bit back a retort and, as his brows came down over narrowed and glacial eyes in the expression she recognized as stubbornly unmoving, she put down the oar. There were, after all, enough major issues to battle about without wasting time over the minor disagreements. Especially at this crucial moment when he might decide the whole plan was foolhardy.

Falconer's Isle was part of a chain of atolls and islands and Alexander rowed past two tiny strips of land before guiding his flat-bottomed boat carefully over a coral reef toward a crescent of dazzling sand backed by a lush growth of palms. He arranged a soft mound of palm fronds in a shady spot for Liz to sit on, then went in search of fresh fruit for their lunch. Liz noted that for once she was not expected to do anything to help.

They had finished eating and were relaxing, enjoying the soft whisper of the trade winds, the scent of the flowers and just being together, when Alexander broke off in midsentence and jumped to his feet. Shading his eyes with his hand he looked out to sea. "The *Avenger*'s sails are on the horizon," he said.

Liz gasped at the sheer beauty of the vessel gliding majestically into view. Sails billowing, the graceful wooden ship rode the gentle swells of the sea as smoothly as a drifting swan. What a photograph, she thought, picturing the wind-bent palm and white beach in the foreground, the sweep of clear blue sea and the magnificent ship . . . but, of course, even if she had a camera, the ship would not be in the picture.

As she watched, spellbound, the words of a long-forgotten poem came to her and she quoted softly:

"*. . . Sandalwood, cedarwood and sweet white wine,*
Stately Spanish galleon, coming from the Isthmus
Dipping through the tropics by the palm-green shores
With a cargo of diamonds,
Emeralds, amethysts
Topazes and cinnamon and gold moidores."

Alexander's hand found hers. "The sight of my vessel has gilded your tongue, Elizabeth."

"I'm afraid the poem isn't mine," Liz said. "It's called *Cargoes* and was written by a man named John Masefield."

"Yet you were moved by it enough to commit it to memory. You reveal a deeply sensitive nature that is at odds with your boyish mien. I suspect that beneath that gamine exterior and hoydon's temper there lurks a well-bred gentlewoman of much understanding and compassion. Tell me, do your tirades conceal a tender heart after all?"

Liz felt her heart flutter as he pressed her fingers to his lips. There was a patient, watchful look in his eyes, as though he were aware of something she had not yet seen.

She wanted to tell him that at that moment she felt more alive than she had ever felt before. That in his presence a heart-pounding mixture of awareness and excitement filled her days with wonder and her nights with passionate longing. That even when he berated her for her lack of womanly virture, or she railed at him for his arrogance, still there was no one more important to her than he. But there was no time to speak her thoughts as he released her hand in order to slide the longboat from the hot sand to the torpid yellow water of the reef-enclosed lagoon.

The *Avenger* drew nearer and she saw the sinister pennant flying from the mast. A bright red flag with crossed cutlasses emblazoned in white at its center and a grinning skull below them.

"I thought the Jolly Roger was black and white," Liz said. "And those are crossed cutlasses, not bones, aren't they?"

"The *jolie rouge* is the name the French buccaneers gave our flag—literally 'pretty red' . . . though some of the Brethren have black flags and some green flags. Some have bones or skeletons. Elizabeth, there is still time to change your mind before she drops anchor. You do realize that once aboard the *Avenger* we shall not only find ourselves in a different time, but also far from this island. Each time I return it is always the same. I climb aboard and go to rest in my cabin. When I awaken the ship is back in the Caribbean."

"I want to go with you," Liz said firmly. "Do you suppose the reason you find yourself back in the Caribbean is because that's where you will find Louis—the man you believe killed you?"

"By God, Elizabeth, you've a head on your shoulders. Come, we must prepare to join my crew aboard the *Avenger.*"

As the longboat skimmed over the surface of the sea toward the *Avenger*, Liz could see the pirate crew hanging perilously over the ship's rail, trying to catch a better glimpse of their captain's passenger. Their shouts of greeting, mingled with suggestive catcalls and whistles, brought to Liz's mind the ordeal of passing a construction site in the twentieth century. She pondered briefly on how little men had changed.

Closer inspection of the *Avenger*'s crew, however,

belied this first impression. The pirates were exotically dressed, bristling with knives, sheathed or tucked carelessly into belts and vivid sashes wrapped about their middles. All of them were as agile as athletes, scurrying aloft for a better view of the woman in the longboat, or descending from the dizzying height of the crow's nest so rapidly their hands and feet seemed barely to touch the shrouds.

A rope ladder came over the rail as Alexander brought the longboat alongside the ship. Liz looked up in some dismay, wondering how she would climb aboard hampered as she was by voluminous skirts and petticoats.

Alexander shouted to his men, "Bring the cargo net."

The rope ladder looked formidable, but the cargo net was a worse humiliation. "I won't go aboard in that thing," Liz said.

"You will." Alexander's tone brooked no disobedience. Liz found herself trussed up in the rope net for the journey from longboat to deck, despite her indignation and loud protests.

She was so angry she did not have time to be frightened by either the swaying ascent or the waiting buccaneers. When she was at last deposited unceremoniously on deck, a huge man with a wild mop of red hair and a face of purest innocence helped her from the net. He grinned vacantly when she thanked him. She knew this must be Alexander's loyal henchman, Tad Bowen.

In the seconds before Alexander came up the rope ladder, Liz was surrounded by crewmen. One man with a particularly evil grin circled her slowly and she jumped when he pinched her bottom. She wheeled around, about to yell at him to keep his hands to himself, when Alexander climbed over the rail.

"Avast, ye scurvy numbskulls," Alexander roared. "Stand aside and let the lady be or damn me if I won't keel-haul the pack of you."

The men jostled good-naturedly, making a path for him to come to her. Ignoring her glowering glance, he announced in ringing tones, "The lady will be treated with respect. I'll cut out the tongue of any man who speaks ill in her presence."

Liz felt the immediate shift of mood on deck. Scowls replaced grins and a snarling undercurrent ran through the outburst of comment. The man with the evil grin stepped forward. "Begging the captain's pardon, but are you telling us this woman is brought aboard for the cap'n's pleasure *only?*" His emphasis of the last word left a chilling echo in the ensuing silence. Too late, Liz realized the risk Alexander had taken in bringing her with him. Female captives, like any other booty, belonged to the entire crew. Alexander was about to break the sacred articles of the Brethren of the Coast.

"You understand me correctly, Woodes," Alexander said. "Elizabeth, this is my first mate. Mr. Woodes, if you have anything to say on this matter, let's discuss it now."

Alexander stood with his legs apart, feet braced against the roll of the ship, his thumb hooked over the sheathed knife on his belt. He stared unblinkingly at his first officer. In the background the disgruntled murmuring grew in volume. "The same goes for the rest of you sea-robbers," Alexander added. His flinty stare swept the assembled men and his shoulder muscles flexed slightly. "Speak up, you scavenging saltwater renegades, or get back to your stations."

"Well now, cap'n," Woodes said slowly. "We thought it a merry jest that you stole Letraz's woman from under his nose. But it's like this, see. We reckoned we'd use her and get rid of her before Letraz comes after her. We don't see no sense in fighting our own kind over a woman. While we're fighting each other, we ain't filling the coffers."

For answer Alexander's fist smashed into Woodes' jaw and the man went sprawling on the deck. Liz gasped and took a step closer to Alexander. He shouted, "Does any other man want to argue?" No one came forward. Woodes rubbed his jaw and climbed to his feet.

"Hark ye, then," Alexander said. "The lady will be aboard for only a short time. Behave yourselves and my shares of the next prize will be divided between you."

The mood of jocularity was restored. Alexander drew Liz's arm through his and led her away. As they went down to his cabin he told her, "The men like not having a woman aboard. 'Tis bad luck."

"What do you suppose Mr. Woodes meant," Liz said, "when he said I was Louis de Letraz's woman?"

The passageway leading to the cabin was dark and she could not see his expression as he answered. "I don't know, Elizabeth. I don't remember this part of my life. What is happening now seems to be happening for the first time. Always before when I returned to my own time it was to an earlier period. Your presence seems to change things—" he broke off, pushing open the cabin door. He didn't finish the thought and Liz knew he had been about to say they had arrived somewhere near the end of his life. The part he could not remember.

Inside the cabin Alexander pointed out a pitcher of cold saltwater set in a tin bowl and suggested she bathe and lie down to rest. He then discreetly departed.

Stripped down to her petticoat and chemise, she

crawled under a scratchy blanket on the hard wooden bunk. Blurred impressions raced through her mind as she began to relax and drift off to sleep. Listening to the creaking of the ship's timbers and the gentle sighing of the breeze in the rigging, she thought of the exotic and colorful clothing of the crew. The fact that everything looked reasonably new—was she expecting rotted boards and time-worn cloth? Some of the men bore fearful scars, which she supposed were legacies of various battles and escapes from the law.

Lying in Alexander's wide bunk, she wondered where the captain was sleeping. Her heart began to beat erratically as she thought of him, alone and unafraid, facing that fearsome band of ruffians. How utterly magnificent he was, she thought. She let her imagination wander to the possibilities of returning with him to Falconer's Island and then, somehow, taking him into her world. He would be a leader, a giant among his peers in any age.

Then she remembered Nick's visit to Falconer's Island. Alexander had been unable to materialize to Nick. Did Alexander exist only in her eyes—was that it? Could she be dreaming even this?

There were dream-like qualities to everything that had happened since she stepped ashore on the island. And, as in a dream, she appeared to have no control over the progression of events. If she had, wouldn't Alexander be with her right now? Rocking soothingly in his bed to the motion of the ship, it was easy to forget the sharp edges of reality that had been distant from the first moment she saw him. The warmth of his touch, the shark he had killed to save her life, the food they had shared, seemed more real than anything.

In the drifting moments before sleep came to claim her she repeated to herself that it wasn't real, it was all but a dream. Then the cabin door opened and Alexander came into the small circle of yellow light cast by a lantern swinging from the bulkhead. His expression was inscrutable but the shadows emphasized his scar and cast his strong features in ferocious lines.

Liz sat up abruptly, clutching the blanket to her breast. Ghost or no ghost, Alexander was now a man back in his own time and ruler of all he surveyed.

"You aren't planning to sleep *here?*" Liz said. Despite the horror in her voice, she realized immediately that she had secretly been hoping he was going to sleep with her. Hadn't she been hoping he would make love to her from the first moment she had seen him? Or was it some other emotion that had preceded desire? Was it possible she had slowly but surely been falling in love with a man dead three hundred years?

Alexander said, "Where else would I sleep? This is my cabin. My men would think my brain addled and my manhood rotted were I to allow a tasty morsel like you to sleep alone." He was carelessly removing his shirt and unbuckling his belt.

Liz watched, feeling a tingling sensation travel upward from her toes.

He moved closer to the bunk, standing looking down at her. "Elizabeth, you have bewitched me with your shrew's tongue and your boy's hips . . . your wild lion's mane of hair and eyes as luminous as tropical pools in moonlight. I love the soft curve of your shoulders and breasts. I love your spirit. I could not be as brave as you were I confined to the puny body of a woman."

Mesmerized, Liz watched him toss his shirt on top of a sea chest and follow it with his breeches. "Alexander, you pay the oddest compliments I have ever heard."

He smiled and sat down on the bunk, picking up her hand and cradling it to his warm mouth. She shivered as he pressed a kiss upon her wrist and looked up the length of her arm. "Why did we come together, Elizabeth . . . if not for love? Ah, fair one, I've waited for you so long. I am spellbound by you, I think of nothing but you. I want you more than I long for life. My blood races when I look at you and there is only one way to quench the fire that consumes my loins . . ." His lips traveled the length of her arm and she did not stop him when he took her mouth.

She felt herself yielding to him, swept forward as breathlessly as he when he enfolded her with one brawny arm and explored every inch of her with his other hand. His kiss was a searching journey to sensations she had never experienced before; to a longing so desperate she felt herself quiver and rake his back with her fingernails.

Slowly and deliberately he outlined the soft swelling of her breasts with his teasing tongue, then found her erect nipples. Her hands went to his head, stroking his thick black hair, as her body moved to a rhythm quickly joined by his. The taut length of him was pressing her to the bunk and the hard swelling of his flesh touched her most intimately. His lips were everywhere; on her eyelids, in her hair, brushing lightly across her throat. "Elizabeth, I adore you. You are my wife. You are the only woman I ever wanted to call wife. I want you with me through all eternity."

Somewhere in some distant reach of her consciousness Liz saw the warning signal flicker, but her blood pounded in her ears and every nerve in her body cried out for consummation of a feeling so intense she thought she would die from it. She could only gasp his name "Alexander . . . my love."

His hands were warm on her thighs and she was

melting with need, the tension of wanting him, loving him, waiting for release.

Then they were together in one searing thrust of his manhood deep into her, filling all of her, driving every other thought from her mind. They moved together, gracefully, urgently, reaching new peaks of desire that surely must send them crashing into oblivion, yet did not. He brought her to the brink of fulfillment and lingered there with her, only to find new nerve endings to bring to an exquisite crescendo of passion that knew neither time nor place, life nor death. Each would forever be a part of the other, from this moment on.

Their climax left them breathless, clinging to each other, floating. His lips traveled from her face to her hair and he was murmuring his love in words old and new to her. Once she whispered, "But we don't know how long we can be together . . ." and he silenced her fears with his kisses. His caress drove away the lurking shadows that proclaimed it was an impossible love, destined to be snatched away from them by time.

After a time Liz fell asleep, cradled in his arms, and knew a feeling of peace that was, in its way, as beautiful as the lovemaking had been. Twice during the night Alexander awakened her with his kiss and made love to her again.

When she opened her eyes to find the cabin filled with sunlight, he was sitting on the end of the bunk, fully dressed, watching her.

"I must go and chart our course, Elizabeth," he said softly, his eyes worshiping her. "But I could not bear to leave you. I wanted to watch you sleep and savor the memory of the night of love you gave me." He gathered her into his arms and their flesh burned where it touched.

Looking up at him, her happiness shining in her eyes, she felt a sudden chill at the sadness reflected in the way he watched her. He put his index finger lightly on her cheek, tracing the delicate bones of her face, as though making an imprint to keep in his memory when he lost her.

"Alexander . . . what is it?"

He tried to smile. "Nothing . . . but the fear that you will stop loving me."

"I can never do that—you are part of me, I would have to stop loving myself."

"Then I shall not be sad. We have this moment, this day." He stood up reluctantly. "I shall return shortly with your breakfast. Stay here and rest. Think good thoughts of me, my beloved, for I would even die for you."

He kissed her mouth with a poignant urgency, silencing her protest, and was gone before she could reassure him. Alone in the cabin she remembered him in every languorous and satiated nerve in her body and could not summon the fearful gloom that seemed to have touched him briefly. Theirs could not be a hopeless love, she told herself contentedly, it was too filled with joy.

Later that morning Alexander took her on a tour of his ship. She learned there were no crew's quarters, the men merely curled up and slept in any part of her 125-foot hull not already occupied. The *Avenger* was built for speed and combat, Alexander told her proudly, and could make fourteen knots under full sail. There were also forty-six oars for use when necessary, which could still move her at three knots without benefit of wind.

"Fire is our deadly peril," he said. "No smoking is

permitted below decks and our stewpot is kept far from our powder stores."

He took her below decks and showed her a small cabin, completely lined with tin except for a heavy glass window on one side. A lantern stood near the window.

"This is the light room. Through that glass is the powder magazine. We illuminate the magazine by means of the lantern on this side of the glass. Another precaution against fire."

Liz peered through the glass and saw the powder kegs beyond.

"Come," he said. "I'll show you the rest of the ship. We have shot for our 12-pounder cannon, and water casks, stored amidships in the hold to help ballast the ship. When we reach port you'll see it takes forty men to work the capstan to hoist some of our stores aboard. The water casks each weigh nearly a ton—and our anchor weighs three thousand pounds."

Liz had already noted that, with the exception of Alexander and Tad Bowen, the pirate crew was small in stature compared to the men of the twentieth century. They were evidently all muscle and sinew, judging by the way they carelessly tossed heavy kegs up on their shoulders and hauled lines to change the direction of the canvas overhead.

She did not mention it to Alexander, but she was appalled at the pock-marked faces, the broken teeth and other evidence of disease and brawling. She remembered Alexander told her the "French disease" was one of the scourges of sailors. At the time this had not registered, but now she realized that was what they called venereal disease.

When Alexander saw her hastily avert her eyes from several pirates who appeared to have had noses and ears slit, he casually informed her they had been punished for stealing from their comrades. He was amazed when she protested the harshness of the punishment.

"I am the most lenient of masters. Other pirate captains slit noses and ears and then maroon the offender."

But the day was too fair, her wonder at her awakening love too intense, for the dark underside of his time to intrude on her happiness.

He spent as much time with her as his duties aboard ship permitted. They talked and teased and laughed and made love. Even when they were not in each other's arms, their eyes consumed each other.

Everything that had gone before the moment she met Alexander seemed like a misty dream, while being with him, loving him and making love, was the clearest reality. She no longer tried to explain what was happening and barely remembered that somewhere, long ago and far away, there had been people involved in the make-believe of film making. She felt that a movie about pirates had not inspired a dream, but rather had cast the shadow of coming events.

Then one night she awoke at midnight with the old prophetic dread and found Alexander standing in the center of the cabin, cutlass in hand. A pale shaft of moonlight slashed cruel light across his face, showing harsh lines and the sinister scar.

He turned, cutlass raised, as she sat up. The scream was trapped in her throat. She looked into his eyes and saw the icy spectre of death.

"Alexander!" she cried. Her fear was not for herself, but for him.

Slowly he lowered the cutlass to his side, the wild light in his eyes dying. "I did not mean to frighten you.

I awoke to some warning voice and thought I must ward off an attack."

Tossing the cutlass back into his sea chest, he gathered her into his arms and stroked her hair reassuringly.

"Alexander, it's the stroke of midnight, isn't it?" she asked against the comforting warmth of his chest.

"Hush, don't worry. I will protect you with my life. My beloved, no one shall ever harm you. And when the fates separate us again, I shall still find some way to come to you. I swear it by this sacred love I have for you."

"Oh, Alexander, I love you so. I'm only complete when your flesh touches mine, when I know you're near."

"Elizabeth, I can feel your heart fluttering like a trapped bird. What a cursed knave I am to frighten you so."

"No, it wasn't you. I've awakened before on the stroke of midnight, feeling the most unutterable dread . . . as though I were suffocating, buried alive. I can't describe it."

"By the saints, that's amazing. For I, too, have awakened at this hour. Of late I have come to believe that perhaps it was the hour of my death."

"You remember more than you've told me," Liz said.

He looked at her, pondering whether to share the vague memory with her. "I remember not a quick, clean death . . . but an ebbing away of my life in a shadowed, smoke-filled trance. I remember looking up at the rising moon, wondering if I would see the new day as the midnight hour approached. Ah, Elizabeth, how I wanted to hurry past midnight to keep that rendezvous that I had to keep . . . it was more important to me than anything that had gone before. I believe I must have died at midnight."

Her hands tightened on his flesh. "Then I shall—" she began, but a hoarse cry of denial broke from his lips and his arms were iron bars, imprisoning her. Before she could say what he feared most, his mouth was pressed against hers, silencing the thought.

When at last he released her, he said harshly, "Tell yourself that I am only a spirit and this is only a vivid dream. Remember it constantly. A dream, Elizabeth. Only a dream."

The next day the dream turned to a nightmare. The *Avenger* had run down an armed merchantman and she was fighting for her life, her mainmast toppled by a broadside, as her out-numbered crew prepared to battle the pirate boarding party.

Bandmen aboard the *Avenger* were beating drums and a trumpet blared as the pirates threw grappling irons. The air was thick with a sulfurous cloud of smoke and the cannon continued to blast away until the moment the first pirates swung aboard their prey.

After taking one terrified look through the porthole, Liz stayed in Alexander's cabin, hands pressed to her ears. Her stomach was churning and she thought of the meal she had eaten the night before. Alexander called it *salmagundi* and said it was made from turtle meat and pigeon, marinated in spiced wine then combined with cabbage, pickled herrings, mangoes, onions and olives . . . and anything else the pirate cook had at hand. She was fortunate, Alexander added, that the ship had recently been in port, or the fare would have been spartan in the extreme.

The food tasted hearty and well-seasoned, but today

Liz wondered if it was the *salmagundi* or the sickening sounds of battle above and around her that were making her so ill.

Hours went by before the sounds faded to an occasional shout and the splintering of a falling mast. Then, unmistakably, Liz heard a woman's scream.

Chapter 15

Liz scrambled up the steep wooden ladder to the deck, peering out of the hatch at the scene of carnage beyond. She gasped as her fingers touched warm stickiness and, looking down, saw a pool of fresh blood on the wood.

Looking around wildly, she saw the entire deck was covered with blood. Several spars had crashed to the deck during the battle and tattered canvas hung limply, but the pirate ship was not badly damaged and it was obvious the hand-to-hand combat had taken place on the deck of their prey.

The sweating backs of two pirates blocked her view of what the rest of the men were doing. She stepped carefully onto the deck, wiping the blood from her hands onto her skirts.

Two women, one considerably older than the other

and obviously a servant, were cowering in a corner of the stern. Liz saw at once the reason for the scream she had heard belowdecks. Several pirates had hauled half a dozen captive sailors from the Spanish ship to their own vessel for interrogation. The prisoners had been stripped and two of them were already covered with bleeding wounds from the torture of daggers and cutlasses. There was no sign of Alexander on deck.

"I'll ask ye again," one pirate thundered, "where did ye hide the treasure? Your ship carried too many musketeers not to have a valuable cargo." He punctuated the question with a vicious jab into the belly of one man, who swayed on his feet, near collapse from loss of blood. His lips moved soundlessly in what could have been prayer.

One of the other prisoners said, "Señor . . . please. The man does not speak your language. Señor, I am the captain and I tell you truly . . ." he fumbled in Spanish for a moment, seeking the words he wanted, then added, "Nothing is hidden. You have seen all of our cargo. I beg of you, kill us with mercy. Do not prolong our agony."

With a roar of rage the pirate turned, swinging his cutlass with such fury that his blow almost decapitated the Spaniard. "There, then, you're dead," the pirate yelled.

Liz closed her eyes, feeling nausea drain her strength. She clutched the nearest pirate, partly for support and partly to attract his attention. "No . . . stop it—for God's sake, stop it," she screamed. She saw that both female captives had fainted.

The pirate with the dripping cutlass in his hand turned and stared at her in surprise. She recognized him now as the first officer of the *Avenger*, the man called Woodes. Two of his shipmates picked up the body of the Spanish captain and heaved it unceremoniously over the side of the ship.

"Get below, wench," Woodes said. " 'Less you want what's coming to them other two when we're finished here."

"Where is your captain?" Liz demanded, pushing aside several grinning pirates to make her way to the first officer. She glared into Woodes' evil stare and prayed she would not lose the contents of her stomach.

"He's aboard the other ship, searching for their valuables. Now get below."

"I'll get below when I'm damn good and ready. You fool, you've just killed the only man who speaks English."

Woodes shrugged. "He wouldn't tell us nothing. Kept pointing to a hold full of tin. Tin's no good to us. They must have something small and valuable hid somewheres." He gestured toward several rough bars of metal lying on the bloodstained deck.

"The women—perhaps they are the valuable cargo," Liz suggested, desperate to keep them talking until Alexander returned. "Maybe if you don't harm them, they will bring a large ransom." She was trying to recall everything Alexander had told her, but the crew were muttering angrily and the atmosphere on deck was one of flashpoint tension.

"We've tried ransom before—don't work," the first officer growled. " 'Sides, the woman is the wife of the governor of one of the islands—her husband died and she was going home. A widow won't bring a ransom. Naw, we went to all that trouble for a cargo of tin. Damn my blood, this is Bartholomew's fault."

One of the other pirates said, "We could try woolding one of 'em—that should make the others talk." There was a shout of agreement from the rest of the crew.

"What do they mean—woolding?" Liz asked.

"Why, missy, that means tying a bowstring around a man's neck and twisting it until his eyeballs shoot out," the first officer answered with a sly grin.

Liz slowly counted to twenty, keeping her eyes fixed on Woodes. "I think you should wait until your captain returns. Perhaps he's found something." Out of the corner of her eye she could see two pirates seizing one of the naked captives.

As though in answer to her prayer a cry rang out from the crow's nest, "Sail ho! Three leagues to starboard."

The ship was bearing down on them fast. Aboard the Spanish ship there was a flurry of activity as pirates swung back to their own ship. Liz was relieved to see Alexander come over the side. He took a spy glass from one of his men and peered through it at the oncoming vessel.

After a moment he lowered the glass and turned to his men. "It's the *Tiger's Claw*. Our old friend Louis de Letraz was no doubt also in pursuit of the Spaniard. What a jest! He will fight us for a cargo of tin. Unless you were able to learn what else of value she carried?"

Liz shoved a burly pirate aside and confronted Alexander, her eyes blazing. "You condoned the torture of the prisoners? You knew what they were doing to them?"

Alexander looked down at her in surprise. "You should not be on deck, Elizabeth. Please return to the cabin."

"Alexander, no, please, this isn't you—tell me you wouldn't torture a helpless man."

His eyes narrowed. "That ship was too heavily armed

for a cargo of tin. They are concealing something of great value. They know they are to die anyway. Their death will be merciful if they save us the time of tearing the ship timber from timber. I am the most merciful of sea rovers."

"But Woodes killed the captain—the only man who speaks English," Liz protested, feeling a cold knot inside her at the expression on Alexander's face. He really believes he is merciful, if he kills them without torture . . . and that torture is justified if they won't—or can't—tell him what he wants to know.

"Tie them to the shrouds, we'll deal with them after I've talked to Louis," Alexander instructed. Two men promptly hauled the captives to the rigging, suspending them by their wrists from the shrouds.

The other pirate ship was closing. She was larger than the *Avenger* and appeared to be jammed with crewmen.

"I suppose you might just as well stay on deck and meet Louis," Alexander said to Liz. "Prepare yourself for a surprise, Elizabeth."

The *Tiger's Claw* was hailed by the first officer and her captain invited aboard to share a bottle of rum and discuss the dilemma of the worthless prize.

Liz saw that the French captain was as tall as Alexander, but leanly built. She could not see his face as he swung over to the *Avenger,* as he wore a large hat with a flamboyant feather tucked into the band. His clothes would have been suitable for presentation at the royal court. Then Louis was on deck, sweeping her into his arms, and she was too astonished to do anything but allow him to hold her. She was looking up into the face of Nick Kane.

Alexander told me he looked like Nick, she thought, but the resemblance is uncanny. Louis had Nick's leanly handsome features adorned with a thin moustache along his upper lip and a small goatee on a stubborn chin, but surely Nick's dark eyes did not have that pitiless cruelty?

Louis was speaking to her in rapid French that was interrupted by Alexander's angry command. "Take your hands off her, Letraz, or by God I'll smite you dead where you stand."

Liz felt Louis' sinewy arms relax their hold. She pulled free and turned to face Alexander, standing uncertainly between the two men. She felt dazed, faint, caught in an almost palpable wave of hatred between the two rivals.

"I have come for my woman, you arrogant dog," Louis said. "And for the prize I have been shadowing for days." His thin lips barely moved as he spoke.

"Elizabeth prefers to remain with me. And as for the prize, you can see for yourself we both wasted our time. That's what she is carrying." He pointed to the metal bars lying on deck. "Tin, Louis. If you need ballast, then take it. I've no use for it."

Liz followed his gaze to the metal bars, momentarily distracted by a memory that hovered elusively on the edge of her consciousness. But her obvious resemblance to someone Louis knew was of more pressing concern. Louis again addressed her in French and she shook her head helplessly.

"She does not understand you, Louis," Alexander said. "She is not who you believe her to be."

"What have you done to her?" Louis demanded harshly. "Have you so ill-used her that she cannot remember her native tongue? Elise, I beg of you . . ."

"Elizabeth," Liz whispered. A strange sense of inevitability weighed heavily upon her. "My name is Elizabeth, not Elise."

Faster than her eye could perceive, Louis' rapier was in his hand, pointed at Alexander's chest. Alexander held a cutlass, but it was pointed downward toward the deck. Louis' voice was a cry of anguish and outrage. "You have bewitched her, you son of the devil. *Mon Dieux,* for this you die."

"Louis, please!" Liz screamed. "I just look like someone you know. Please, let me explain."

Alexander did not flinch as Louis' rapier brought a spot of blood through his shirt. "He will not understand, Elizabeth. He believes you are his cousin, Elise, who ran away from a forced marriage in France to join her buccaneer cousin in exile. Tell me, Louis, will you run me through while my own weapon menaces only the deck? Or will you fight me honorably, your rapier against mine?"

Louis' cold eyes flickered again in the direction of the metal bars lying on the deck, then he glanced toward the Spanish prisoners, hanging from the shrouds. "I will fight you, whoreson. I will fight for Elise and I will fight for the prize. But first we will learn what the Spaniard is really carrying, so that I will know whether to dispatch you quickly for presuming to carry off my cousin, or slowly for adding the insult of taking my prize and lying about her cargo."

"The Spaniard carries only tin," Alexander said. "All of her officers are dead except for the two we have strung up. The rest of her crew are either too stupid or too far gone to question."

"You always were too soft," Louis said with a contemptuous curl of his lips. "I will question your prisoners and find out in short order what cargo they carried. The sport of splitting hides will put me in a proper frame of mind to deal with you, you strutting scoundrel."

The thought that had been trying to intrude into Liz's mind broke through her dazed senses as Louis strode toward the Spanish prisoners hanging from the shrouds.

"Wait!" she cried. "You ignorant fools!" She was remembering Falconer's Island, the radio message from Tahiti in response to her request for information about pirates. The Falconer family had dug for buried treasure, but found only . . . "Rough silver," Liz shouted. "That isn't tin. Those are ingots of rough silver. It looks like tin because it hasn't been polished. If they have a hold full of it, then it's worth a fortune. There's more than enough for you to split."

"Silver," Louis repeated. He bent to pick up one of the bars and weighed it in his hand. "The Spaniard was too heavily armed to transport only a cargo of tin."

"The prize is mine, Louis," Alexander said coldly. "My men are weary from a long battle and in no condition to fight you for what is rightfully theirs. Therefore, I accept your challenge. We shall duel with rapiers. If I lose, the prize is yours. If I win, your ship agrees to withdraw."

Louis paced the deck for a moment, considering. He was a splendidly impressive adversary. His bearing and proudly held head bespoke an aristocratic ancestry, while his movements were those of a man who lived constantly with danger and relished its challenge.

Alexander stood waiting; equally in command of himself and his world. His breeding and courage were written in every line of his magnificent body, in his level gaze and composed expression. A vibrant aura of invincibility radiated from him that dazzled Liz with its impact, making her forget it was a mortal body that faced cold steel and the unmistakable threat of death in the merciless eyes of his opponent.

"Very well, knave's whelp," Louis said. "I can tell my crew the Spaniard carries only tin and they will let you be. But, of course, the matter is elementary, since I shall be the victor in the duel. Have your men wash away the blood, so your deck is less slippery."

"Go below to the cabin, Elizabeth," Alexander said.

"She stays on deck," Louis said. "When I have sent you to your maker, she returns with me to the *Tiger's Claw.*"

"She goes below—" Alexander began.

Liz interrupted, "Alexander, it's all right. I'll stay. But please allow the women prisoners to leave."

Alexander put his hand to his brow, brushing back a lock of black hair. He drew a deep breath. "Elizabeth, I'm beginning to remember events I had forgotten." He placed himself between her and Louis, speaking softly so that only she could hear. "At the same time, I feel myself slipping backward, caught between your time and my own. I must take you back to my Pacific isle. I am afraid I will forget who you really are."

"Don't worry about that now," Liz whispered. "Don't fight him. There must be another way. Can't you let him have the Spanish ship?"

"My men would mutiny. They fought for that prize and I've no right to deprive them of their share." He wiped his brow again, blinking.

He's been fighting, too, Liz thought, and he's weary from it. How can he fight Louis after battling strenuously for hours to capture the Spanish ship? "Alexander, let him have the ship. You were right, the cargo is tin. I only said I believed it to be silver so he wouldn't torture the prisoners."

Alexander smiled. "But you were right. If I had been thinking clearly I would have realized it was silver. Besides, the disputed prize is not the real point of our duel. We fight for you, Elizabeth. You see, my beloved, I remember now that Louis fell in love with his cousin Elise the moment they met again. Not only for her beauty and grace, but perhaps because she represented a life of elegance and charm he would never know again. His love and need of you are, alas, almost as great as mine."

Liz could see Louis, out of the corner of her eye. He was rolling up the cuffs of his immaculate shirt. "Then let us go back. Back to my time. Now—at once, before it's too late."

"Elizabeth, my love, we can't go back—nor even forward," Alexander said heavily. "I can only face this moment. Was it not always thus?" He gave an odd little smile.

When she clutched at him desperately, he called curtly to Tad Bowen to come and hold her.

Liz found herself sitting on the blacksmith's lap, barely able to breathe as he kept his muscled arms about her middle. The two female captives were carried below and the decks were quickly cleared of debris and swabbed.

The crew of the *Tiger's Claw* lined the rail to watch their captain fight, while the crew of the *Avenger* hung from every conceivable vantage point in the rigging for a bird's eye view of the duel.

After watching for a few seconds as Louis and Alexander parried and lunged, the blades of their rapiers ringing and clashing, Liz could not bear the suspense. The fear for Alexander's life was too much. She felt as though her heart were beating in her throat and it might at any moment escape into her mouth. She closed her eyes and wished she could close her ears to the sound of the duel.

She heard the labored breathing, occasionally a

grunt or a curse, and the shouted encouragement of the audience. Once she heard Louis say, "*Touché*, you hen-hearted sneak. You have been practicing. But Louis gives no quarter this time, he has your measure."

Behind closed eyelids, Liz could imagine the scene taking place on deck and she ached with fear, not only for Alexander, but for Louis; feeling an old familiarity of acquaintance because of his uncanny likeness to Nick. She could not open her eyes as the clashing of steel came closer, then receded. They have fought each other before, she told herself, and Alexander bettered Louis—hadn't he cut off his ear? Liz realized suddenly that Alexander had not yet cut off Louis' ear, for the Louis she had just met clearly had a pair of ears. Alexander had been mistaken—he had confused various sequences of events. Could he, therefore, be wrong about dying while he slept at midnight—was he to die now, in front of her? And if he did not die, then must Louis die? And was it true that Alexander was somehow slipping away from her? Would he revert to being the barbarian he was before and forget their moments of tenderness together? Her body was rigid with fear and her thoughts raced in several directions at once.

She felt Tad's huge body tense suddenly and, opening her eyes she saw that Alexander was down on one knee, fighting desperately to deflect the wickedly slashing blade of Louis' rapier. There was a trail of blood on the sleeve of Alexander's shirt, dripping over the fingers of his hand holding the hilt of the rapier.

It seemed certain that Alexander had lost. Fatigue was taking its toll and his style of fencing, while recklessly brave, was not in the same class as the polished swordsmanship of Louis.

Louis was playing with his opponent now, taunting him with the blade, coming within an inch of administering the *coup de grace,* then withdrawing. He flicked the blade close to Alexander's scalp, lifting a lock of black hair and sending blood streaming into Alexander's eyes. Liz struggled to free herself from Tad's grip, but he held her tightly and she was powerless to move. She was crying in great frightened gulps and had never felt so helpless before in her life.

Alexander shook his head and struck out blindly, deflecting Louis' blade with a lucky stroke. Louis was caught by surprise and hesitated for a fraction of a second, giving Alexander time to leap to his feet. Now Alexander fought angrily, his strokes rapid and his movements so swift that Louis blinked in bewilderment as he tried to decide which way Alexander would swing his blade next in his unorthodox self-taught style.

Alexander saw an opening and lunged. His blade skimmed down the side of Louis' head, removing his left ear as deftly as he might slice meat. Louis fell to the deck, his hand clapped to the side of his head, his face pale. Alexander's rapier tip hooked the hilt of Louis' rapier and it went flying across the deck. Alexander stood over him, poised for the final thrust.

Liz screamed. "No—don't kill him!" For a moment the scene froze in her mind, sounds receding. She was remembering that Alexander had told her he spared Louis' life because of the plea of a woman. Not remembering the events in his life after he met Elise, he believed it was the Lady Amelia's cry that stopped the fatal blow. But it was Elise who cried for mercy.

Alexander looked at her sadly, with resignation in his eyes. She had caused him to spare his enemy, who would now have a second opportunity to kill him . . . and would succeed.

Chapter 16

"I didn't think it would be like this," Liz said. "The savagery, the appalling cruelty."

Alexander stood looking out of the porthole at the angry swells rolling toward the ship. "You made me spare him because he reminds you of your Nicholas. You still love him." His voice was heavy with despair. "He is a mortal man while I . . ."

". . and worse, the callous acceptance of it all." Liz sat on the bunk, her uneaten dinner growing cold beside her. The heavy seas and consequent rolling of the ship had done nothing to ease the nausea she had felt all day.

"Fragments of memory of my last days have been returning to my mind. I did not want to face it. I knew that a woman's voice caused me to spare Louis after I cut off his ear." Neither Alexander nor Liz appeared to notice that they were each conducting a one-sided conversation.

"I haven't heard the women scream for some time," Liz was trembling and could not stop. "Are they dead? Oh, God, Alexander, how could you let the crew have them like that? One of the women was old enough to be your mother. It all sounded so romantic—like those old swashbuckling movies—when you talked about it. But in reality . . ."

She had been locked in the cabin for hours, listening to the heart-rending cries of the two Spanish women. Alexander had brought her meal and told her curtly that a woman who sailed the waters of the Caribbean knew full well what to expect. She did not dare ask if he had taken part in the ravishing of the women, He was too hurt and angry that she had interceded on Louis' behalf.

"Perhaps I should have given you to Louis. Sent you to the *Tiger's Claw*. Perhaps that was what you really wanted." He regarded her with a lost, hopeless gaze that sliced into her heart.

He looked down at his feet as he spoke. "I shall die soon, Elizabeth, but you will not be with me. I remember a state of being suspended—perhaps between life and death . . . weakness, great lethargy, my life tides ebbing. There was smoke, darkness . . . choking . . . alone. I was alone. Louis must have left me for dead, yet I lingered on to die at the stroke of midnight, all alone."

"Alexander," Liz whispered, overwhelmed by the force of her feeling for him. There was an expression on his ruggedly handsome features that she had never seen before. Not defeat, that was too bitter a pill for a man of his iron will to swallow, but a stoic acceptance of that which cannot be changed.

"It was foolhardy to bring you here, Elizabeth," he said heavily. He turned to stare morosely out of the porthole. "You belong in a different time and place. You belong with the man you truly love . . . your Nicholas. Just as Louis won the fair Elise."

Liz sprang from the bed and grabbed his arms, spinning him around to face her. "Look at me, damn it—stop looking out of that porthole." She had taken him by surprise but he quickly shook her free. "Alexander—it's you I love. Only you."

"We are heading into a storm and I must see to my ship," he said coldly. "How can you love me and hate what I do?"

"Don't let me detain you," Liz said, tossing her hair back over her shoulder with as much hauteur as she could summon. "And don't bother making excuses about a storm when you really want to return to the sport of raping two helpless women."

For a second she thought he was going to strike her. His eyes pierced her with the impact of sword thrusts and his mouth twisted savagely. "I did not touch the women, but it would be more than my life is worth to stop the men. This is not a navy ship—on most pirate ships there is no captain. I am their leader because I know when I must discipline them and when I cannot. The taking of women prisoners is part of their plunder. Shall I tell you what happens when we take a ship? The first place the men go is to the ship's stores, to see if there are any mercury compounds aboard." He paused to allow the significance of this to sink in and when Liz did not respond he clarified for her, "To treat the French disease, Elizabeth, which most of my men have picked up from whores in waterfront brothels. Women are only a necessary evil to the Brethren."

"Those women who were aboard the Spanish ship

were not prostitutes. Why should they be punished? Oh, what's the use of talking to you. You have no compassion in your soul—" She stopped, drawing in her breath sharply.

Alexander gave her a cool and mocking smile. "Perhaps, my beloved, I have no soul at all. Merely a spirit doomed to wander the earth endlessly, searching for my lost love. Ah, Elizabeth . . . why are we quarreling when I love you more than . . ."

"Life?" she finished for him. "Oh, Alexander, what have we done? What hope could there ever be for a mortal woman and a ghost?"

"And what hope would there have been for us had we both lived in the same age?" he demanded savagely. "Does not every love affair end in parting? What difference whether the parting be because of death . . . or disillusionment?"

They stared at each other, his face twisted with pain even as he denied its existence, the zig-zag scar standing out whitely against his sun-darkened skin. The harsh lines of his barbaric experience were etched deeply into the noble features. He had faced trial and deprivation bravely, for they were old adversaries he knew and understood. But this surge of tenderness, the yearning to protect and care for this woman to the exclusion of all others, this was an emotion so overwhelming that it bewildered him, suppressing rational thought. He knew that because of his love for her he would take chances, make mistakes, destroy himself. Yet his love for her was the shining peak of his existence, no matter what price he would pay for their all too fleeting moment together.

Liz watched him, her own feelings of love battling the doubts and fears, the questions in her mind raised by the revelations of the brutality of his life. He spoke cynically of love—was that because he wanted to make their parting easier, or did he really mean it? "You're right, Alexander, as always," she said. "We always knew our time together would be short."

The wind howled as though in mournful lament and they were both flung against the bulkhead as a towering wave caught the ship.

"Stay here. We must shorten sail," Alexander said. "Tie yourself to the bunk if the seas become heavier, or you will be injured. I shall return to you as soon as I can. Meantime, keep the door bolted. The men are in an ugly mood because I have not yet convinced them the ingots are silver. Perhaps the storm will be the diversion we need."

For the next two days the *Avenger* battled moutainous seas and shrieking winds that tore the canvas to shreds. The decks were constantly awash with icy water and, despite double-lashings, a cannon broke loose and went skittering about the deck injuring several men before it was washed overboard. Men and equipment were flung about as the ship rolled and pitched and came close to capsizing so often that Liz stopped praying for deliverance and instead resigned herself to accepting a watery grave.

Alexander fought to keep the ship turned into the wind, taking the helm himself. There was no time for him to go to Liz but he sent Tad Bowen with a meal of soggy bread and a measure of rum.

Liz was now battling seasickness along with everything else and shuddered at the offering. "No, thank you, Tad," she said. She had looped a blanket around the bunk posts and fastened it under her shoulders, harness-fashion, to keep her from being flung from the bunk as the ship rolled. With the porthole hatch closed, the tiny cabin was as claustrophobic as a coffin.

In her misery she longed for the nightmare to end, convinced it was all a dream. The terror of the storm, the weakness of nausea, her aching bones and the feeling of suffocation in the cramped quarters drove all thoughts of Alexander from her mind. Her lantern went out and she was left in murky darkness, which added to her fear. At last, exhausted, she slept.

She awakened to the sound of gentle waves slapping the hull and bright sunshine flooding the cabin through the open porthole. About two miles away was land, a bustling settlement. Several other ships lay at anchor.

Alexander was sitting on the sea chest, watching her. "I heated water so that you may bathe. We are anchored off the island of Jamaica. The settlement is called Port Royal. Many vessels have put in here because of the storm, including your friend Louis."

Liz uncoiled stiff limbs. "He isn't my friend."

"You begged for his life."

She reached for the sponge floating in the bowl of water he had brought. "What happens next, do you remember?"

He shook his head. "Everything is fragmented in my mind from this point. I believe that there was a land battle; the sacking of a town. Louis started the whole thing by deciding he wanted to attend the ball given by the Grindwalds. Then we were on the run, because a Royal Navy squadron came after us. I decided to take the *Avenger* into the Pacific and lie low for a while . . . Elizabeth, I believe as soon as the ship is repaired we should sail for the Pacific. Take you back to my island and back to your own time. It was a mistake bringing you here. I see my life through your eyes and I am ashamed. It is a feeling I do not like."

Liz held the sponge to her throbbing head. "What became of the two female prisoners?"

He looked away. "We lost them—in the storm."

"What do you mean, lost them?"

"They must have jumped overboard. Damn my eyes, don't look at me like that. 'Tis a miracle any one of us survived. We went through the storm the natives call *hurucano.*"

"Would you please leave while I remove my nightgown and bathe?" she asked with icy politeness.

"I have seen you naked," he growled, not moving.

"Alexander, leave me alone, please. I need time to think . . . about us."

He jumped to his feet and caught her to him. "Don't think, Elizabeth—feel. My love for you, my need of you. No two people ever have clear sailing all the time in their love, they have to accept the storms and the doldrums as well as the warm tropical nights. I won't give you up now. I can't."

His mouth would not be defied, finding hers and claiming it as only he could. His hands were warm and seeking and she resisted for only a moment. He whispered into her hair, "I was jealous of Louis, I wanted to kill him for the way he looked at you."

Liz clung to him, feeling a familiar surge of need that was honed by memory and touch. When his arm went under her knees to lift her to the bunk she could only whisper, "Alexander . . ." and open herself to him completely.

She loved the way he touched her, so delicately, as if she were a flower that could only be gently coaxed into opening. Each touch was a call that she responded to from the deepest part of her being, coming closer to him, coming out of herself to meld with him.

When she finally felt him plunge deeply and heavily into her, when she knew that he could not bear to pull away again even a hair's breadth from her, she felt a wonderful endless joy. There was nothing, no one, in the world but this. Every horror and fear that pressed in on them was momentarily stopped, imprisoned and they knew the perfect freedom from time and trouble that all lovers seek but few ever find.

To banish time—that was the only thing she really wanted. To exist no where else but here. As if he could read her thoughts, Alexander cocked his head gently listening to the toll of the ship's bell.

Alexander smoothed her hair back from her brow. "We are each the fruit of our own time, yet we came together like two rivers blending at the sea. Can there be a place where neither of us is bound to time and circumstance? Or are we forever doomed to sacrifice one world for the other?" He sighed. "Am I dreaming you, or are you dreaming me?"

She sat up, looking down at him with her eyes filled with love. "Alexander—this much we know. We are here together, now. I don't want to go back to my life without you. Why can't we change the way it was?"

He looked puzzled. Her fingers were trapped in his hand and he kissed them individually. "I no longer know how it was. I am so besotted by you I know only how I want it to be."

"Don't do any of the things you did before. Don't go near Louis. Don't go back to Falconer—I'm sorry, I mean Bartholomew's Isle. Give up piracy. Let's make a new life for ourselves and live it as long as we can. We could go to America . . . there are settlements along the east coast."

"You would give up your world for mine?" he asked with profound wonder in his voice. "Yet you believe us to be barbarians, after only the briefest glimpse of our times. Ah, Elizabeth, I fear you would grow to hate me. You put a high price on life . . . it troubled you greatly that we killed the Spaniards. Yet we must kill in order to live. You say, give up piracy, as if only pirates killed. Elizabeth, I could take you to the villages along the coast of Cornwall and Devon in my own England and show you the villagers lining the shore on a dark and stormy night, waiting with axes and crowbars for the wreckers' wind to blow a ship onto the deadly rocks. Aye, and women and children helping to murder the surviving sailors who came stumbling ashore. Clubbing them down in cold blood, for the sake of the cargo that would be washed up and any valuables on their persons."

Liz shuddered. "And we think our times are lawless. But you wouldn't have to kill, Alexander, there would be another way to live."

He gave a short laugh. "How long before Elizabeth is called a witch and tied to a dunking stool, or burned at a stake? Or we both go to a debtor's prison . . . or starve? My family lost all of their property, Elizabeth. Piracy was all that was left to me for I would not submit to serfdom."

"It can't be so hopeless. There has to be a way—" she broke off as there was an urgent knocking on the cabin door.

"Go away," Alexander roared.

"It's a messenger, Cap'n," a voice called. "Waiting for a reply."

Reluctantly Alexander uncoiled himself from the pleasant tangle of her arms and legs. He pulled on his breeches and went to the door, disappearing into the narrow passageway beyond.

Outside the cabin door was a familiar figure. Alexander sighed as he recognized the Scholar.

"If you've come to warn me that the *Tiger's Claw* is

also at anchor here, it will avail you nought. I must bide here until my ship is repaired and seaworthy. We were severely damaged in the storm. You can inform Louis—"

"He went ashore," the Scholar interrupted. "Our ship is in the next cove and I must make haste to return, for there's talk of sailing without Louis. I will delay the men as long as I can. I thought perhaps you could convince him we should not tarry here."

"God's teeth! Why did he go ashore? I can understand him being forced to shelter from the storm, but the last time we were in Port Royal between us we sacked the town. And I came as close to dancing on a hangman's rope as I'd ever wish."

The Scholar shuffled his feet. "You know how he is. The stories about you and the planter's wife, Lady Amelia . . . Louis was always angry that you concealed her from him. Then when you made off with his cousin Elise . . . I don't know if that's the reason he did it, or if it was just his usual love of danger."

"For God's sake, man, what are you trying to say?"

"We anchored yesterday and Louis went ashore to see how heavily armed the town and harbor were. He came back late last night and told us we'd be here another twenty-four hours because he was going to a ball. A ball!" the Scholar repeated incredulously.

Alexander swore under his breath. "Has he gone mad?"

"At the Grindwald plantation," the Scholar continued. "To present the Lady Amelia to Port Royal society. It seems Louis caught a glimpse of her riding through town and overheard conversations about the ball. It's to be a masquerade, with masks removed at midnight. Louis was in a tavern, drinking ale with another of the Brethren, who made the suggestion that Louis go to the ball. It was a wager and Louis accepted. I tried to stop him, but you know how he is."

In the gloom of the passageway Alexander searched the Scholar's face. "You've come to me before, when Louis' foolhardiness threatened all of the Brethren. I've always trusted you. But I can't help but wonder, knowing how Louis felt about Elise, if this isn't a plot to lure me away from the *Avenger* while Louis recaptures his cousin. Do you swear before God and all that is holy to you that Louis has gone ashore to Grindwald's ball—that he is not waiting to board my ship the moment I go ashore?"

"I swear to you he's gone ashore—to the Grindwald plantation. May God strike me dead if it isn't so."

"Very well. You would not lightly make such an oath, superstitious sailor that you are. Go back to the *Tiger's Claw*. Tell the men that Louis will be back in time to sail on the early tide tomorrow."

Alexander went back into the cabin and looked at Liz for a moment without speaking.

"What is it?" Liz asked, feeling apprehensive.

"I must go ashore. That fool Louis is going to endanger all of us. You see, Elizabeth, our ships are indistinguishable from any merchantmen unless we run up our flags. We could have lain safely at anchor here while the sailmakers restored our canvas and the carpenters nailed up broken spars. But Louis heard that Sir Miles Grindwald is giving a ball to present his bride to the other planters and officials on the island—and Louis plans to be one of the guests."

"But why?"

Alexander shrugged. "A wager. He has always been recklessly daring. He takes foolish chances for the sheer thrill of it. Then, too, I cannot entirely discount the considerable charm of the Lady Amelia. Apparently he saw her in town and he has never forgiven me for hiding her from him when we took the *Avenger*. It may possibly be his way of showing me he is indifferent to the fact that you chose me over him . . . he now feigns interest in Amelia. It has always been thus with Louis and me. What I do, he does, what I have he wants. He must outdo me in every respect: finer prizes, more treasure. If I sacked a city, he sacked two cities." Alexander paused, wondering whether to tell her the rest.

"Let him go then, it's his neck. Please, don't force any confrontations with Louis. Can't we just leave?"

"We can't leave until the *Avenger* is seaworthy."

"Who brought you the message? Perhaps it's a trap?" Liz asked, feeling buffeted by fate once again. No matter how they tried, it was inexorable, she thought, that rushing toward some nameless horror.

"There is a man aboard the *Tiger's Claw*, I call him the Scholar." Alexander said, answering her question. "When he believes Louis is acting rashly, the Scholar informs me. Especially when Louis' actions bring danger to all of the Brethren. I must warn him—" he broke off, he teeth biting his lip in annoyance.

"What do you mean?" Liz asked quickly, "Danger to all of the Brethren? Warn him about what? Alexander, what aren't you telling me?"

"During the storm," he said slowly, "we sighted a Royal Navy squadron. We saw them only briefly and quickly changed course. But no matter which of these islands they were bound for, eventually they will come to Port Royal. Miles Grindwald's younger brother is a Naval officer. Even if he is not aboard one of the vessels, I'm sure if they reach Port Royal in time for the ball, the officers will attend—because of the Grindwald's Navy connections."

"How long until the *Avenger* is seaworthy?" Liz asked, a knot of fear in her throat. "Will the Navy ships recognize the pirate ships for what they are?"

"My men are working with all speed, but we can't sail before the morning tide at the earliest. Perhaps the Navy squadron will not look too closely at our ships in their haste to go ashore for the ball. We will probably be safe after dark, unless Louis alerts them to our presence by being caught at the Grindwald plantation. Louis does not know about the Navy frigates, or even he would not be so reckless as to announce our presence to a vastly superior force."

"Take me with you then, if you must go to the ball. You would be less conspicuous with a partner."

"No. It is too dangerous. Besides, I plan to be in and out in a trice."

Liz glared at him. "Are you sure it's Louis you're concerned about? Or is it really the Lady Amelia? Are you risking your life for her sake? Are you afraid Louis will carry her off and show you up? I saw you fight a fierce duel with Louis, now you tell me you must go after him to save him from the Royal Navy."

"Damn me, you're applying a woman's logic to it, and that tinged with jealousy." Alexander's fist crashed into the bulkhead beside him in anger. "I expected more of you, Elizabeth. I tell you again, Louis will endanger all of us if he is discovered."

"Go ahead then, risk your life. But I'm going with you even if I have to swim ashore. You must do it all exactly as you did before. Louis will kill you."

"Nevertheless, I must warn him of the approach of the Naval squadron. The lives of his crew are at stake.

Besides I have no desire to see Louis fall into the hands of the law, despite our personal feelings for each other."

Liz at last recognized what was written in Alexander's gaze. Fearing nothing on earth himself, only a deep concern for a friend's welfare could put that particular expression in his eyes.

Liz's breath escaped slowly. She stared at him, lips parted, as she finally understood. "You really are worried about Louis," she said, and it was not a question. "Alexander, how many times in the past has Louis had an opportunity to kill you and yet spared your life? Or you his? You've been rivals, yes, but it sounds to me as if it is an affectionate rivalry. You were his protégé, who grew to be a leader in your own right. But everything you know, you learned from Louis. I detected a certain pride in you in the way he looked at you. I didn't watch all of your duel—but it seemed to me that when you were down on the deck on one knee he could have killed you then, but wanted only to teach you a lesson. And when I screamed at you not to kill him, was it really my cry, or your own feeling for him that stopped you?"

Several conflicting emotions were now racing across Alexander's face as he took this in. "When I was to be hanged," he said slowly. "Louis' men attacked the town. I thought it coincidence, but what if he was coming to my aid?"

"Yes, yes. But there's a new element this time. A woman, Amelia. Louis will never believe your story of wanting to warn him about the Navy, he will think you go to save Amelia."

Alexander made a strangled sound, deep in his throat. "No, Elizabeth, I think not. Lady Amelia is not a woman either of us would die for. You say you saw the way Louis looked at me . . . well, I saw the way he looked at you. I've never seen Louis look at a woman in that way. If one of us is to die for love, it will be for love of you, Elizabeth." He leaned back against the bulkhead, staring at her strangely.

Inside her head a voice was screaming that this had to happen and that there was nothing, nothing she could do.

Chapter 17

Lanterns were strung from the trees of the Grindwald plantation and the flames glowed like jewels against a black velvet night. The ladies in their ball gowns were almost as dazzling. Everyone was masked, the ladies carrying masks on ribbon-wrapped sticks, and the men wearing theirs. Sir Miles Grindwald had decided to have a masked ball and traditional midnight unmasking partly for the sense of intrigue and partly because the presence of a Royal Navy squadron in the Caribbean meant there was no fear of a pirate raid.

Miles' younger brother was captain of a Navy frigate in the squadron presently sailing for Port Royal and it was hoped that he and the other officers would arrive in time for the ball.

Lady Amelia looked bewitching in a royal blue satin gown that set off her fair hair. She giggled and bubbled behind a white satin mask. Receiving their guests beside her, Miles was also resplendent in silk and satin, with several lace-edged handkerchiefs tucked into pockets ready to press to his aristocratic nostrils whenever he was faced with someone, or something, he found unpleasant.

The guests danced in the great hall and moved outside to the cooler air of the lawns and gardens, wandering in couples beneath the colored lanterns.

Since Miles had been forced to spend more of his life than he intended caring for the plantation, he had endeavored to re-create his home in England. Many a hapless slave had been beaten because the lawns refused to grow as lushly green in the tropical climate as they did in England's misty rains. Nor would he accept the fact that some English shrubs and flowers would not grow. The island produced dozens of beautiful flowers and shrubs, but Miles wanted lilac and holly and would not settle for orchids and wild orange trees. He did not hear the multitudes of native songbirds trilling in the branches of mango and ceiba trees as he longed for the call of nightingales from the depths of the hedgerow that encircled the park-like grounds of his home in England.

As their hired carriage came to a halt in front of the brightly-lit house and a footman sprang forward to hold the horses, Liz felt both apprehension and excitement. Alexander was calm at her side, but he exuded a roguish vitality she feared would give him away. They were dressed richly but not flamboyantly, masks in place, and had waited until the festivities were well under way before arriving. Liz picked up the skirts of her rose-colored gown as they went up the steps to the front doors and the sound of music and laughter.

As they had guessed, their hosts were now mingling with the guests rather than standing at the door receiving. They moved quickly to the hall, where a minuet was beginning.

"We can sit on the sidelines," Alexander whispered. "And watch for Louis. Mask or no, I'd recognize that sea rover at fifty paces."

"But I want to dance, Alexander," Liz murmured. "And you'll find him more quickly if we move about."

"Ah, so you still do the same dances as we? I did not want to embarrass you by asking."

Liz' eyes were bright behind her pink silk mask. Strangely, she felt she would be able to follow the graceful steps of the dance. It's because this is all a dream, she thought. In a dream one can do anything. What a pity the waltz hasn't become popular yet. I'd love to spin around the floor in Alexander's firm embrace.

As he led her out to join the dance, she whispered, "Where is Amelia?" and Alexander nodded toward a small, voluptuously curved woman in a bright blue gown. Liz frowned. She had hoped for a less attractive rival.

The musicians struck the opening chords and Alexander was bowing to her. He danced with the same grace he exhibited while striding the deck of his ship or swinging over the side of his unfortunate prey, despite the fact that he was more muscular than most of the planters and merchants who made up the guest list.

Liz loved the way her skirts swung and billowed as she moved easily into the minuet. At the end of the dance she was surprised to hear a nearby conversation that indicated the minuet was a new dance, only recently introduced.

"Where did you learn to do that?" she asked Alexander as he brought her a crystal goblet of punch.

He smiled. "We don't spend all of our time at sea."

There was a flutter of excitement through the guests, and she felt Alexander stiffen at her side. Several Naval officers were at the door being greeted by Amelia and a slightly-built, effeminate looking man.

Someone nearby was saying in an authorative tone, "Of course, my dear sir, the government *encouraged* the buccaneers while they were preying on the Spanish galleons. Our people simply didn't have the men to patrol these waters and the buccaneers were keeping the Spaniards busy. But they got out of hand, as we all knew they would. The Royal Navy will make an example of a few of them and we'll be safe from land raids at least, though there are so many of the pirates now, they attack every ship, no matter what flag she flies."

"I understand the captain of one of the frigates is Miles' younger brother," someone else put in. "Not much family likeness is there? Can't imagine old Miles aboard a ship. I heard that with the dowry Amelia brought him he will be able to restore the ancestral home in England. That is, if he can ever find a buyer for this white elephant."

"The plantation would be easier to sell if Miles hadn't been plagued by slave uprisings. He drives them too hard . . ." the voices drifted away in the direction of the Naval officers.

Liz said, "The Lady Amelia is very pretty. I saw her glance in your direction a couple of times. She hasn't guessed your identity, I hope?"

Alexander's steel gray eyes flashed behind his mask. He too had seen Amelia turning her head repeatedly in his direction. Had she not been myopic, she would no doubt have recognized him merely from his muscular frame and superior height. He kept maneuvering Liz out of range of Amelia's nearsighted gaze. Aloud he said, "I do not believe she recognizes me. But I am of the opinion the Scholar was mistaken about Louis' reckless plan, or else we have walked into a trap."

"What do you mean?"

"Perhaps Louis wanted the Scholar to send me into Miles' hands. He may have allowed the Scholar to believe he planned to come here when in reality he had no such intention. I should have considered how devious is the mind of that scurvy knave."

"Let's go now then," Liz said. "Don't tempt fate by waiting for him to appear."

"Perhaps . . ." Alexander said thoughtfully, "I will first pay my compliments to our hostess. So the evening will not be wasted. She can inform me as to the course the Navy ships will set, so that we may sail in a different direction."

"No! Don't be a fool—" Liz began.

He smiled. "You need not fear, Elizabeth. My heart is yours alone."

"What I fear is that she will betray you," Liz said, fluttering her fan furiously. Some of the accessories of the day had their uses.

They had both been distracted long enough to miss Amelia Grindwald's steady progress toward them. Before either of them realized she was approaching, she had moved to Alexander's side. Her ostrich feather fan came down lightly on his arm, tapping him to attract his attention. "What an impudent rogue you are," she said in a throaty whisper, "to dare come here tonight. Do you not see that Miles' brother and half of the Royal Navy are here?"

Alexander bowed to her. "How could we miss your presentation ball, my dear?"

Amelia's darting eyes swept up and down Liz. "How dare you bring one of your filthy harlots to my house?"

Liz bridled, but before she could speak Alexander moved to circumvent a possible scene. "Amelia, if there were not more important matters on my mind than your ill-bred jealousy, I would teach you a public lesson, here and now. As it is, methinks you and I should withdraw for a private conversation. Elizabeth, my dearest, please forgive me. You know what it is I must learn from our hostess. Will you wait here?" He seized Amelia's plump white arm and propelled her forcefully toward the nearest door.

The second Alexander disappeared, a man appeared at Liz's side. He moved soundlessly, slipping into the seat beside her with the sinuous movement of a snake. Behind a scarlet mask the man's eyes were as cold and empty as dark mirrors.

"I was afraid Alexander would never leave your side, my dear cousin. You see how I cater to your disastrous forgetfulness by addressing you in English, instead of our beloved native tongue?"

"Louis," Liz breathed, recognizing the slightly accented and reproachful voice.

"I knew he would not dare leave you aboard his ship," Louis continued, "for fear the Scholar's message was a ruse to get him ashore while I kidnapped you. I know that sea rover better than he knows himself. He would trust no one else to guard the fair Elise—even to the point of bringing her into the lion's den so that he himself may protect her."

"Louis, please—believe me, I'm not your cousin. I can't even speak French. I just look like her."

"So my lovely Elise still insists she has no memory. You cannot remember an interlude with Louis, therefore it did not happen. *Bein.* I understand. But *ma cherie,* I understand also that the brigand Bartholomew carried you off and you were forced to submit to him, so that he would protect you from his crew. But you are safe now. I will kill that cur for his insolence."

"Louis, you are endangering both yourself and Alexander by being here. Surely you've seen the naval officers? There is a squadron of ships in Port Royal, enough to blow the *Tiger's Claw* and the *Avenger* and all the other pirate ships out of the water."

He shrugged indifferently. "That scurvy dog left your side to dally with the Lady Amelia. No doubt warning that doxie I may come and carry her off. A gallant, our friend Alexander. Forever trying to protect the honor of women no better than they should be. Oh yes, I realize he carried you off because he could not see a well-bred lady fall into Louis' hands . . . Alexander knows what usually happens to the women I capture and did not understand that I would have guarded your honor with my life. That I had begged you to be my bride."

Liz's eyes widened at this announcement and she glanced about to see if they were being overheard, but the hum of conversation and the sound of the music and tinkling glasses ensured they were not.

"Ah, Elise," Louis murmured, his hand closing over hers, "there was never before a woman I would have killed Alexander for . . . until you came along. I have always had a grudging respect . . . indeed, a slight fondness, for the crafty rascal. But I must kill him for dishonoring you. You *will* be my bride Elise. We are two who are bound by tradition and family ties. And did you not tell me yourself that with the new clique in power at Court that I might possibly buy back the king's favor? My love, we shall return to France covered with glory . . . not to mention laden with treasure. I have amassed a king's ransom, Elise. More than enough to close the Court's eyes to my family's past indiscretions. And after I have dispatched Alexander, I shall also take possession of the cargo of silver ingots which rightfully should have been mine."

Liz listened with a growing sense of dread. She knew that Louis had, indeed, returned to France, where he married and produced a daughter who then married Falconer. Had Elise been Louis' bride? Liz searched the crowded room for Alexander. There must be no confrontation between the two pirates. She had to do something—anything—to keep them apart.

"Louis, could we go somewhere private and talk? There is a great deal you don't know that I must explain," she said breathlessly. Alexander had laced her into a corset so that her waist measured barely nineteen inches and she could hardly breathe.

Behind the scarlet mask sudden hope flared in the emptiness of Louis' dark gaze. "As soon as Alexander returns. Tonight's duel will be our last, I promise you."

Liz's heart began to pound as she caught sight of Alexander. He came through the door, striding purposefully, but Amelia was behind him, tugging at his sleeve with a delicate white hand to detain him. She was speaking to him rapidly behind her fan. He paused, looking down at her to reply to her whispered plea. He had not yet seen Louis, Liz was sure.

"If you start a fight with Alexander here, you'll both be captured," Liz said. She put her glass of punch down on a nearby table, unsure whether a wave of dizziness was the result of the unaccustomed drink. She had eaten as little as possible of the food aboard the *Avenger,* choosing the faintness of hunger to the queasiness caused by the food and constant motion of the ship.

She had noticed too that both past and present were becoming a confused kaleidoscope of detail in her mind. Frequently she would awaken in the night feeling totally lost, as though she were slipping into a void. Only Alexander's comforting arms pulled her back from the brink of some bottomless pit awaiting her.

Louis is going to kill Alexander, she thought now, feeling the old terror surge again as she stared at the table where she had placed her glass. A clock under a glass case was ticking away the minutes toward midnight. Midnight . . . when the masks would be removed . . . when Alexander would die?

"Louis," she said, urgency making her voice shake, "I will go away with you. If you promise not to let Alexander know you are here. Meet me outside in a few minutes. Give me time to leave without arousing his suspicion." She ignored the distant warning that if she left Alexander there may be no way she could return to her own time. For Alexander she was willing to sacrifice everything else.

Louis was on his feet immediately "Very well. Though I know not why you wish me to show mercy to a man who ill-used you. I will have a carriage brought near to the French doors on the terrace so that you will not have to exit through the front door and attract attention to the fact that you are leaving."

"Go now," Liz said urgently, as Alexander started toward them. She felt faint. Closing her eyes for a second, trying to concentrate on what was happening to her, she experienced a feeling of complete disorientation. She could not remember in that split second who she was or where she was.

"Elizabeth!" Alexander's voice. She opened her eyes

and looked up at him. "Are you all right? You look pale. Will you be able to find your way to the carriage, while I go after Louis?"

"No! Don't go after him. Please, Alexander, sit down beside me before you attract attention to yourself. Louis is not going to carry off Amelia. You were right—he came here for Elise, being certain you would not leave her aboard the *Avenger*. Alexander, let me go with him, he won't hurt me. I can't let you die for me." She waved her fan, hoping the movement of the air would dispell her sense of drifting, of dreaming, of nothing being real.

Alexander's hand was warm on hers. "Elizabeth, what is happening to you?" There was fear in his voice. "You are not Louis' cousin. Don't you remember who you are and where you came from?"

She blinked at him. Alexander. Must get him away from here. Away from Louis. Louis will kill him. Dear Alexander. My own true love . . . I will even give you up to save your life. "Go back to your ship, Alexander. I will come to you there." Her voice seemed to be echoing in some hollow cave. She was on her feet, swaying, the room spinning dizzily out of focus.

Alexander swung her up into his arms. "Excuse us,' she heard him say. "The lady feels faint. Make way there, please,"

Then a shrill female voice. "It is Alexander Bartholomew behind the mask. Miles! Seize him—I tell you it is the pirate Bartholomew."

Struggling to the surface of consciousness, Liz opened heavy-lidded eyes as Alexander began to run for the door. The way was barred by several Naval officers. Alexander hesitated, placing Liz down on her feet but keeping his arm around her waist to support her. The dance floor quickly emptied as frightened guests ran for cover.

There was a gasp as one of the officers pitched forward on his face, a dagger protruding from between his shoulder blades. Behind him, rapier in hand, stood Louis de Letraz. A second rapier came flying over their heads and clattered to the floor a few feet away from Alexander. "You are endangering my woman, you cowardly dog," Louis said loudly. "I must, therefore, save you both."

"Try to get to a carriage, Elizabeth . . ." Alexander whispered, shoving her aside as two men sprang toward him with drawn swords.

Dazed, Elizabeth found herself leaning against the wall as Alexander and Louis, side by side, fought off the Naval officers and several guests who had recovered their wits sufficiently to find weapons.

Miles Grindwald was jumping up and down, well away from the clashing swords, screaming, "Shoot them! Shoot them! Fetch pistols," while Amelia was protesting shrilly that the ladies might be hurt.

Despite the peril, several of the ladies were murmuring to one another that the two intruders were dashing rascals and more than a match for their opponents. The two pirates were excellent swordsmen and fought with flamboyant flourishes and energetic grace. They were steadily cutting their way through the officers, who fought desperately to keep them from reaching the front doors.

Louis held his rapier at arm's length, flicking it in small contemptuous circles to deflect the blade of his opponent. Glancing out of the corner of his eye at Alexander, Louis drawled, "This is most tiresome of you, *mon ami*. You know how I hate to soil my clothes with bloodstains." His thin lips flattened over his teeth in what could have been an expression of amusement as he sidestepped gracefully to avoid a lunging sword, then dispatched the wielder of that sword with showy efficiency.

Alexander brought the hilt of his rapier to his lips briefly in mocking salute to Louis' prowess, to the amazement of the two officers dueling with him. Before they recovered their wits, his blade was again forcing them to retreat.

"I see you have been practicing, Louis," Alexander said. "I trust, therefore, you will be able to retain your remaining ear."

Louis gave an elaborate yawn, patting his lips with his elegant fingers, the lace cuffs of his shirt fluttering. His rapier was warding off a second naval officer who sprang to take the place of his fallen comrade. "My scarfaced subordinate believes his immortality is assured because he caught Louis with his guard down and deprived him of an ear. Perhaps when I am finished here I will put my mark on your other cheek to teach you a lesson, you insolent wretch."

As though responding to some unseen choreographer, at that instant both buccaneers leaped forward, right knee bent, and with awe-inspiring precision switched from defensive parries to lethal thrusts. Their opponents, distracted by their nonchalant exchange, fell back under the onslaught of blades that slashed too rapidly to be followed by the eye.

Liz still lingered, watching with fearful admiration, despite Alexander's having told her to leave.

Lady Amelia watched too, her plump breasts rising against her low-cut bodice and her expression a combination of cold fury and erotic arousal. She still seethed that Alexander had rejected her amorous advances and, had he been able to see her expression, he would have recognized the truth in the adage that hell hath no fury like a woman scorned.

Alexander and Louis maneuvered the red-faced officers toward the banquet table and, still moving as one, leaped to the table to gain the advantage of height. Dishes of silver and pewter went clattering to the floor and a flagon of wine sent its blood-red trail winding over pale linen. Amelia turned to follow their progress and in doing so brought Liz into her range of vision.

"Miles—the woman—have the footmen hold the woman who was with the pirates," Amelia screamed.

Liz picked up her skirts and ran, fear giving her strength. Don't think, a small voice hammered inside her head, just run. She was outside, the cool air reviving her. She had run through the terrace doors and Alexander and Louis were now fighting desperately at the archway leading to the front door. As she ran, Liz prayed that Louis had had time to bring the carriage to the driveway outside the French doors leading to the terrace.

She paused at the top of the terrace steps, panting. A carriage and pair of horses were waiting. Liz scrambled into the driver's seat and picked up the reins.

She laid the whip across the horses backs just as the two pirates came down the steps, backing away from the four men still pursuing them, rapiers clashing against Naval swords. Alexander glanced over his shoulder and saw her. "Louis—our carriage awaits us," he said, panting.

The two men leaped into the carriage and she felt the reins taken from her hands. A hail of pistol balls exploded around them.

Louis' arms were around her, pulling her down into the open carriage, as Miles Grindwald ran from the house. She saw the pistol in his hand, watched him take careful aim as she sank into oblivion.

She was in a blurred and misty world of moving shadows and pale flickering images. Drifting, dreaming, floating endlessly toward some distant place she must reach or all would be lost.

They did not appear to hear when she spoke their names. She was outside their conversation. Out of range of everything but the rushing wind and spinning universe.

"You are mad. She is my cousin, Elise. I love her and will marry her. How dare you presume to love her?" That was Louis de Letraz, coldly angry.

"Louis, I cannot explain to you who and what she is. You would not understand. Believe only this, she must be taken to an island in the Pacific. Here, look at your chart. At this latitude and . . ."

"You are finished, whoreson. There is a pistol ball buried in your scurvy flesh. Your ship has sailed without you, and there is a price on your head. Do you believe I will take you back aboard the *Tiger's Claw?* Even if we reached my ship, you would not last the night."

"I shall not die. I will cross the isthmus by land. I can cross that narrow strip of land between the Gulf of Darien and the Pacific ocean while the *Avenger* beats her way around the Horn."

"Strong men have died attempting that journey. There is a steaming jungle, filled with poisonous reptiles and insects, as well as hostile Indians. You are wounded and have lost much blood. You will die."

"Perhaps. If I remain here my death is a certainty. As slow and miserable a death as Grindwald can devise. I am his runaway slave, I possessed his bride, and now I have killed his brother. Louis, I beg of you: take Elizabeth to my Pacific isle."

"I shall take Elise back to France. As my wife. It was always our destiny."

"Apart from the hold full of silver ingots the *Avenger* is presently transporting, I have doubloons and Spanish gold buried on that island. Enough, Louis, to buy back your family's honor and allow you to live a life of pleasant luxury. My only condition for telling you where the treasure is buried is that you promise to take Elizabeth to the island and wait half a year for me to join you. If I live, I shall meet you there and she can choose between us."

"You are a daring rogue, Alexander. I have always respected your courage. I should cut our your heart for presuming my Elise would welcome your attentions. But I believe you did not know she was my betrothed when you kidnapped her. Come, the moon has gone behind a cloud. I will take you to the *Tiger's Claw.* We shall sail to your treasure isle together."

"No, Louis. I know that Tad would not have sailed without me. He will find one of the Brethren to transport the two of us to Darien for the land crossing to the Pacific. The *Avenger* will meet us on one of the atolls in that chain of islands where my isle is situated. My first officer is loyal and has orders to do so. Louis, if you chart a course southward for the Horn also, the Naval squadron will not follow you. They will be informed I am sailing for Darien to attempt a land crossing to the Pacific and they will come after me."

"No doubt your blacksmith will have little difficulty

finding a ship to transport you, providing they do not know a Navy frigate is in pursuit. But how then will you draw them from us?"

"A farewell message to the Lady Amelia. The final insult to all of the injury I have caused Sir Miles."

"Your wound has addled your brain, Alexander. A more foolhardy quest I have never heard. You would do all of this for love of my Elise? I would not have thought you so selfless."

Liz was struggling to be heard, but her lips moved soundlessly. Her arms reached into the vastness of space, dispersing wisps of mist and fleeting shadows, but finding no substance. Everything was rushing away from her, as though sucked into a black hole. Then she was spinning, falling, crying out for her lost love. Alexander. Her last memory was of the pain and desolation of losing him.

The crackle of the radio awakened her. She blinked in the white light of dawn. The air was heavy, oppressive. She moved toward the radio with leaden limbs and it was several seconds before the message became clear.

". . . sending the outrigger. Should be there within the hour."

"No," Liz said. "I don't want to leave. I must stay here."

"Miss Holly, you can't stay there. It's unusual to have storms this time of year, but there's no doubt there's a big one heading your way. We can see it on the satellite pictures coming in."

After the disembodied voice signed off, she went outside. There was no wind yet, but the sea was dark along the horizon and the sky the color of granite behind gathering clouds. White caps were forming and the surf crashed against the reef with increasing frequency.

She sat down on a rock and stared at the sea. Had it all been a dream? Could there be life after death? Alexander was a man so dynamic in life that, if it were possible, his spirit would live on through the centuries.

Did he reach his island? Or did he die of Miles Grindwald's pistol ball during the desperate attempt to rendezvous with her? Louis de Letraz returned to France, was given the island, eventually became respectable . . . marrying and producing an heir. Was it possible that they had all reached the island and Louis had indeed killed Alexander there? She did not think it likely.

Nor was it likely that she . . . or Elise . . . reached the island either. Alexander had kept his rendezvous, not half a year later as he promised, but three centuries later.

Louis would not have killed Alexander while he slept. For all their rivalry, they had been friends of a sort. It was more probable that Alexander had died in his sleep of the mortal wound made by Grindwald's pistol ball as they were fleeing from the plantation.

The sails of the outrigger were on the horizon. She stood up and called his name, "Alexander . . . please . . . come back." She ran along the beach, calling into the rising wind. But only the sound of the lonely sea, dashing in fury against the land, answered her.

He was gone forever, she knew it for a certainty. How could it have been otherwise for a mortal woman and a ghost?

Chapter 18

Honolulu airport was jammed with tourists, blinking as they stepped into brilliant sunshine and the sensual caress of the trade winds; grinning in delighted embarrassment as dusky beauties draped flowered leis around pale mainland necks and planted kisses on gray *haole* cheeks.

Liz made her way through a covey of tour directors in bright Hawaiian shirts busy herding their charges into waiting buses. She took a taxi directly to the travel agency in Waikiki Beach.

"I want to reserve the next free period on Falconer's Island. As soon as possible."

"It's booked for the rest of the season," the travel agent said. "And Mr. Falconer hasn't given me the go-ahead to make reservations for next season."

"Then I have to meet Mr. Falconer. It's very important."

The agent was putting together tour packages and didn't look up. "I can answer any questions you might have, but I can't give you another reservation."

"I want to meet Mr. Falconer."

"He doesn't see anyone. I told you—he's a recluse."

"How old is he? What does he look like?" She thought: this is ridiculous. You know he isn't Alexander—Alexander is a ghost. How does one conjure up a ghost? But Falconer owns the island . . . isn't there just a chance?

"Let me speak with Falconer on the phone then. I promise I won't do anything but thank him for letting me stay on his island." What do I hope to accomplish, she wondered. If I hear his voice . . . I'd know that voice anywhere.

"I told you—no. I'm sorry."

Liz took a hotel room, developed the pictures of the island and presented herself to the travel agent again the following day, spreading the prints on his counter.

"Very nice."

"Far better than any you have in your brochures on the island."

"Agreed. But you still can't meet Mr. Falconer."

"I'm getting desperate. Desperate enough to resort to desperate measures."

He looked up warily. A middle-aged couple were going through travel folders on the counter and a younger couple were studying posters on the wall. "I hope you aren't going to make a scene. It isn't my fault that Mr. Falconer is a hermit."

"I'm going to find someone to take me back to the island. Without a reservation or a booking or anything. I just came to tell you."

"That would be foolish. The storm veered away, but

it hasn't dissipated. I don't want your death on my hands."

"Then just tell me where Mr. Falconer lives. I promise I won't tell him you told me. And if he refuses to see me, I'll give up. But at least let me try."

The travel agent sighed and gave in.

Falconer lived on the big island and Liz was on a plane that afternoon for the short flight from Oahu to Hawaii.

She had a two hour drive from the airport to the sugar plantation where he lived, across volcanic fields and then through mile after mile of sugar cane. The house was a sprawling ranch-style structure surrounded by masses of flowering trees. A burly Hawaiian responded to the chimes of the doorbell.

Liz smiled brightly. "I'm Liz Holly. Mr. Falconer is expecting me." If he's Alexander he's expecting me . . .

The Hawaiian looked puzzled. "Mr. Falconer doesn't see people."

"If you would just tell him I'm here?"

He hesitated.

"Please, it's very important."

He motioned for her to step into a flower-filled room and then disappeared through a bamboo screen.

Liz waited nervously. She had not called Falconer, deciding a bold approach was best. What exactly am I hoping for, she wondered. That Falconer is somehow Alexander? But Falconer is a descendant of the Falconer who married Louis de Letraz' daughter . . . if indeed this particular Falconer was even part of that line, which was doubtful. Then what?

The Hawaiian returned, a small smile on his lips. "Mr. Falconer says he'll see you if you're pretty. I told him you were. But you can stay only five minutes, otherwise you'll tire him."

"He's been ill?" Liz asked. But the man was already moving through the bamboo screen. She followed to a long veranda running the length of the rear of the house. Filtered sunlight came through open slats in the roof and yellow and white ginger trees moving in the trade winds sent changing patterns of light over the wood decking of the floor. Several rattan chairs were scattered about and, at the far end of the veranda, a chaise longue.

At first Liz thought there was only a plaid blanket on the chaise, but then she saw it covered a still figure. A very old and frail-looking gentleman, with wisps of white hair and faded eyes, who bore absolutely no resemblance to Alexander. Her heart sank.

"Thank you for seeing me, Mr. Falconer." She drew one of the chairs near to him and sat down.

He gave her a tired smile. "They won't let me have any visitors nowadays. I'm glad you came."

"I stayed on your island. It was beautiful. I wanted to thank you."

His eyes brightened. "A paradise . . . some day I will go there again myself."

"Have you spent much time there?"

"Not for many years. I did when I was a young man. They say it's too primitive for me now. Too far from their doctors and fancy machines that keep me alive . . . but I'll fool them and go back to my island some day."

"Did you ever see . . . anyone else on the island?"

"Tell me, why did a pretty young thing like you want to spend her vacation all alone?" he asked, seemingly oblivious to her question.

"An unhappy love affair," she answered frankly.

He nodded sagely. "And what . . . or who, did you believe you saw on my island?"

She was momentarily taken aback. Everyone is an amateur psychologist, she thought. "Did you ever see anything?"

He shook his head. "And you didn't either. Some man let you down and you were seeking an escape from the pain he caused you. You sought it in a dream, perhaps you transformed the man who hurt you, perhaps you sought another man who could love you. When you are lonely and isolated it is not unusual to experience your wishes as realities, the way certain dreams seem more real than waking . . ."

"The travel agent said the island was booked for this season and you weren't taking reservations for next season. Please . . . I have to go back."

"It would be better for you to go home and begin living in the real world again."

"Won't you at least allow me to make a reservation for the first opening?"

"I'm sorry. It's out of my hands. The French government is re-claiming many of the islands in the Tahitian group—the ones that are privately owned. There are plans to open Falconer's Isle for tourism. But you'll have to wait until they put in the proper facilities."

She stared out at the heartbreakingly beautiful flower gardens, her soul in her eyes, and after a moment he relented and said, "If you can find someone willing to allow you to go there during their reserved time, or if there is a cancellation, I promise the island is yours. I'll have my man phone the travel agent."

Impulsively, she picked up the limp and wrinkled fingers lying on the arm of the chaise. She squeezed gently. "Thank you. You don't know what this means to me. But I'm so sorry you're losing your island."

The faded old eyes were watering slightly. "I shan't live to see it pass out of my hands . . . and who knows, perhaps I will go there before I die." He paused, then reached out to pat her cheek. His touch was as dry and lifeless as an autumn leaf, blown on the wind. "There'll be another young man. A real one. One who won't hurt you. But you won't find him if you go looking for a dream."

His Hawaiian servant returned. "I'm sorry, Miss Holly, but Mr. Falconer must rest now. If you'll come with me, the cook has refreshments for you before you drive back."

Liz was already planning her return to Falconer's Island as she sat in a plant-filled kitchen sipping passionfruit juice and eating tiny coconut-iced cakes. The Hawaiian served her, then sat down at the table with her.

She smiled at him happily. "Mr. Falconer is going to let me go back to his island."

"Nobody is going to Mr. Falconer's island," the Hawaiian said. "Not no more."

"What do you mean? "

"The island blowed away. We got word this morning that there's nothing left of any of the small islands in that region. The storm has wiped out all the vegetation . . . high tides hit the beaches and all the sand is gone . . . there's nothing left but bare volcanic rocks and the radio message was that some of those are submerged now. I didn't tell the old man, it would break his heart. He's kept going because he thought one day he'd go back to his island."

Liz did not remember leaving the house. She was driving the rented car back to the airport along a deserted road, still dazed from the realization that there was now no way she could ever find Alexander again.

Trying to believe the whole thing had been a dream did not help. Nor did telling herself she was acting like a fool. Only the knowledge that there was nothing else she could do brought a measure of resignation. The old man was right, life did have to go on. She would have her work. Her friends. The world was full of promise for those with the courage to challenge it.

Everything old Mr. Falconer had said was logical. More than that, it was reinforced by the fact that the filming of *The Black Pirate* had brought about her trip to the island in the first place. With pirates on her mind, she had merely had a desperate fantasy about a pirate. *A dream. Say it to yourself every day, Liz, until you believe it.*

Believing it, why then, did her soul cry out for Alexander? Why was she so certain that she knew him and that he was a real man?

Chapter 19

Maggie was waiting for her at the airport when she arrived back in Los Angeles. A newly svelte Maggie, the result of two weeks at a famous spa. Along with her new figure there was a new expression in her eyes, an uneasiness.

"You look like a new woman!" They both said at once, then laughed and hugged each other.

"You're OK now?" Maggie said as they made their way to the luggage carousel.

Liz looked at her curiously. "I'm fine, Maggie. You ask that as though I've been ill. Why?"

Maggie did not return her stare. "You were upset when you left. Liz. And . . . Nick came to see me."

"Ah," Liz said. "I see. It *was* you who told him where I was."

"I was worried about you, all alone on that island.

You were stretched tight as a bowstring, ready to break."

Liz studied the suitcases coming slowly into view, not speaking, feeling angry that Maggie had betrayed a confidence.

"Nick was worried about you. He came to see me again after he visited the island." Maggie volunteered.

"But he wasn't worried enough to be here to meet me."

"He had to leave for a few days. He asked me to tell you."

"It doesn't matter. Nick and I are through anyway."

"Are you up to running the studio without him? I got the impression from him that you were ill."

"I'm not ill," Liz said irritably. "I've just come to my senses about Nick, but he's so damn conceited he thinks I must be out of my mind because I'm no longer interested in him."

"He said you were . . . acting strangely—on the island."

"I didn't expect to see him there, that's all. I wish you hadn't told him where I was."

They made strained small talk while Maggie drove her to her apartment.

"How about coming out for dinner? Or I'll fix you something while you unpack. I bought you a few staples," Maggie suggested.

"No, thanks. I just want to crash. I'm beat."

"OK. Call me when you feel like company."

Liz did not call her. She did not call anyone. She had no interest in going back to work. The photonovel had been abandoned. Alexander haunted her waking and her sleeping hours. She saw him everywhere.

The following weekend, after calling first to be sure

Nick was not there, Liz went to his apartment to remove all of her belongings. He had left the usual clutter. Including a pair of crotchless panties and a pink jar of something called Love Cream that certainly did not belong to Liz. The panties were generously sized, indicating that the lady who lost them was wide in the hips.

Liz moved aside a lipstick smeared champagne glass in order to clear a space on the coffee table to write a note to Nick. She scribbled that she had picked up her things and that the key was on the dresser. He was welcome to pick up whatever he needed from the studio and perhaps later they could get together and decide on the custody of items purchased with joint funds—the Hasselblad, the processor.

She took the note and her key into his bedroom, avoided looking at the devastated bed and tried to close her nostrils against the stale and overpowering odor of chemical-based perfume. Propping the note against the dresser mirror, she felt only distaste. Nick no longer had the power to make her miserable.

At least, she told herself wryly, her dream love had opened her eyes to all of Nick's frailties. A turning-point in your life, Liz. No more Nick. But the end of the affair was not causing this deep-down desolation. That was caused by the hopelessness of her love for a dead man. You're really cracking up, Liz . . . yes, Doctor, I'm aware of my problem. I'm in love with a dead man . . .

She was about to leave Nick's apartment when the phone rang. Looking at the phone, she felt a moment's curiosity. A woman? The one who wore crotchless panties?

Picking up the receiver she was vaguely disappointed

when Elliot's voice came over the wire. "Nick? Where are my pictures? I've got a deadline to meet. Nick, are you there?"

"No, he isn't. I'll leave a message," Liz said.

"Liz? Is that you? When did you get back? Does Adam know you're back?"

"Adam? You mean Nick?"

"I mean Adam. He's been driving me and everyone else crazy, trying to find out where you'd gone. When Nick took off suddenly we figured he'd gone after you, but then he came back alone."

"Eliott, Nick and I are through. I'm just picking up my things. I'm going away as soon as I've talked to Nick about dissolving our partnership in the studio."

"Liz, it's none of my business, but shouldn't you see a lawyer first?"

"We just rent the studio. If it comes to a hassle with Nick, I'll just let him have all the equipment. I've got an old Nikon that was mine back in college, it got me started once, it can again."

There was a pause. "Liz . . . it may not be quite that easy to walk away from."

"What do you mean?"

"Nick borrowed heavily to invest in *The Black Pirate*. He used your joint enterprise as collateral."

"You mean I'm responsible for the debts too?"

"It wouldn't hurt to see a lawyer to find out. The film is in big trouble. It's running over schedule and the costs have been astronomical. They should have gone on location, but they haven't been able to wrap up the scenes here. A couple of extras were hurt when the deck of the ship—a mock-up, of course, collapsed. Everyone connected with it is jumpy as hell. To top it all off, Barry and Adam are feuding again and Adam quit."

"Elliot, this really doesn't concern me. What did you want me to tell Nick—I'll leave him a note."

"That's OK. I'll call back."

Until the moment she announced she was leaving, Liz had not given any serious thought to her future plans. A vague idea came to her now. Return to Falconer's Island was impossible, but what about the Caribbean? If she could see Port Royal, Jamaica, perhaps the dream of Alexander would fade. She would see the places she had seen with him and they would bear little resemblance to her memory.

Her spirits lifted as she drove back to her own apartment. A trip to the Caribbean. That was the answer. Something to work and plan for . . . but first she would have to go back to work. There was the loan to Maggie to be repaid, to say nothing of what Nick had borrowed to invest in the film.

She forced herself to think about present problems and plans, blotting out the vision of Alexander's clear-eyed gaze, the way the muscles of his back rippled when he swung an axe, his way of smiling slowly, as though discovering something wonderful for the first time.

The following morning she was finishing breakfast when Nick's key turned in the front door. He had a strained look about his dark eyes and there was no teasing banter in his voice when he greeted her. "We've got to talk, Liz. I got your note. You can't just walk out on me. There's a lot more involved than our personal relationship, babe."

"Don't worry, I'm not going to get into a community property hassle with you. The studio is yours. You can have all the equipment. I'll sign it all over to you. Since we're only renting the studio, you can just close it down if you wish. You never did like the idea of being tied down. That way you can take off at a moment's notice."

He looked properly chastened. "Don't let it end like this, Liz. We've been too much to each other. Gwynna meant nothing to me . . ."

"Gwynna doesn't matter any more. Nor any of the others. I'm sorry. I just stopped loving you. What you do, where you go . . . I wish you well, but quite honestly, I just don't care."

A small muscle twitched in his jaw. "I was hoping you'd run the studio for a while. I won't bother you—I've been tied up with the movie. And . . ." he hesitated, giving her a desperately engaging grin, "I could use a little financial assistance from your drooling Basset hounds and chubby babies."

"Oddly enough, I'm the one with the gypsy feet now. I don't want to run the studio. I'm going traveling."

He sat down on the edge of her bed, fingering a silk blouse she had bought, impulsively, in Hawaii. "Nice. This new? I like the dress you're wearing too. What happened to you, Liz? You're different. The way you look—everything about you."

"I came to my senses, that's all."

"Would you do me one last favor—for old time's sake?"

"What is it?"

"Talk to Adam Eastman."

"What? Oh, Nick . . ."

"Just try to persuade him to come back and do the stunts—and the dueling scenes. Babe, we won't bring in the movie without him. He and Barry Gerrard never liked each other, but the fact is, the longshots of Adam doubling Barry are the best scenes. There was an uneasy truce between them and everything was going fine until Gwynna decided to stir the pot by going after

Adam. She knew that would make Barry mad. It's been an on-again, off-again thing with Gwynna and Barry for years."

"Gwynna," Liz sighed. "She really has no equal as a predator, does she? You and Barry and Adam. What makes you think I can persuade Adam to come back when everyone else has obviously failed?"

"He was really smitten with you, babe. He made no secret of the fact. I think maybe that's what irked me . . . why I went home with Gwynna that day. She and I were both trying to get even with you and Adam." His jaw hardened, remembering. "You always were a little fool when it came to sex. Why can't you see it has nothing to do with love?"

Liz looked at him evenly. "It has everything to do with love, Nick. If you don't understand the relationship between love and sex you're missing more in life than I imagined."

"Well, sure—sex with you was different, because I love you. We shared everything, didn't we? Admit it, Liz. Babe, I'm counting on you, I really need your help. Just talk to Adam."

"Nick, this whole *Black Pirate* investment was your idea. I'd really rather not have anything to do with it."

His teeth came down over his lower lip. He reached tentatively for her hand, but she jerked it away.

"Liz, babe . . . the papers I signed to get the loan . . . the money I invested . . . We were a partnership and the bank wants us both."

"Damn it, Nick, you had no right to do that." She slammed her breakfast dishes into the sink, eyes blazing.

"If you would just keep the studio going until the movie is finished. And if you could just persuade Adam to come back . . ."

"Get another stuntman," she snapped. She would have to keep the studio going, of course. Her own good name was at stake if the loan were not repaid.

"We could try, but Barry is hard to double in the dueling scenes. And we need Adam in Hawaii—for climbing the rigging and . . . Hell, Liz, we *need* him."

"But even if you get Adam back, won't Gwynna be a problem again?"

"Well, it wasn't just Gwynna. You see, the director decided Barry and Adam didn't look right for the part. He had them both shave off their moustaches. Then he wanted longer hair. He tried having them wear wigs, but Adam kept losing his in the action scenes. I don't think he liked wearing it and didn't try to keep it on. Anyway, he grew his hair longer for the part and, I don't know, it was strange, without the moustache and with the longer hair, dressed in costume, there was something about him. A magic—I guess what they call star quality. He was outshining the star, there was no doubt of it every day when we looked at the rushes. The director felt it, Gwynna felt it. Barry felt it and resented it. He began to deliberately pick fights with Adam, and tried to humiliate him. I got Barry to agree to cut out the funny stuff if Adam will come back, and Liz, Adam *will* come back if you ask him."

"You seem positive enough to make me suspect you've made a deal of some sort," Liz said.

"I talked to Adam yesterday. Fortunately he hasn't cut his hair yet. He said if you stood to lose the studio because of him, then he'd come back. But he wanted to hear it from you."

Her breath was expelled in exasperated resignation. "If he goes back, will the movie be completed and can we pay off the loan?"

"I know it, babe." Nick's eyes gleamed with victory,

but Liz didn't care. Once the debt was paid, she would be free of Nick Kane forever.

"All right. Tomorrow I'll re-open the studio, start calling on agencies again. And I'll talk to Adam Eastman."

She called Elliot, who told her Adam Eastman lived with his foster father in a ramshackle house on the beach that threatened to collapse under the onslaught of every high tide. Old Gene Eastman had bought the property back in the old days, long before the Coastal Commission and restrictions on beach building came into effect. After his accident, all of the steps and stairs had been converted to ramps for his wheelchair.

Liz had no trouble finding the house. Apart from the ramp leading to a sagging deck, it was the only unpretentious structure on the stretch of beach long ago taken over by people who were able to afford extensive remodeling of the modest houses that formerly occupied the area. What caught her eye first, however, was the skeleton of the boat rising from behind a screen of oleanders in the back yard.

The hull was finished and had been lovingly layered with enough coats of varnish to give a silken patina that glowed warmly in the sunlight. Closer examination revealed that the "skeleton" effect of unfinished spars and masts and varying lengths of rough planks lying on deck appeared a deliberate attempt to call attention to the fact that the boat was unfinished. Liz remembered that Elliot had told her Adam had been working on his boat for years, but would neither finish it nor sail it on his dream voyage because he would not leave Gene behind.

A second boat, a small catamaran, lay on the beach in front of the house. There was no sign of Adam.

The front door was on the ocean side of the house. Liz rang the bell and waited. She heard the sound of a wheelchair coming toward her and saw the silhouette of the man propelling it. The sunlight was bright on the sand behind her and the hallway was dim. She could not see his face, but saw that he was a man of enormous stature, from the width of his shoulders and the size of his head. His long arms seemed muscular and the chair approached rapidly.

Then his face was in the sunlight and Liz stared, a pulse beginning to throb in her temple. Bright red hair was touched by silver, but the face was cherubic and the eyes serene. He did not wear a beard, but there was no mistaking that baby-face and those huge hands. She was looking at the living image of Tad Bowen, Alexander's faithful friend and fellow pirate.

Chapter 20

Gene Eastman smiled at her, his eyes lighting up appreciatively. "A pretty girl is always a welcome visitor . . . but I've a hunch you are a very special visitor, indeed. Adam described a lady photographer who made a great impression on him. Yup, a mass of tawny hair, eyes that glow with a soft violet light. Sort of half-shy half-cheeky smile. You can only be Miss Liz Holly."

Liz stood frozen, staring at him. She had never heard Tad Bowen utter a word, but the physical likeness was uncanny.

Gene misunderstood her thunderstruck expression. He chuckled. "I guess it's hard to believe Adam and me is related. Because we ain't—not by blood. He's my adopted son. He'll be back soon. Please come in and wait. He'll have my hide if I let you get away. I mean, that is, if I guessed right and you *are* Liz Holly?"

"Yes, I am. I'm sorry, I didn't mean to stare . . . it's just that you look so much like someone I once knew."

"God help the poor soul," Gene said with another chuckle, "I hope he's got more brains than me."

Liz followed him into a neat, simply furnished room that had a clean, scrubbed look to it. The hardwood floor was waxed to a mellow golden shine and a picture window framed an uncluttered view of beach and sky.

"We hoped you'd call," Gene said. "Adam didn't dare expect you'd come in person."

"You were expecting me?" Liz asked, surprised.

Gene plumped the cushions on a chair for her and she sat down. "Well, we hoped. Nick was here. Told Adam about your photography studio being in hock because you invested in *The Black Pirate.*"

Liz tried to hide a grimace.

"Never cared much for Nick Kane," Gene went on. "He and Adam and Elliot were friends in school and they kept in touch over the years, but we haven't seen much of him for the last couple of years. Reckon I know why, now."

"I don't understand." Liz blinked, seeing Tad Bowen's brawny arms swing his giant's body up the shrouds of the *Avenger*. There was a smaller window in the rear wall of the room through which the masts of Adam's unfinished boat were visible.

"Shoot," Gene said. "Me and my big mouth. I meant because of you. You bowled 'em both over."

"But I only met your son, briefly, on two occasions, in connection with *The Black Pirate*. He doesn't really know me."

"That's all it took," Gene said with a grin. "Kismet, I reckon."

"I think perhaps you misunderstood what Adam told you."

"I'll make you a cup of tea," Gene said. He plugged in an electric kettle on a small cabinet that appeared to contain everything he might need within easy reach. The cabinet had the same gleaming patina of the hull of the boat and was obviously also Adam's carpentry. Glancing around, Liz saw the doorways had been widened, and everything was placed at a height suitable for a man in a wheelchair. Gene did not appear to have heard her comment.

His big hands busied themselves with teapot and cups while he chatted as though they were old friends. He told her of his early days in the circus and how Adam's parents had been high-wire artists who died together in a fall when Adam was a baby. "I think he gets his grace from them. You notice how graceful he is, Elizabeth, I mean for a big man? Weren't nobody else to take care of him, so I took him into my trailer with me. Spunky little kid. Deep, too. A real deep thinker. Now I won't fool you, he's no angel. I mean, he's a man and he's never taken a wife. When he does, it will be forever. I know him. There'll be none of that merry-go-round of marriage and divorce for Adam. I used to worry, when he became a Hollywood stuntman. But he saw it all for what it was. Make-believe. Shoot, I knew that Gwynna Duvalle would never get her claws in my Adam. He'd never be husband number eight. Elizabeth, I'm glad you and Adam—" he broke off, giving her a sheepish grin. "Reckon I'm talking out of turn, huh?"

Liz felt embarrassed. "I think perhaps you've misunderstood why I came here. I came to ask Adam to do the stunts for *The Black Pirate.*"

Gene looked comically woebegone. "Oh . . . I hoped, well . . ."

Liz moved quickly to cover his dismay. "I understand Adam's dream is to sail around the world one day."

"Yup. That's his dream all right. Only I don't reckon he's ever going to finish building that damn ketch. Oh, he thinks he's fooling me, but he ain't. He won't finish because he thinks I can't get along without him if he leaves."

He rolled across the floor to her, balancing a china cup and saucer on the palm of one hand; sugar, milk and sliced lemon on the other.

Liz took the cup and the milk pitcher, thanked him and added, "Then why don't you go with him?"

A slow smile spread across Gene's features. "Elizabeth, I knew I was going to like you. Minute I set eyes on you."

Over the sound of the surf advancing on the beach they heard a man's voice, singing an old sea tune, the refrain growing louder as he approached. Liz's heart pounded in time with the footsteps leaping up the ramp, coming along the wooden deck, through the front door . . .

He stopped abruptly, a delighted smile lighting up his steel gray eyes. His hair, grown long for the film, hung thickly about his shoulders. Hair so black there was no hint of brown or blue. His eyebrows were heavy, dark. Skin swarthy from the sun and a cleft appeared in his cheek as he smiled a slow, wondering smile.

Why hadn't she realized before? Why hadn't she seen the resemblance? Because, Liz, she told herself in shocked recognition, *you never really looked at him before.*

She was half out of her chair, her eyes wide, held by a mesmerizing gaze that made her blood pound in her ears. The only thing missing was the jagged scar on his cheek. She almost cried aloud the name that sprang to her lips, "*Alexander!*"

Adam crossed the room and took her hand. His touch was warm, fingers strong, blunt; his palms broad and callused. "Elizabeth Holly," he said, with vibrant wonder in every syllable. "You came."

Adam had been fishing. He had red snapper and yellowtail. Liz was invited to dinner and she surprised both Adam and Gene by offering to clean and cook the fish. She laughed at Adam's look of amazed disbelief. "I promise I won't mangle your fish. After all, it's only fair. You caught it, I'll cook it."

Gene said, "You told me she was a rare one, Adam. Not one of those libbers."

Liz continued to smile but she replied quietly, "Don't let my fish-cleaning abilities fool you, Gene. I'm a modern woman in every respect."

Gene produced wine and crusty bread, while Adam put together a salad. Once, during the meal, he stopped eating and looked at Liz and said softly, "If I wake up and find this is all a dream—" and Liz's heart was too full of wonder to reply.

Later, when the two of them walked along the deserted beach, watching the moon sail in lonely splendor across the dark sky, Liz told him, "Adam, I have to be honest and tell you that I came to ask you to finish *The Black Pirate*. Nick and I stand to lose everything we own if the picture isn't completed and released."

"I'll be back on the set tomorrow," Adam promised. "But tell me something. I sense a shift in your attitude toward me. As though now you would be willing to get to know me. When I came home today you looked at me as though really seeing me for the first time. Come to think of it, I guess you were, since the last times we met I was costumed and your eyes were filled with tears

Nick Kane put there. No—don't talk about him now. You know, a couple of times during dinner I had the strangest sensation . . . like what we were doing, we'd done before. I suppose it was because I've wanted to see you again so much, I imagined how it might be. Liz—I don't know exactly what I'm trying to say."

She turned toward him. In the moonlight it was easy to imagine a scar like a lightning bolt on his cheek. His voice sounded different only because he used modern language, the timbre and almost musical cadence were still there, now her ears were attuned to hear it. The same noble head upon broad shoulders, the proud bearing, the aura of invincibility that blazed from the spirit of Alexander, was present also in the mortal body of the man at her side.

But he isn't Alexander, a small voice warned, he's Adam. Even if he is a reincarnation of Alexander, he has no knowledge of what went on before.

Adam said, "You've been on my mind constantly from the first moment I saw you. I thought I'd go crazy, wanting to see you again and not knowing where you were. I kept thinking about how you looked that day of the sail ripping stunt. You were standing by the window and the sun turned your hair into a golden halo. When you turned around there were violet shadows in your eyes and I thought I'd never seen sadder—nor more beautiful—eyes. But you looked right through me as if I weren't there. I wanted to rip off that fool mask I was wearing for the movie and yell at you, Hey Look At Me—I'm Adam and I think I just fell in love at first sight."

Liz smiled. "I had a lot on my mind that day. Besides, I outgrew masked men when I stopped reading Captain Marvel."

"You're too young to remember Captain Marvel,"

Adam said. They stopped to sit on some rocks and he leaned forward, watching her, his eyes caressing each vulnerable plane and hollow of her face sculpted by the moonlight.

"I didn't see past your mask and moustache that day," she admitted.

"You disappeared behind your camera, too. I would have come down that sail in slow motion if I could have got you to move the camera away from your face and see me as a man instead of a stunt. But you were so aloof, untouchable. The next times I saw you, Nick was with you and you looked like your heart was breaking. I was beginning to despair that you'd ever meet the real Adam Eastman."

"I've met you now. And I'd like to get to know you."

"If you're still involved with Nick—" he began.

"I'm not. It's over."

She felt his sigh of relief as he took her hand and they started to walk again. "And you, Adam, I have the right to know about Gwynna Duvalle. I warned you—I'm a modern woman and I don't believe in different rules for men and women."

He squeezed her fingers. "Gwynna hasn't entered my mind from the moment I met you, Liz. And before that, our relationship was somewhat one-sided. She used me to make Barry Gerrard jealous. It's a favorite trick of hers."

"Would you do me one favor?"

"Anything."

"Call me Elizabeth."

He stopped, whirled her around and into his arms, hugging her with fierce exuberance, but not attempting to kiss her. "Of course. Elizabeth. Now, about tomorrow . . . Elizabeth, tomorrow! And tomorrow after that—all of a sudden, there are tomorrows!"

Chapter 21

Adam was unprepared for the magnitude of his feelings for Liz. At first the old question posed itself. Was he so taken with her because she was involved with Nick? The old rivalry? They had both always fallen for gutsy women with fragile beauty and sharp intelligence, but whereas Nick immediately set about cutting such a woman down to size, Adam gently probed to find a certain indefinable quality that had always eluded his searching. Until Liz.

He was not sure what the missing factor had been before, or even what it was now. He knew simply that it was present in Liz. In meditative moments he wondered if it were a melding of old souls who had come together before. There were times when they were together that one would answer the other's question before it was asked. Or both would begin to express the same thought simultaneously.

Very late one night as they walked along the beach, a freighter silhouetted against the still horizon called a mournful farewell to the land as she glided out into the vast silence of the sea.

Adam said softly, ". . . *sandalwood, cedarwood and sweet white wine. Stately Spanish galleon, coming from the Isthmus. Dipping through the topics by the palm-green shore . . .*"

Liz caught her breath. He felt her hand tremble in his and, just as he knew she would, she finished ". . . *with a cargo of diamonds, Emeralds, amethysts. Topazes and cinnamon and gold moidores.*"

They were silent for a moment, aware of each other, of the sea, perhaps of destiny itself. Then he took her in his arms and in their embrace there was the quiet wonder of finding each other among the millions on earth. He hesitated on the brink of telling her of his most secret yearning—then quickly decided that if there were to be a choice, he would choose her—but for the moment he did not want to approach that particular dilemma for fear of spoiling the magic of his discovery of the woman with whom he wanted to spend the rest of his life. So he held her in his arms and closed his eyes to shut out the sight of that beckoning temptress, the sea.

It seemed to him that at night when a great stillness fell upon the sea he could almost recall lost memories of another time. He could not explain the affinity he felt for the ocean, or the ships slipping their moorings to go out to conquer her. Yet he knew that, for him, the answer to his yearning was not aboard one of those vessels. He had to go with the wind. It was a command from deep in his soul that could not be denied, merely postponed. Somewhere out there, with the wind in the sails and the heaving deck beneath his feet he would find, perhaps, the unsolvable answer to life itself. But was there a woman . . . even Elizabeth . . . who could understand such a need?

Slowly he began to run his hands over her back, smoothing her hair, gliding his fingertips over her shoulders to the tips of her breasts. Her nipples became hard under her light blouse and he wanted her so much that holding back made him tremble.

She felt his sudden shivering. "Oh, Adam," she breathed, "I've never felt this way about any man before." She nestled into him, rubbing her cheeks against his chest wanting to absorb all of his warmth into her.

His mouth moved gently over hers, down her neck and shoulders and then he buried his face in her breasts. She moaned softly and he helped her lie back against the sand. Now his hand grazed her stomach and trailed downward. Suddenly she stiffened.

"What's wrong?" he whispered.

"Oh, nothing, no, don't stop—" her words begged him to go on but the strain in her voice prevented him. He saw that her face was awash with confusion and pain.

"Oh Elizabeth, my sweet Elizabeth," he rocked her. "That animal has made you so afraid. Don't worry, it's not going to be like that, I'm never, never going to hurt you." And he held her against him until her fears abated and her body softened.

"Forgive me, Adam," she said. "I didn't realize how upset I was. . . ."

"It's just going to take time," he answered. "And we've got all the time in the world."

Because he asked her to, Liz visited the set of *The Black Pirate*. She felt the tension immediately.

Everyone seemed to be arguing with everyone else.

Gwynna refused to come out of her dressing room and refused to let anyone in, including her brother Colby, who usually was the only one allowed near her when she was having a tantrum. Colby was red-eyed and red-nosed from a cold and wandered around like a lost soul, blowing his nose so hard that his thin body shuddered.

He scurried about making a great show of keeping track of costumes, props and a collection of antique weapons rented for the film, along with the replica of the galleon that had housed them.

Colby complained peevishly about wastefulness and the cost of renting costumes for extras who stood about all day waiting for shooting that never took place. He wailed that the director was striving for authenticity at unnecessary expense; that cardboard cutlasses and plastic pistols could be made to look as realistic as the genuine article.

Since Adam had to go and change into his costume, Liz found a shadowed corner in which to wait, trying to make herself as inconspicuous as possible. She was most curious to see Adam in action. Several times she had almost addressed him as "Alexander," and she wondered if his appearance in costume would heighten that illusion.

There were times when Adam spoke to her that she was startled at his use of modern phrases; she worried and wondered if she loved him for himself, or because he was so heart-wrenchingly like her dream of Alexander.

Yet as the days passed by and she saw him in his own environment, she began to realize that although Adam and Alexander shared a physical likeness and the same fearless boldness in facing all of life's challenges, there were deeply rooted differences between the mortal man and her memory of the ghost. Adam constantly surprised her—he was even more caring, more loving than she dared hope. He accepted her as she was, no differently than he accepted himself. He was simply and fully a man, and made her feel his equal in every way.

She searched the set for him and was glad to see him approaching through a knot of scriptwriters.

The script had evidently been revised so many times, no one was sure exactly what was current. The previous director had been fired and replaced. Barry Gerrard had not yet arrived.

Nick was deep in conversation with the camera crew, but his eyes narrowed when he saw who Adam was talking to. Nick sauntered over to them. "Liz, Adam." His voice expressed anger, despite the fixed smile. "What's this? She was just supposed to convince you to come back to work to protect her vested interest. You wouldn't be moving in on my territory, would you, old buddy?"

"Elizabeth tells me all ties are broken," Adam said evenly. "And even if they weren't, a woman isn't anyone's territory . . . old buddy." Adam turned to the director. "If you're ready for some dueling, let's break out the rapiers."

Nick shrugged with exaggerated indifference and answered for the director. "The other stuntman isn't here yet. I'll let you know when we're ready for you." He gave Liz an eloquent glance before moving away. Adam's hand tightened on her arm.

She turned to him, smiling. "It's all right! Don't let him get to you. Once the film is finished I'll be free from him forever."

They sat down to wait and Liz studied the set, which was supposed to represent a pirate stronghold and bore surprising resemblance to enclaves Liz had seen while with Alexander.

Gwynna's dressing room door opened and she peered near-sightedly around the set. "Someone said Adam is back. Darlings, is Adam back?" When someone answered in the affirmative, she floated toward them, surrounded by swirls of white silk. Her eyes showed pinpoints black disapproval when she saw Liz. "Adam, darling," Gwynna gushed. She bent to kiss him, but he turned his face away, stood up and took her hand instead. "Hello, Gwynna, you remember Elizabeth Holly?"

"Darling, the set is closed. We've had so much trouble with spectators, we've simply had to ban everyone."

"Elizabeth and I will leave as soon as I've done the duel."

"But I thought Barry said he was going to do the dueling today. Colby . . . where is Colby? Colby, darling, didn't you tell me it was all arranged for Barry to duel today?"

Colby sneezed into his handkerchief and fixed her with a bleary eye. "They've switched scenes again. In this scene the pirate has to jump from that balcony. Barry can't jump that far."

"Barry can do anything Eastman can do." Barry's voice cut across the set, high and angry. "But the director and producer would faint if I attempted it. Insurance underwriters, Gwynna, necessitate the presence of our stalwart stuntman; not my inadequacies." He strode toward them, an impossibly immaculate pirate, considering he was supposed to be escaping from a filthy jail cell.

Sans moustache and with longer hair, Barry Gerrard should also have looked like Alexander, Liz thought.

But he didn't. Whereas the loss of moustache on Adam revealed ruggedly masculine features, with a high forehead, firm chin and expressive eyes, in Barry Gerrard's case the moustache had been a focal point for a face that was too handsome to be interesting.

Barry's rather cold blue eyes flickered from Adam to Gwynna and then to Liz. He nodded briefly in her direction, with an expression that said he was trying to remember who she was.

Adam was saying, "Good. If Barry is going to duel, you won't need me. Elizabeth and I are going sailing."

Barry turned angrily to Colby. "Why did you tell Gwynna I was going to do the dueling scene? When I asked, you said the underwriters wouldn't go for it."

Colby sniffed daintily into his handkerchief and waved a beringed hand as though trying to brush away a repulsive insect. "I probably didn't make myself clear. I haven't been feeling well. Gwynna, darling, I thought I told you Barry could *not* do the duel."

"For God's sake, we could have it done while you're all arguing about it," Adam said, exasperated. "Where the hell is Sam?"

Sam, the other double, arrived fortuitously. The director began to instruct those taking part in the scene, while Barry and Gwynna disappeared into her dressing room. Colby sneezed, gave everyone a watery look of reproach, then sat in the director's chair to watch the duel. Nick was behind a camera.

For Liz it was impossible to watch Adam and Sam fencing without remembering Alexander and Louis on the deck of the *Avenger.* Although the rapiers being used by the two stuntmen had protective tips, they were real swords. The two men had to make the duel look as though it were to the death and, frighteningly, that was the impression they gave. Liz closed her eyes and turned away, seeing on Adam's face that same reckless disregard for danger she had seen displayed by Alexander. Despite the fact that Liz still tried to tell herself everything that happened on Falconer's Island had been a flight of her own imagination, a sense of foreboding persisted as she listened to the clashing of steel. She adored him so much she felt certain something would take him for her.

Adam is in danger. The thought hammered on her brain each time steel rang against steel. She opened her eyes and saw that Adam was about to make the dangerous jump from the balcony to the street below. He was poised on the wooden rail, balancing like a tightrope walker, as he warded off the lunges of the two jailors pursuing him. One of the two men was Sam, and most of the action was between him and Adam, while the other jailor mainly circled and slashed wildly with his sword. Adam was supposed to continue parrying the thrusts of his two adversaries until the very second he jumped to the street below.

Liz felt her heart pound. Adam's words came back to her, from a life-time ago. *I just had a narrow escape from a messy death on the set . . . one of those fancy chandeliers came down . . . missed me by inches . . .* Liz jumped up, hand on her throat.

At the same instant the rail beneath Adam's feet gave way, sending him crashing to the ground.

Liz felt as though she were running in slow motion, everything seemed frozen into immobility. The cries of alarm and horror were far away. She could not see how or where Adam had fallen because of the crowd of extras gathering around him. She caught a glimpse of Barry and Gwynna, framed in her dressing room doorway; of the two men on the broken balcony, staring down with horror on their faces, still clutching their rapiers; of Colby Duvalle pressing his handkerchief over mouth and nostrils; of the director's hand raised in an anguished gesture, as though to stop the action in midair.

As she fought her way through the gaping extras, she was thinking how she and Alexander had tried so desperately and vainly to detour from the path fate had laid out for them. A tiny demon of destiny danced excitedly in the back of her mind, shaking a malevolent fist.

Chapter 22

Adam was sitting up, massaging life back into his wrist and attempting a rueful grin, when Liz pushed through the crowd to his side.

"I'm OK. Just sprained my wrist, that's all. I've taken too many falls not to know how to relax and keep the bones intact. It was just the surprise of that rail giving way that caught me unaware."

"But what if you had fallen on the blade of the rapier," Liz breathed.

"This really is too much," Colby Duvalle was saying to no one in particular. "That's the same balcony Gwynna did a scene on yesterday. What if the rail had given way then? Gwynna isn't a stuntman."

"If you'll recall," Barry cut in, "I was on the balcony also."

"And wouldn't have lifted a finger to save her."

Colby sniffed. "Gwynna, I insist you stay off this set until they have re-built it from the ground up." He glared at everyone around him.

The director shouted to be heard. "Adam, go and get that wrist X-rayed. The rest of you—clear the set. There'll be a meeting after lunch."

Adam looked at Liz. "I told you we should have gone sailing."

"I'll drive you to the doctor," she said.

"An ace bandage will do it, but I'd like you to drive me home."

"See a doctor, Adam," the director insisted. "I want to see his report before you continue working."

As they were leaving they passed Nick, who was still holding a portable camera. There was a look of satisfaction on Nick's face that Liz knew. She had seen it many times in the past and knew it signaled the acquisition of another memorable Nick Kane picture. She felt a slow chill rise up her spine.

"Nice going, Adam," Nick said with a mocking slant to his mouth. "The fall is even better than you jumping. And I got the whole thing on film."

Adam's soft response was drowned by Barry's voice, "Which you'll not use, goddamnit, because I'm the star of the film, not some clumsy, pratfalling stuntman."

"They decided to suspend all further shooting here and go on location," Adam told her late the following day. "The entire cast and crew are leaving for Hawaii in a few days." He had come to her studio and watched as she went through proofs of shots she had taken that day.

"You're going with them?" Liz felt her circulation slow down. "What about your sprained wrist?"

"It isn't bad. Won't slow me down much. I've been

thinking. There are two ways we can handle this situation. One, I stay here and they get another double for the great Gerrard. Or . . ." he paused, searching her face with eyes filled with longing. "You can come with me to Hawaii."

He picked up her hand, holding it as though afraid she were going to be snatched away from him. "As my wife. Elizabeth—marry me. Tonight—tomorrow, let's not wait. I love you. I've known it from the moment we met, in some deeply mysterious way that I'm not sure I can explain to you. The moment you walked into my life I knew why I'd never settled down, why every other woman I'd ever known always disappointed me . . . because I was waiting for you. Elizabeth, I'm a man who has tried to hide an affectionate heart and a romantic spirit behind a tough-guy exterior, because I was afraid there was no one out there. . . . I guess what I'm trying to say is that I feel some answering chord in your make-up knows and understands how I feel about life."

Liz listened silently, feeling her love grow until she was afraid she would swoon like some long-ago lady caught in a declaration of love she had so longed for that the reality of it overwhelmed her.

"Please," Adam was whispering, "say something." He grinned to hide his tension. "Even if it's only goodbye."

"Adam, there's something I have to tell you," Liz said. "And I'm afraid when I do you'll think I'm crazy." She put her fingers to his lips to silence his protest. "But before I tell you, I want you to know that I love you. I want to be with you, always. With you I feel a sense of permanence that doesn't require anything other than being near you. I know we would never hurt each other. I don't even need to be your wife, but I would like to be. To make that commitment, that statement—to the whole world. It's funny, I was so blindly infatuated by Nick, yet I never knew the emotional security with him that I feel with you. I thought marriage would give it to me . . . but of course, it wouldn't have."

Adam said, "How can I tell you how much I love you? I feel I've waited all my life to experience the feelings I have for you."

"Adam—wait—I told you there was something you should know. It's a sort of fantasy, I suppose, that came to me when I went away. I had a dream—at least, I think it was a dream. You were in it, and so was Gene. Even Nick. All playing different roles. I was very upset and emotionally wrung-out when I went away and perhaps the total isolation of the island played tricks with my mind and memory, I don't know. But I'm afraid it was somehow a warning of what might happen now, in the present. Coming events casting their shadows . . ."

She began, haltingly at first, to tell him everything that had taken place. Then, as she became caught up in the narrative, re-living the vivid details of her time with Alexander, the words and images flowed and became almost as real to Adam as they were to her.

When she was finished, he sat silently for a while, still holding her hand, watching every expression that crossed her face and illuminated her eyes, sometimes with delight and sometimes with fear.

"Adam, I think it was wish-fulfillment, but I can't shake a sense of foreboding. Of something terrible about to happen to you. I couldn't bear it if I lost you twice. Before I went away I was so blinded by Nick I wasn't really aware of you. That's why the dream was so strange . . . you must have made more of an impression on me than I realized, during those brief meetings. I've been thinking about all the incidents and mishaps that have plagued the filming of *The Black Pirate*—most especially the times you were hurt or nearly hurt. And then I think of Alexander—killed while he was still a young man."

Adam drew her into the comforting warmth of his arms. He didn't laugh or mock her, as Nick would have done. "I promise I'll be careful. But I do have to finish the film. Apart from the fact that I hate to quit in the middle of something—even though Barry Gerrard has done everything short of firing me personally—there's also the investment you and Nick have in *The Black Pirate*. I want you to be free from any financial entanglement with Nick. Besides, he and I go back far enough that I don't want to see him lose his shirt, either."

Liz watched him as he spoke, feeling a surge of tenderness that was tinged with foreboding. Adam held his head high, proudly, defiantly, that same way Alexander had faced life . . . and death. She felt she knew Adam as intimately as she had known Alexander, although they had not yet consummated their love physically. Still, their minds and hearts had already coupled in that mysterious way that only true soulmates ever experience.

"Adam, it's hard for me to put you and Nick and Elliot together as friends. You're all so different."

"They used to call us the Three Musketeers in college. We drifted apart when we got out, but our paths crossed from time to time. We met again in Vietnam, just before the fall of Saigon. Elliot was a reporter. Nick, as you know, was a news photographer and I was flying refugees out."

Liz' eyes were glazed, staring. "You saved his

life—he saved yours. Or, more likely, you both saved his camera and film. You have one of those peculiarly masculine friendships that is part rivalry, part competitiveness and part concern for each other."

Adam looked at her strangely. "What makes you say that?"

"Alexander and Louis had the same relationship."

"Nick and I were college friends who grew in different ways as we got older. Nick represented a carefree time of my life. I guess any affection I felt toward him was because of that. He's become hard, unfeeling, over the years. Elizabeth, don't try too hard to put us all into the roles you think we played in your excursion into the past."

"Was it all just my unhappiness, do you think?"

"I believe there are more things in heaven and earth than are dreamed of, that human desire is more potent than we know. I believe it was more than a dream; perhaps you are extraordinarily sensitive to the dark feelings people hide. But listen, you haven't told me if you'll come to Hawaii with me."

"I'll come, Adam. But let's wait to get married until we get back and the film is finished . . . and everything is settled with Nick."

A week passed before all the arrangements for transporting crew and equipment were complete. During the lull in filming, Nick was at the photography studio every day and called Liz every night. Now that it was all over for her, the excitement of the chase was on again for him.

Adam was shooting several stunts for another film company and Liz saw him only in the evenings. She did not tell him of Nick's renewed and persistent courtship.

Returning to her apartment one evening, she found

Nick sitting on her doorstep. He smiled engagingly. "Hi, babe."

"Nick, I've had a hard day."

"I've been thinking. About Adam and me and you."

"I don't want to discuss him with you. I'd like to relax in a hot tub for a while. Besides, I'm expecting him later."

He took her key from her and opened the door. "You ever wonder who it was who sent you to Gwynna's house that day you caught me with her?"

"Elliot Moore, of course. But the answering service must have given me an old message, because Elliot hadn't called that day."

"It wasn't Elliot. I asked him. He'd *never* left a message for you to meet him at Gwynna's house. You were sent there by someone who knew I was there. Adam Eastman. I just wanted you to know he isn't the honest and upright citizen you think he is. He resorts to underhanded methods to gain his ends, just like the rest of us. He had the hots for you and was mad at me for beating his time with Gwynna. *Voila,* two birds with one stone."

"I don't believe you. Adam wouldn't . . ."

"He'll never admit it. But who else could it have been? Come on, Liz, he caught you on the rebound. But you're going to discover he has feet of clay, too. You know what they say about the devil you know being better than the devil you don't know."

"Nick, just go. I don't think I can stand to hear you utter one more cliché tonight. I just stopped myself from answering that people in glass houses shouldn't throw stones."

He laughed. "See? We understand each other, Liz. We know each other through and through. Look, I've even decided that if physical faithfulness is so important to you, then I'll quit whoring around. You've got my word."

"Nick, it's too late. Don't you see, you only want me now because I don't want you."

"Adam ever tell you how hard he fell for Gwynna Duvalle? Elliot wanted him in the article because he thought there was going to be a headline type romance between the living legend and the humble stuntman. Only Gwynna really wanted Barry Gerrard. She's wanted him for years. She and Barry came to Hollywood about the same time—two kids with nothing but their looks and burning ambition. They had a torrid love affair then. But Barry married his first wife, an established actress, and Gwynna married her producer. Still, she carried the torch for Barry through seven husbands. Adam was just a substitute for Barry to her."

"They're both free now, so perhaps they'll get together. Nick, I'm really not interested. I'm going to Hawaii with Adam. The director believes Adam's stunts will be wrapped up in a couple of weeks. When we come back we're getting married."

Nick's jaw hardened. "OK, babe. Fine with me. I just hope your bridegroom comes to you in one piece."

"What do you mean by that?"

He shrugged. "Nothing. He seems accident-prone lately. Probably getting too old for his job."

The following evening Elliot Moore appeared at Liz's apartment. "Adam here yet?"

Liz shook her head. She had expected to spend the evening alone with Adam and extended the door to admit Elliot somewhat reluctantly—although she had come to like Elliot and regard him as a friend.

He swaggered into the room, eyes darting about and

nostrils twitching in a hound on the scent look that Liz had learned to associate with him. There was a two-day stubble of beard on his heavy jaw and a nicotine stained cigarette butt stuck to his lower lip.

"I'm glad he isn't here. Wanted to see you alone, Liz." He dropped into the nearest chair. His clothes looked as though he had slept in them. He stared at her silently until the pause embarrassed her.

"How are you doing with the articles?" she asked, to break the silence.

He gave a deprecating shrug. "Been working on my novel. My new one—not my really big one. This one is a practice book, to see if I can finish the big one. I've got a lot of stuff I can't use in my articles, so I'm fictionalizing it. Liz, I'm worried about Adam."

A cold hand closed over her heart. "What do you mean?"

"Something's fishy. I can smell it. I've always had a nose for a story, and there's one behind the filming of *The Black Pirate* that may be more than any of us bargained for."

"Adam is in danger?" Liz prompted, her throat dry.

"Someone is deliberately trying to sabotage the film. I've been trying to talk Adam out of going on location to Hawaii, but he won't listen to me. I thought maybe you'd have more influence."

"Did something happen to Adam?"

"No—no, don't worry. But remember the balcony rail that collapsed? It had been partially sawed through. That chandelier almost hit him when it fell in the ballroom scene. Yesterday someone spilled oil where he was supposed to run and jump from one building to the next; he was lucky he didn't fall between the two buildings. Look, Liz, Barry Gerrard doesn't like Adam, he thinks he upstages him. I'm not making any accusations, but it sure looks like someone either wants to get Adam out of the movie, or stop production altogether. It seems like every time something like this happens, it's always in an area where both Barry and Adam have rehearsed earlier. Barry diverts attention from himself by saying it could easily have been him who came close to being hurt . . . only it never is Barry, it's always Adam."

Liz stared at the wall over his head, remembering that the previous night she had awakened at the stroke of midnight, trembling with the old nameless fear. "But surely Barry would stand to lose a great deal of money if the film were abandoned?"

"He can afford it. He's the only one of the backers who can. It might even be a tax write-off for him. Gwynna is wealthy from all of her marriages, but she's also extravagant. Barry shrewdly invested most of his loot. He didn't want to make the film in the first place, but the affair with Gwynna had flared up again and he agreed to please her."

"I'm afraid Adam has his mind set on finishing the film. I don't think he'll listen to me, either."

"Try," Elliot urged. "I know he's stubborn and doesn't want to quit. And Nick keeps after him to stay on because of your investment. Nick thinks maybe the trouble is because it's an independent production and they've been using a lot of non-union people. But I think it's more complicated than that. I pick up an undercurrent of seething emotions around Barry and Adam and the Duvalles. Eventually I'll ferret out the story, but in the meantime I don't want to lose the best friend I ever had."

The door bell rang before Liz could reply. "That will be Adam now," she said, jumping to her feet.

Adam listened silently to Elliot's recital of his fears

and premonitions and to Liz's plea that he bow out of the film; then he slipped his arm about her waist and glanced reproachfully in Elliot's direction.

"Elliot is hoping for something dramatic to happen. To climax his articles. Come on, Elliot, tell Elizabeth how disappointed you were that the big romance you hoped for between Gwynna and me didn't materialize. Why don't you just resurrect the old stories about Gwynna and Barry being starcrossed lovers, instead of scaring Elizabeth with those tired old jinx tales."

"Have you told Liz that the most dangerous stunts you'll have to do will be in Hawaii? That Barry wants to fire you, but the other backers—including our good and true friend, Nick, won't let him? Why take unnecessary chances?"

"Nick—" Liz began fearfully.

"He's exaggerating. Elliot, some day someone's going to break you in half for stirring up trouble. It may be me."

Elliot sauntered toward the door, turned and glowered at them. "Okay, okay, I did my best. Guess I'll just take a trip to the islands, too. Might as well be on hand when it hits the fan. And it's going to, Adam . . ." He was still grumbling audibly when he went through the door.

Adam silenced Liz's protests with his lips and his caresses and she did not have time to notice how his expression suddenly closely resembled that of Alexander, at the moment he told her he was going ashore in Port Royal, where Miles Grindwald's pistol ball awaited him.

Liz sat on the beach watching the director set up the marooning scene. Adam would be brought ashore in a longboat, left on the deserted beach with only his knife as a means of survival. Adam would be in the boat coming through the treacherous Hawaiian surf, but the close-up would be of Barry Gerrard, contemplating his fate with twitching facial muscles and a soulful gaze.

Gwynna had a great fear of tropical sunlight, dreading the ravages of sunburn on her pale and translucent skin. She remained in her hotel room adjacent to the beach. Barry stood in the shade of a cluster of palms, talking to two young Hawaiian girls who would find the marooned pirate.

Liz's eyes drifted out to where the sailing ship lay at anchor, thinking again how remarkably like Alexander's *Avenger* the ship was. The "shore boat"—a power boat used for transporting actors and technicians back and forth from beach to ship, was also in use. The healthy, clear-skinned crew of actors and extras bore no similarity to Alexander's scurvy, pock-marked and scarred band of ruffians.

Indeed, the reality of the film was less convincing than her fantasy of Alexander. But her feelings for Adam were growing stronger day by day. Her fear for his safety had been somewhat allayed by the fact that since their arrival in the islands there had been no further accidents. Even the crew was beginning to relax and decide the film was not jinxed after all.

Nick was amusing himself with a new script girl and, except for an occasional questioning glance in Liz's direction, always when Adam was absent, appeared to have temporarily given up the chase.

Gwynna was as temperamental as ever, and complained incessantly. Since her brother had not accompanied them because he was being treated for a sinus infection, everyone hoped that when Colby arrived he would be able to placate her. Adam told Liz that in his brief acquaintance with Gwynna it had soon become evident that Colby was the only man in Gwynna's life who was indispensable.

"He caters to her every whim. I've seen family devotion, but never like Colby's. I believe she'd fall apart completely without him."

"Perhaps that's why her marriages went sour," Liz suggested, feeling sorry for both Gwynna and Colby, without knowing why. "Perhaps she made it clear she needed her brother more than she needed her husbands. Will she marry Barry, do you think?"

Adam glanced in Barry's direction. The handsome actor was laughing at something one of the island girls had said. "I think it's too late for them. Perhaps I'm wrong. I'm not exactly Barry's confidante."

"Because he's eaten up with envy of you. Oh, Adam, you *are* the pirate. I believe if you'd agree, the director would get rid of Barry tomorrow and you'd be the star."

Adam grinned and ruffled her hair. "You're prejudiced." He stood up as the director called for him to take his place in the longboat.

When an argument between Barry and the director began over the way Adam, doubling the star, would be flung from the boat, Liz wandered away.

That night she awakened again at the stroke of midnight, every nerve in her body screaming and throbbing with fright. She thought for one moment that she was aboard the *Avenger* and Alexander, cutlass in hand, was watching her from the shadows. Even when she flooded her room with light and recognized the modern furnishings of the impersonal hotel room, the fear persisted, holding her trapped in a suffocating sense of inevitability.

Chapter 23

The dancers swayed sensuously to the throb of the drums, hands gracefully telling the story of the dance as their hips moved in a more primitive message. Bare feet caressed the black sand; ankles, wrists and throats were encircled with flowers. Leis swinging over golden breasts were all that the women wore above the waist, as the scene was supposed to be taking place long before the islanders were taught by the missionaries to cover themselves.

Barry Gerrard, as the pirate saved from the barren atoll by the islanders, was seated beside their chief. A brawny team of cooks had just lifted the whole roast pig from the *imu* and were unwrapping *ti* leaves. Waiting diners and beaming chief were torn between their desire to watch the dancers and seeing the meat unveiled.

"Look at their faces," Adam whispered to Liz, "the

audience will almost be able to smell that aroma of roast pork."

Liz wore a brightly colored cotton muu-muu and she had tucked a ginger blossom behind her left ear. Nick had pointed out that the flower should have been placed behind her right ear, since she was unattached and looking for a man.

"Or perhaps," Liz said with a flash of fire in her eyes, "I should wear it on the back of my head? I understand that indicates the end of a love affair."

"The flower is in the right place," Adam said, joining them. "On the left—where you'll wear my wedding ring."

Nick had shrugged and backed down.

As they settled down to the feast scene, Liz tried to put aside the nagging sense of impending disaster that had been clawing at her for days. Once again, the filming of *The Black Pirate* seemed plagued by mishaps and accidents.

Much of the film of one day's shooting had been damaged when it was mysteriously dropped into the lagoon. No one knew how the cans of film came to be anywhere near the water. Then when the scene lost—that of Adam being brought ashore through the surf in the longboat—was scheduled to be re-shot, it was discovered that a hole had been punched in the wooden hull of the boat.

But most chilling of all was the fire that erupted in the grass shack where Barry had taken one of the island girls for a midnight tryst. The shack had been built on the beach, supposedly a shelter for the marooned pirate. Barry and the girl swore there was no way they could have started the fire, that they were not smoking, and the whole structure burst into flames as though touched by a torch.

Although Barry and the girl had been able to plunge through the burning palm fronds, the girl had been burned on the arms and was in the hospital. Barry was untouched, although the crew felt that Gwynna's fury at his peccadillo was probably more punishing than the flames might have been. It was generally agreed among the crew that Gwynna would have been impossible to handle if Colby had not arrived.

The growing atmosphere of tension and distrust came to a head when Barry accused Adam of burning the shack. "I think he wants to make it a life-time job, doubling me in this film," Barry said. "He gets paid, no matter what. I've got my own money in this film. I'm tired of his insolence. He acts like he was the star instead of some two-bit stuntman."

There followed the inevitable arguments. Everyone was aware that the film was becoming more and more Adam's triumph. When he swung up the shrouds of the ship, wielded rapier or cutlass, or leaped over the rail of the buccaneer vessel to plunder a rich prize; he was a dashing and colorful figure out of another time, stripped of modern inhibitions. He became the pirate in a way Barry Gerrard could not even hint at. Even Nick had secretly approached the producer with the suggestion that Adam should take over completely and another part be written for Barry. But that would have been the final humiliation to a star of his stature, and more importantly Barry was one of the principal investors.

In her fury at Barry's infidelity, Gwynna sided with Adam and refused to consider firing him, as Barry wanted to do. Gwynna had come storming on to the set and had startled everyone by pulling a pistol from the belt of the nearest extra and hurling the heavy gun at Barry Gerrard.

Barry ducked and the pistol fell with a resounding thud on the wooden floor. There was a moment of dead silence. Everyone stared at Gwynna, who was a study of white-hot rage from her narrowed eyes and grimly pursed mouth to her quivering shoulders and heaving breasts. "You swine, Barry," she shrieked, her gaze going around wildly as she searched for something else to throw at him. "Adam didn't set that fire and you know it. What really happened—did you and your little playmate smoke a joint and forget where you put the match? If you're going to play around you should be more careful where you do it. Little grass shacks are highly flammable."

Bending to pick up the pistol she had flung at him, Barry gave her the famous smile that had captivated women for more years than anyone cared to remember, especially Barry. "Beautiful Gwynna, light of my life; I'm glad this wasn't loaded."

"Next time it will be," she promised, stamping her foot. "There are pistol balls and cannon balls in that old sailing ship and perhaps I'll load one."

"Not a cannon, I trust, my love." Barry moved in closer, dodging her swinging fists, and captured her in his arms.

Colby took a step toward them, clucking disapprovingly. "Gwynna, if you must throw things, please don't throw the antiques. You might have damaged that pistol."

Gwynna squirmed in Barry's arms and, looking over her head Barry said, "Clear the set. Let me talk to her. And Eastman—you're not fired. You can stay on."

"Don't do me any favors," Adam growled.

The director pleaded, "Please, Adam. Let's go somewhere and talk this over privately."

Unexpectedly, Nick cut in. "No one goes anywhere

until Barry withdraws the accusation he just made. Adam has an apology coming."

When she heard about the incident later, Liz was surprised to learn that Barry had apologized for accusing Adam of starting the fire. She wondered if Nick had defended Adam for the sake of their former friendship, or because Adam had become more important to the success of *The Black Pirate* than Barry.

Most of what happened during the shooting of the film came to Liz second-hand, as she had soon realized her presence was an irritant to Gwynna, and Liz preferred to see Adam alone when he was finished for the day.

In a strange way, Liz even felt a little sorry for Gwynna. It was obvious that the rumors about her long-lived attachment for Barry had not been exaggerated, and Liz had known the pain of lost love in that short time before she met Adam again. In Gwynna's case it was also obvious that Barry did not return her devotion. He was too narcissistic and insecure to care for another human being deeply. He needed constant reassurance from a variety of females as to his virility. The closest he came to singling out Gwynna for special attention was his striving to be sure she always saw him as larger than life.

Elliot Moore arrived to continue his series of articles and, finding Liz alone at lunch one day, joined her. He summed up what Liz had suspected about the relationship between the two superstars. "They can see themselves in twenty-year old movies and it's like time has stood still for them. Who else has to compete with his own self at his most youthful, vital time of life? For Barry and Gwynna it was also the time they met and fell in love. But they don't realize that those two kids no longer exist—how can they realize it when they are there on the silver screen in all their shining make-believe glory? Gwynna wants Barry but all he really represents is her lost youth, while Barry can't accept an aging Gwynna, even though he's still attached to her. As attached as it's possible for a man who's in love with himself first and foremost to be."

"It's all rather sad," Liz agreed. "How much of it are you going to use in your articles?"

"A fraction probably. Like all research. I've been thinking about writing a novel—a *roman à clef*—to use up all the stuff I won't be able to put into my articles, because of the possibility of someone suing me. Tell me—I haven't seen Adam yet, how is he hitting it off with Barry nowadays?"

"There have been several unpleasant incidents. From what Adam tells me, they have come close to blows a couple of times."

By the day of the luau, an uneasy truce had been negotiated.

"Shall we stay for the food afterward?" Adam asked Liz.

Liz shook her head. "The dance is finished, that's all I wanted to see. I'd rather have a picnic on the beach than get involved in all the arguing that's bound to start again."

"Good, I've already ordered a picnic basket," Adam said.

They split a pineapple, ate cold meat and cheese and papaya. Adam twisted the cork from a bottle of wine. The quiet cove lay bathed in moonlight, the palms rustling in harmony with the lapping of the sea against black volcanic rock and the distant rhythmic breaking of the surf against the reef.

Sharing the food and the quiet beauty of the moment, they spoke to one another of their hopes and fears and dreams, speaking in the quick breathless sentences of lovers who resist the passing of each precious moment in each other's company, wanting to delay every second.

Liz pressed for details about Adam's unnamed boat and he told her that she was right in assuming it had been close to completion for a long time. "I never gave her a name because I didn't want Gene to know how close to being seaworthy she was," he confessed. "I guess everyone has a dream. Mine was to sail around the world. But if it doesn't actually come true, that doesn't diminish the dream or the pleasure I had building her."

"You will go on your voyage, Adam. And Gene and I will go with you. I've been thinking about it, and it can work. You'd have to widen the cabin door and rig up a hoist of some sort to raise the wheelchair so Gene could go on deck—but it could be done. He's stronger in his arms and hands than most men, he could be very useful. I'm not sure how useful I could be . . . but I'd like to go with you anyway. I could record your dream voyage in photographs."

Adam's face was in shadow and he was silent for a moment, deeply moved.

"You're right," Adam said. "We could do it. Gene would love it—and think what an inspiration he'd be to other handicapped people through your photographs. I've never told you how much I wanted to sail on that dream voyage. I never dared hope I could have everything . . . you and the voyage and not leave Gene alone."

"Adam—about *The Black Pirate* . . . I know you're only doing it because of Nick's loan—but I did some calculations on the value of our equipment and so on, and I believe if Nick and I really worked hard for a few months, then sold everything, we could pay off the loan."

Adam pulled her into his arms, kissed her mouth and let his lips drift lightly across her cheek to her hair. "There's only a couple more scenes they need me for. I'll have to re-do the longboat scene we lost, then the climax of the burning of the ship. I can put up with old Barry if you can stand Gwynna sniping at you."

"I honestly don't know what I did to her, to earn such dislike. It really reinforces the reincarnation theory, doesn't it? That if you meet someone and instantly feel hostile toward them, for no apparent reason, then you must have been enemies in another life? Gwynna looks just a little like the Lady Amelia Grindwald—same figure and coloring at least, and Amelia lost her pirate captain to Elise."

"My darling Liz—you are so sensitive. Really you let it get to you too much," Adam said. "If you'd prefer, you could go home tomorrow. Wait for me there."

"No," Liz said quickly. "I don't want to go without you. I wish you'd come, too. I can't shake this feeling of something terrible about to happen. I feel we're running out of time, that I'm going to lose you. I keep making plans for the future and I try to hold on to them, but when I'm not with you I'm filled with despair and can see only blankness ahead. It's like the feeling I had toward the end of my dream of Alexander . . . of being in limbo, not able to reach him . . ."

His lips and hands were warm, reassuring, as he tried to dispel her fears. "I'm not going to die, Elizabeth. I have too much living to do. Besides, didn't you say Alexander died of a pistol ball in the back—put there by Sir Miles Grindwald? Where is Sir Miles in your present cast of characters? If Nick is Louis and I am Alexander and Gwynna is the Lady Amelia, who is Miles?"

Liz ran her hands down his back, assuring herself of his nearness. "Barry Gerrard, perhaps?" she suggested. "He resents you so."

"He's not going to kill me. Have me fired maybe, but he doesn't hate me enough to kill me."

His mouth found hers again and she closed her eyes and forgot everything but the tide of passion that united them. Adam had been exercising almost superhuman restraint. His caresses had been the wondering, worshiping touch of a man treasuring the knowledge that he has found the woman who will share the rest of his life, knowing that haste was unnecessary, that passion would unfold as naturally as the petals of a flower.

Since that first time, each time they were alone, Adam held back; stopping just short of consummation of their love, sensing her need to approach the act slowly. She needed time to become familiar with his touch, his kiss. He knew that she wanted to give herself to him completely, but in those first days it would have been for his pleasure more than her own and Adam loved her too much to take from her without giving.

She murmured his name and trembled slightly as her fingers closed over his hand and guided it to her breast. Her nipples were taut as his hand went gently under the soft swelling of her breast and found the silken areola.

Liz's need for him was overwhelming. When she felt the hard length of his body close, his lips warm against her mouth, his tongue exploring, her own response was a melting need and a sharp tensing of inner muscles that quivered with desire for fulfillment and release.

Almost with a will of their own, her hands moved

slowly over his chest, downward to his manhood. When he groaned and she felt his body tense as he fought again for control, she whispered, "Adam, I love you. I'll always love you."

Gently he pulled the muu-muu over her head and she lay back in the moonlight, watching him as he removed his jeans, her eyes luminous. Then his flesh was vital against hers, pulsing with life and love and the joy of their coming union. He was kissing her fiercely, hungrily, without restraint, and she was responding with an ardor that matched his own.

They were in a breathless world of sensual pleasures that went soaring toward delights neither had ever experienced before. His hands cupped her breasts, took her throbbing nipples into his mouth, sending a heightened longing racing through her body. She raised her hips to meet his thrust and they were one in an exquisite moment of exultation that seemed to spur them both over the earth. Breathlessly they rose and fell in a harmony that had no beginning and no end, it had always been theirs, a continuation of every other expression of their love for each other. They were two parts of one whole. Together, joy and pleasure were doubled and fear and pain were dim shadows that vanished. They were immortal.

Release came for them simultaneously, a tingling ascent to the pinnacle of passion and then a spinning weightless fall to the comforting intimacy of sharing an afterglow that promised this was only the beginning of desire.

The climax of the film was about to be shot and although Adam would have preferred that Liz not be present, she was so filled with anxiety for him that nothing could keep her away. Since Gwynna would not be in the scene, Liz did not see how anyone could object to her presence..

Adam had re-made the longboat scene that morning and the burning of the ship would be his final scene in *The Black Pirate*. Liz wended her way carefully through the technicians and prop men setting up the scene. Adam was talking to a special effects man who was explaining to him how the scene would appear in its final form, after the special effects had been spliced into the live action. Liz waited until Adam saw her, then went into the circle of his arms.

"Are you sure it's safe?" she asked for the hundredth time.

He grinned. "A feather bed," he said, using the stuntman's term for an easy job.

"But the fire . . ."

"Gas jets—carefully controlled. Why don't you go up to your room and start packing? I'll be through here soon and I'll come up to you."

"What if your clothes catch on fire? What if you fall over something? Adam, the flames may be controlled, but they are real flames. Fire is unpredictable."

"My clothes have been sprayed with a fire-retardant chemical. I won't fall. Elizabeth, you've got to go now, they're ready to shoot. Please—don't worry. You saw me go over the whole thing this afternoon."

"Without the fire," Liz murmured, but Adam took her firmly by the hand and led her to the sidelines, then resumed his position on the mock-up of the deck.

A mast behind him had been rigged to explode into flame and crash to the deck. Timing would be crucial and Adam had already been through the action several times, on a split-second schedule, to insure that he would be on the exact spot planned for him. Marks had been made on the deck and he would reach the last of these at the same instant the blazing mast fell.

Liz sat down, her hands gripping the arms of her folding canvas chair, her body tense, her mind a plethora of frightening images. Alexander had never told her exactly what had taken place in his last hours. Everything was chillingly clear up until the moment Miles Grindwald's pistol ball smashed into Alexander's back and Liz fainted. After that Liz's only recollections were of fragmented snatches of conversation.

Trying to visualize what had happened, Liz reasoned that the badly wounded Alexander, accompanied by the faithful Tad Bowen, boarded a friendly pirate ship sailing for Darien—once there to attempt to cross the isthmus and reach the Pacific ocean. Darien, she learned later, was Panama; but of course, at that time there was no canal and ships had to take the long sea route around Cape Horn. The narrow strip of land Alexander would attempt to cross was a dense jungle, populated by both human and animal predators, as well as venomous snakes and dreaded yellow fever-carrying mosquitoes.

Meanwhile, the *Avenger* would be sailing for the Pacific on the long and dangerous voyage around the Horn. The *Tiger's Claw* would also sail for the Pacific island where Alexander had buried his treasure, and where Louis and Elise would wait the promised half-year to see if Alexander survived.

But Alexander wanted to draw the Royal Navy squadron after him, to allow both the *Avenger* and the *Tiger's Claw* to escape. Therefore he sent a message to the Lady Amelia, sure that she would betray him to her husband. The Navy squadron would then follow the ship bearing Alexander and Tad to Darien.

Liz shivered, seeing it all as clearly as though she were there. Alexander, weak and perhaps delirious from loss of blood and probably infection, lying in a pirate ship engaged in a desperate battle with navy frigates. The choking smoke . . . the screams of the wounded, and the crash of falling spars overhead . . .

Tad would have been helping defend the ship, Alexander would have been alone. Through the port-hole, if he were lying in a cabin, he could measure the distance from horizon to moon . . . watching the mid-night hour approach.

What had he said? . . . I remember not a quick clean death, but an ebbing away of my life tides . . . He was dying from his wound in a burning ship . . . perhaps suffocating in the smoke—

Liz closed her eyes tightly, squeezing back the tears. She felt certain that her dream of the past and Alexander was meant to aid the future and Adam. The past rushed away and then back again as the director called for action and flames leaped from the make-believe ship on the set. Her eyes were wide now and her fear was a throbbing bubble in her throat as Adam began to fight for his life.

Cutlass in hand, he leaped from the burning quarter-deck to do battle with three wildly slashing ruffians. Cannon balls were slamming into the ship and Adam was dodging imaginary splinters that would be dubbed in later. Even without the added special effects, the scene was terrifyingly realistic. Liz winced and prayed silently as Adam leaped from one vantage point to another, perilously close to the flames.

She was on her feet, following the action with frightened darting eyes, feeling that something was horribly wrong. Liz had watched Adam rehearse the scene earlier, without the fire and explosions, and on the surface it appeared that it was going well. But Alexander's words kept echoing around her mind like some faraway warning signal. His last memory was of smoke, fire . . . she was sure of it.

Then she saw it. The last of the marks on the deck . . . in the rehearsal the last mark was closer to the helm. Someone had erased the chalk marks and moved them directly under the mast that was rigged to fall.

Liz opened her mouth to scream a warning when, incredibly, the director yelled, "Cut!"

Like magic, the flames went out. Adam held his position. The two remaining attackers froze; the third man lay where he had fallen. Liz blinked. It was as though the world had simply stopped.

Then Barry Gerrard, dressed in an identical costume to Adam's, came on the set. He and Adam changed places. The director raised his hand for silence. "We've decided to come in for a close-up of Barry here, then a long shot of the exploding mast."

Liz found her voice, "Wait, wait, please. You'd better check that mark on the deck. From where I'm standing, it doesn't appear to be in the same place it was during rehearsal."

Adam came to her side and she gripped his arm as though to assure herself he was really there.

The director recognized the mistake instantly and pale and shaken, berated the crew for their carelessness as he measured the distance between chalk marks.

"Old Barry might have been in trouble, if you hadn't been alert enough to notice the mark," Adam said. There was an odd questioning look in his eyes.

"Adam, I thought you were doing the complete scene. The way you rehearsed it earlier, you would have been under that falling mast instead of Barry."

"A last minute change," Adam said thoughtfully. "Just a few minutes before you arrived on the set the director told me he'd cut and Barry would take my place. I guess Barry felt the scene was an important one and he wanted a close-up."

"If the mark was deliberately moved then," Liz said, "the person moving it wouldn't have known about the change. Adam, do you realize someone might have wanted you to be hit by that falling mast? Why, you could have been killed—"

"Chalk erases easily, the original probably got wiped off and someone was careless. Let's forget it. I just wrapped up my part in the film, Elizabeth, so let's go and celebrate."

Adam slipped his arm around her waist, his eyes sending her a message that drove away her terror.

They planned a quiet evening alone for their last night on the island and when there was a knock on her door she called, "Come in, Adam."

There was a pause, then the door opened. Colby Duvalle stood on the threshold. "I'm sorry to disturb you, I thought perhaps Adam was with you."

"I'm expecting him. What is it? I thought you were all finished with him." She felt another wave of apprehension. "It isn't for another stunt is it?"

"No, no. Nothing like that. It's just that I've been taking inventory of some of the props. We rented most of them and in the interest of economy, I thought I'd return what we no longer need. I wondered where he put the cutlass he used last night. It's not important."

He took out his handkerchief and pressed it to his nostrils. "Excuse me. I can't seem to shake this sinus condition." He blew his nose daintily and then went out into the hall and closed the door.

Liz stared at the door, feeling the blood rush to her ears and begin to pound. The image of Colby Duvalle was still there, as though imprinted on her mind. The diminutive body clad in almost effeminately-cut slacks and shirt, the silver hair and aristocratically aloof features; a slightly disapproving slant to the eyes, but most of all, the handkerchief pressed to his nostrils, as though to shut out an unpleasant odor. . . .

She stumbled against the bed in her haste to reach the phone. She fumbled, re-dialed and listened to the phone ringing in Adam's room. There was no answer.

Downstairs in the hotel lobby she found Nick and a cameraman sipping drinks and talking. They looked surprised as she burst into the conversation. "Have you seen Adam? Where is everyone—did Colby just go by?"

"Hey, babe, simmer down," Nick said, pulling out a chair for her. "What's wrong? You look like you've seen a ghost."

The cameraman said, "Most everyone is watching the dailies. Except for Barry and Gwynna, they weren't in the scenes shot this morning."

"They're probably taking advantage of the lull to catch up on a little fun and games," Nick said. "Gwynna and Barry disappeared in the direction of her room after lunch. Unless . . ." he broke off, his dark eyes flickering over Liz calculatingly, "unless it wasn't Barry I saw with her, but Adam?"

"It wasn't Adam," Liz said coldly, ignoring the chair he offered. She left them, staring after her, and ran outside to the crowded beach area in front of the hotel, trying to remember what Adam had told her he would be doing. He had been evasive, saying merely that he would meet her for dinner and they would spend a quiet evening alone.

There was no sign of him on the beach, nor in the hotel bar or the restaurant. The afternoon was hot and guests were in air-conditioned rooms. Liz went back to her room to wait, pacing up and down.

At last she went to the phone again and dialed the room number of Elliot Moore.

"Elliot—Liz Holly. Listen, how much have you learned about Gwynna and Colby Duvalle in your research for your articles on Hollywood? Where did they come from, originally—it was some European country, wasn't it? Do you know anything about their early life?"

"Not much," Elliot admitted. "They arrived in Hollywood in the fifties, although Gwynna doesn't like to talk about those days since it dates her. Why?"

"Will you do me a favor and not ask questions for now? Find out all you can about Gwynna and Colby's early life. I know her biography has been done by every fan magazine, but they all tell her story since she came to Hollywood: the films, mostly her rich husbands and enormous divorce settlements. I want to know about Gwynna and Colby in their pre-Hollywood life. Elliot, I can't tell you how important it is. Will you do it?"

There was a pause. "It's funny you asking this at this particular time. Remember I told you I was thinking of doing a novel? A *roman à clef* on Gwynna? Well, just the story of all her husbands and lovers was fascinating enough, plut the added poignancy of the hopeless love for Barry all these years. But I have a friend in the Department of Immigration and I wanted to learn more about their early life in Europe so I asked him for details. Just birthplaces, birthdates, that sort of stuff, since I didn't want to get him in any trouble. But he gave me a very curious piece of information. I'm not sure if it's what you're after, or whether I can use it, even in a novel. Listen—we'd better not discuss this on the phone. Let's get together, and if you tell me why you're interested in their early life, I'll tell you what I turned up."

"I could meet you later; right now I'm waiting for Adam. I haven't seen him all afternoon and I'm getting a little worried. I'll call you again as soon as I find him and we can meet somewhere."

Half an hour later, after she had called Adam's room half a dozen times, he appeared suddenly at her door. She fell into his arms, shaking with relief.

"What is it, Elizabeth? What's wrong?"

"Oh, Adam, I was deathly afraid something was going to happen to you."

Afterward, it seemed that in that split second they were both holding their breath, that the very air around them was heavy with tension. Neither of them spoke as the warm stillness of the afternoon was rent by a heart-stopping scream of terror. The scream was repeated, over and over again in growing hysteria.

Outside in the hall Adam collided with Nick. "What happened? That sounds like Gwynna," Adam said.

"It is," Nick replied grimly. "Help me find Colby so he can quiet her before the police get here. Someone just killed Barry Gerrard."

Chapter 24

Elliot's voice was low, urgent, whispering from the telephone receiver into her ear. "Did the police let Adam go yet? OK, calm down. I talked to the detective in charge and he said Adam would be released soon, at least until they complete their investigation. Listen, I've got news. The Duvalles are registered aliens. Gwynna and Colby aren't their real first names, though Duvalle is their real last name. Her maiden name was Heinrich. Duvalle was her married name at the time she applied for an immigrant's visa."

"Of course," Liz breathed. "I should have realized before."

Elliot went on, *sotto voce,* "They let everyone think they were brother and sister, when in reality they had been married to each other."

"Sir Miles and Lady Amelia Grindwald," Liz said.

"What? Liz, don't say any more on the phone. I think I know what happened this afternoon. Maybe you can fill in some blanks. Let's go for a ride so we'll have some privacy. The hotel is crawling with cops and reporters. I've rented a car. It's a red Thunderbird. Meet me in the garage. Give me half an hour. I've got to talk to someone first."

As she dressed, Liz asked herself if there was really anything particularly sinister about Colby and Gwynna continuing to live together as brother and sister after their divorce. Strange, perhaps, but Hollywood was full of stranger stories.

Gwynna had married and divorced seven or eight husbands, perhaps she needed the constancy of her relationship with Colby. Perhaps Colby had discovered latent homosexual tendencies and, although romantic love died, they remained friends.

But then Liz remembered the contorted look of hatred on Colby's face the night of the party, the times he had caused friction on the set, and his peevish dislike of Barry, Adam and Nick. It was a fact that he was never seen in anyone's company other than Gwynna. A man's voice had called Liz's answering service sending her to Gwynna's house on a wild goose chase and Colby insisted she go upstairs. She thought of his misty, glassy-eyed stare. He knew Gwynna was in bed with Nick.

He still loves her, Liz thought. Impotently, perhaps, but obsessively. He must have gone through the torture of the damned as Gwynna went through her parade of husbands and lovers. But the one man Gwynna had always wanted had been Barry Gerrard. He had been the first—and the last.

Liz hurried along the pathway winding through

coconut palms toward the underground parking area. The humidity had increased and there was a distant rumble of thunder. Raindrops came on a gust of wind and a tiki torch lighting the path blew out. A couple of guests reversed their direction and raced back to the hotel for shelter from the approaching storm.

It had been agony waiting for half an hour to pass and even now she was early. The garage area appeared to be deserted. Looking around for the red Thunderbird Elliot said he had rented, Liz felt a stab of foreboding.

A concrete pillar loomed ahead. She stopped beside it; glanced around. She was still alone. Stopping to examine each red car, she continued to ask herself unanswerable questions.

Where had Adam been all afternoon? The police had taken him downtown for further questioning because Barry had been killed by the cutlass Adam had used in the burning scene, which he swore had been returned to the galleon with the other weapons in the shore boat.

All Liz had learned of the actual murder was that Barry and Gwynna had made love and he fell asleep. When she emerged from the shower in the adjacant bathroom, she discovered his body in her blood-soaked bed.

Liz saw the red Thunderbird across the aisle, parked so that it faced her. Elliot was at the wheel, in a curiously stiff and upright pose, watching her approach.

"Elliot!" Liz called, quickening her pace. The light was too dim for her to see the warning in his eyes. She opened the passenger door of the car and looked directly into the muzzle of an ancient pistol clasped in the trembling fingers of Gwynna Duvalle, who crouched in the back seat. Liz recognized the pistol as being one of the collection aboard the galleon. Single shot, but lethal.

"Get in," Gwynna ordered. Her eyes were wide, and green mascara stained her cheeks. Her normally coiffured hair was in straggled disarray. Her voice shook with rising hysteria.

Liz slid into the front seat as Gwynna prodded Elliot with the pistol. "Drive," she ordered.

He turned on the ignition. "Gwynna—let's just go back inside and talk this over," he said. "Bigamy isn't a capital offense—"

"Bigamy?" Liz exclaimed.

"She and Colby were never divorced," Elliot said.

A sound that was half wail, half animal panic, broke from Gwynna's lips. "We'd lose everything. All of my ex-husbands are waiting to pounce on me. Every settlement, all the alimony. Besides, then they would know I couldn't marry Barry because Colby wouldn't give me a divorce—" she broke off, realizing she was thinking aloud, and prodded Elliot again.

Elliot accelerated and the car leaped forward.

"Where are we going?" Liz asked, her eyes fixed on the gun jammed into Elliot's back.

"Down to the beach where they did the filming. I guess Colby is there."

They drove in tense silence for a few minutes, the wind swaying the car. "Liz, I'm sorry I got you into this. I went to talk to Gwynna and she pulled the gun—"

"Be quiet!" Gwynna shouted. "Don't talk to each other."

Trying to collect her wits, Liz thought of all those bigamous marriages—but Gwynna had not "married" Barry because Colby would not stand for it.

The beach used for filming was only minutes away from the hotel by car, but hidden from the highway by a dense growth of trees that swayed in the wind, giving glimpses of whitecaps on the sea beyond. Clouds had blotted out the moon.

When the car came to a stop, Gwynna leaped from the back seat, keeping the gun pointed at Elliot, and screamed, "Colby!"

A dark figure near the water's edge straightened up. The shovel in his hand glinted as the moon showed itself briefly between racing clouds.

Gwynna began to speak before Colby reached them, her voice a series of whimpers that were almost lost in the sound of the wind. "Colby, darling, what shall we do? They know what will happen to you. What if we lose all our money? What if we're deported? I can't go back. I won't."

Colby Duvalle was a dainty but menacing figure in the darkness. "Calm yourself, Gwynna. Don't say another word."

"But he knows about Barry, too," Gwynna wailed.

Liz heard Elliot's swiftly indrawn breath and realized what must have happened. Following his reporter's instincts, Elliot had been unable to resist the urge to confront Gwynna with what he had discovered, wanting her reaction and her story. Gwynna had been hysterical about Barry's death. Colby was here on the beach, burying something in the sand . . . bloodstained clothes? Somehow Elliot had tricked Gwynna into revealing more than he had already uncovered. *Including the fact that Colby killed Barry Gerrard.*

It made sense, Liz thought. How could anyone have killed him without Gwynna's knowledge? And there was only one man she would lie about to protect.

"You fool," Colby's voice was shrill with fury. "He was guessing, but you have confirmed his suspicions."

"Hold on," Elliot said, a thin edge of desperation in his voice. "When I went to see Gwynna I had no idea you killed Barry. I bought the story of an intruder . . . I even thought maybe someone had mistaken Barry for Adam, because of all the incidents that almost killed Adam . . ."

Liz thought, but we were wrong. Barry was the target all along. Colby was trying to keep Barry and Gwynna apart, first by sabotaging the film, then by causing him to have an accident. Of all Gwynna's husbands and lovers, Barry was the only real threat. Shut up, Elliot, she thought in panic, as she realized he was talking to gain time but was actually damning himself with his own knowledge.

"Listen," Elliot babbled on, "all I had was the fact that you two were still legally married. I figured Gwynna must have known who killed Barry—she was there—and perhaps she was being blackmailed to keep quiet about it by somebody who had found out she was a bigamist. I never thought it was you, Colby, for Christ's sake. . . . Hell, Barry was only one of—"

Elliot did not finish what he was about to say as the pistol in Gwynna's hand exploded.

His body jerked with the impact of the pistol ball, then slid slowly out of the car. One arm was still over his head, reaching grotesquely toward Liz, who watched, disbelieving.

Liz flung open her door and stumbled from the car. She had taken only one step toward freedom when Colby caught up with her, the handle of the shovel raised above his head.

The next second consciousness left her in an explosion of shooting lights and excruciating pain.

She was in a blurred and misty world of moving shadows and pale, flickering images. Drifting, dreaming, floating endlessly toward some distant place she must reach or all would be lost.

The others seemed unaware of her presence. She was outside their conversation. Their voices floated, barely within reach.

"It's all right, my dear," Colby was saying. "I'll take care of everything. Eastman is already a prime suspect. I heard he was being released pending the issuance of a warrant, so he would have been at large when Moore was shot. It all fits, you see. Moore had proof that the stuntman killed Barry—the result of a long-standing feud. Moore is therefore killed by Eastman to keep him quiet."

Colby Duvalle's voice was flat and cold, absolutely without emotion. Liz struggled to command her frozen limbs to obey her brain's command, but she could neither see nor feel. Only sound penetrated the icy fog in which she was wrapped. Colby Duvalle . . . always cold, aloof, apparently without emotion, yet all the time he seethed with violent passions that only occasionally showed in his eyes.

A strangled sob, somewhere nearby. Gwynna?

Then her voice, shaking with terror. "I didn't know . . . I didn't know it mattered so much to you. You always laughed about it. My first marriage . . . Colby, darling, you encouraged me to do it. You said there was no need to get a divorce because we looked so much alike everyone here just assumed we were brother and sister. You even suggested I divorce the producer to marry the hotel heir. When I asked you to give me a divorce to marry Barry, you said it was too late, that I'd be deported for bigamy. Colby, my dearest, why didn't you tell me how you really felt—why?"

"Why, my love? Why what? Why, when I can't make love to you? Why could I stand by meekly and allow all of those men to possess you? Because I loved you. It was enough just being with you. Because I was too proud to tell you of my agony. Why . . . why did I kill Barry Gerrard? Because, dearest heart, he was the only man alive who might have taken you from me. I couldn't have born living apart from you. Oh, I'd thought about killing him, many times. I tried to warn him off, tried to stop that stupid film from proceeding. But every time I arranged a not-too-fatal accident for him he would be on the sidelines and his stand-in took his punishment."

There was a sudden chilling laugh that rang with madness. "That swine Gerrard, I believe he needed a stand-in for everything, including death itself."

"I'd never seen you . . . like that," Gwynna's voice was a whisper. "That terrible rage—Colby, darling, in some dreadful way it excited me, it made me want you."

"Coming into the room and finding him on top of you like that. Always before it was *you*. . . . Somehow I could bear that. *You* doing it to *them*."

"I would never have left you. You know I can't manage without you, how much I need you."

"Years ago, my beautiful Gwynna, your Barry Gerrard told me I had better make other arrangements. That he didn't want me around you. That it was 'unhealthy' . . . our attachment. I was so afraid of losing you. . . ."

"Oh, Colby, darling. My darling, if only you could have loved me."

"I love you with my heart and spirit and soul, Gwynna. Only my sorry flesh cannot respond to you."

"I only needed their bodies. I never loved any of them. Only you, my dearest. I married for wealth and I took lovers for . . ."

"Hush. Don't say any more. I can't bear it."

"Not even Barry. Not even him, Colby. Even though he was the only one I ever really submitted to."

"Shhh. We must see to it that they believe he was killed by Adam Eastman. And make sure Eastman never comes to trial."

"But how?"

"You will take a message to him, my love."

Their voices faded and Liz was falling through space, tumbling endlessly. Everything was rushing away as though sucked into a black hole. She reached frantically for something to cling to but her flailing arms found only wisps of mist and floating shadows.

Adam! His name echoed out in the far reaches of the universe and she was desolate with the pain of losing him. Adam, how shall I find you? How can I bear losing you a second time? There was no strength left in her body, her struggles became more feeble. On the last edge of awareness, there hovered the certain knowledge that she had done all of this before.

Chapter 25

The sound of creaking timbers and the sour smell of bilgewater were the first sensations that broke through the blackness. She was rolling helplessly with the surge and pull of the sea as the old wooden ship rose and fell on increasing swells. Storm waves were washing against the hull and the wind shrieked through ancient masts and spars.

Complete darkness surrounded her. Her head throbbed and there was pain in her legs that could have come from her cramped position or from a fall into the hold of the ship. She had no recollection of being brought here, but knew she was aboard the ship that had been used in the filming of *The Black Pirate*. She was alone.

Memory returned slowly. A confused fragmentation of past and present, of dreams and nightmares.

Colby and Gwynna. Colby had killed Barry and

Gwynna had covered for him. It was not difficult to imagine why she claimed to have been in the shower. She had washed away Barry's blood and the two of them had then schemed how to pin the murder on someone else.

The memory of Elliot being shot came shrieking through her mind and she was numb with a feeling of loss that momentarily blanked everything else, including her own predicament, from her mind. Elliot . . . with his eager curiosity, his questing badger look, his Great American Novel that would now never be written.

Then she remembered the conversation she had overheard in her semi-conscious state. Adam! Liz sat up, bumping her head. She crawled about in the darkness, fumbling with her hands to distinguish objects around her. Several boxes and crates. A sodden length of rope. Something cold and metallic.

Her searching hands found human hair, slid downward to touch a lifeless face. For one agonizing second she thought it was Adam's body, then her fingers touched a heavy stubble-covered jaw, passing over protruding teeth. Elliot Moore. There was no doubt he was dead.

She sobbed aloud, from grief and from fear, wanting to wake up and find it had all been a nightmare, refusing to accept the spectre of death beside her.

Colby killed Barry. Gwynna killed Elliot, the dreadful truth pounded her senses until all she could do was lie in the darkness, retching.

Minutes passed. Gradually the painful thumping of her heart in her throat subsided. A terrible anger was born, somewhere deep inside her, and with it an overwhelming desire to see the Duvalles pay for what they had done.

For a moment she indulged her fury by imagining the immaculate and effeminate Colby and his nymphomaniac wife cowering before her accusing testimony. Then she realized that her most pressing need was to warn Adam of their plans to frame him for both murders.

The movement of the ship was becoming wilder. She was flung against the bulkhead, wincing with pain as stars exploded again in her head.

Searching the inky darkness for a glimmer of light, her eyes at last found the thin lines of a square above her head. Faintly outlined was a hatch cover. Too high to reach.

She tried to drag one of the boxes into position beneath the hatch cover, but realized it was too heavy. Her hands searched the deck for the metal object she had touched earlier. A crowbar. She was panting with exertion by the time she had pried the top from one of the boxes and started to unload the contents.

When the box was half empty, it was light enough to drag into position. She scrambled to the top of it, reached for the hatch and found it securely fastened.

Down again to find the crowbar, fumbling in the wet darkness. Her stomach churned with the movement of the ship. Don't think about it! Think about Adam. I must reach Adam before Colby does. She was poking at the hatchcover with the crowbar, trying to find an opening where she could apply leverage.

It flew open suddenly and hammered down again in the wind. She reached for the deck with one hand and kept the crowbar in the other hand to protect her head from the falling hatchcover.

The wind sliced into her lungs. The rain had stopped. Cautiously she made her way to the rail, fighting the roll of the wet and slippery deck. Tied to the stern was the power launch that had been used to transport th crew back and forth, the "shore boat."

She looked around, searching for whoever ha brought the shore boat to the ship, but the deck wa deserted. She was about to make her way aft when sh saw the dark shadow riding the surf toward the ship. A second boat was approaching. The man at the oars wa only a silhouette, but she recognized him instantly Adam.

By the time the longboat reached the ship, Liz ha thrown a rope ladder over the side. She called his nam and he looked up and saw her.

"Are you all right?" he yelled over the sound of win and sea as he grabbed the rope ladder.

She did not question how he had known where sh was until he was at the top of the rope ladder. Then, i that moment of eternity when he was on the rail, sh remembered fragments of conversation she had eithe dreamed or heard in a semi-conscious state.

Colby's voice, ". . . see to it they believe he wa killed by Adam Eastman. And make sure Eastma never comes to trial."

". . . you will take him a message, my love."

"Adam!" Liz screamed at the same second the pistc exploded.

The ship rolled and Adam pitched forward on th deck. Liz dropped to her knees beside him, franticall running her hands over his chest and feeling th spreading tide of sticky wetness.

Six feet away, clinging to the capstan, stood Colb Duvalle, aiming the ancient pistol a second time. Th moon slid out from behind a cloud, sending its pal light on Colby's thin-lipped smile and the antiqu weapon he had rented for the film.

But the gun takes only one pistol ball; he has to re-load, Liz thought. Adam groaned and stirred. "Can you walk?" she asked against his ear. "I'll help—hurry." Too late she realized she should have armed herself before leaving the hold. She had unloaded similar weapons in order to lighten the box she had climbed upon.

She pulled one of Adam's arms over her shoulder and he stood up, swaying. They staggered across the slanting deck and fell down the nearest stairway. Colby appeared at the top of the stairs as they hit the bottom. The pistol exploded again, stabbing the darkness with fire.

The pistol ball slammed into the bulkhead beside them, sending splinters flying.

Stumbling along the narrow passageway, Adam panted, "Take the next stairway back up on deck. I'll lead him below." His right arm hung limply and blood soaked his shirt.

Even if she had been willing to do so, the storm hatch was down over the only other stairway. There was only one way to go, downward.

For Liz, time seemed suspended between past and present. She was with Alexander again and he was dying from Miles Grindwald's pistol ball, but in reality she was dragging Adam down into the bowels of the ship, to the lower deck, provision room, past the water casks. They gained precious seconds only when Colby Duvalle had to stop to reload the pistol.

She clung to Adam, finding strength she did not know she possessed to help him. They reached the water pumps and could no longer hear the sound of Colby crashing after them.

Adam slipped to his knees, fell forward on his face.

Liz strained to turn him over, trying to avoid the smashed bones of his shoulder. Her face was wet with tears.

"Elizabeth . . ." she had to bend close to hear his words. " . . . want you to know where I was this afternoon." She had to bend close to hear the words.

"I don't want to know. You must know I never imagined you killed Barry."

"Want you to know . . . just in case," he persisted. "Looking for a wedding ring. . . . Elizabeth . . . you've got to get to the boat—"

"No," she said fiercely. "I won't leave you. Adam, the pistols and all the weapons are in one of the holds, remember? We have to find a place to hide you and I must get to them . . ." She broke off as they heard Colby crashing about above them.

Huddling over Adam, she bit her lip to keep from crying out as something slammed into the deck above their heads. Then Colby's voice rose above the sounds of storm and ship. "Where are you? You might as well come out. Come on, I won't kill you if you come out. I know Eastman is wounded. His blood is on the deck. Come on, woman, I'll help you."

Liz was shivering violently. She felt Adam's body tense as he tried to struggle free of her restraining arms. She considered the possibility of somehow encircling Colby. If she could get behind him, perhaps she could hit him with something. But what if he found Adam first? She discarded the idea. She and Adam must stay together. They must not separate this time. . . .

All at once a picture of Falconer's Island flashed into her mind, irrelevantly, bringing with it tantalizing glimpses of half-forgotten images that she knew were significant, if only she could remember more clearly . . .

The wind was dropping and the ship rolled less erratically. Liz crouched beside Adam, staring into the darkness. There was a thud somewhere and the sound had a final ring to it that made Liz hold her breath. After that there was only the creaking of the ship and the dying whisper of the wind.

"Adam," she said, but he was unconscious.

Several minutes passed before she heard the roar of the power boat. Moments later she was aware of a difference in the way the ship rolled. They were drifting.

"Adam, the ship has broken free—or he cut it loose . . . we're moving," she said. But Adam could not hear.

She strained her eyes into the darkness, looking down at him helplessly. He was losing so much blood. She tore off her shirt and pressed it to his wound, trying to stop his life from pumping out onto the deck.

Then she smelled the first acrid hint of smoke.

Alexander's words seemed to come to her across an eternal expanse of time . . . *fire is our deadly peril.*

Looking down at Adam, she saw the tiny red glow of the illuminated digits of his wrist watch. Eleven fifty-five. Five minutes to midnight. Her heart began to pound and terror ran along her veins in an icy flood.

". . . I remember not a quick clean death . . . but an ebbing away of my life in a shadowed, smoke-filled trance. I remember looking up at the rising moon and wondering if I would live to see the new day as the midnight hour approached. Ah, Elizabeth, how I wanted to hurry past midnight to keep that rendezvous that I had to keep . . . that was more important to me

than anything that had gone before. I believe I died at midnight."

Laying down Adam's head as gently as she could, Liz stood up. She retraced their steps, coming to an abrupt halt at the locked door to the provision room. Touching the door, she felt intense heat. Dropping to her knees to avoid breathing the deadly smoke, which crept from beneath the door in a choking cloud, she crawled back down to Adam. He was still unconscious.

She looked around wildly for a way out. Oh, Alexander, is this how you died? Bleeding from a pistol ball, trapped in your burning ship? Did the navy frigate catch up with you and your ship caught afire during the battle, as you lay dying? But at least this time we are together . . .

"Elizabeth . . ." She jumped, startled. Adam raised his head, gritting his teeth to force himself to consciousness. "I smell smoke . . ."

"Colby set the ship on fire. The provision room is full of smoke and the door is so hot he must have set the fire there."

Adam struggled to sit up. "Maybe I can break through . . ."

In the darkness his silhouetted profile was so like Alexander that it seemed to Liz she was whisked backward as memories became present reality. She was recalling her tour of the *Avenger*.

Alexander had said, "Fire is our deadly peril and the terror of every sailor. We permit no open flame below decks." *The powder magazine is lighted by a lantern that shines through a heavy glass window in the light-room—which is lined with tin.*

Liz almost shouted the words, "Adam—I know how we can get to the deck! We must go to the powder room—"

"What?" Adam said with a weak grin, thinking she was looking for a bathroom.

"The magazine. Next to the powder magazine there is a lightroom, where the lantern is kept. There's a door from the lightroom that leads to a stairway up to the deck. Come on, we must hurry before the hold fills with smoke."

She pressed her shirt to his shoulder, acutely aware that he winced but did not cry out. Then he was on his feet and she was guiding him through the murky darkness.

"I don't remember seeing anything like what you describe," he said when they came to the water casks.

"We've gone the wrong way. Come on, back the other way. Elliot told me this ship is an exact replica of a seventeenth century fighting galleon. It would have to have a lightroom. I'm sure of it."

What time was it? She didn't dare look at Adam's watch and her own did not have a luminous dial. Their progress seemed painfully slow and the smoke followed relentlessly. They could hear the crackle of the flames overhead now and the sound of crashing timbers.

"Look—there it is, the magazine. Adam, can you make it?"

The powder magazine was in darkness. Adam was breathing unevenly, but kept moving with dogged determination.

Liz pressed her hands to the bulkhead, moving swiftly around the room. On the third wall she touched the glass. "Adam, it's here—the glass window to allow the light from the lantern to shine into the magazine."

"Over here . . . cannonballs," Adam called. "Can you smash the glass with one of them?"

It seemed to Liz, as she hurled the cannon ball through the window, that along with the sound of shattering glass and the call of wind and sea came a rich, full-bodied shout of laughter and triumph. She felt a new rush of energy. They had to make it.

They stumbled out on deck to the sweet clean breath of the wind. Admidships the vessel was burning fiercely.

Adam clutched her arm. "Look, Colby was so sure we would burn to death he didn't bother to cut the longboat loose." The boat still bobbed alongside.

The ship had already drifted out of sight of land in the swift storm tide. It would have been impossible for the injured Adam to swim that far.

Liz wondered fleetingly if Colby Duvalle had left the longboat as evidence the two of them had gone of their own choice to the ship.

The pounding sense of panic did not leave her until they were in the boat and she had paddled a safe distance from the burning ship. The pressure of her makeshift bandage had slowed the bleeding of Adam's wound and he remained conscious.

"The storm is subsiding," he said. "A fishing boat or a plane will see the flames from the ship. Don't tire yourself by rowing."

Liz put down the oar and lay next to him, gently removing his hand so that she could hold the bandage in place.

"Oh, Adam, I love you," she said. "We'll be safe now." She looked up at the moon, sailing in lonely splendor across the night sky, and her breathing relaxed. "It's past midnight."

Dear Reader:

Would you take a few moments to fill out this questionnaire and mail it to:

Richard Gallen Books/Questionnaire
8-10 West 36th St., New York, N.Y. 10018

1. What rating would you give DREAMTIDE?
☐ excellent ☐ very good ☐ fair ☐ poor
2. What prompted you to buy this book? ☐ title ☐ front cover ☐ back cover ☐ friend's recommendation ☐ other (please specify) ______________
3. Check off the elements you liked best:
☐ hero ☐ heroine ☐ other characters ☐ story ☐ setting ☐ ending ☐ love scenes
4. Were the love scenes ☐ too explicit ☐ not explicit enough ☐ just right
5. Any additional comments about the book?

____
6. Would you recommend this book to friends?
☐ yes ☐ no
7. Have you read other Richard Gallen romances? ☐ yes ☐ no
8. Do you plan to buy other Richard Gallen romances? ☐ yes ☐ no
9. What kind of romances do you enjoy reading?
☐ historical romance ☐ contemporary romance ☐ Regency romance ☐ light modern romance ☐ Gothic romance
10. Please check your general age group:
☐ under 25 ☐ 25-35 ☐ 35-45 ☐ 45-55 ☐ over 55
11. If you would like to receive a romance newsletter please fill in your name and address:

____

____

____